I0629082

Whispers

of Life

A Novel by

D.C. McLaughlin

Copyright © Kathleen Florio 2014

All Rights Reserved

Cover Design: H.A. Kennedy
Author Photo: H.A. Kennedy

ISBN: 978-09895910-5-8

This is a work of fiction. Names, characters,
businesses, places, events and incidents are
either products of the author's imagination or
used in a fictitious manner. Any resemblance
to actual persons, living, dead, or undead, or
actual events is purely coincidental.

DEDICATION

To Joanna, my thrice found friend. Never give up skating and I'll never give up dancing!

ACKNOWLEDGEMENTS

Rarely is a book published which is not the result of a collaborative effort of a team of people. This book is no different. The story may be mine but without other people involved it never would have seen the light of day. And they deserve recognition for their efforts.

First and foremost I would like to thank Demi Stevens formerly of the Shrewsbury Public Library and now master and commander of the "Year of the Book" program. She is a multi-talented individual with all the skills necessary to bring a fledgling writer from first draft to final polished published book. If it wasn't for her tireless efforts and patient tutoring, this book would still be just a dream on a PC. I have learned so much from her. I hope I will continue to learn more.

Secondly I would like to thank Dr. Karl Eltz of Eltz castle in Germany. I contacted him when I first started looking for a castle to model Schloss Lowentore after. I expected to talk to the tour guide. Instead I got a member of the family who owns the castle! He was extremely patient and gracious in letting me ask all my crazy questions about modern life in a German castle. He cleared up many misconceptions I had. Yes, I did take some dramatic liberty by adding a hedge maze to Castle Lion's Gate. That seems to be more of an English and French custom. German castles do not have labyrinths. But castle Lion's Gate is pure fiction loosely based on Eltz. I cannot thank Dr. Karl Eltz enough for being so forthcoming in my research.

Once again I am grateful to my long suffering hubby for supporting me through the whole writing process and being my first and best fan. He has never wavered in his support of my writing dreams. In fact he has always pushed me to write more and is thrilled to see when my latest endeavor hits the bookstore shelves. But then it was my words that first made him fall in love with me!

Thanks also go out to my family and friends who have stood by me from the first book to the latest. Those closest to me make the whole effort worthwhile. Thank you for nurturing the love of reading in me from an early age.

PROLOGUE

Tonight I think I die.

Farran stood before the ancient doors to the tomb which held the eldest of his race.

To anyone else this idea would have seemed ludicrous. Since he was a vampire, wasn't he already dead? But no, he was simply undead. If he did not step carefully in the next few moments, his lord and master might promote him to full dead.

Had he a living heart it would have beat a staccato of fear in his breast. Had he body temperature, his hands would be wet and clammy with nerves. If he had needed oxygen, his breath would have come in short quick bursts. Breathing was something any vampire could fake well enough. It was not necessary in this instance.

But he was a vampire. And he was afraid. He tried to no avail to control his trembling.

One did not simply march up to God and tell him he should have made Eve's breasts bigger. One did not tell God anything of the sort. And yet, in a way this was exactly what he was about to do, advise an elder on the wisest course of action.

If he angered his master, he would be squashed like a bug, like the insignificant insect he was. He would have to be extremely careful as to how he worded his proposal.

Tonight I could die.

He cursed his inward thoughts. His mind was not helping to process words rationally.

Farran forced himself to breathe to have something else to focus on. He pulled up to his full willowy six-foot height. He ran a trembling hand through cropped spiked white hair. He took another deep breath and clenched his hands tightly into fists. Then he forced the breath out and tried to vent all his anxiety with it. He made himself push the great doors before him wide open and walk into the room beyond in what he hoped was a confident manner.

"Farran," a loud voice boomed from the inky darkness.

He tried his best not to search for the source of the voice with his eyes. Farran knew Kane would only be seen if he wished. And sometimes the sight of his master only unnerved him more. His appearance was never the same twice. Kane tricked the eyes and confused the brain enough to unsettle even the most grounded of people.

But Farran could not be distracted from his purpose.

"My Lord," Farran replied in what he hoped was the most respectful and obedient of tones.

"I've been told you wish to make a suggestion to me." The disembodied voice thrummed from what seemed all about him.

"That is true, my Lord," Farran affirmed and bowed low.

"Hmmm," the voice replied.

Farran wasn't exactly sure what emotion this sound conveyed.

"You may proceed," the voice intoned.

"Thank you my Lord," Farran gave another very low bow and took a deep breath to compose his thoughts. "I have been told you wish to awaken to the world and take up your kingdom again now the humans have reached sufficient numbers for harvesting."

"Who told you this?" was the reply from the dark depths of the room.

Farran cast his eyes to the floor before him. "My Lord, it is common knowledge," he said quietly spreading his arms wide.

There was a long silence.

"Continue," the deep voice finally said.

"All Nosferatu call you Lord but the vampire legions across the world are scattered. Some have clans. Most do not. In order to be successful in your endeavor, the vampires must unite into groups that support each other. And you."

Farran thought he heard something like scornful laughter rumble through the room's walls and floor.

"They refuse to unite," it told him. "They bicker and squabble amongst each other. How do you propose we convince them to set aside petty differences?"

"My Lord, you must take the first step," Farran said. He fought the urge to flee as he said this. If he angered Kane with these words, his existence would be over in mere seconds.

But the expected strike from his master never fell.

"And your solution is...?" Kane said.

Farran swallowed the icy spider of fear that inched up his throat. "A gesture," he said quickly. "You should bond yourself with a Nosferatu female."

Another sinister rumble radiated through the room.

"What you propose is disgusting and degrading to me. I am insulted!"

Before Kane could continue, Farran plunged onward.

"I am not suggesting a carnal bond, my Lord. This is to be a business arrangement. If you make this gesture, it will symbolize bonding the very ancient to the days to come. It ties the past to the present and future. If the mate chosen for you is the right stock with the right history, all the scattered Nosferatu will swear loyalty to you in one fell swoop."

There was a very long silence.

"I suspect you already have a certain mate in mind?"

Farran nearly fainted in relief he was allowed to continue. "I do, Lord."

"And?"

Farran bit his lip. *Here comes the ticklish part!* he thought to himself as he wrung his hands nervously. "Well she's not exactly Nosferatu – yet! She's a human who has angered many of our kin by killing an elder."

"Which elder?" Kane demanded.

Farran swallowed once. "Hector."

Kane made no reply for a long moment.

"So...Hector will not be joining us in the Rising." Kane said in the softest of tones.

"I'm afraid not, my Lord,"

He was silent for one long pregnant moment.

"That is very disappointing," Kane said finally. "He was my favorite son. Hector was the only spawn I truly had hope for. He was the most similar to my own kin."

Kane heaved a long sigh. "He will be missed. Now I truly am a god among insects."

Farran fidgeted even more. Maybe this grandiose plan of his wasn't so great after all.

Kane turned his attention back to the issue at hand. "And you want me to mate with Hector's killer? His assassin?"

"She is yet mortal," Farran interjected. "I'm sure she does not want to be converted. It would be a special kind of revenge not to kill her outright. She could prove useful. If she was caught and transformed...and you bonded yourself to her..."

"All would bow down and worship me as the true god of the Nosferatu," Kane's heavy voice finished.

"Yes!" Farran beamed half in relief, half in joy. He had managed to make his case and was still alive.

"And how many vampire children have you spawned, Farran?"

Kane's words stopped him. "None, my Lord."

Farran waited for the axe to fall.

"It seems you are rather overdue," Kane's voice judged him.

"I...I...was waiting for the right occasion," he stammered shivering.

Kane uttered a brief sigh as if he was disappointed in him. "Very well. Do it!"

"At once, my Lord!" Farran tried to keep from smiling

"If she displeases me, I will simply devour her and kill you. Do you understand?"

Farran nodded in agreement but his already pale face blanched whiter. He fled from Kane's presence.

* * *

Are you sure about this?" Bartal asked gravely.

Mykhalo was seated in a plush leather chair in the sitting room of his historic Pennsylvania home. A small table held a Tiffany reading lamp and a now empty wine glass.

Bartal stood next to the bar. Out of all the crystal, he chose a shot glass for vodka.

"I am. I've given it a lot of thought." Mykhalo unbuttoned and rolled up the sleeves of his starched white shirt. "Besides you know he's been dying to get hold of a sample to study. This may be his last chance."

Bartal nodded curtly. "It will be his last chance." He tossed down the shot and came to stand beside his friend's chair.

Mykhalo smiled at his words. "That's what I've always loved about you Bartal, your infernal optimism!"

The door burst open and a young man stepped through. The sides of his head were shaved and the one streak of hair left on top was slicked with gel and styled into a Mohawk. He wore sneakers and worn faded blue jeans with the knees torn out. A matching jeans jacket clad his torso with the sleeves ripped off and frayed. Safety pins and metal chains adorned every piece of clothing. Only one thing did not match his attire. He carried an old black leather doctor's bag clasped tightly by the handle.

"Ah Dr. Sullivan," Mykhalo greeted the youth with a smile. "Today is your lucky day! I've decided to give you your wildest dream. I'm going to let you draw my blood to poke at in the lab."

The young man Mykhalo had called doctor just moments before froze in place and his eyes bugged out briefly.

"Seriously?"

Both Bartal and Mykhalo nodded.

"Has Hell frozen over or somethin'?"

They shook their heads in denial.

"It has come to my attention that my time is short and if there's ever a chance to do this, it's now or never."

The young man blinked a few times before he finally recovered.

"Well then. Let's get to it, shall we?"

He came to the side of Mykhalo's chair. As he knelt, he opened the doctor's bag and took out supplies. Lastly he donned a pair of surgical gloves. His hands moved with confidence, sure of the task they were about to do.

Bartal cleared his throat loudly and the doctor stopped.

"Shouldn't you have a nurse to draw the blood?" he grumbled.

"No!" both Mykhalo and Dr. Sullivan replied with some heat.

The doctor looked to Mykhalo. He bowed his head and waved at the young man.

Dr. Sullivan turned to Bartal.

"Have you ever heard the English saying, 'Too many witches spoil the brew'? I have many...unique...samples in my lab."

"The fewer people involved in this the better," Mykhalo added. "And the doctor has been betrayed many times."

Bartal grunted. "It just seems you make more work for yourself, that is all."

Dr. Sullivan nodded. "True. But to draw a sample of vampire blood from an undead host can be very challenging. Too challenging for a mere nurse."

Bartal's heavy brows furrowed. "Why is that?"

"My kind typically have no blood pressure," Mykhalo said. "Isn't that true doctor?"

Dr. Sullivan nodded. "The blood draw will be difficult even with my experience. I will be lucky if I do not have to use your jugular. We shall see. Now, can we get on with the task at hand?"

He tied the tourniquet snug. Mykhalo uttered a single long sigh and rotated his arm so the tender part faced up.

The young doctor paused one moment, large gauge needle poised and ready. Their eyes met. "Are you absolutely sure about this, sir?"

"I am," Mykhalo told him resolutely. "Go ahead."

The young man nodded. He took a deep breath as if to prepare himself.

The doctor prayed Mykhalo's veins wouldn't act like human veins. He hoped he wouldn't have to chase it about with the bevel of the needle as it rolled away from him, or "blow" which meant it would bleed around the needle shaft, or collapse the minute he struck home, vanishing away from his probe, or the blood would clot almost immediately as it flowed into the medical tube.

He thrust the needle into the pale blue vein hiding just below the surface of the vampire's milk white skin.

Mykhalo never flinched. Bartal turned his face away with a grimace of disgust.

The doctor was lucky. The vein behaved itself and did nothing he feared it might.

Both mortal and vampire watched silently as the medical tube filled with dark red blood. Dr. Sullivan switched the red topped tube with a purple top one which he only allowed to fill a small amount. He kept switching tubes and swirling them about before adding them to the tube rack in his bag.

"How much do you want me to take?" he almost whispered to the vampire.

"As much as you think you'll need," was the reply.

"How about enough for a transfusion?" His eyes flickered up and down, half afraid he'd asked the question which must never be asked.

Bartal turned and gave him a sharp look. Almost as quickly Mykhalo waved his reaction off.

"If you think it might prove useful then by all means."

There was a long pause.

Dr. Sullivan nodded briefly and without a pause, pulled out a large transfusion bag with the other. He worked quickly and attached the line to the bag in smooth motions showing none of the apprehension he felt.

"Make a fist," he instructed. "Good. Now keep squeezing and releasing regularly."

Mykhalo did as instructed.

Dr. Sullivan risked a glance to Bartal. The bearded man gave him a stormy look. He turned his eyes back to Mykhalo. The vampire seemed fascinated by the flow of his own blood into the bag. He tilted his head as he observed the whole process. Mykhalo's eyes began to lighten in color.

"Thanks," he whispered softly to him. "You have no idea what this means to me."

Mykhalo smiled slowly and turned his pale gray eyes back to the doctor.

"I have an inkling," he told him. "Now you can go and play mad scientist."

The doctor gave a hard look to the transfusion bag to make sure everything was progressing as it should. He then rummaged about in the bag until he produced another rubber tourniquet which he awkwardly tied about his own arm.

"What are you doing?" Mykhalo asked, not comprehending.

It made perfect sense to Bartal. The big man knelt beside Dr. Sullivan and tied the tourniquet around the doctor's arm exactly as he had done to Mykhalo just moments before.

"I'm taking a lot of blood from you," the doctor explained as he pulled out another intravenous line and affixed a needle to the end. "I can't exactly give you bottled water and cookies."

He prepared another large needle like the one in Mykhalo's arm.

"Stop!" Mykhalo told him. "Don't waste the needle."

Dr. Sullivan looked up, Mykhalo offered the glass which previously held wine.

"Please don't give me a transfusion of your blood. It will still be distasteful from a glass rather than your jugular. Blood cools so quickly. But if you insist then I prefer to drink it this way."

"I do insist."

He put away the other needle. Then took a deep breath and stabbed his own vein wincing as he did so. Bartal held the glass. They all watched as the doctor's blood ran down the tube and into the wine glass.

"This is so unnecessary," Mykhalo told them. "I'm still not hungry."

Bartal sniffed scornfully.

"We can't afford to take the chance, my friend. Drink your medicine." he scolded and handed him the glass filled to nearly overflowing.

Mykhalo acquiesced. He raised the wine glass to his lips and drank deeply. Dr. Sullivan busied himself with cleaning up the medical supplies now the transfusion bag was full.

Mykhalo lowered the glass when it was almost empty with a grimace of distaste, revealing red-stained teeth. "Dante!" he wagged a scolding finger at the youth. "You really must stop smoking!"

CHAPTER 1

We were about an hour away from landing in Munich when Bree spoke to me again.

"Mom?"

Bree's voice was at my shoulder, soft and low in a secretive sort of way. "Yes, Hon?" I turned to regard my daughter. Her face twisted in confusion as several emotions played across her pale features.

"Do you still believe in God after...after what happened?" she said

I smiled reassuringly to her and stroked her bright red hair. "Even more so now than before."

Bree sighed and fingered her iPad. "I guess Sekhmet's done with me now."

My brows wrinkled. "Now why would you think that?"

Her green eyes turned back to me, wide and innocent. "Well, we did what She wanted us to do. She's done with us now. Right?"

Her eyes begged me for clarity. I sighed heavily and gazed out the window at the clouds.

"I'm always amazed when something horrible happens in a person's life, their first reaction is to insist there is no God. How could God hurt them like that if He really is love?"

I sighed again.

"Fools! They're so eager to leave Him but does He ever leave them? No."

I turned my attention back to my daughter.

"Maybe Sekhmet is done with you and you are ready to respond to a different face of God. Maybe She has no plans of leaving you just yet. We shall see. Just wait and we shall see."

"Okay," Bree said and then she laughed quietly. "The last time you gave me that advice you turned out to be dead right!"

"See? Sometimes mothers are right after all," I chuckled and tousled her bright red hair affectionately.

I tried to sleep. But sleeping on an airplane never worked for me. I always found myself waking up at the slightest sound. Bree busied herself by pecking away at her iPad while cruising the 'net. She kept herself amused like this for a little while. Then I noticed her start to grumble.

"What is it?" I sighed and gave into wakefulness.

She sat back in her chair and frowned. With a furtive glance she asked in a hushed tone, "Ma, have you ever wanted to....to be a vampire?"

I straightened up in my seat and looked her full in the eye.

"What a strange question."

"Yeah I know." Bree rolled her eyes, made a face and nodded.

But then her eyes met my own. "Uh…well? Have you?"

I found myself momentarily at a loss for words.

"I…uh…never gave it much thought actually."

"Well think about it," she nodded. "Then tell me. It's important."

We held each other's eyes for a long pregnant moment.

Bree was absolutely right. If we were just ordinary people the question would be an incredibly odd one.

But after what we both had so recently gone through…

"No, I do not want to be a vampire," I said with quiet conviction and certainty to my words.

Bree's eyes never moved from my face. "Why? Tell me." she said and then after a short pause she reiterated, "It's important."

As I searched for a way to put my thoughts into words, Bree continued, "Don't you want to be young, beautiful and strong forever?"

"The price is a little high!" I sniffed in scorn.

I thought harder and Bree waited, her eyes searching the emotions as they played across my face.

"A vampire's life is not forever. It's never forever. It's just a tease, a lie of immortality. They all eventually die. No. Cancel that. They all eventually *get killed!*"

I sighed and thought harder.

"I don't want to live so long I end up watching my family and friends grow old and die right before me. I'd miss the sunshine. And having to kill people to live….what does that do to you inside after a while? How does that twist you into a person you never wanted to become?"

I thought of Brittany.

"And what if you killed a dear friend? No, I do not want to live with that."

Bree nodded, thinking hard.

"It's just...I've been cruisin' all these vampire sites on the 'net and people are saying how much they long to be a vampire…how romantic it is and how great it must be to not worry about anyone's feelings but their own…"

I stopped her there. "From everything Mykhalo told me, that's not necessarily true."

Bree nodded again.

"And what do you think my little Bookworm? Do you want to be a vampire?"

"Heck no!" Bree laughed. "I think all those vampire wannabes are some really sick twisted people! They've got issues!"

I laughed. Bree turned back to her computer screen, signed out, put the machine away.

"Besides," she continued. "You'd have only one food group to choose from. And, after a while, doesn't all blood begin to taste alike? I'd have a fit if I could never eat cheesecake or ice cream or pho' again!"

I laughed louder.

We both lapsed into a comfortable silence.

"Ma? There's still vampires in the world, right? We didn't get them all did we?" Bree said eventually.

"Oh I am absolutely sure we didn't get them all." I grunted and shook my head ruefully. "There's more out there!"

Bree frowned again eyebrows furrowed in concern. "Somehow I just knew that would be your answer!"

She was quiet for another moment. I could sense her mind was full of worrisome thoughts.

3

"Then…what do we do? I mean it's a pretty good bet more will come after us. Do you have any spells or tricks or something that might work?"

Now my mind really started to spin. I remembered what Mykhalo told me on his last night alive that now I and my daughter would be a magnet to more creatures of the night. I had to prepare myself and Bree for the eventuality. I still had to protect my daughter in any way I knew how, and magic might be a very effective means to an end. What did I know? All the spells I'd worked in the past probably didn't apply. I knew love charms, spells to give one success and yes, I did know some magic for protection. But somehow I suspected protection from a vampire would need to be a spell with an extra punch.

"We need to find a priest and get a lot of holy water, "Bree muttered to herself.

"That's it!" I exclaimed suddenly in triumph. "I can teach you how to make holy water!"

Bree gave me a confused look.

"You can do that?" she asked. "I thought you needed a Catholic priest."

"Poppycock!" I dramatically waved her comment away. "No priest needed. Any dumb fool can make holy water! All it takes is intent."

Bree blinked a few times, an incredulous look on her face. "How many supplies do I need?"

I smiled at my daughter. "Very few at all."

She smiled in return and an eager light came into her eyes. "Show me!"

I hailed the flight attendant and requested water. She brought us two clear bottles with a label which suggested purity. I turned to Bree after she had walked out of ear-shot. "Do you still have your pendulum on you?"

Bree immediately rummaged in the backpack stashed under her seat. She pulled out her own pendulum with a victorious smile a minute later. It was a simple point cut from iridescent opalite stone with a metal clasp attached to a leather cord.

I nodded my approval and busied myself unscrewing the lids from her water bottles.

"Now you remember the golden rule when it comes to asking anything of a pendulum, right?" I tested her.

"Of course!" Bree was ready with the answer. "Whenever you ask a pendulum any question, it must be as simple as possible, meaning questions which can only be answered with yes, no or maybe. And when asking the question, don't have any preconceived notion of what answer you want or the pendulum will give you just that answer."

I smiled. "Nice to know you pay attention. Now. Hold the pendulum over the open mouth of the bottle and ask what charge it is, negative or positive."

"But shouldn't we put it in a glass? Won't the plastic throw off the answer?"

I shook my head. "It doesn't matter the container is plastic. It will still work. Now go to it."

Bree took a deep breath and closed her eyes clearing her mind from all distracting thoughts. I closed my eyes to mere slits as I watched and saw her aura flair briefly. I smiled.

Bree opened her eyes and turned her attention to the bottle in front of her. She held the leather cord high overhead and straightened the pendulum until its point was suspended without moving above the open mouth of the bottle. Her eyelids drooped and her lips silently moved.

It didn't take long. Almost imperceptibly the cut opalite began to swing. Slowly at first but then faster and in bigger sweeps it began to swing in a diagonal line over the mouth of the bottle. It took only a couple of minutes for this to happen.

I saw Bree murmur a quiet thanks and she stopped the motion of the pendulum with her hands.

"Very good," I said. "Now what did it tell you?"

Bree sighed and replied at once. "It said the water has a negative charge."

I nodded. "And now I want you to change the negative to a positive charge."

She blinked at me, confused. "Uh…okay. How?"

My smile only increased. "Simple. You put your intent into it. Concentrate on changing the water's charge from negative to positive. That's all. Go ahead and do it."

She looked doubtfully at me. Bree turned her attention back to the open bottle of water. She took another deep sigh and grasped the bottle with both hands like it was a sword hilt. She sighed, closed her eyes and fell into a meditative state. Again I saw her lips move and once again I saw her aura flair. She stayed this way for a couple of minutes. Then she opened her eyes and let go of the bottle. Bree peered intently at the water for a moment. Then her eyes turned to me.

"Um…its looks just the same," she said.

"Well what did you expect?" I laughed. "A puff of smoke like a magician?"

Bree chewed her lip in concern. "But how do I know it worked?"

I smiled. "You're trying to change it metaphysically not physically. You're not going to see the change with your eyes. Take out your pendulum again and ask the same question as before. But remember to try not to doubt yourself or expect any outcome. Go on."

Bree frowned but obeyed. She sighed closed her eyes and concentrated like before. It took a bit longer this time to center and clear her mind. Then she opened her eyes and set up the pendulum like before.

At first nothing happened. We waited patiently both knowing pendulums could not be rushed. Then the stone began to swing. Its motion was different than the last time. This time it swung in circles. The circles grew progressively bigger and bigger until the arc encompassed the bottle like a cowboy's lasso around a prospective target.

"Congratulations Bree," I told my daughter proudly. "You now know how to make all the holy water you need."

"Well that was easy!" Bree smiled. "Wish all spells were that simple."

She laughed easily and I drank in the happy sound of my daughter's mirth. *Amazing!* I thought to myself. All I needed was to hear the sound of my daughter's joy and I was home.

"What happens if I drink it?" she asked me.

I shrugged as if it was no serious matter. "Then you will have drunk holy water. That's all. It won't hurt you in any way."

6

She grinned, tickled with herself for mastering this newly discovered skill.

I sighed to myself as I watched her. My mind drifted onto more serious things. I wished I knew if Wiccan holy water had the same effect as the Catholic equivalent. I wished I could test it somehow. I didn't speak these doubts to Bree. I didn't want her to catch the same disease of hesitation I had. I wanted her to be sure of herself and believe what she had just created and learned really would work as a weapon against vampires. Belief in one's actions might just be the tipping point between whether something worked or not.

We both had to believe in ourselves.

CHAPTER 2

Bree yawned and stretched as our plane taxied to its designated runway at the Munich airport. We were both weary of the flight. I wondered how long it would take for our internal clocks to adjust to the time change.

"I can't wait to get outta this flying box!" Bree said. I smiled in complete sympathy. It seemed the newness of her first plane ride had worn off long ago.

I looked out the window and sighed in relief. The rolling stair contraption was being pushed up to the plane for the passengers to disembark. *Good!* I thought to myself. I hated those folding tunnels they herded you through like lemmings! I wanted to feel the wind of a foreign country on my face.

I placed my baseball cap over my head and adjusted the dark sunglasses on my face. My eyes thus shielded, I looked over the other passengers as we stood up and gathered our things.

I wondered if I needed to worry about any of them following us.

Bree and I both shouldered our backpacks. We'd chosen to pack light. Besides, we really only intended to stay for the funeral and then head back to America.

It was windy and chilly when we first stepped out of the plane. I clutched my light jean jacket closer and Bree squealed in shock of the breeze.

We made our way down the stairs, the wind buffeting and tugging us every which way.

Bree called me and tugging on my sleeve, pointed to the tail end of the plane.

Workers busily unpacked cargo from the bowels of the airliner.

Two men rolled out a black casket.

Mykhalo's coffin.

Bree and I made our way toward it.

One of the workers turned the casket a little sharper than the other expected as they pushed it off of the ramp and the load tipped off the dolly. There was a shout as hands tried clumsily to catch it.

A man's voice bellowed right behind us which made me jump nearly out of my skin.

I'd been trying to memorize some German words on the plane but I needed no translation to tell me the gruff voice had called them both idiots!

I turned to see a man of singular appearance behind me. He looked like a Russian gentleman from long ago, cleaned up and stuffed into modern business attire. He had a long but fastidiously groomed brown beard and mustache. His brown hair had gray wings at the temples and he wore it long enough to tie back in a short ponytail. The wind threatened to rip his hair loose from its bindings. He was dressed in an overcoat which barely hid the suit underneath and he stood only a shade taller than me. But his black eyes glittered dangerously as he stalked past us, face dark as a storm cloud.

A rather heated exchange took place between the 'Russian' and the airline cargo workers. I think they were speaking German but it was difficult to say.

"Ma," Bree hissed in my ear, tugging again at my sleeve.

I glanced at her face and saw her gesture behind us with her eyes. I turned to look.

Two black stretch limousines with tinted windows pulled up, flanked by the swankiest hearse I've ever seen-with diplomat flags set at the corners. Silently, men who looked like secret service agents disembarked wearing black shades. Their faces were utterly emotionless and cold.

"Uh Ma..." Bree began in a tremulous whisper. "Are we in trouble with the German government?"

"Not that I know of!"

"Uh.... German Mafia?"

"I don't think so!"

"Uh-hunh." she grunted. "Then what do they want with Mykhalo's body?"

"I'm not sure but I mean to find out," I said and strode forward.

My momentum was halted by one of the men in black. He simply stepped in front of me and motioned me to stay where I was. He didn't touch me.

I didn't like his cold expression.

"Are we being kidnapped?" Bree whispered.

The thought *had* occurred to me. What would I do if indeed we *were* kidnapped?

I hadn't the foggiest idea!

Unnerved as I was, I tried to look past this man's shoulder to the confrontation just beyond us.

The airline workers were very upset now, gesturing and shouting angrily at the 'Russian.' Finally the bearded man produced a document from the front breast pocket of his over jacket and practically flung it in their faces. One worker snatched it out of the air before the wind could take it and scrutinized the paper, scowling darkly. He finally relinquished his charge. He threw the document back in the 'Russian's' face, motioned to his partner and retreated inside the plane for more cargo, grumbling loudly.

The 'Russian' wadded up the paper and stuffed it back into his jacket with one hand. With the other, he gestured to the men in black. Four came forward and carefully commandeered Mykhalo's coffin.

I could no longer stand by and watch.

With a grunt of force, I shoved past the man impeding my way and strode up to the Russian who seemed to be in charge.

"What are you doing with Mykhalo's remains?" I demanded tartly.

The Russian spun on his heel and for the first time, actually seemed to see me. My appearance seemed to startle him. He stared for a breathless moment and then his mouth split wide and he began to laugh.

A chill went down my spine when our eyes met. A coldness squeezed my heart when he laughed. My Wiccan senses were all in an uproar over this one warning, screaming, tugging at me to get away.

But why I did not know.

Then I realized I'd had much the same reaction when Mykhalo first stepped into my bookstore in Sleepy Pines, Pa.

But this person couldn't possibly be a vampire! He was out in broad daylight, the sun's rays fully lit his face and he seemed completely unaffected. Yet the warning in my gut screamed *Get away!*

He was not a vampire. But he was *something* sinister, my instincts assured.

But what? He seemed familiar even though I knew I'd never met him.

"Pardon me, but I see nothing at all to laugh at!" I declared, insulted by his reaction.

He managed to control his laughter at last and wiped the tears from his eyes with hands encased in black leather gloves.

"My apologies. I'm so sorry my manners are in such bad taste at a time like this. I am Bartholomew Sebastian. You must be Mrs. Susanne Miller who I've heard so much about."

He offered his gloved hand to me to shake.

I did not know what to make of this character. For a long moment, I considered refusing to take the offered hand. But then I slowly and suspiciously relented.

I felt my little hand disappear entirely into the gloved paw of this bear standing before me. He smiled and squeezed my hand in a frighteningly, crushing grip.

His teeth were white as Mykhalo's.

He pumped my hand twice then suddenly jerked me towards him. I felt the bristles of his beard tickle my cheek and his breath ruffle my ear as he whispered one word privately to me.

"Hoffe," he said.

Then pushed me back to a safe distance and released my hand.

We regarded each other silently for a long moment.

He had spoken Mykhalo's safe code word.

Why then did I still not trust him?

The silence was becoming awkward. I had to say something.

"Who told you about me?" I finally managed to force out in a faltering voice.

His smile disappeared momentarily. His face turned to regard the coffin his men solemnly bore toward the black hearse. When he returned to me his smile had grown sad.

"You knew Mykhalo?" I asked in a softer voice.

He nodded.

"He was my oldest and dearest friend." he replied. "Mykhalo sent me word before he died that I was to collect you and your daughter at the airport and see to your every comfort during your stay here. I am here at his request."

The tension between us lessened somewhat.

"How long have you known him?" I asked.

The corners of his mouth twitched upwards briefly.

"Such conversation is better suited for a more secure setting, Mrs. Miller," was all he would tell me.

One of the men in black, the one who had stopped me before, came up to Bartholomew and whispered something into his ear. He gave a nod and a grunt of acknowledgement before turning back to me.

"So sorry to rush you off, Mrs. Miller, without a proper introduction to my men but we need to leave now. So if you please..."

His gloved hand gestured to the waiting limousine. The man in black held the door open for us.

Bree and I exchanged uncomfortable looks. I glanced to the hearse. Mykhalo's coffin had been loaded and they closed the doors. The men in black seemed to be in a hurry to get going.

I took Bree by the hand and we entered the spacious, leather upholstered compartment. Bartholomew entered behind us and closed the door.

I could tell Bree was not comfortable around this strange bearded man. She huddled closer to me like a much smaller child and fixed him with a suspicious glare.

I looked out the window. Mykhalo's hearse pull ahead of us and we swung smoothly into line behind it.

I turned my attention back to the Russian looking man in front of me.

"What about customs?" I asked. "Don't we need to show our papers to some official?"

Bartholomew smiled at me quietly.

"Of course, Madame," he told me.

Our limo pulled up to the airport gate and a stiff looking German with an expression as if he never smiled, rapped on the tinted window. The tone of his voice was not pleasant.

Bartholomew sighed impatiently as he pushed the button on the automatic window and abruptly pasted on a smile as he hailed the German official cheerfully. The man's scowl disappeared instantly when he saw Bartholomew's face and the two began a lively chatter in German. Presently Bartholomew motioned to my daughter and I. I recognized the word "American" in his speech.

"Give me your passports, please," he ordered us.

We silently handed them over and Bartholomew passed them to the guard. The man looked at our photos on the passports and then peered into the limo at both of us and nodded. He strode away.

"This should only take a moment," Bartholomew said.

Barely had he finished speaking when the man returned and handed him back the stamped passports, which were quickly passed back to us. The German and the 'Russian' resumed their lively conversation and I got the distinct impression they were exchanging small talk on each other families and when would be their next get together over a tankard. The window finally rolled up. Bartholomew waved goodbye to his friend and the limo continued peacefully on its way.

"That's it?" asked Bree. "That's 'customs?'"

I snorted.

"The process is usually much more time consuming, my dear."

"Not when you have diplomat status." Bartholomew graced us with another huge smile.

Man! He seems to have a lot of teeth! Like a crocodile! I thought to myself.

I heaved a tense sigh.

"Can we talk now?" I asked tersely.

"For the moment we are safe." he nodded. "I'm sorry to have to force you to endure another long trip. I'm sure you are very tired after your plane ride. It will take us several hours to get to our lodging. At least here you can stretch out and sleep more comfortably than on a plane."

I nodded quickly, not caring about the small details.

"What would make me more comfortable right now are some answers to my questions."

The man across from me grunted in amusement.

"Mykhalo warned me you wasted no time in getting to the point!" he chuckled. "Very well then. What will put your mind at ease, Madame?"

"Well, for starters, are we your prisoners?"

He really did laugh at this; a big, deep, rumbling laugh. I felt Bree shiver at my side and cuddle closer. I put a reassuring arm around her.

"Heavens no, Madame!" he chuckled. "You and your daughter are our honored guests! You are both to be afforded every luxury which is within my power to provide for you during your stay. You may stay until the funeral is over and then return to America. Or you may stay longer. Whatever you wish."

I nodded silently, taking this in.

"Who are these men in black with you? Are they your henchmen?"

"They are my apprentices, nothing more," Bartholomew grunted.

"And your profession is…?"

He smiled at this, a wide smile which could have meant many things.

"Right now my profession and that of my apprentices is seeing to you and your daughter's safety during your stay."

"So...you are bodyguards...so to say?"

He waggled his head in a non-committal way.

"If you like."

"Are we in danger then?"

His black eyes glittered at me.

"You were a dear friend of Baron Mykhalo Von Ludwig." he informed me. "Not only did Mykhalo acquire many shadowy friends during his long life but he also accumulated quite a few enemies. Those who wanted to hurt him may now wish to harm you. This is why such measures as my 'men in black' as you so quaintly put it, are necessary. We will strive to keep you both as safe as possible. But it would be

15

good if you do not close those eyes in the back of your head, so to speak. Mykhalo's funeral will attract much attention, some genuinely sympathetic. Some not so. Keep your guard up, Mrs. Miller."

I was silent while I digested this information. I finally turned my eyes back to his.

"How old are you, Bartholomew?"

I knew I was taking a risk asking such a question but I had to know.

Bartholomew's eyes glittered and the corners of his mouth twitched.

"Suspicious and persistent." he mused aloud almost as if to himself. "Good qualities to have. I shall have to watch myself around you! Please call me Bartal."

I raised my chin defiantly.

"What about my question?"

Bartal's only reaction was to knock on the window behind him. The limousine came to a silky, silent stop.

"Another time perhaps. Good day, Mrs. Miller." he said with a courteous nod and he stepped out of the limo and entered the one ahead of us, past the hearse.

Bree sighed in relief at his departure and wriggled away a bit.

"Ma," she muttered softly.

"What babe?" I said as I arranged myself a bit more comfortably on the plush leather.

She waited until her silence forced me to look into her eyes.

"He's older than Mykhalo."

CHAPTER 3

"Mom! Mom! Wake up! You've gotta see this!" Bree shook me.

The ride had been long with only two brief stops for bathroom breaks. Compared to the plane, the limo was too comfortable. I always slept easier in a car anyway and this made it all too easy. I had spent most of the ride stretched out on the plush leather, snoring away.

"What is it?" I moaned, not wanting to be disturbed.

"We're here! We're here!" she babbled. "We just pulled through two honkin' big iron gates around a stone wall."

I groaned and sat up, rubbing the grit out of my eyes.

"Mom! We get to stay in a *castle*! A real castle! How cool is that??" Bree squealed.

"A *what?*" I retorted, still not quite awake.

"Look! Just look!" Bree exclaimed. Her window spun down with a soft, automatic hiss.

My eyes followed her pointing fingernail, painted with glittering red nail polish.

The limo climbed a cobblestone road at a sedate pace towards the square archway of an ancient castle. Two large winged statues of African lions sat watch at the corners of the arch. All who passed beneath earned expressions half regal, half disdain.

I turned my wondering eyes back to the castle. At first glance it looked brick but as we drew nearer I saw the walls were simply made from dark colored stone. The castle was perched on a small hill surrounded by larger hills built into the bend of a river beneath.

I expected most castles to be great sprawling, glistening white affairs but this one seemed to shoot straight up into the sky, piercing the clouds with all its spires like conical witch's hats. Beneath most were octagonal watch houses painted white with windows framed in red. The white watch houses stood in stark contrast against the dull brown stone walls. It was both ominous and welcoming at the same time.

We drove beneath the arch. I got the distinct feeling the protective stone spirit of the castle had wrapped its stoic arms about us and swallowed us up, hiding us from the rest of the modern world and its frenzied designs. Modern life meant nothing to these stones which stood for centuries untouched. And would continue to stand while the world sped by.

I gazed upon the glory of this magnificent old structure. My mind flashed back to one of the many conversations I'd had with Mykhalo.

"Any castles?" I inquired.

"Just a small one in Bavaria. The heating bills are astronomical in winter!"

"Any secret passageways hidden in bookcases?"

"That property has many secrets," he stepped closer to me. *"Maybe you'll get to investigate it someday."*

It occurred to me that nowhere in his response did he suggest he'd be by my side. A deep sadness came over me at this realization. I felt very much alone.

I turned to look at my daughter.

She was nearly giddy with glee. Bree's head was out the window like a happy dog, craning to catch every inch of the colossal building we would be staying in.

"This is *so friggin' awesome*! A real castle! I wonder how old it is. Does it have ghosts? Hey! Maybe someone died in the dungeon ages ago! I can't wait to run through the halls!" she bubbled, delirious in her excitement.

I forced myself to have a more carefree attitude for my daughter.

"That's right!" I told her. "Go ahead and act like a total, uncultured American! What will the locals think?"

Her head suddenly popped back into the limo. Her red hair looked like it had been brushed with an eggbeater.

Silly spawn! was all I could think.

"Hey! Something just occurred to me!" she told me. "What if this is just a teaser? What if they're really going to put us up in a small cottage nearby? You know, the servant's quarters?"

I snorted.

"I don't think Mykhalo would jest with us like that." I told her as I rummaged in my backpack for a hairbrush.

"You really need this. Let's make a good first impression to the servants," I advised. "And please try to behave with some decorum for starters."

She plopped herself down on the seat and attacked her hair.

"I don't quite think I'm dressed right for this place.

"Ditto!" I laughed.

A little late now to change."

The limo swung closer to the stone walls and began to slow.

I glanced out the window.

Is this what Mykhalo called a small castle?

Bree passed the brush back to me and I turned my attention to my own long tresses.

"I'm sure there are places inside which will be off limits to us. This is probably a big tourist attraction in the summer," I muttered thinking aloud. "So *don't touch anything*! Everything inside is probably several centuries old. Heaven forbid we break it!"

"Ooo! Right. Hadn't thought about that," Bree said suddenly serious. Then she wriggled and bounced on the seat, clapping her hands.

"A castle! I can't believe it! Wait 'til the girls back home hear this one! I better take lots of pictures." She hugged herself in excitement. "This is almost as good as being a real princess!"

"Well you've always been that to me, dear," I chuckled in motherly pride.

"Even without the castle and crown." I didn't really care whether she heard me or not.

"Now all I need is a prince to go with it!" she giggled.

I shot her a warning look.

"Didn't anyone tell you? Princes are extinct."

"No they're not!" she laughed. "I know at least two. Dad and Mykhalo."

"Yes, and they're both dead." I muttered with a heavy sigh.

"Killjoy!" Bree sniffed.

She was absolutely right. I decided to shut up and not rain on her parade.

The limousine door opened and afternoon sunshine poured into the black tinted shadows inside our compartment.

Bartal appeared, blocking out the light. He bowed as if we were important dignitaries and held out a gloved hand to me. I wordlessly took it as expected. I stepped out of the limo and Bree followed close behind.

"Mrs. Susanne and Sabrina Tempest Miller, welcome to *Schloss Lowentore.* Or Castle Lion's Gate in English," he stated with pride.

We were finally afforded an unimpeded view of the castle. It stretched high overhead, festooned by nature with climbing rose vines and ivy. It seemed to have multiple levels. There were winged lions on the corners of its many rooftops. The windows gazed dispassionately back at us and I felt an awareness regarding us with unblinking eyes.

Was it the lions who watched us? Or the castle itself? I didn't know. I was in the presence of something far older than I've ever known. If I'd been alone, I would have asked permission of the spirits within before entering. But I was unable to do so tactfully in the present company.

Two immense, winged African lions framed the main doors. They seemed to have been gilt at once time, or fashioned from bronze which had weathered and tinged green by countless years.

A quick glance at Bree and I saw she also noticed this detail.

"Your bags will be brought in later. Come. Let me introduce you to the staff." Bartal ushered us through the great doors.

It was everything I expected of a castle. Vaulted ceilings and expensive woodwork everywhere I looked. Large paintings of previous occupants hung on the walls and their eyes regarded my daughter and I with silent, lofty expressions.

The staff was lined up and Bartal introduced them to us one by one. They were quiet and polite, almost devoid of personality. I supposed this was how castle servants were expected to behave. I must confess their names went in one ear and out the other; I was so overwhelmed.

It was strange to be the center of attention here. I suddenly felt small and peasantly, like I wasn't supposed to be here. I didn't deserve all this royal attention.

Somehow, when Mykhalo had said all the arrangements had been taken care of, I had never expected *this!* I was totally unprepared. How was I expected to act? Was I supposed to shake the servants' hands, curtsey in reply to the women's curtsey, or just remain aloof and not even acknowledge them with a nod? Somehow my own mother skipped this chapter when she taught me manners. *What an oaf I must seem to them.*

The introductions complete, the servants dispersed. Bartal asked the butler to show us to our quarters.

But then a door banged and Bartal's apprentices wheeled Mykhalo's coffin into the hall.

Everyone, even the servants, froze. There was a long, uncomfortable pause. The women made the sign of the cross and uttered a breathless prayer.

Hans, the butler, barked instructions in German and motioned the men down the hall.

Bartal's men obeyed without a word.

Without a thought I followed.

The sitting room was not far down the hall and was smaller than expected. Golden lion statues stood in each corner, guarding the chilly room.

Mykhalo's casket was positioned in front of a fireplace. The room held several black ribboned bouquets and their perfume filled the air.

"He will rest here until the ceremony," Bartal said in a soft voice.

He turned to those in the room and commanded them with a look. Everyone except the butler, four of the men in black, my daughter and I were ushered out.

The doors shut.

We stood in absolute silence around the coffin for one long, breathless moment. Then Bartal said two words to his men.

I gasped and gave them a shocked look.

21

As I have said before, I don't speak German. But I'd been scouring a German to English dictionary on the plane. I understood just enough to know he'd said, "Open it."

"NO!" I exclaimed. I rushed to the casket, held the lid down before they could get there.

"I must protest! This cannot be allowed!" I fumed at them.

Bartal sighed heavily and stepped forward. I warned him away with an icy look.

"Mrs. Miller," he began in a soft, placating tone of voice. "I understand your misgivings. Really I do. But I must insist on this. Many people doubt Mykhalo is really dead. Many doubt there is a body in the coffin at all. I am one of those. I would much rather you and I view his remains than someone who only wished him evil all his long life. Please. You must permit me to do this. I must know beyond any question of doubt that he is there. Please Mrs. Miller, stand aside."

For a long moment I could do nothing. My thoughts spun wildly.

My family had never agreed with the open casket ritual at funerals. It bothered them too much. But then I remembered Sage explaining the custom to me. With some people, a person dies and no one sees them again. They just disappear from their lives. And while this is good for some because the last memories of their loved one is when the departed was alive and thriving, this does not sit well with others.

Some people need to see the body without the spirit to truly believe their friend has left the mortal coils of life behind. They need to look on their face to bring closure to their emotions. Otherwise how do they know their loved one is really dead? How can they stop expecting them to walk in the door someday? They never really came to grips with the fact their friend is gone.

I relaxed a bit. I gave Bartholomew one last suspicious glare and then backed away from the coffin. Bree gathered me in her arms and I clung to her I buried my head in her shoulder and hair as if I were the child.

Abruptly, every forensic show came to mind. Pictures flashed in my head of bodies in different stages of decomposition. I shuddered. I tried to block the thoughts but they kept coming in a steady stream of horrific images. It was different when the bodies were of strangers. It had been interesting then.

This would certainly *not* be interesting!

I didn't want to see Mykhalo that way. I vowed not to look when they opened it. I buried my face in Bree's red hair.

I heard the smallest of creaks and a hiss when the casket lid opened.

And then there was silence.

My own heart pounded loudly in my ears.

Bree stroked my hair reassuringly and I felt her hand twitch.

"Mom, you should look," she told me. "It's fine. He's really not bad. Please look. It's okay, really."

I pulled away and looked into her face. There was no lie in her eyes.

I took a deep breath and turned around.

Mykhalo lay before me in the coffin. He looked the same as in life. He just looked like he was deep asleep. A pre-dusk sunbeam broke through the high window and fell across him. He didn't burn away into a bony pile of ash at the sun's touch. It lit up his face and glistened on his pale yellow locks. His skin looked almost warm.

I approached the coffin, walking as if in trance. I must have looked like I was going to faint because both Bartal and Hans took me by either arm.

"Let go. I'm fine," I shrugged them off.

I had to touch him one last time.

I laid a hand gently against his face.

It felt cool, like a smooth piece of white marble. I let my hand trail down his cheek to his neck. All was cool to the touch. The blush of life was gone.

My fingertips brushed a cord of leather around his neck. I looped it around my hand and drew it forth, believing it to be his talisman of Bavarian earth.

I was wrong. It was my pentacle.

I remembered I placed it around his neck sometime during the night. I was surprised the mortician had chosen to leave it there.

I choked briefly on emotions. Quietly I replaced it underneath the collar of his fine shirt, hoping the others hadn't seen.

I bent low over Mykhalo and kissed him on the forehead.

23

"You are whole once more. Be at peace." I whispered gently.

I withdrew myself and stepped away from the casket. Some dim sensation told me Bartal and Hans whispered prayers in German.

Without taking my eyes off Mykhalo's face, I nodded.

The men in black stepped forward and slowly, reverently, closed the lid. I watched the shadows obliterate the sunshine on Mykhalo's face.

I thought I saw his eyes open before the lid came down.

And then the coffin shut with a final resounding snap.

Mykhalo hadn't really opened his eyes at all. It was just a figment of my imagination.

CHAPTER 4

He didn't hear Farran enter the room and walk silently behind his chair. He couldn't have because Ainsley Wainwright was snoring on his computer keyboard. Limp strawberry blonde hair pulled loose from his customary pony-tail and blue light from the monitor reflected like a mirror off his balding head.

Farran frowned at the back of the British tech he'd chosen to align himself with. Ainsley disgusted him in so many ways. He smelled bad, his hygiene was always questionable, he was a slob and totally unaware of the effect any of these traits had on the people with which he came into contact. Farran found him so abhorrent he frequently contemplated killing the bloke except he didn't want to touch him to do so. He would have murdered him long ago except for the fact Ainsley had his uses. Despite many flaws, he was a wizard in all things computer and a gifted photographer and videographer.

Ainsley was also known as a "flea" in vampire circles. Any vampire could get the wretch to do anything they wanted simply by dangling the prospect of turning him into an undead. There was nothing Ainsley wanted more than to become a creature of the night. The possibility of this was remote at best. The more probable scenario was one of the Nosferatu getting fed up with the little weasel's pleas and taking him permanently out of the picture.

Until this happened, he belonged mostly to Farran. The vampire kept him busy as a day-walking gopher. He gathered information, ran secret errands and generally did the dirty work Farran would rather not sully his hands with. And Ainsley was all too happy to be a vampire's messenger boy. It made him feel invincible and important. Poor, stupid mortal had no idea he was always one mistake away from dying like any normal human.

"Ainsley!" Farran declared in a loud voice.

The computer guy jumped, startled out of slumber like a kid caught sleeping in class. He slammed his spine back into the chair with a screech and a groan of the worn out piece of furniture. His glasses were crooked, and there were impressions of keys on his cheek and crisp crumbles in his hair.

"Farran!" he exclaimed in an overly dramatic tone of voice. "When did you get here?"

Farran allowed himself to reveal a small smile. "You said you had news for me?"

"Hunh?" the tech guy mumbled in confusion.

Farran sighed as he waited for Ainsley's brain to catch up.

He began to sputter and mumble nervously and he rummaged through the pile of papers on his desk while his thoughts scrambled to remember what he had forgotten.

"Ah yes!" he finally declared in triumph and began busily pecking away at his computer. "Remember the American woman you wanted to settle a score with? Susanne Miller I believe her name was."

Farran frowned and growled in irritation.

"What of it?" he snarled. "I am not permitted to set foot in America. Remember?"

Ainsley only shook his head and grinned.

"No need. No need, my Lord," he said in a very placating and yet triumphant tone of voice. "She has come to us. Wasn't that nice of her?"

He cast a furtive, shaky glance back over his shoulder at his master and then turned his attention back to the keyboard and the screen.

"I have video of her. Here she is getting off the plane in Munich…"

Farran leaned over the table and peered at the computer screen with renewed interest.

Sensing his chance, Ainsley's mouth twitched and he redoubled his efforts with the videos he had shot.

"She's staying with Bartal at Lion's Gate castle. Here's video of her arriving there."

Ainsley risked another quick peek at the vampire. It seemed Farran was riveted to the screen.

"Can you zoom in on her face?" he asked.

Ainsley's fingers stabbed at the keys with renewed vigor. "Your wish is my command, my Lord!"

Farran ignored his words and continued to glare at the screen, his eyes absorbing every detail he saw there. Slowly his hand came up and his finger pointed to a figure on the video.

"Who is this? The girl with her?"

Ainsley twitched in eagerness to do his lord's bidding.

"That is her daughter, Sabrina."

Farran continued to stare, mesmerized by the figures on the screen. Ainsley kept switching between both short videos making sure to zoom in on the faces.

Farran was silent for a very long time as he absorbed the images. Finally he spoke in a whisper.

"We have a choice," then he corrected himself in the very next sentence. "Kane has a choice."

"Uh…my Lord?" Ainsley asked half fearfully.

"How old is the daughter?" he asked in a louder voice.

Ainsley's thoughts scrambled. "A mere adolescent. Not old enough quite yet to drive in her country."

Farran began to pace the room as he thought. He licked his lips hungrily and slowly smiled.

"She's young and naïve. This is her first trip out of the country. She doesn't speak the language. She's ill equipped to handle anything…"

"She's very young and fresh," Ainsley said trying to join in on his master's thoughts but not quite sure where he was going with this train of thought.

"She'd be a much better mark," Farran began to smile widely. "Look at her hair! She's a rebel. It would be so easy to lure her away from mommy dearest, catch her, turn her and present her to Kane."

Ainsley smiled in what he hoped was an encouraging way.

"And you do so like little girls!" he added with a giggle.

Farran stopped and slowly turned to face Ainsley.

The tech turned back to the screen and began to feverishly peck away. "I take it you'll want to know everything about this girl, yes?"

"Yes, and Ainsley…"

At this Farran was right behind the computer guru, digging his fingers painfully into the tech's shoulders.

"Don't ever presume to tell me what I do or don't like again. Ever."

CHAPTER 5

Bree and I were given adjoining rooms. The bedrooms were immense. Each was equipped with its own fireplace and canopy bed which would have fit four people easily. And, just like in the sitting room, both rooms were guarded by four brass lions in the corners. Their figures frozen in mid roar, a paw raised to threaten whoever disturbed them.

It was late in the day when we arrived at Schloss Lowentore so a servant brought us a small evening meal to our rooms before bed.

I'd slept so much in the limo I thought I would be awake all night. But a fit of sudden fatigue hit about an hour after sunset. I was barely able to roll myself into the thick blankets before sleep took me.

I awoke several hours later. The moon was in its crescent phase but the night was cloudless and the white beam from its slivered face awoke me.

I sat up and looked around at the great room lit in moonlight.

I suddenly felt the need to move about.

I disentwined myself from the covers and placed my bare feet on the wooden floor. The polished wood did not seem as cold as expected. I strode to the nearest lion and stroked its cold, metal mane distantly. I watched my fingers caress its heavily muscled form and come to rest on the pad of its one raised paw. My fingertip rested there, encircled by the beads of its exposed claws as if we were shaking hands.

What's with all the lions? I thought to myself.

My heart was beset then with an irresistible urge to see Mykhalo's coffin.

I turned and left the opulent bedroom.

I didn't remember the way from the bedroom to the sitting room. But my feet had a surprising new sense of direction and within moments, I was in the room before his casket.

My hands lovingly caressed its smooth black surface, watching the way the moonlight played across my fingers. The top of the casket was so well polished I could see my reflection in its curved, ebony surface.

"Zan," a voice whispered at my shoulder.

Startled, I spun on my heel and glanced about the room wildly.

But I saw no one.

I was all alone in the room.

Well, except for Mykhalo's coffin...and the brass lions...and the flowers.

I turned back to the coffin and regarded my reflection with a new interest.

As I looked at my dim image, I saw another, less distinct, move suddenly behind my left shoulder.

My heart began to pound in fear.

"Zan," again the breathless voice whispered just behind me.

I froze in terror. I was afraid to turn around. But I had to see what was behind me.

Slowly, holding onto the casket for support, I turned my head and looked through the black curtain of my hair.

Mykhalo stood just three feet away. He seemed misty and insubstantial, like a ghost.

"Zan," he said. "Would you love me if I wasn't a vampire?"

It was then I awoke and sat up with a start and a gasp.

I was all alone in the great canopy bed in the enormous bedroom.

It was only a dream.

* * *

The next morning we had a sumptuous breakfast in our pajamas on the castle veranda overlooking the rose garden. Hans served us far too much food, after which we retired to our rooms to shower and change for the funeral.

30

I'd just recently bought a black dress appropriate for funerals when Brittany died so I believed I was set for attire. I piled my long black hair on top my head with the assistance of many hairpins. I donned the dress, stockings and black heels, which I rarely wore and made my way to the sitting room.

Bartholomew was talking quietly to Hans in German. Both were silenced by my appearance.

For a long moment no one spoke. I felt my face begin to turn red.

"Is something wrong?" I asked and began to look down at myself, almost expecting my slip to be showing.

"You mean to wear that?" Bartal said stiffly.

I looked back at him blinking stupidly.

"Isn't this appropriate?" I said. "I'm sure it's not Rodeo Drive but..."

My face was now burning hot.

Hans and Bartal exchanged knowing looks. The Russian spoke quietly to the butler who nodded and immediately left.

"The dress is adequate, my dear, and so is your hair," Bartholomew explained slowly. "The whole appearance though is just a bit...flat."

I blinked a few more times before I ascertained his meaning. I was wearing no jewelry.

The only necklace I brought with me was my spare pentacle, which I didn't think was appropriate for the occasion.

Hans reappeared.

"Ah!" Bartal breathed, rubbing his big hands together. "I believe this will remedy the situation quite nicely."

Hans bore a black, velvet jewelry box in his white-gloved hands. He smiled and with a polite bow, opened it for me.

A choker of several strands of white pearls with a centerpiece of large black pearls interspersed with tiny diamonds winked at my amazed eyes. Matching earrings and bracelet accompanied, all of white and black pearls.

I could only stare dumbfounded at the jewels. Some dim sensation told me in a strict but silent voice not to ask if they were real.

Bartal easy removed the choker from its velvet bed and placed it gently around my throat while I recovered my wits.

"There! Now you look more the part of the bereaved loved one," he said and came back around to view the front. "Every woman should own at least one strand of pearls."

I decided not to tell him the closest thing I had was the strand of mother-of-pearl beads Bree made me, which I treasured highly.

My shaking hands somehow found a way to don the earrings and the bracelet.

"Much better," Bartholomew looked me up and down with a critical eye.

My hands were still stroking the smooth roundness of the pearls which embraced my neck.

I suddenly got a quick flash in my mind's eye of a woman; tall, slender, laughing blue eyes, head wound with long, white-blonde braids. Her skin was alabaster except for rosy cheeks and red lips. Her gown perfectly complimented her golden hair. Roses of every size and color surrounded her. Their perfume was heavy in the air.

The vision lasted only an instant and then left me with the feeling of warm approval.

"Who was the last person to wear these pearls?" I asked in a whisper.

"That would be Sofiya, Mykhalo's mother." Bartholomew smiled quietly, almost wistfully.

My eyes met Hans'. His professional look fell away and he looked at me narrowly.

"You saw her," he whispered, in a heavily accented voice. "You have the sight."

A chill went through me. Hans suspected there was more to me than met the eye. Could he be trusted?

Bartholomew dismissed him curtly.

With a flash, the professional wall returned to his face. He bowed slightly to us both and left.

"Do not concern yourself with Hans," Bartal told me as if he sensed my worries. "He has seen quite a few strange things while in the Baron's employ. He is not given to spreading rumors or gossip."

I absorbed this information quietly.

"Does he know...about Mykhalo? About what he really is...I mean...was?"

Bartal smiled, approached the black coffin, and stroked it sadly with a gentle, gloved hand.

"Hans has always known Mykhalo's secret. He was raised here in the castle. His father was the butler before and his grandfather was Mykhalo's gardener."

Bartal sighed and folding his hands behind his back, turned to face me.

"All the staff here knew what Mykhalo was. Most of them were raised with the knowledge. You see Mykhalo 'collected' people during his long life, especially during the war."

Here he lost me.

"What do you mean 'collected'?"

Bartal's face wrinkled.

"Maybe the word 'collected' is not correct in this instance. What I meant to say is the Baron helped a great many people and repaid them by seeing that they were employed, safe from threats both political and from the shadow-world. In doing so, he amassed a large 'extended family' so to speak, of people around him. During the war he was very busy rescuing people; Jews who did not want to leave Germany, people who spoke out against the Fuerher, people left homeless by the bombing. He brought them here and helped them get back on their feet. He protected and hid them as well as he was able. Some left to follow their own dreams and careers. Some remained out of loyalty to what he did for them. They have all stayed close throughout the years. They have been there when he needed them and he has returned the favor. It made for a loyalty and devotion which has spanned several generations."

I looked at the door which Hans had just exited.

"Now what will happen, now Mykhalo is dead? Are they all out of work?"

Bartal smiled and laughed briefly.

"No my dear. Things will continue as they always have. This castle will be opened to the public for summer tours and weddings as normal. Castle Lion's Gate doesn't make a huge amount of money doing this

33

but Mykhalo made wise investments to insure this would continue. Some of his 'family members' work for a bank, another is an accountant and still another works for the stock market. The money is there and very secure. The Baron assured us no one would be left to fend for themselves should hard times come."

"And....what is my role in all of this?"

Bartal smiled and put a reassuring arm around my shoulders.

"You and your daughter are now important members of this odd little family. I'm sure your purpose will eventually rise to the surface. But for now all you need know is you have friends in very high places. You are well protected here."

His words did little to comfort me. I felt as if I was in a gilded cage. I had no idea just how much or little I could trust him. And although he was meant to see to my safety, I felt there was a lot he was hiding from me.

"Now if I could trouble you for some assistance," Bartholomew said.

I turned my eyes back to him. He held a tie in his hand.

"It's a little difficult to do this with my beard."

I smiled and walked up to him to comply.

He held his thick beard out of the way while I worked on tying his tie.

I looked past his shoulder to the shiny, black coffin which held Mykhalo. The pearls which rested on my neck felt cool and smooth as my skin moved under them.

"So, did you know her? Mykhalo's mother I mean."

As I said this I drew up the tie. The motion was quick, as if I wouldn't stop when I reached his throat.

He took a startled gulp of air and our eyes locked and held.

I hadn't asked his age. But in asking him the question, I was implying I suspected his age was not the span of any normal human's.

He was cornered both by my words and my hands on the tie around his neck.

His eyes looked into my own. For a long breathless moment, neither of us spoke.

34

Bartal finally placed his hands on mine and unfastened them from around his tie.

"Thank you for your help, Madame."

He took two steps back and regarded me warily.

"I knew Sofiya," he finally confessed. "I met her several years before she got consumption and died. She was a saint of a woman. Her husband was most unworthy of her. Mykhalo was a lot like his mother."

He paused, considering his next words.

"She would have idolized you and adored your daughter."

I raised my eyebrows in surprise.

"Idolize and adore are strong words. What makes you think she would feel that way about us?"

The corners of his mouth twitched upward briefly.

"Because you are independent and strong women. And most importantly, you and your daughter are both *free*. That was something she always wanted. The only way she got to be free was by dying."

He sighed sadly and striding up to me, placed both hands on my shoulders.

"Wear those pearls with honor. They should only grace the neck of an incredible woman. Mykhalo thought you worthy of them. I know he was correct in this."

I bowed my head and stroked the pearls lovingly.

I was beginning to feel hemmed in by the serious mood of the room.

Bartal informed me he would go and see how Bree was coming along with her wardrobe.

I felt I had to say something to lighten the mood.

"You know, you'd have an easier time with ties if you took a little of the beard off. What is it with you Russians and long beards?"

A confused look crossed his face for an instant to be replaced by a huge smile.

"Not all Russians have long beards, my dear. And besides, I'm not Russian."

On this note, he left the room leaving me to deal with my own shock and embarrassment.

CHAPTER 6

Bree came down shortly afterwards. I had dreaded the scene to come. I was certain something in her attire wouldn't be appropriate for this gathering and I was right. But Bartal had corrected her appearance.

Bree came down the stairs in a tasteful black dress and minimal, (for her at least) jewelry. They had even gotten her out of army boots and into modest heels. In fact the only thing rebellious about her appearance was her shocking red hair.

She slunk up to me like a beautiful bird insulted when her wings had been cut.

"They wouldn't let me wear my bangles!" she complained in a soft voice. "And they wanted to color my hair back to a more 'realistic' shade. But I wouldn't let them!"

"Good for you dear!" I chuckled. "You're not old enough yet to conform to the real world!"

She started to agree then stopped herself. I could see the wheels turning in her brain, trying to figure out if I had just slighted her by suggesting she wasn't an adult yet.

"Is this going to be our life now, Ma? More funerals than parties?"

I gave a heavy sigh as the humor left the room with the comment.

"Could be dear. Better be prepared to wear more black."

Bree sniffed her disapproval.

"This is gonna be a small to-do, right?" she asked. "I don't think I have it in me for an all-day affair."

"I have no idea but I certainly hope so," I said as I did some last minute preening in front of the mirror. "I'm not exactly looking forward to a huge swareé with tons of people I don't know speaking in a language I don't understand. Maybe bit by bit I could handle it but not all at once."

Bree nodded her complete agreement.

Finally it was time. We assembled with Bartal and the entire castle staff in the spacious foyer and waited in silence while Mykhalo's black casket was solemnly wheeled out into the courtyard. Exiting the castle, escorted by Bartholomew and his 'apprentices,' I found a surprise awaiting us.

Instead of a large black hearse, there was a horse drawn version with black curtains and glass sides. The four horses wore black plumes on their black leather harness flashing in silver trim. I was further surprised to see the horses were not black but had an odd shade of liver dappled coats with cream-colored manes and tails.

I leaned over to Bartal and whispered in his ear, "Shouldn't the carriage horses be black?"

He nodded briefly and replied to me in a low voice.

"That would be customary, yes, but these are Mykhalo's. He has bred them for generations. It would be inappropriate to draw his hearse with any other breed."

The coffin was loaded quietly and the glass doors with ornate black curtains closed. Bree and I were escorted to a limousine which followed. Bartal and one of his apprentices climbed in with us. He was introduced as 'Sigmund' Bartal's second in command.

The pavement rang with the sound of the horses' hooves and we swung slowly out to follow the carriage's progress down the hillside.

Bartal told us we would stay in the limo until we reached the town proper. And then we would exit the vehicle and parade slowly down the city streets on foot until we arrived at the church and the cemetery. He told us the street had been blocked off for the funeral.

Bree and I exchanged the same look. We were both thought we shouldn't have worn heels. I hoped the church was close and we wouldn't have to walk miles to get there.

All too soon we arrived at the town. The limo pulled to a quiet stop and Sigmund and Bartal got out and conversed briefly.

I could tell Bree was getting nervous. I patted her arm and smiled.

"Don't worry my little Bookworm," I said. "I'm sure it will be a little church with a small turnout. This will be over in no time."

Sigmund motioned silently for us to get out. Quietly we obeyed.

Bree and I stepped out of the limo and froze. Both sides of the city street were lined with a sea of people. All were dressed in black and all were somber of face. And all were staring directly at us.

You could have heard a pin drop.

"Come, come my dears. Do not be afraid. They are simply here to pay their respects. Take my arm, Mrs. Miller," Bartal reassured.

I needed his arm because my knees were knocking! Bartal offered his other arm to Bree but she scooted around to my opposite side and clung close like a much younger child.

Bartal patted my hand with his big-gloved paw as if this was nothing, We followed the carriage as it clip-clopped down the city street.

I tried to look straight ahead as I marched by his side. I felt the eyes of the multitude as I passed. Bree's hand trembled on my arm.

"I thought you said this was going to be a small ceremony!" Bree hissed to me from my side.

"I thought it *was*."

Bree growled softly at my side.

As we advanced, something incredible happened. All the men bowed their heads and removed their hats out of respect as the hearse passed. Ladies curtseyed, crossed themselves and kept their faces downward. From time to time I saw a woman risk a glance upward into my face as I passed. Many looks of what I hoped was sympathy seemed to be aimed my way.

As we marched slowly along, I also risked a glance upward. From the balconies overlooking the street, more people gathered, all removing their hats and crossing themselves.

I also saw here and there, scattered on the tilted rooftops, Bartal's men in black. They were heavily armed with machine guns and were looking at the crowds instead of the solemn procession.

"Why all the firepower?" I hissed at Bartal, hoping Bree hadn't heard.

"Just in case," he said with another pat on my arm. "Although anyone wishing to harm you would be crazy with this crowd. They would jump on him quicker than my men could shoot them. Mykhalo was well loved in this town."

"He also had his share of enemies," I muttered.

"I thought they could only come out at night," Bree hissed.

"Right you are, little one," agreed Bartal. "But they have human spies during the day keeping them informed. They are what my men are looking for."

I glanced behind us at the limousine following us and noticed the German flags fluttering in the gentle spring breeze.

"Diplomat status has its perks."

Bartal nodded.

"It has come in handy many times. Especially in matters of personal security."

We continued onward, the silence broken only by the sound of the horses' shod hooves and the occasional cough from the crowd. Another glance behind showed me the respectful throng lining the city streets had fallen in and were marching along with us to the church.

I wondered how big the cathedral was.

I didn't have to wonder for long.

Our solemn parade turned a corner abruptly and the church loomed high above our heads. It was made in a medieval gothic style with gargoyles spitting outward from the corners of arched roofs. A dazzling array of filigree architecture and statues of the saints and angels reached or gazed up to heaven.

We stopped momentarily just to look in wonder at the monstrous building before us – huge, opulent, imposing.

"Whoa!" breathed Bree at my side. "This will *not* be a small ceremony!"

She looked frantically at the enormous crowd gathered.

Bree never liked to be closed in with a large crowd of people. Neither did I but I'd learned to bear it out of necessity. Bree still struggled.

Her hands trembled on my arm as Bartal left to converse with the hearse driver some of his other men.

I noticed the crowd was hanging back from us. Although whether it was out of respect for my daughter and I or because of the obvious presence of law enforcement, I couldn't tell.

"Here's what we'll do," Bree whispered to me in a trembling, but vainly jesting manner. "When we get inside, I'll say we have to go to the ladies room and when we get there, we'll crawl out the window or something, pop off these damned heels, and make a run for it! Whaddya say, Mom?"

Now every mother, I don't care what race or religion, should be able to give what I call 'the maternal death glare' at a moment's notice. You know the look, the one which stops offspring in their tracks and sends them muttering meekly to do your bidding.

I decided now was such a time and I turned this glare on Bree with a vengeance.

"Sabrina Tempest Miller," I began in a quiet but a withering tone of voice. "If you bail on me right now, I swear to you I will put you on a plane back to the States *alone!* And if you think that is the worst I can do, you are sadly mistaken! Now be respectful and get into the church before I leave you there with the nuns!"

Bree began to whimper, "But I was just jo..."

This earned an even sterner glare.

"Yes Mom," she squeaked and hung her head.

I turned my attention back the horse-drawn hearse ahead of us and refused to look at her.

Bartal came back to us.

He motioned us into the church behind the casket. We silently obeyed. Two of Bartal's apprentices came forward and ushered both Bree and myself to our respective pews at the front. Bartal sat next to me. We quietly waited while the church filled.

I could see Bree at my side, turning and looking every which way, taking in the ornate church's decor. For some reason, the inside of the church had become unimportant to me. I focused only on the shiny, black casket before me.

They had opened the lid to expose Mykhalo's body to everyone.

I'd been okay until this point. Again I looked on his face, so peaceful, serene. He looked like he was just asleep. I wanted to shake him awake. I wanted to run out the door with him hand in hand, laughing and joking into the bright sunshine and leave this strange, melancholy crowd behind.

I did not want him to be dead.

The organ's music filled the air. Small sounds like the shuffle of shoes and the cough of someone behind me echoed within the huge cathedral. I could feel the magic of its reverence humming all about me. I didn't care. I only wanted to be outside and alone with the casket, not here with my grief on display to the whole world, a world which wasn't even my own.

I huddled within myself and tried not to feel anything.

The church must have filled completely because the organ music swelled. A priest in white robes came out followed by his choirboys. Behind the last, a tall blond man, dressed impeccably in an Armani suit bowed his head in respect.

Some dim sensation in my mind told me this last person didn't belong. My eyes focused on him and followed his progress up to the dais. He moved more smoothly than other people. He stood at the head of the coffin looking reverently down upon Mykhalo's face. And then he turned and looked directly at me.

My voice caught in my throat and I choked back the exclamation. Tears started to flow. I couldn't stop them. Handkerchiefs were thrust to me from both sides. I clutched them desperately. I tried to control my emotions. This was a funeral. I was expected to weep.

The man looking at me was transparent as smoke. I recognized him.

It was Mykhalo.

He smiled sadly at me.

I wanted to vault the pew, dress and all, and run to him. But I kept myself seated. I looked nervously at Bree. All she could see was her mother crying. She didn't see Mykhalo's spirit standing next to his coffin. One glance told me Bartal didn't either.

I swallowed with difficulty. I told myself not to make a scene. I stared at Mykhalo's ghost and waited for him to vanish.

He remained where he was. I looked deep into his misty eyes and got the sincere impression he intended to stay for the funeral. Only I could see him.

I took a deep breath to steady myself. It didn't work. After the fourth breath I felt somewhat more composed.

I repeated internally, 'I can get through this. I *will* get through this.'

The priest spoke in German. Bartal softly translated his words for me. I half listened. My eyes were locked on Mykhalo, partially expecting him to disappear at any moment.

The funeral ritual passed me by in a fog. What the priest said, standing for hymns, kneeling for prayers, it all seemed useless posturing and made no sense to me.

Then came the public viewing of the body. A long line formed. One by one many came to the coffin and gazed upon Mykhalo's silent form. Some made the sign of the cross, some knelt and offered a brief prayer, and others just stood and stared at his form and said nothing. Many from the line, came to me afterward. Whether I understood or not, they offered words of condolence. Bartal translated as best he could.

The elderly people were very nice. Many of their sentiments began with "The Baron helped me during the war..." It was easy to see how grateful they were to him and how sorry they were for me. Many of the town shopkeepers begged me to stop by their establishment later and sample a little of their wares 'on the house'.

A strange little, bowed woman who needed two canes to walk, shuffled up to me after viewing Mykhalo's remains. Her eyes were bleary, her face withered. Her hands quaked with every step. Bartal told me she wanted to see me. Her trembling hands reached out and I took them. I leaned my face close so her bad eyes could see.

"This is Fraulein Geissler, the oldest woman in the town," Bartal introduced.

She peered closely up into my face.

Then she said something in German which sounded very ominous. I only recognized the word, 'America'.

Confused I looked into Bartal's face.

"She says you are not going to return to America just yet. We have need of you here. The Baron still has a lot to say to you."

My eyes immediately flew to the ghostly image of Mykhalo over her shoulder. He only smiled at me.

When I turned my eyes back, Fraulein Geissler smiled widely as if she knew who I had seen.

I knew then her eyes may have been fuzzy, but her sight was keen.

"What about my daughter, Bree?" I asked.

I waited while Bartal translated.

The old woman looked at Bree briefly. She grunted and waved her hand as if Bree wasn't important.

"She says, she'll be fine."

She began to hobble away. Abruptly she stopped and half turned as if she had just thought of something. Her voice raised so many could hear as she called back over her shoulder to me.

There was a confused titter among those gathered as if she had said something which might have been funny but they weren't exactly sure.

My expression urged Bartal to translate although he looked just as confused as anyone else.

He turned back to me.

"She says you should wear more turtlenecks."

* * *

The people streamed on and on. More people were in the viewing line than in the entire church. It took quite a while to go through them all. All their faces and names began to blend together in my mind into a confused sea. It was like trying to meet and speak to each and every person who assembled in the square for the pope to give his daily blessing. I don't think I remembered half of who they were and what they said to me.

But one man stood out among the throng. I did not need a translator for him because he was British. Besides, Bartal was engrossed in conversation with the last person I had shaken hands with.

He was a short man. He had to look up to me. He was slightly round in appearance and his face was pasty, with a fat nose sprinkled by a scattering of red freckles. His lackluster hair, what little he had of it, was a pale, strawberry blonde which he wore in a short ponytail. His watery blue eyes were the most riveting. They were large, bulbous and bloodshot as if he never slept. They also seemed to be constantly darting about as if he was nervous or afraid of being caught doing something he shouldn't.

"Mrs. Miller!" he said as if we were old friends. "I'm so glad to meet you finally. I've heard so much about you. I wish we were meeting under happier circumstances."

I was instantly suspicious.

"And you are..." I said.

"Oh yes. How rude of me to not tell you my name first! I am Ainsley Wainwright. Let me offer my sincerest condolences to you in your loss."

Instantly, Mykhalo's ghost was by my side. He glared at this little man with not the kindest of expressions.

Ainsley Wainwright clutched my hand with both of his and pumped it all too eagerly. His skin felt oily and spongy. I was grateful when he released it and I waited for an opportune moment to wipe my hand off on the fabric of my skirt without being obvious.

"And how did you hear about me?" I asked slowly.

He seemed to have lost track of our conversation's topic already.

"Hmmm?" he abruptly raised his eyebrows and I saw his eyes dart about as his mind accessed my question's answer.

"Oh! Mykhalo and I go way, way, way back. He spoke of you often, very fondly too I might add," he assured me.

Somehow I doubted the truth of what he said. And if I hadn't, the sight of Mykhalo's shade rolling his eyes and shaking his head certainly convinced me.

"And how long will you be visiting this lovely country?" he asked.

I knew better than to give him our entire itinerary.

"Oh, we will probably hop on a plane the minute the funeral is over. I do have a business to run back in the States after all," I said and inwardly chastised myself for not being more vague.

"Hmmm," he mumbled. "That's not what the little old lady said."

This little, fat, weasel was really starting to annoy me!

"And the little old lady is certainly not my travel consultant, nor does she buy my plane tickets." I told him and then kicked Bartal in the shin, hoping he'd rescue me from Ainsley's greasy presence; which he did, in a hurry the minute he saw who I was talking to.

I breathed an immense sigh of relief when Ainsley was ushered quickly away from me.

45

"Thank you," I said and meant every bit of it.

"Who let him in?" Bartal growled in irritation.

"You know him?" I said.

"Unfortunately," Bartal gave a long-suffering sigh. "Please let me know if he bothers you again and I will take care of it."

I nodded. Bartal was beginning to prove his worth in spite of the fact I still felt he was holding something back. I would just have to pry it out of him at a later date, someplace more private than here and now.

Bartal stopped having people come up to me after this happened. I think he sensed I was getting a bit overwhelmed by so many people and would very soon need my space from the crowd. Another point in his favor.

The church ceremony soon ended. The priest sprinkled holy water upon Mykhalo's peaceful form and no – he did not burn to a crisp. He just lay there with holy water slowly making tracks down his serene face. The casket was closed. Six of Bartal's 'apprentices' came forward and served as pallbearers. They carefully bore the black casket out of the church and into the cemetery. There, between two very old headstones with worn letters, a grave had been dug and the coffin was set upon the framework which held it above ground. There was no tent set up over the grave because it was a bright sunny day. There were mounds of large bouquets everywhere and their perfume hung thick in the air.

More words were spoken in German over the casket and passages from the bible read. The priest finally closed his book and, cradling it next to his chest, gave me a meaningful look. Bartal passed me three roses; one yellow, the other two red.

He looked at me and said quietly, "For the three of you."

He then nodded to the casket.

I sniffed and approached. For a long moment, all I could do was stand at the side of the casket. Bree stood by my side with her arms around me for support. Bartal stood at the head of the casket with both of his gloved hands on the surface. His eyes were closed and his lips moved in a silent prayer. He opened his eyes and I saw they were glassy and wet. Then he cleared his throat, crossed his arms behind his back and he was once more, a man in control of his emotions.

46

I felt the tears come again. I wished I had worn one of those big, black, mourning hats with the black veil which before I had always thought to be so silly. Now I understood the veil. It was to give the woman wearing it some privacy from the crowd.

"May you be as welcome in the Summerlands as you are into Heaven." I whispered softly so only Bree could hear. She smiled and gave me a tight squeeze.

I stepped back into my place among the crowd.

Mykhalo's spirit appeared right in front of me. His ghost put his hands upon my shoulders and kissed me on the forehead. I did not feel his hands. But I felt the kiss as if he were real and tangible. He then smiled and vanished from my sight.

The funeral was over. I was numb from all the emotions. The crowd around me was backing away and started to dissipate. I just stood there and watched as they lowered Mykhalo's casket into the earth. Automatically, without even thinking about it, I bent over and grabbed a handful of earth and tossed it into the grave. I watched it land with a dry splat on top of the roses. Bree mirrored my action and then Bartal. I stepped back. And then one of Bartal's men, Sigmund, came forward and tossed a handful of earth into the crevice, crossing his chest afterwards. Each one of my bodyguards came forward and contributed a handful of earth.

Bartal touched me lightly on the arm and whispered in my ear.

"Mrs. Miller, I know this has been an ordeal for you. If you wish some space, there is a flower garden adjoining this cemetery. I will take you there now if you wish and guard the entrance so no one bothers you for a little while at least. I think you need to breathe a bit."

He gestured in the direction of the garden. I nodded and mouthed my thanks. My eyes went to Bree as he accompanied me.

"I'll be okay now Mom," she assured. "I'm better now we're outside. You go, please. I'll be waiting."

She gave me a quick hug and released me before the emotions could take over.

I gave a deep sigh and followed Bartal immediately.

In the space of a very few steps, I was ushered through an imposing, tall, oak door with heavy, ironwork hinges which spoke not a word as it swung back. On the other side was a beautiful garden, with a fountain, clustered with spring flowers bordered by a very high stonewalls.

Bartal stepped inside the door and closed it behind us.

"Now," he began in a lighter tone of voice. "Go anywhere you wish but stay within sight of the door."

I sped toward the fountain's edge. Once there I stopped to observe the statue. It was in the shape of a rearing unicorn. Water sprang from its mouth. From the pitting on the statue I could tell it was very old. At first I was shocked the fountain would sport an image of a mythological beast being it was on church grounds. But then I remembered the unicorn was used many times as a representation of the Virgin Mary because of its attraction to purity. It was also a symbol of healing especially when coupled with a spring or a pool hidden in a forest glade.

Healing was what I sorely needed.

I had been restraining myself all during the funeral, crying but not crying the way which would have consoled me. I felt I was going to explode from all the restraint. I wanted to scream my grief to the heavens in such a way it would have made my throat sore. But I did not. I had swallowed the majority of my pain because there were too many people about. I wondered why it was the custom of funerals to surround the bereaved with people. All I wanted was to be alone with my pain.

At least this Bartal fellow seemed to understand me.

I gasped quite suddenly. The gasp turned into a moan and then a sob and before I knew it, I was crumpled on my knees, hanging onto the fountain's side for support, weeping bitterly. I felt the release I so desperately needed at that moment and inwardly I thanked the unicorn for the blessing of my tears.

I have no idea how long I cried. The grief and the tears seemed to envelope me and take me away to a dark and very private place. When at last I came back to myself, I found I was kneeling on the ground. I felt weary and spent from all the tears. There was a hollow place deep within my heart which was somehow now at peace.

I wiped the tears away from my cheeks and looked up through bleary eyes. Bartal was standing far away but I could tell by his expression he too was feeling the same grief. The wall of control had disappeared from his countenance.

"How long have you been standing there?" I muttered almost to myself.

He quietly came over to me and, taking me by the arm, helped me to a nearby bench framed by rose bushes. For a long moment he sat close to me, holding my hands in his large bear paws, sharing my grief silently. He seemed he was on the brink of saying something truly meaningful but was unsure how to phrase it exactly.

"Mrs. Miller," he finally began in a very gentle tone of voice. "When Mykhalo and I first met…well it was supposed to be a brief meeting. You see I was charged to kill him."

The breath caught in my throat. Before I could say anymore, he plunged on.

"Obviously that never happened. Something stayed my hand. I have no idea what. I tried three times to obey the orders I was given and three times I failed. Twice I tried to kill him secretly. He never knew about the first two attempts. The third attempt…I just rushed him face to face. I expected him to fight back."

A knowing smile flickered across my face.

"Let me guess. He didn't try and stop you, right?"

"How did you know?" his expression was incredulous.

"Because I tried to off him too after he killed my daughter's best friend and I had the same problem. Mykhalo must have had a powerful guardian angel!"

Bartal dropped his head and his laughter mirrored my own.

"What I'm trying to say is…" he blundered onward. "Is that I have known Mykhalo for many more years than you…"

"Centuries perhaps?" I prodded. I still was curious about the details of their relationship but I wasn't in the mood to poke around now.

"Yes, a few centuries…" Bartal acquiesced some. "And I have never met a more kind and noble spirited person. I was sure it could not exist in any human let alone a vampire and yet here he was. I quickly became his friend in spite of the danger to myself over disobeying orders and he has been my closest confident for most of my life. I can see how he loved you and how much you loved him although your

49

relationship was short. Mykhalo seemed to encourage a deep loyalty in all those he befriended."

He paused and furrowed his brow over how to phrase his next words.

"What I'm trying to say is you're not alone here. I too miss my friend very much and I would give anything to have him back this very instant even if that meant having to share his affection with you. It would be worth it just to have him happy and back in my life."

I still did not know this Bartal very well. For all I knew, their supposed friendship could be just a big pile of malarkey.

But his words felt genuine to me and I wanted to believe everything he said.

"What are you really trying to say, Bartal?"

Bartal took a deep breath and then drew his face so close to mine our foreheads almost touched. He looked down at the ground and closed his eyes.

"Please stay," he said squeezing my hands tightly. "Don't go back to America the minute the funeral is over. I want to get to know the woman my friend loved and I want you to get to know me. Let us console each other. Maybe we can heal from this without either of us being alone."

I pulled back in surprise and some fright.

"Bartal! My love just died and you…!"

He suddenly dropped my hands, jumped to his feet and backed away from me.

"No! Not that! I didn't mean that!" he paced a small circle and ran a frustrated hand through his hair as if he had just said the complete opposite of what he had meant. He turned his back to me and placed his hands on his hips.

"I loved a woman once many, many years ago. She is dead now. I will not tread down the same road again. Do not ask me to say any more," he said still with his back to me.

He took another deep breath which made his shoulders heave. He turned around to face me. The controlled expression had once again taken up residence on his face.

"I would ask you, Mrs. Miller, to please extend your stay here, at least until Mykhalo's will is read. I and my men will look after you and your daughter. You will be afforded every luxury that Lion's Gate castle is equipped to provide you. I assure you both will be safe. Please give me a chance to show you some proper German hospitality."

He held out his hand to me as if apologizing.

I paused thinking hard. He was asking me to make a major decision now on top of everything I had already been through this day? My heart was tired. I just wanted to skip the whole issue.

I heaved a great sigh and closed my eyes. My chest hurt and my eyes burned from the salt of my own tears.

"All right," I surrendered. "Bree and I will stay until after the will is read and then we will go home."

CHAPTER 7

The rest of the day was a blur. Somehow we returned to the castle and Bartal ushered me into the sitting room with Bree. I wanted to be around no one but my daughter. Bartal was there but purposely distant. He seemed to think his new job was keeping people away so I could grieve in private. Apparently this chore kept him quite busy.

The rest of the evening was like a fever dream. I remember crying intermittently and then seeming almost fine the next. Bree held me a lot. She wouldn't leave my side. I know I ate something but I could not recall what. Bree waited on me hand and foot. I felt bad about it but couldn't tell her to stop. I finally excused myself, telling Bree I felt like turning in early. She sat on my bedside holding my hand and rubbing my arm lovingly until I drifted off to sleep.

I wanted the real world to go away.

I wanted Mykhalo back.

I awoke, or at least I thought I awoke, sometime later. I had rolled over onto my side facing the tall, heavily curtained, windows. The bright light of the full moon should have been streaming onto my face. But there was something blocking it.

A person stood next to my bed. It wasn't Bree.

But I was not frightened for it was only Mykhalo.

He stood there in the moonlight, hands in his pockets with the moonlight shining through pale hair turning it into silver gold.

"Good evening, my love," he said. "I hope I didn't startle you."

And he smiled at me in the dark.

"But I thought you couldn't speak," I began and then stopped myself. "Oh! Am I dreaming?"

He nodded.

"This is the only way I can have a private conversation with you."

It wasn't real. It was just a fantasy.

I didn't care. I gave in to the dream body and soul. Right now I wanted it this way. I would deal with reality later.

I smiled in return.

I held out my hand to him. He slid his hand into mine and seated himself on the side of the bed next to my reclining figure. His hand felt warm and alive.

"I can touch you!" I breathed in amazement.

Mykhalo's smile widened.

"I can do more than touch you," he said as he stroked the side of my face lovingly.

In the space of a blink, the suit he wore was gone.

I raised my eyebrows. I held up the covers invitingly and he crawled in beside me.

"Let's see, how do I thank you for making me warm again?" he whispered.

"Well, I guess biting me on the neck is no longer an option," I chuckled and snuggled closer to him. "But I'm sure we'll figure something out."

I melted into his warm touch as he traced his lips down my neck. I had no idea how long this was going to last but I was going to enjoy every bit of it and fight not to wake up in the best part.

I didn't wake up. Our private moment seemed to last forever with each one of us exploring each other's form and desires. Mykhalo asked for more of the 'sex magic' thing and I was only too happy to oblige.

Finally, completely exhausted and spent with each other, we lay entwined within one another's embrace and watched the moonlight outside the window.

"I hear you will be staying for a little while," he murmured at last into my hair.

"Does it please you that I willingly accept your gilded cage?" I replied.

He turned my chin so I could look him in the eye.

"This is no gilded cage," he assured me. "This is yours for as long as you want. I know you will return to Pennsylvania someday. It is your soul's home. And there's no one better than myself to understand the pull of the land on someone raised there. Bavaria will always be my home. Pennsylvania will always be yours. Nothing can change that."

I tilted my form so I could peer closer into his face, to see the emotion before he chose to hide it.

"Will you return with me when I go, as a ghost?"

"I'm not sure." His face became furrowed with worry. "It depends on what gets accomplished between here and then. I linger because of you."

"Why?" I asked. "What is left unfinished?"

"I promised to tell you all my secrets." His silver eyes met mine. "I have not yet kept that promise. You have questions about my life. I need to answer them. You cannot leave until I clear them up. I like to keep my promises."

"Then Fraulein Geissler was right," I said.

"More than you'll ever know," he replied.

His look became distant all at once as if someone else was talking inside his head.

"I need to leave you soon and you need to wake up," he whispered. "But I want to tell you something first. Please trust Bartal. He speaks the truth when he says we were close friends and he really does have your best interest at heart. He does have many skeletons in his closet but I could think of no one better to defend you and Bree against certain supernatural forces who may want to harm you. You can discuss vampires openly with him. He has a great amount of knowledge which comes from personal experience in that department. He knows little about magic so you may have to educate him on it. But please believe me, he really can be trusted."

He quietly slipped out from under the covers and was once again clothed with a thought.

He held my hand and stroked my hair tenderly.

"This is not a frivolous romantic fantasy," he whispered to me bending close. "You will remember every word of this when you awaken. This is important. Your safety and that of your daughter's is vital me now. That is why I linger here. I love you, Zan Miller."

He bent over and kissed me on the lips.

My body was suddenly bathed in warmth. When I opened my eyes once more Mykhalo was gone. It was morning and the sunlight was flooding the room and my bed.

It was just a dream after all.

* * *

I rolled out of bed and dressed in a hurry. My predicament was very quickly getting too big for me to handle. I had to tell somebody, someone I knew I could trust. My daughter was the only person I thought I could confide in right now.

I gently rapped on her door and peeped my head in.

"Bree honey. Are you awake?"

A long yawn greeted me.

"Yeah, I just haven't committed to rolling outta bed yet," she moaned.

"I have to talk to somebody. I..." I stopped short as I looked about her room.

Where it seemed every other room in the castle had been decorated in statues and images of big maned African lions; this room's walls and even the bedclothes were decorated in images of lionesses.

"What is this thing he's got with the lions everywhere?" I said.

"I dunno. I found a note on the bed the first night which said Mykhalo specifically asked for the room to be decorated this way. He thought it would make me feel more welcome. I guess any nobleman is due his own odd eccentricities, eh?" she yawned again and rolled over onto her belly.

"What's up, Ma?" she said.

I sat down on the bed next to her and told her everything. Well, not exactly *everything*! I decided to leave out the part where I bedded Mykhalo.

By the time I was done, Bree was wide-awake and sitting up on the bed hugging her legs to herself.

"So my step-vampire dad is still hanging around but he's a ghost this time. That is *sooo cool*!" she breathed.

"Enough of that!" I scolded. "What do we do about this?"

Bree pursed her lips and waggled her head from side to side.

"Depends. What do you want to do with this?" she asked.

I was taken aback for a moment. Then I began to think about it. This was why I had told her everything; so I could get somebody else's opinion on the situation.

I sighed and set my jaw.

"I want to have it out with Bartal," I said finally. "I want to ask him everything I've been afraid to ask. Like what his age is, how long has he known Mykhalo, is he a strange new variety of vampire and if not just what exactly *IS* he?"

"So what's the problem?" Bree said. "We wait until breakfast when we're alone in the room with him and you ask."

"You want to be there?" I said in surprise.

"Well of course!" she replied blinking at me. "You need me to back you up and keep him from weaseling his way outta any corner you put him in. You're not doing this alone, Ma!"

I gathered my daughter into my arms and squeezed her tight. I realized Bree had been tolerating my hugs much better as of late.

Hmmmm, I should play the grieving widow more often, I thought to myself.

"Mom," Bree said suddenly.

"Hmmmm," I muttered back.

"Aren't you hungry?" she suggested.

"Famished!" I said.

"Me too. Let's go and have a talk and some gnosh."

I laughed and released her.

Bree dressed and brushed her hair and we headed down to the spring patio where we had enjoyed our last meal together.

The table was already set for three. Almost as soon as we had seated ourselves, Hans brought out our food and set it before us.

"All this lovely German cooking is going to make me fat!" I commented.

Hans smiled and bowed politely.

"I'm so glad you enjoy it. I will make sure to relay that to the chef," he replied. Hans made to leave and then turned about.

"Herr Bartholomew will be joining you presently," he told us and then left.

Bree exchanged a knowing look with me. I motioned for her to wait for a bit before diving into her food.

We didn't have long to wait.

Bartal came into the room all smiles and cheer.

"Ah, there are my honored guests! Please, don't wait for me. Go ahead and enjoy your food before it gets cold."

He picked up the German paper next to his plate. "And how did you two sleep?"

"Some slept better than others," Bree muttered making me choke on my orange juice.

I kicked her under the table and she squeaked.

Bartal's eyes lifted from his paper and his gaze darted between us.

"I'm sorry. Am I missing something?" he asked.

Hans came out and placed his plate in front of him. It had an odd looking, large link of sausage on it which was a rather unusual and dark shade of purplish red.

Bartal thanked Hans and made ready to dig in.

Bree noticed it too and being less polite than her mother, had to burst out with, "What is *that*?"

Bartal turned his eyes to her.

"Blood sausage. My favorite," he replied. "Don't you have this in the States?"

Bree turned her shocked expression to me. Her eyes seemed to say, 'Now would be as good a time as any.'

"Bartal, you told me yesterday at the funeral I could ask you some questions when we were back at the castle," I began.

"Yes, yes," he replied as he began to shovel neatly cut portions of sausage into his mouth. "Ask away."

"Anything?"

He gestured with his fork as if it were nothing.

"Of course!" he said as he took a swig of his coffee.

I exchanged looks with Bree and
took a deep breath to bolster my resolve.

Okay, here goes, I thought to myself.

"Are you a vampire?" I said.

The knife clattered loudly onto the plate as he dropped it. Bartal stopped eating and looked at me. Then he looked at Bree.

"What? Just because I like to eat blood sausage you think I'm a vampire, eh?" he began in an insulted sounding tone of voice. "There are many cultures in this world that use blood as a food source. The Eskimo with their ptarmigan blood soup, the Europeans with their blood sausage..."

"And you are avoiding the issue," I said in a stern tone of voice. "Answer my question. Yes or no?"

Bartal carefully finished his mouthful and put down his knife and fork. He fastidiously wiped his mouth with his handkerchief. He folded his fingers on the table before him and looked me directly in the eye.

"No, I am not a vampire. You have my word on this."

We held each other's gazes as if it was some odd version of a staring contest.

"My daughter here says you are older than Mykhalo. Just how old are you, Bartholomew?"

His eyebrows twitched.

"I am around four hundred years of age," he replied steadily, his food forgotten.

I could see him waiting for my shocked reaction. He must have been disappointed because all I did was sigh as if I had expected the answer.

"If you're not a vampire, then just what exactly are you?" I asked. "Why does my inner sixth sense warn me to stay away from you because you're dangerous?"

The corners of his lips hopped upwards ever so slightly.

"Because I *am* dangerous, Mrs. Miller."

I nodded, not questioning this one iota.

"What are you then?" I said raising my voice.

He straightened in his chair.

"What are *you*, Mrs. Miller?" he asked quietly.

This question threw me for a moment. "I beg your pardon?"

His eyes narrowed with the gravity of the inquiry. "You were more than in love with Mykhalo. You *made* love to him, is that not so?"

I was floored by the brashness of his statement. "I don't see where it's any of your business what I..."

"Yes or no?" he persisted, now raising his voice like an army commander at me.

I flapped my jaw wordlessly for a moment. Then I raised my chin like it was a dare and with my eyes flashing dangerously, I replied in kind.

"Yes," I finally said.

Bree's eyes bugged in surprise. "You bedded a vampire and lived? Way to go, Ma!" she said.

This earned her another one of those 'maternal death glares'. Bree shut up.

I turned my gaze back to Bartal. His eyes were narrowed and he nodded angrily.

"Mykhalo didn't take lovers! Not after the first few attempts, two centuries ago proved disastrous! He felt it was too dangerous for them," he said harshly. "So what makes you different? What are *you*, Mrs. Miller? In order for me to answer your question, you must first answer mine."

There was a long silence between us. Finally I relented. "I'm a witch."

"That goes for me, too," Bree included, sticking her hand into the air like a schoolgirl.

Bartal did not react at first. Then he began to laugh softly to himself.

"So that's the reason, eh? He finally gives up his search to find the one witch who will save him and she falls at his feet. How ironic."

He shook his head. "I already knew you were a witch. I just wanted to hear you say it."

He sighed heavily. "You remember the day at the airport when I first laid eyes on you?" he said as if it was years ago when it really was only two days.

"Of course," I replied. "You laughed at me."

Bartal sniffed again and nodded. "I laughed because from the first moment I laid eyes on you, I knew you had bedded him. All those years I had pestered him whenever he got all melancholy on me, which was often, I told him all he needed was to bed a strong, independently

60

minded woman. I said if he did that, he would feel better. And then I saw you and I knew. I knew it had happened."

He shook his head and sighed sadly. "He talked to me right before he died and said his end was coming. I begged him to let me be with him when he died but he refused. That wounded me deeply. After all we had been through together, he didn't want his best friend there by his side? And then I saw you and I understood why he didn't want me there."

He paused a moment thinking back over the years. "Every man, vampire or mortal, needs to bond with someone in a physical sense. It heals, strengthens and better equips them to move forward on their path. It's just not healthy to deny yourself that vulnerability toward *someone* for too long. It's necessary."

He sighed again sadly and leaned forward. "I want to thank you for ending his life," he said.

Bree held up her hand again. "Uh, it was me...sort of. And why would you want to thank us for it?"

He smiled and hung his head. "Because it came at just the right time."

He glanced up and gave up an apologetic look when he saw both of our expressions.

"It's complicated," he explained. "You see, when a vampire gets to be around four hundred, they start to go through a change. The vampire blood takes a stronger hold and begins to strangle out the human consciousness. Pretty soon the human they once were does not exist anymore and all that is left is strictly vampire. Mykhalo could feel the change coming and was getting extremely worried about the safety of his human friends. That's why I say he died at just the right time."

We both just sat there blinking at him, food forgotten, while we absorbed this information.

"But it still doesn't explain why you are four hundred years old if you're not a vampire." Bree interjected. "Just what are you exactly?"

He sighed and I saw the wall go up again. He looked at me for a moment.

"You're not getting out of it this time, Bartal. Answer my daughter's question," I demanded of him. I was not leaving my chair until I understood just who we were dealing with.

"I'm a dhampir," he said simply.

This meant nothing to me but realization dawned on Bree's face.

"That explains a lot!" she said.

"No it doesn't!" I fumed. "What the hell is a dhampir?"

Bree got all giddy from knowing something I didn't. "A dhampir is half vampire, half mortal. They have all the powers and none of the weaknesses. That's why they can come out in the sunshine and eat food and everything. They were usually employed as vampire hunters in the old days. I read about it on the 'net."

I nodded and turned my eyes back to Bartal. "Do you drink blood as well?" I asked, deciding it just might be an important thing to know.

Again I saw the edges of his mouth twitch. "I only drink the blood of vampires," he reassured me. "Human blood is unpalatable to me."

"Well that's…reassuring to know," Bree added.

I ignored her words. My thoughts had already jumped ahead of this point in the conversation. I nodded to him, thinking hard.

"And just who were your parents?" I asked.

Bartal pushed himself back in the chair, withdrawing his presence further from me, uncomfortable with the spotlight within which I caged him.

"That's what I'd rather not tell you," he said slowly. "It would only upset you being as you know of the one and have met the other."

I stared at him for a long moment. And then all the mysterious dots about Bartal finally connected.

"You're not Russian because you're Hungarian," I said slowly.

He nodded with a look of shame and dread on his face.

"That means your parents were…" the food suddenly turned to sand in my throat.

"Oh…my…God!" I exclaimed, standing up so abruptly, my chair fell over.

"Ma what…?" Bree began.

All the pieces of the puzzle had finally fallen into place. The vampire who had kidnapped both my daughter and I, the one who had tormented and sliced me with a dagger and chained me up in his 'torture theater', the one who had forced Mykhalo to kill every member of his own family, the one who has caused so much pain and suffering to countless other people throughout the centuries, came to my mind in an instant.

I knew why Bartholomew's eyes looked so familiar and why he had such brilliantly white teeth.

"Bree, we're sitting across the table from the son of Hector and Elizabeth!"

Hans, hearing the clatter, burst into the room with one of Bartal's apprentices.

Bartholomew Sebastian Bathory, for that indeed was his full name as I now surmised, said nothing but waved them out of the room.

"Now don't get so upset, Mrs. Miller. Think!" he tried to reason with me. "Why would Mykhalo have entrusted your safety to me if I was a threat to you? How could I be his dearest friend if I had other motives? Think! Please sit down and finish your breakfast before it gets cold and I will try my best to explain."

I sat down but my appetite had vanished.

"My parents 'designed' me for the purpose of hunting vampires who got out of line."

"Like Mykhalo?" Bree suggested and he nodded.

"Exactly. Every society needs some sort of police force. So I was it," he told us.

"Assassin more likely!" I murmured in a soft voice.

Bartal shrugged as if it didn't matter. "If you like," he replied. "I've been called worse."

"Then why didn't you kill Mykhalo if you were supposed to be this grandiose vampire slayer?" asked Bree.

"He tried," I interjected. "He tried three times and failed just as I tried and failed after I found Mykhalo had murdered Brittany."

Bree turned her eyes to look me in the face.

"I was trying to protect you. I'm your mother. It's my job." I told her.

Bree swallowed with difficulty.

Bartal tried to explain his actions to Bree.

"I made the mistake of meeting Mykhalo first," he said. "And the goodness of his heart shone through. I had convinced myself all vampires were bad. Now here was one who tried to deny his nature and do good things. The better I grew to know him, the more highly I thought of him. Here was a man with all the qualities of honor, morality and justice I endeavored to aspire to. And yet he was an undead! I couldn't find it within myself to kill him. I tried to warn him of my parents' designs whenever I was able and took the fall for him many times so he could escape. His friendship was that valuable to me. Just as I assume it was for you."

He fell silent to let us think on all he had just said.

"So Elizabeth was mortal when she had you?" Bree asked.

Bartal nodded.

"She wanted to take the blood oath sooner but Hector wouldn't allow it until a few years after she had borne his child. As it turned out, events in politics began to escalate against her right then. The enormous number of women she had slain for her 'beauty treatments' finally came to the notice of the nobility. They decided six hundred suspicious deaths of women on her estate was too blatant a transgression to be ignored as a strange excess of a certain nobility."

"The history books all say she was walled up in her room as punishment until the day she died," Bree stated.

Bartal gave a rueful grin and a snort. "History books are written by the powerful. That was a lie!" he told us, anger lacing his words. "They found some peasant woman of about her age who looked similar enough to her to pass and tried *her* and locked *her* into the room. She proclaimed herself innocent of all crimes and remained unapologetic until the day she died. The real Elizabeth had been spirited away by Hector as soon as they saw the way things were going. She took the blood oath soon after."

Bartal fell silent. We all regarded each other for a long moment.

"Um, I need to make a point here," Bree said. "Mykhalo killed your mother and then we helped him to kill your father. Shouldn't that make you want to kill us as well being as we had a rather big hand in Hector's death?"

I agreed with her. She made a very good point.

64

Bartal smiled again and bowed his head respectfully to Bree. "Your daughter is very perceptive, Mrs. Miller," he said softly. "And you have every right to know the truth of the matter."

He sighed and leaned back in his chair. "I was designed with a purpose in mind and raised for that specific purpose. No one asked me what I thought or what I wanted to do with my life. I would have chosen any career but that of a vampire slayer. I did not want this task no matter what talents made me so well suited."

He sighed heavily again and hailing Hans in German, requested more coffee. Silently, Hans obliged. Bartal remained quiet until his cup was refilled and then he began again.

"I had very little contact with my parents as a child. I was raised by nurses and trained by special tutors in the skills I would someday need. My mother played the part of overseer much better than of a loving parent. As a little child, I barely understood who she was to me and harbored little affection towards her. As a young adult, I had many problems with the things she expected me to do and I did witness some of her brutal excesses. I found them shocking and needless in every regard.

"Hector, my father, I knew even less well and felt even more disinterested in him as far as affection goes. I found him forceful, demanding, egotistical and completely unable to be reasoned with when it came to anyone's opinion other than his own. I did what I was trained to do without pride or sense of duty, simply because it was a chore expected of me. I remember one of my earliest longings was to have out of my situation and just live a normal life; one where compassion was permitted and affection towards friends and others encouraged and maybe a little joy in one's profession would be considered a good thing.

"Meeting Mykhalo opened a whole new world for me. Here was someone who understood my pain. Because of him I began to question things in my life that before I wouldn't have dreamed of doubting. I especially began to question the ideals of my parents and where I fit in the grand scheme of things. Mykhalo taught me how to live like a human not just a predator. I will always be grateful to him for it."

Bartal took a deep breath and finished off the remainder of food which was on his plate. "Knowing how Hector treated you both, I can understand your inclination to distrust me. But I can assure you from personal experience, he was no kinder to even his own blood kin. He treated everyone this way. He was well over five hundred years old when you met him and his personality was pure Nosferatu. He loved me no more or less than you and I was his own son!"

Bartal wiped his beard fastidiously and wadding up the napkin, placed it on his plate to signal he was finished with his meal. "Hate me if you wish, Mrs. Miller. You certainly won't be the first or the last to do so. But I'd much rather have a more pleasant relationship with you and your daughter. Now I've met you, I see what Mykhalo was so attracted to. He was lucky to have had your affection for the short time he was able.

So my job now is to keep you both safe from the attention of any supernatural threat. Unfortunately, you are already on their radar."

This earned a glare from me.

"How do you know this?" I demanded.

Bartal took a swig of coffee and swallowed carefully before answering. "I'm sure you were not aware of it but there were certain…individuals at the funeral who were not there to offer condolences. They were there to see proof of Mykhalo's death and to size you both up. I recognized them and my men kept most of them away from you. But some did get in."

He took a long swallow of his coffee before continuing. "Here in the castle, you are quite safe. But I would caution you to watch your step when you leave to do any sightseeing. They are waiting for you to get careless. They are here and they are watching."

I thought of the greasy Ainsley and shuddered. The way Bartal was speaking, I had more than just him to worry about.

"Is it safe to do any sightseeing at all?" I asked. "I'd hate to come all this way and not see Bavaria, just to be stuck here in this castle the whole time. Although I've seen very few rooms, I'd also like to explore it as well."

"Sightseeing can be arranged for you." Bartal reassured. "I can make sure two of my apprentices will be with you at all times, one to drive and another to serve as interpreter. But I would highly recommend not staying out too late after sunset if I were you.

"As to the castle, I think you have noticed certain rooms are off limits and others are locked. However, I was told by Mykhalo to give you free rein of those rooms. He wanted you to discover all his secrets."

He called Hans to him and then spoke with him briefly in German. Hans nodded politely and left. Presently he returned with a metal loop with some very old keys strung onto it. These Hans offered to me.

"Congratulations, Mrs. Miller," Bartal said with a smile. "You are now the chatelaine of Lion's Gate castle. I think you will find there is more of interest in the basement than just the dungeon."

CHAPTER 8

Farran was so eager to pitch his new proposal to Kane. He thought his idea of converting this American woman was good but now he had seen her daughter, he was infused with a new excitement. He felt certain Kane would go for his idea and choose the girl. Farran didn't care he would have to give up his first vampire conversion to his lord and master. He looked forward to enjoying the entire process of converting an innocent into the ways of the Nosferatu. He didn't even care this young adolescent was, in his opinion, a little old. The younger the victim he could get his hooks in, the better he enjoyed it. But he much preferred the prospect of playing with this Sabrina girl than her mother. He found innocence so tantalizing and exciting.

Kane had moved his new abode to a basement storehouse just outside Munich. News of his awakening was starting to spread and every time Farran showed up at this compound, there were more and more vampires gathered in the adjoining rooms. They were waiting, waiting for their lord and master to show himself, to grant each a private audience, to look upon them and treat them like they were something special.

He felt their jealous gazes on him as he strode through the adjoining rooms. They noticed how each set of doors he came to, he was granted immediate entry, going deeper and deeper into the bowels of the compound, closer to the one glorious presence all wanted to get to but were always denied. He, Farran, strode through all to the very end.

Farran paused before the last set of doors and cast a look backwards at the other vampires who had been ahead of him, awaiting an audience. He smiled, bowed mockingly at those gathered and then walked right through the doors. He could practically feel his back sting with the acid from their venomous eyes. A vampire's jealously knew no equal for it was timeless.

The doors closed behind him with a solid final sound. Farran looked about him. The spacious room was sparsely decorated as far as he could tell. It seemed Kane still preferred barely lit rooms. No problem really for someone with vampire eyes. But it did make seeing details slightly more challenging. Farran wasn't sure if the statues along the walls really were statues, or undead sentries.

"Farran," Kane's voice spoke into the dark room. "What a pleasant surprise."

Kane's voice hinted he was anything but surprised.

"What do you think of this look?" Kane asked him.

Since his last visit, Kane had experimented with trying to hold a shape for longer and longer periods of time. He was getting better at it although his facial features did seem very mirage-like and shifted into another form before they had solidified with the last. He felt it was still aggravating to look into his master's face for any length of time because of this. His eyes were still not sure what it was they saw. He was sure if a human tried to look at his face they would probably end up with a severe headache. As for Farran, he just found it a very disturbing visual exercise.

"My Lord, your faces are getting better," he told him quite honestly. "But no one has worn clothes like that for three hundred years."

Kane made a sound of disappointment. "A shame. I liked the...what do you call them? Ruffles," he replied morosely.

There was no answer Farran could give which wouldn't get him in trouble so he just chose to drop the subject and move on.

"My Lord, I have something you might want to see," Farran told him. Without waiting for an answer, he strode to the nearest table and opened his laptop computer. He felt Kane's presence sweep nearer like a cloud of mist. He tried not to shiver or fumble with the computer. Farran was uncomfortable with this technology which he predated by several centuries. But more than this, he did not want to seem an idiot in front of Kane.

He breathed an immense sigh of relief when he successfully managed to turn on the laptop and load the videos Ainsley had recorded.

"This is the woman I told you about," he explained, pointing to the figures on screen. "But it seems fate has smiled upon us. We have two possible conversions to choose from, the woman Susanne Miller or her daughter Sabrina."

The misty face form floated closer to the screen.

"Fascinating invention!" Kane breathed at first and then his foggy eyes latched onto the moving figures on the screen.

Farran waited for a reply as his master observed the two short videos. And he waited and waited. Farran began to get nervous as the minutes stretched onward.

"I was thinking, my Lord..." he began tremulously. "The daughter would be an easier target for conversion. She is out of her element here. She does not speak the language, she does not know the area, she is naïve to the ways of the world..."

Abruptly Kane interrupted in an authoritative tone of voice. "The mother."

Farran was startled into silence for a few breathless moments.

"But Sire," Farran began, trying to remember his manners. "The spawn would be a much easier a victim..."

"I said I want the parent!" Kane announced in a louder, more commanding tone of voice.

Farran's mouth flapped uselessly like a fish out of water before he was able to actually form words.

"But my Lord! I don't understand..." he stammered.

"And I don't need you to," was Kane's terse reply.

Farran's mind scrambled as he tried to find some way to make use of this denial.

"My Lord...what if the child causes trouble?"

There was a sound from Kane which seemed to be a growl.

"The child is no good. She is a casualty of war. Cannon fodder. If she gets in your way, get rid of her."

Farran's mind was still frantically trying to make use of what he had just heard.

"You're the one who likes to play with toys!" Kane growled at him. "I am not victim to the same perversion as you. I am only interested in the mother. Now go and get her for me. I command you. And remember...I have dined on your kind before."

He let the sting of his thinly veiled threat hang in the air between them. Farran's eyes bulged wider and his gaping mouth snapped shut. He turned to the laptop and clapped it roughly closed. He tucked it under his arm and fled from his lord and master's presence.

* * *

We were in the limo again heading down the hill from the castle taking the road to town. It was just the two of us this time. Bree had asked to stay behind to investigate the castle and the gardens. She was so eager to explore her new surroundings. We had been informed there was a very old garden maze on the property. Being from Pennsylvania, we were used to mazes. But the ones we had in the states were made in cornfields. Bree had only seen garden mazes in movies. So Bree stayed.

"Have you ever been to the reading of a person's will?" Bartal asked me.

I was told my presence had been requested.

"Not really," I replied without looking at him.

Bartal nodded and continued. "I believe it is very likely Mykhalo mentioned you in his will. I would like to warn you, Mrs. Miller, whatever he left you, there may be an adjustment period you may need help to get through. And by that I mean legal adjustment. I am here to shepherd you through the process."

Okay, I wasn't expecting that! I had totally forgotten about the onerous paperwork assigned with the death of a loved one. There were forms which must be filled out, ownership of property which must be transferred and many more things I had completely forgotten about in my grief.

"Is this will...legal?" I finally asked him.

"Of course," he smiled knowingly.

"But...I mean...how could it possibly be...since he is...*was*...a vampire?" I asked.

Bartal laughed and waved a hand as if it was no matter.

"The world does not, and *should not* believe in vampires. Therefore the will was drawn up as if Mykhalo was the blood kin of a noble and inherited all this property and wealth from relatives down through the centuries."

"And if it got out this will was for a three hundred year old vampire?" I inquired.

Bartal guffawed. "Then the will would be declared null and void and the legal world would be thrown into a tailspin. Not to mention if it got out into the papers! No, my dear, as far as the world is concerned, vampires aren't real and those who say they are surely must be crazy. That is the way it should stay."

I frowned and thought hard about this.

"I take it the entire will is written in German?"

"Of course," he replied. "Do you speak German?"

My frown increased and I shook my head in denial. "Other than the typical 'please' and 'thank you' no I don't. Pennsylvania Dutch was the jargon my parents spoke when they didn't want me to know what they were talking about. They never taught it to me."

"There is a rather large difference between Pennsylvania Dutch and German languages," Bartal interjected. "They are similar in some ways but they are definitely not the same."

I sighed and this time I crossed my arms in front of me.

"So I guess I'm not going to know anything anyone is saying, eh?" I muttered dismally.

I was starting to dread this whole ritual to come.

"Do not worry!" Bartal smiled and patted me reassuringly on the knee. "Many people who will be there speak English and I will translate any information pertinent to you. You have very little to be concerned about."

As he said this, the limo pulled into the parking lot of a very official looking government type building. Its architecture resembled the famous buildings of ancient Rome. The lawns were immaculately tended with beds of spring flowers everywhere.

The limo found a spot and slid to a silky stop.

"Come now, Mrs. Miller. You have nothing to worry about. This is just the business end of death. It is necessary, not enjoyable."

He exited the limo and held a hand out for me. I hesitated, and then placed my hand in his and allowed myself to be led on Bartal's arm to the cold looking building. I noticed small groups of other people, all dressed in black, who seemed to be making their somber way to the same door. Silently we entered the building. I shivered and Bartal must have noticed for he squeezed and patted my hand to bolster my courage. I took a deep breath and followed the small group of other people who seemed to know exactly where they needed to be.

We entered a room which looked like it was meant for board meetings. A smiling official greeted us, shaking our hands each in turn as we entered the room. He seemed to know every person's name before they were even introduced. There was a long table with plush, high leather chairs arranged about it. We all took our seats around the great table. Bartal seated himself beside me.

I felt very inadequately dressed to be in this crowd. They all were in business suits and ties, appropriately dressed as if for a political cabinet. I felt small and insignificant. The chair seemed to swallow me up as if I was a little kid in an adult's office. I was very uncomfortable with corporate life. I risked a glance at Bartal. I must have looked ready to bolt. He flashed me a quick, confident smile and a nod and once again patted my hand in a 'you can do this' sort of way.

I risked a glance about me at the faces of the other people gathered. I noticed many were eyeing me in a curious but not an unfriendly manner. Many smiled and nodded in my direction. I took a deep breath and forced myself to relax a bit. No one had given me an angry look or threatening gesture. We were all here for the same thing. It was all in my head, a paranoia of my own imagination.

Why was I so on edge?

Those who knew each other spoke quietly among themselves. Others seemed to look anywhere but at another person.

We waited. And waited. I looked at the clock anxiously. Twenty minutes ticked by while we sat there waiting for stragglers. Finally a tiny, thin man with spectacles perched on the end of his sharp nose entered the room. He clutched a stack of papers to his chest and a briefcase. His movements were quick and nervous like a scared mouse in a room full of cats. The official left the room and closed the door behind him. The latch turned with a final sounding snap.

The little man went at once to the chair at the head of the table. He placed his briefcase on the table and as he opened it, he cast a quick glance about the assemblage. He said something I didn't understand. Bartal leaned close and translated softly in my ear. He was the attorney presiding over the will proceedings.

He rummaged about in the briefcase, mumbling inaudibly. Finally with a declaration, he seemed to have found what he was looking for. He pulled out a large legal folder, clapped the briefcase shut and put it on the floor. He opened the file and glanced around again at everyone gathered.

Bartal told me he asked if we were all ready to begin. Without waiting for our heads to nod, he began to read from the papers in front of him. People held their breath and leant forward to catch his quickly spoken words. Bartal translated softly at my ear.

Most of the language was in legal speak. I barely understood anything which was said, even when translated. I understood when something read pertained to a certain person from everyone's reaction. The reading went on and on, page after ponderous page of legalese. Bartal continued to translate but I ceased to listen. The words were so dry and uninviting. I was glad I hadn't chosen to go into the legal field. Nothing seemed interesting to me about it.

I had almost nodded off when I realized the nervous little man had stopped talking and was looking directly at me. In fact everyone in the room was looking at me.

Had I fallen asleep and snored? Were people insulted by this strange American woman's rudeness that she couldn't even stay awake during legal proceedings? What had happened?

I looked to Bartal but his clarifying words had suddenly stopped and he was staring at the little man as if stunned.

"What…did I…miss?" I said in a whisper.

This seemed to jar Bartal out of his stupor. He arose at once and gave me a reassuring squeeze on my shoulders as he went up to the little man sitting at the head of the table. They exchanged some words.

The attorney began to pass to him several stacks of paper which Bartal proceeded to tuck securely under his arm.

Everyone at the table was still staring at me. I couldn't decipher what emotion was on their faces.

Finally Bartal came back to me with reams of papers tucked securely, as if they were gold bars, under one arm. He touched me on the shoulder and said in a soft but a firm voice, "We are done here. Come with me at once."

Wordlessly I obeyed. I could still feel their eyes upon me as I turned my back to them. Before I could exit, the attorney addressed me in a loud tone of voice in heavily accented English, "Congratulations, Fraulein Miller. You are now a very rich woman."

Bartal shoved me out the door.

"What was all that about?"

Bartal hissed at me to keep quiet. "I'll tell you when we get in the limo."

I have never seen Bartal so nervous and jumpy. The chauffeur opened the door for us and Bartal rattled off something stern and shoved me rudely into the vehicle. He followed behind and slammed the door shut.

Finally, he uttered a huge sigh of relief as we left the parking lot.

"Will you please explain to me what just happened?" I demanded tartly. "What did the attorney mean by that? He had to have been joking."

Bartal rubbed his face and suddenly began to laugh out loud.

"I expected Mykhalo to leave you something but I never expected that!" he laughed. He removed his hands from his face. "Mykhalo just made you the main beneficiary of his estate."

I paused for a long moment.

"I...think...I know what it means," I said slowly. "But please repeat it in plain English. I've had enough legalese for one day."

Bartal just laughed and clapped his big hands together.

"You own most of the castle, properties all over the world, several coffee plantations, numerous stocks and bonds, you now have a Swiss bank account and just about all of his holdings."

My jaw dropped.

Before I could recover from my initial shock, Bartal continued.

"Where were you planning on sending Bree to college? You have enough assets now to pay for all of her schooling before she even attends one day of class. You know Heidelberg is one of the oldest universities in Europe and has an extensive foreign student program. Just a suggestion, my dear."

It was a good thing I was seated! I had to remind myself to breathe. My heart was doing funny things.

This has to be a joke! I remember thinking to myself. I just blinked stupidly at Bartal and flapped my jaw uselessly for the next few moments. He continued to laugh. I'm sure the expression on my face was priceless.

I took a deep breath and tried to recover my wits a bit.

"Show me the Swiss bank account forms," I was finally able to demand.

He nodded, changed seats to sit beside me and began to rifle through the papers. He found the ones he wanted and passed them to me. Even though it was in another language, I was able to piece together the official logo of the Swiss bank, underneath was Mykhalo's full name with title and underneath this was my full name. Across from both of our names was a balance number with more zeros behind the first digit than I had ever thought possible.

Oh. My. God. I remember thinking. *This is real.*

I let the papers slide through my hands and fall like spring flower petals buffeted by the wind on the floor about my feet.

Bartal started laughing again.

CHAPTER 9

To say I was in shock after the reading of the will would be a severe understatement. I kept pinching myself and looking at the papers Bartal had given me. I told him I knew nothing about running a coffee plantation or managing stocks and bonds or how to keep a castle running. Apparently there was some clause in the reams of paperwork which stated Bartal was to be my guide and ease me into the responsibilities slowly and gradually. This both reassured me and made me nervous. My world of financial responsibilities had suddenly grown exponentially.

Telling Bree was another matter altogether. I tried to do it myself but in the end I needed Bartal's help. I guess I was still trying to figure out how to emotionally handle the news myself.

Though I did remember to warn Bartal off pressuring Bree about colleges.

I decided what Bree and I really needed was time to ourselves to adjust to our new life. We could decide later what to do with our now possibly brighter future.

We wanted to spend a few days getting to know our surroundings. There were areas of the castle and grounds Bree still wanted to explore and I felt much the same way. I also got the feeling Bree wanted to do her adventuring away from Mommy. So I allowed her the liberty of being chaperoned by one of Bartal's suits, a young man from the Netherlands named Sigmund.

While Bree was otherwise occupied, I decided to investigate the castle's inner sanctum. The keys to those off-limits rooms tempted me. Bartal led me down a hallway and past many rooms cordoned off to the general tourist public. Then we went down another series of hallways which only the servants were allowed to traverse. Finally we came to a pair of great, black-stained oaken doors which looked like they may have been centuries old.

"Explore the rest on your own, Mrs. Miller," Bartal told me as he swung one door open with a grunt and a shove. "These are Mykhalo's private chambers. Only myself and Fraulein Strauss are allowed down here. Fraulein Strauss is our head maid and one of the more highly trusted individuals. She has been with us nearly thirty years. There is nothing dangerous to you in these rooms. They can, however, be rather spooky. Like all old castles this one has its share of ghosts."

I shivered as the cooler air from beyond the door swirled around me. I wondered how many ghosts the old castle had.

Bartal passed me his cell phone. "If you are afraid or confused as to how to get out or for any other reason, don't hesitate to call. Here is my number. Mykhalo wanted you to know all his secrets. Most are locked away here," Bartal waved ahead of him. "The physical ones at least."

I sensed him looking at me but I could not tear my eyes away from the dark tunnel before me.

"Remember you are safe here. Enjoy yourself."

He passed me the heavy ring of keys and then left.

I noticed he flipped the bolt on the opposite side, locking me in. This made me slightly uneasy. I forced myself to keep from shivering and turned around.

I was in a long hallway with vaulted ceilings. Chandeliers made of deer antlers swung above and the windows were high off the ground, large enough in let light in but too high to see out of. Smaller versions of the great doors I had just passed through, lined each side of the hallway.

As I walked down the hallway, I had a feeling of descending. I surmised the door at the end of the hall was the dungeon and probably Mykhalo's bedroom. I wasn't interested in seeing that just yet. So I made my way back up the hall. I stood there and tried to decide which door to open first, the right or the left.

"Eeeny, meeny miney moe..." My voice echoed in the cavernous hall. It quite took the humor out of the moment.

I chose left.

I was surprised to find the door had an old style latch but no lock. A quick glance informed me all the doors were the same in this hallway, latched but not locked. Only the great doors I had come through were bolted.

I threaded the brass key ring through a belt loop on my jeans and prayed its weight wouldn't pull my pants down.

I took a deep breath and pressed the heavy wrought iron latch.

With a deep creak and a hiss the door fell easily and obediently away from my hand. A gentle gust of cool air stroked my face and a smell which reminded me of a museum assaulted my nostrils. I stepped through the door and understood the aroma.

It seemed to be an art room. The walls were lined floor to ceiling in paintings and many more leaned against the walls covered in white sheets. At first glance, all the paintings seemed to be portraits. But the lighting in the room was bad. So I strode to the far end of the room and drew back the curtains from four enormous windows. I promised myself I wouldn't turn around until I had let the proper amount of natural light into the room. This done, I turned about and gasped in shock.

Every single portrait was of Mykhalo.

There were pictures of him in all phases of life. Those nearest the last window were of an adorable white haired boy with rosy cheeks and marble smooth skin. One had him mounted on a shaggy white pony in a stable yard with chickens and straw scattered on the cobbles. Another had him mounted on a chestnut horse which looked like a thoroughbred, seemingly preparing to ride out on a foxhunt. Still another showed him holding the bridle of a wild-eyed black mare.

In all the equestrian paintings, he wasn't smiling. He looked grim and sad with haunted eyes. Even in the portrait of him as a child seated on the white pony, his expression seemed frightened and nearly ready to burst into tears. I wondered if his father was nearby while the portraits were being painted.

Mykhalo's expression remained sadly stoic in all except the last painting. In that one, horse and man gazed at each other. A flame colored chestnut with a wide blaze and expertly braided cream mane, the horse's eyes were quiet and trusting. Mykhalo looked much as when I'd known him. Except his golden hair was tied back in a black silk bow, lace at his throat and cuffs where his hands held the bridle. He looked toward the horse with pride and adoration. And he was actually smiling.

"Must have been your favorite horse," I whispered to no one in particular.

There was another painting of Mykhalo in full noble regalia – head to toe in blue, white and gold, with lace at cuffs and neck. Each hand rested on the head of a gigantic great Dane. One was a harlequin color with blue eyes, the other slate gray. Both dogs regarded the painter warily while Mykhalo smiled down upon them.

"His favorite dogs," I whispered again.

I strode about the room looking up at the walls of all the portraits of Mykhalo. In some he stood, dressed in the proper clothing of 17th century nobility, in some he was seated, others were just paintings of his bust.

The next set of portraits were done after he became a vampire. The skin of his face became grayer, an almost blue pallor and his eyes became harder, colder. Centuries sped by on canvas. In each painting, he adopted the proper garb of the time. The painting from the 1960s was very interesting. He added a new flair to wearing a ponytail. I smiled sadly.

I passed a tall shape leaned against the wall, covered in a sheet. Expecting another painting, I was surprised to discover a full-length mirror.

I passed on to free other paintings from their ghostly wrappings.

All were of Mykhalo. Some pen and ink, others charcoal pencil. Some pastel, others a soft watercolor wash. Still others in bold strokes of oil paint.

"You find the collection disturbing. Why?" a voice whispered at my ear.

I must have jumped ten feet at the sound. I spun about and searched wildly for the source of the voice. But I was alone in the art room.

Then I noticed the reflection in the mirror was not my own.

Mykhalo stood regarding me quietly from inside the mirror. He seemed to be standing in a shaft of sunlight. It lit his golden locks like the mane on a lion. His black Armani suit stood in sharp contrast.

"Do not be afraid," he smiled at me reassuringly. "But why do the pictures bother you?"

"A whole room full of nothing but pictures of yourself? Well…it just seems a little egotistical that's all."

His smile deepened. "Maybe for a normal person, Zan, but not me. Think! I went for nearly three hundred years without being able to see myself. Think of how that might change things for you. After a while you begin to question the reality of your own existence."

"Is that what all this is?" I said. "Reaffirming to yourself you're really real?"

"Perhaps," he said. "After each portrait was complete I would spend hours looking at it. I think I was looking for some sign of age in the artist's handiwork."

He sighed sadly. "All I ever found was another portrait of a vampire."

"You reflect now," I said.

"Yes, but I still can't see myself. Ironic don't you think?" he almost laughed.

His eyes became suddenly serious. "The only time I can see myself is when I am close to you. Then I can see me shining in your eyes."

I stepped closer to the mirror. He reached out his hand. I mirrored the gesture. But all my fingertips touched was cold, hard glass.

I dropped my eyes, too wounded by raw emotion. My current situation burst into my thoughts.

"So… I have sex with you and you repay me by making me your beneficiary?"

Mykhalo uttered a short laugh. "Please tell me you don't *really* believe that's the reason I left you everything!"

I risked a look up at him through the strands of my hair. "Then tell me the real reason."

He was silent for a long moment.

"You made me human again."

"Yeah, for what, like five minutes before you died?" I sniffed almost in scorn.

But Mykhalo wasn't laughing.

"Zan," he breathed softly. "I would rather be a simple human mortal for five minutes and die in the arms of someone who loved me than be immortal, living off the death of others for three hundred years. That's why I put you in my will. No matter how short a time it was, you saved my life. And you were the only person who could."

It felt like someone squeezed my heart, stopping it from beating. Tears came to my eyes.

"I miss you, Zan," he said. His other hand reached up and he tried to stroke my face through the glass. His eyes were shining wetly.

"I wish I could hold you again. Just once more."

"Ditto," I replied trying not to cry.

I sighed, and the sigh turned into a sob which doubled me over. Quite suddenly I felt faint. The next instant I was crouched on all fours in front of the mirror sobbing harder than I dared at the funeral. I could see Mykhalo's reflection crouched beside me and I felt his frustration at not being able to touch or comfort me.

"Why are you here?" I finally managed to gasp out.

I felt confusion in the silence from him. "You want me to leave?" he asked softly.

"No!" I flung my head back in agony. "I want you to be alive and here for me to touch and hold. And you're not. You're just... not! You're not anything anymore."

I gasped and sobbed raggedly a couple more times before I could trust my voice again. I watched my tears spatter on the highly polished marble floors.

"Why are you here?" I asked again. "You're only a ghost now, a tease of your own reality. Why are you here? Are you trying to torment me more?"

"Zan, I love you," he started in a voice which shuddered with emotion.

"Shut up!" I was almost screaming at the mirror now. "You're not real. You're dead! So why are you still here?"

He was silent.

I closed my eyes and took a couple more deep breaths before I began again in a whisper.

"I have to move on. I have to adjust to you not being here, to you being dead. Hanging around as a ghost isn't helping me cope with your loss. It's not helping me mourn and grieve over you. I can't move on. It's just prolonging the pain. So why are you still here?" I stared at the floor for one long moment. "Are you trying to torture me more?"

I took another deep breath before I could trust myself to look up into the mirror. I expected his reflection to be gone, chased away by my thorny words.

But Mykhalo remained, now standing. His face was pale and blank. But his eyes were wet with unshed tears. "Do you want to know what happens when you die, what comes next after the spirit leaves the body?"

I had a feeling he was going to tell me whether I wanted to hear it or not.

"First you're allowed to attend your own funeral. This is so the spirit can accept the reality of its own situation. Next you move on to paradise. Or at least you're supposed to. I don't know that part yet because I stopped just short of entering the doors."

I dashed the tears away from my face. All right. He was correct. He had my attention. "What happened?"

He smiled and bowing his head, stuffed his hands in his pockets. "I asked a question. A question I probably never should have asked of the spirits guiding me."

I swallowed with difficulty. "What question could keep you out of paradise?"

He smiled as if in regret and shook his head. "Will Zan and Bree be safe from any paranormal danger from now on?"

The breath stopped in my throat. His last thought before entering heaven was to our safety. I bit my lip and clapped a hand over my mouth. "And the answer?"

Mykhalo's face twisted in worry and confusion. "Well, that's just it. There was no answer. Neither yes or no."

He flapped his arms helplessly. "So this planted the seed of doubt in my mind. I had to come back in whatever form I was allowed, to try to protect you both."

Mykhalo stepped as close to me as the mirror would allow. "Zan you're in danger. I don't know who it is. I have my suspicions but nothing certain. I can't get in anyone's mind. Well, sometimes I can get in yours but not always. I don't think you going home would help. It might just make it easier for them. Stay here. Please, please be careful. I have no idea how I can help you best in this form. I will try everything I can."

He stepped closer to the surface of the mirror. "They're hunting you, Zan," he paused until my eyes met and locked with his. "I see shadows all around you. Following you, whispering about you, going away and coming back. The darkness wants you for its own. I can't allow that to happen."

"Who's they?" I thought of the greasy fellow I met at the funeral. "Do you mean like Ainsley Wainwright?"

His eyes grew stormy. "Possibly. Probably. I wouldn't be surprised if he turned out to be a vampire's errand boy. But I don't know any details yet."

He paused another moment. "That's why I'm still here. I'm not trying to hurt you. I'm trying to protect you and Bree. Please, you've got to believe me."

I reached out and touched the mirror's surface. My frustration at my new situation suddenly seemed insignificant. "I believe you, Mykhalo."

"Promise me you'll be careful."

I sniffed and rose to my feet. "I promise."

CHAPTER 10

Bree and I decided to go into town to do some shopping. Bartal arranged transport.

Blonde haired, stony-faced Sigmund with his pitch-black shades would act as our driver. Bernard had a better mastery of the language and would act as our translator if needed. With dark brown hair and sparkling blue eyes, he spoke with the barest of accent. He seemed just as eager for an outing as we were.

As we drove into town, Bernard pointed out historical sites. We decided to visit them another day. This day was for shopping.

In the city square, Bernard recommended a coffee shop and local bakery to visit later in the day. Sigmund parked the limo and went to visit a newsstand while Bernard ushered us around. He led us to the spring festival on a wide street reserved for pedestrians and people on bikes. Every lamppost was festooned with garlands of flowers and ribbons in bright spring colors. Music of every sort filled the air. We dined at an outside patio and watched as a colorful procession of acrobats filed slowly down the street.

We visited a nearby shop selling clothing. Unfortunately it was all very current styles made for teenagers and ultra-thin people. Nothing there screamed 'Bree's mother' but everything called 'Bree.' I had to restrain her from going nuts with the credit card or she would have bought everything in the store. Especially now she believed money was not an issue!

We stopped in a few more shops along the way, meandering slowly taking in all the sights. We easily lost track of time. We exited one shop to find it was dusk.

I shivered at the change in temperature. Something inside me whispered we should head back to the castle. I had a creeping sensation we should not be here after dark.

But Bree wanted to buy pastries from a man with a pushcart. It wouldn't take long so I decided to indulge her yet again.

Big mistake. I wish I had known.

My feet were tired from all the walking so I told her and Bernard to go ahead while I sat down to rest on a bench underneath a street light. It was well within view of the pastry cart so Bernard escorted Bree while I hastened to give my feet their well-deserved rest.

I was only two feet away from the bench when I collided with someone, spilling my bags.

I stooped to gather them as the person above me apologized in German.

"That's okay. No harm done," I assured him.

"You are an American!" the voice switched languages in surprise. "Here let me help you."

I started to protest but my words died on my lips as I met the stranger's eyes.

He had a strangely angular but oddly handsome face. His eyes were ice blue and his short hair was dyed white and spiked with hair gel. And his pale face was streaked in theatrical paint to resemble flames.

Something inside me shivered.

"Here you go. Nothing breakable in there I hope," he said as he handed the bags back to me.

His English was perfect. There was only the slightest hint of an accent but from what country I could not tell. It sounded vaguely British.

"No, just clothes," I said.

I noticed his hands were gloved.

The man was tall, maybe just a tad taller than Mykhalo but much thinner. With his frame and pale almost blue skin amid the face paint, he reminded me of a concentration camp prisoner. Except there were no hollows around the eyes. He almost looked like a longer version of Governor Tarkin from the first "Star Wars" movie.

"Excuse me but what's with the face paint?"

He smiled easily with teeth as white as his skin.

"I am the after dark entertainment of the spring fair," he explained. "I am a fire eater and dancer, hence the face paint and odd costume."

He gestured smoothly to the rest of his body.

It was then I noticed he wore a tight body suit of silver painted in orange and gold flames which accented his already lean build.

"But where are my manners? My name is Farran. And you are?" he said with a theatrical bow.

I remembered my conscience's warning this time and refused to give my full name.

"Zan," I said briefly.

"Zan?" he repeated. "What a unique and intriguing name for an American. I am pleased to make your acquaintance."

He took my hand, and lifting it to his lips, dropped a kiss onto the back of it.

Again I shuddered inwardly and did not know why. Was this part of his theatrical manner or was he this way with every woman? I smiled politely at this touch of formality, but removed my hand from his light grasp.

"I must hurry. My show is about to start, Miss...Zan. But I would be honored if you would stay and watch. There are many fire dancers but none has a performance like mine. Won't you please stay?"

I cast an apprehensive glance at the darkening sky above us.

The man called 'Farran' seemed to guess my thoughts.

"I am sorry but my show cannot be fully appreciated until it is full dark. Fire is less impressive in the daylight. Don't you agree?"

I looked back to him. I did not want to stay. I was uncomfortable in his presence. I wanted to collect my daughter and leave.

But I thought I could say yes and slip away quietly when the crowd gathered; just melt away like the morning mist.

I turned my eyes back to him and forced myself to smile politely and nod once.

"Excellent!" he breathed in pleasure with a wide grin. "You will not be disappointed. I have a good feeling about this. I suspect tonight will be a show of shows!"

He bowed with a flourish and pranced away into the center of the street.

I sighed in relief of his departure. I was glad he wasn't a real actor, just an acrobat for he seemed to overdo everything.

I cast my eyes about for Bree. She and Bernard were still talking to the man with the pastry cart.

I looked back to find Farran fussing with several small boxes set up around his performance space. They began to spew a heavy fog. Dry ice, I suspected.

Then music poured from a shadowed alcove, loud instrumental music which boomed and thrummed through one's feet. Laser lights shot across the square and Farran began to move in time. He struck a dramatic pose in the center of the square. Two long rods appeared in his hands. He swept in a smooth circle then somersaulted lightly end over end. When his feet landed, the tips of the rods sprang into flames.

A sound of surprise rippled among the crowd along with scattered applause. Four other dancers dressed like Farran ran into the circle and began to take up their places about the inside edge of the gathered townspeople. Two sported dancing ribbons, the other two fire rods as well.

The smoke from the dry ice was getting thicker as was the audience.

I cast my eyes about for Bree. She and Bernard had made their purchase and were winding their way back to me. Bree was distracted by the show. Bernard suddenly adopted a watchful stance, looking everywhere but toward the show.

I stiffened. Bernard knew something was wrong.

Mykhalo's words came back to me from before. *"They're hunting you, Zan."*

I began to make my way toward them.

The crowd had quickly grown thick. All were mesmerized by the performance before them. They had also become loath to get out of my way. It was harder to see Bree and Bernard over all the heads in front of me.

My sense of danger increased.

"I see shadows all around you, following you, whispering about you,"

The music rose and banged, deafening as a rock concert. Laser lights flashed and tendrils of dry ice smoke invaded the crowd. Dancers spun and leapt about, sliced by the laser lights then suddenly thrown into shadow. Fire licked from their hands and ribbons snaked through the air. I called for Bree but my voice was drowned by the music.

And then I lost sight of Bernard.

I twisted, turned and hopped to see over the people in front of me but I could not see him anywhere.

"The darkness wants you for its own."

Where was Bree?

I looked back to Farran. He was dazzling the crowd with his acrobatics, dancing as he juggled two fire pots on chains about his body, rippling with serpentine skill around the leaping flames. His eyes were nowhere near me. He concentrated on weaving his art.

Then I saw Bree.

One of the ribbon dancers entered the crowd and cleared a little space in which to perform. Bree stood at the edge of the crowd. The ribbon dancer beckoned her as she spun and flowed, inviting Bree to come and dance with her.

The look on Bree's face was one of suspicion, as if she knew something was not quite right but couldn't figure out exactly what it was. While she stood there confused, the dancer came nearer and nearer. There was something sinister and threatening about her movements.

I hurriedly pushed through the people in front of me to get to her. Somehow, winding, weaving and forcibly shoving people aside, I came nearer, approaching Bree from behind.

The ribbon dancer was quite near her now, near enough to entwine Bree in spiraling ribbons. The dancer reached out seductively towards Bree. My daughter mirrored her motion.

The dancer switched one of the ribbon sticks to her other hand and reached out for my daughter with the other.

It was then I saw the moon white eyes in the dancer's face shadowed by wild dark hair and teeth so white they glowed. Their fingertips touched.

I screamed Bree's name.

At that very instant a dark shape separated itself from the crowd and crashed into my daughter, knocking her away from the sinister dancer.

I shoved the last few people separating us and spun to face the dancer as a mother wolf would protect her cub.

But the dancer retreated into the crowd, melting into the fog and dark with a flash of inhuman eyes. I heard her scornful laugh and the sound chased a shiver up my spine.

I turned back to Bree.

She was splayed on her side on the ground. She had raised her torso up, frozen in position, staring at the person who collided with her. He was now crouched on the ground at her side. Music pounded and lights flashed so I couldn't get a clear look at his features. He seemed thin and youthful, slightly taller than Bree. His clothes were ripped for fashion and his spiked Mohawk was plain to see. But his eyes glittered in the moving light and I could not tell just what color they were.

He shouted at Bree above the din of the music. "Get out of here! There's suckers everywhere here and they want you both."

Before either of us had time to react, he picked her up and put her on her feet again.

I grabbed Bree by the hand and the young man clutched my arm firmly. I reeled as I felt a jolt from his touch. Before I had any time to react, he ordered us to follow him.

My mind was spinning. My thoughts focused on one very unimportant detail.

The stranger with a Mohawk had an American accent.

"Don't look! Just run!" I ordered my daughter and gave her a warning tug.

I cast a wild glance behind me. Through the black strands of my hair and the laser light slivered smoke from the dry ice, I saw a strange thing.

Farran appeared from out of nowhere, clutching the vampire dancer by her hair and with an arm around her waist, jerked her away from us into the smoke and thunderous music. He made it all look like part of the dance but I knew it wasn't. To the crowd he was approaching her from behind and kissing her passionately on the neck. They weren't close enough to see the fangs he bared just before he buried his face in her throat.

The smoke swirled and flowed, obscuring anything else.

I didn't wait to see more. Some dim part of my mind told me we shouldn't trust a stranger to guide us away from the threat. But I was just thankful we were moving in any direction away from Farran and his cronies. I wanted to keep it that way.

The guy in the Mohawk pushed us in front of him and pointed in one direction. "Go that way! I'll keep them from following. Run!"

I took my daughter by the hand. We didn't wait to hear more or question why. We just did as he said. We ran away from the crowd, away from the smoke, away from the entertainment with its strange vampiric dancers.

After a short sprint Bree paused to gasp. "Where's Bernard?"

"Keep moving!" I shook my head as I panted.

Bree nodded and bolted with me hot on her heels.

The two of us jogged through the lamplit streets to try to avoid the shadows. I finally had to call for a stop to catch my breath.

"Are we safe?" she gasped, bent over.

"No, not until we find Bernard!"

Bree cursed suddenly.

"What?" I questioned, too agitated to scold her.

"My cell phone is gone!"

I did a quick check of my person.

"Mine too. Crap!" I muttered between pants. "I hope Sigmund is where we left him. We're not about to hike out of town in the dark to the castle by ourselves!"

"Sounds like something some really stupid characters in a horror movie would do just before they're killed!" Bree agreed. "We need to get to a phone."

I nodded.

"Preferably one in a well-lit, populated area."

Bree straightened from her bent over crouch to look carefully about her.

"Hey! Where's Mr. Mohawk?"

It was then I noticed 'Mr. Mohawk' as she had nicknamed him, had suddenly gone missing. It was just my daughter and I on the dark street.

I frowned. No, I didn't want to trust this guy we'd just met. But even I had to admit I felt more helpless with him gone.

"Well, there's a restaurant over there that's still open," she said pointing.

I peered in the direction she gestured and frowned.

"Just our luck!" I growled. "The two streetlights before it are burned out! Double crap!"

"We gotta try it." Bree sighed. "I don't feel like staying in one place too long. I'm not sure that vampire is dead. And where there's one there's probably more."

"You're probably right. Okay, you go in front and don't let go of my hand. Hear me?" I cautioned her.

She nodded and slid her palm into my own.

"I'm stuck to you like glue," she whispered.

We headed toward the brightly lit restaurant. The shadows before it looked ominous and deep. I let Bree look for trouble ahead while I searched the shadows behind for any less than friendly pursuit.

We entered the shadowed part of the street. I tried my best to think and behave like an owl, hoping to borrow some of their useful night vision. We progressed along pretty well for some time.

Until Bree tripped over something on the sidewalk.

"What the..." I began to hiss.

Bree started to scream but slapped her free hand tight over her mouth to keep the sound from coming out.

Our other hands were still linked. I felt hers begin to shudder and sweat.

"Ma, I think I know what happened to Bernard," she said in a trembling voice.

I crouched down to peer through the dark at the barely lit thing lying on the sidewalk between us.

Bernard's body, face twisted in agony, and what was left of his blood draining from two pinpricks on his neck.

We sprang away in horror from the sight.

Bree met my eyes in the dark. I saw mirrored there in her wetly shining wide eyes, my own fear. Then suddenly her eyes shifted to a spot just beyond me and widened even more.

"MA! Behind you!" she shouted.

At the same moment, she pulled me towards her and down. I hit the street hard and rolled to the side trying to look at what Bree had been avoiding. Bree was grappling with a shadowy person. It looked female from the wild hair flowing about and seemed to be dressed in a cat suit. The strange woman was much stronger than my daughter and easily spun her until she was held from behind. Bree's attacker pinned one arm behind her and wrapped the other tightly about Bree's throat, pulling her head to the side preparing to bite her neck.

Bree flailed with her free arm at the side pocket of her backpack. No sign of fear on her face, just frenzied determination.

I saw the vampire's teeth flash in the dim light.

"Bree!" I screamed.

There was an answering scream as the vampire forcibly flung my daughter away from her embrace as if touched by acid.

Bree used this opportunity to snatch a bottle of water from the side pocket of her pack. Faster than I thought possible, she had the cap off and was squirting the contents on her attacker. The vampire began to writhe in agony and smoke, shrieking in pain.

Bree scrambled to her feet, took my hand and we bolted from the scene.

"Are you bitten?" I gasped as we ran in the dark.

"No," she replied and held the empty bottle aloft in triumph. "I've been drinking holy water every day."

I have never felt so relieved in all my life!

"That's my girl!" I said with a laugh.

We had almost made it to the safety of the next lamppost and the restaurant when a tall, lean figure blocked our path. I recognized the person.

"Farran," I said.

Before I could say or do anything else, he slapped my daughter hard across the face and she crumpled like a sheet.

Furious, I turned on Farran. He merely tapped me on the forehead.

At his touch, my entire world went dark.

CHAPTER 11

Bree woke up to cold cobblestones beneath her cheek.

"Mom?" she said quietly as she raised her head and looked around. No answer.

It was still dark. She was alone on the streets of a strange German town.

"Mom?" she called louder and sat up.

'Hush little one! You're still in danger,' a voice spoke inside her head.

Slowly, Bree crawled to her feet. She scrutinized every shadow with suspicion.

There was a scuffle to her right and she spun to face the sound. Yellow eyes glowed from the darkness before her.

Bree's heart pounded in fear.

Then the eyes seemed to hop down several levels. They blazed and hovered only a few inches off the cobblestone street. The creature approached, growing progressively smaller until it stood right at Bree's feet.

The dark thing with the ominous yellow eyes uttered a plaintive, "Meow."

Bree heaved a sigh of relief and felt her fear evaporate. "Never been so scared of just a cat!" she muttered to herself.

'No talking!' the voice in her head scolded. *'Follow the cat.'*

She shut her mouth and obeyed. The cat led her through a maze of nearly black alleyways. She should have lost it several times. But always the feline stopped and waited, its eyes shining a beacon even when there was no other light to see.

Finally the alley led them onto a main thoroughfare. The cat stopped, looked at Bree, meowed one last time and vanished.

Bree stepped out of the alley. She was greeted by a very familiar looking limousine. Sigmund stood in front talking to Bartal. Their conversation was hushed but angry.

"Bartal?" Bree called out. "Where's M..."

This was all she managed to get out before they grabbed her and forcibly shoved her into the limo as if she was being abducted. Bartal climbed in with her. Sigmund jumped in the driver's seated and stomped on the accelerator.

"Hey!" squawked Bree. "What's going on? Where's Mom?"

Bartal barked orders to Sigmund in another language. The limo's speed redoubled. Bree braced herself as they careened wildly around a turn. The tires shrieked in protest of the rough treatment.

"What the Hell is going on?" she demanded. "Where's my mother?"

Bartal sighed heavily then faced Bree with the sternest expression she'd ever seen.

"Sabrina, your mother has been taken."

At that very second, everything stopped for Bree. She forgot to breathe. Her heart stopped beating. She forgot to blink. Time itself stopped.

Her jaw flapped uselessly a few times before she was able to force a sound out of her lips.

"What do you mean...she was...taken?" she whispered.

"Sigmund saw a vampire take your mother. He wasn't able to stop him," Bartal reported. "Bree, your mother is gone."

Bree took a sudden breath and then words began to spill out like flood waters breaking a damn.

"You're lying!" she shouted. "We have to go back for her. We can't let them do that. Turn this thing around. We have to get my mother back!"

She hurled herself at the door controls just as Sigmund hit the lock mechanism.

"NO!" she screamed. "Turn around! Go back! We have to get her. We can't just leave her there with them. Mom! Mom!"

Bartal growled and tried to grab her arms. But Bree turned on him. He finally spun her around in his arms so she couldn't punch him in the face.

Bree screamed for her mother over and over. She didn't even feel the tears as they streamed down her face like rain.

Bartal hugged her tight, half to keep her from hurting him, half out of his own frustration.

"We've lost her, Sabrina. She's gone."

* * *

I awoke to cold and darkness. I gasped and sightlessly knew that my breath condensed in the cold, a plume of surprised heat from my warm lips. My brain scrambled to figure out what could have happened. I knew I didn't normally sleep on cold, hard concrete in a dark place. My thoughts raced trying desperately to piece together the events leading up to my present situation.

My last thoughts were of Farran's eyes – cold, gray, angry and inches away. Then he tapped me lightly on the forehead and darkness had consumed me.

My next thoughts were of Bree collapsed in a heap on the dark German street, lamplight throwing wrinkles on her clothes into stark contrast against her smooth skin.

Was my daughter safe? I had no idea.

Bartal had tried to protect me. But he failed. Something had gone horribly wrong. Bernard was dead. I had no idea where Sigmund was. More importantly, I didn't know where I was.

I knew it was late spring outside so the fact the room was so cold either meant I was in an air-conditioned place or I was far underground. I didn't hear a fan or an engine running so that left the far underground choice, probably a cellar for storing beer — if I was still in Germany.

Then my animal instincts shrieked a warning in my brain.

I was not alone.

Something or someone else shared the room with me.

I reached out with my senses trying to ascertain what sort of life form I was imprisoned with. I heard no sound of movement. My gut told me it was human not animal – but not the right kind of human.

I heard a barely discernible breath across the room to my left. I knew in my heart the other person was a vampire.

Yes, this was definitely not Buffy's world!

I sat up and my fingers scrabbled on the hard floor beneath me, searching for the parameters of the room.

"Your animal instincts serve you well, my dear," spoke a male voice in the darkness. Its calmness only served as further warning of the danger I was in. "You know I'm here in spite of the dark, whereas I need no light to see you. You glow like a pillar of heat before me."

I found the wall behind me and crouched, facing the voice. I tried to sound fierce and angry. "Where am I and why have you brought me here?" I demanded..

But my voice betrayed me. It shook and trembled like a frightened, cornered rabbit.

"Where are you?" my jailer repeated.

The voice paused for a low, sinister chuckle. "As to where you are, I have no intentions of telling you. And why I have taken you..." He paused for effect. "That will soon become obvious."

There was a slight scuffle of footsteps made for my benefit so I could track his movements. I knew vampires could move without a sound if they truly wished. My captor was just prolonging the inevitable.

"But there is no need for us to be strangers."

There was a click. A beam of white light, the kind from a hooded lamp used to fix cars or interrogate prisoners, shone down into the exact center of the room. The light threw my jailer into stark black and white contrast. He stood before me slivered in dark shadows. His sockets were shaded black pools but his eyes shone clearly, gleaming out of his skull-like face.

"Farran!" I recognized him at once.

He smiled and bowed his head slightly. His voice had the same accent as before but now it changed in tone. Deeper, more ominous sounding. "I am glad to see you have such a close relationship with your animal side," he said. "I chose well. The Master will be pleased."

"What master?" I said.

He started to approach. I scrambled to my feet. I slid along the wall, my hands leading the way, refusing to take my eyes off him. I didn't want him near me. He was trying to corner me like a sheepdog.

My fingers and body finally found a corner of the room and there I felt trapped. Farran was still advancing on me. I wanted him to keep his distance. So, when he came close, I slapped him. The blow was hard enough to spin his head to the side. This only seemed to amuse him.

"Just try and do that again," he mocked.

I was happy to oblige. But this time he caught my hand and pinned it to the wall. I tried to spin out of his grasp but he caught my other hand and pinned it as well.

I could see my struggles only served to excite him more.

I stilled and did my best to glare daggers into his eyes. "Let...me...go," I demanded slowly.

Farran simply chose to ignore me. Instead he inhaled deeply, like a dog sniffing its prey.

"Did you fight like this with Mykhalo?" he whispered. "Or did you let him do whatever he wanted?"

I growled and tried to kick him. He pressed his hip against mine to stop me. The close proximity of his body only served to further frighten and infuriate me. I did not like his touch.

He however, seemed to enjoy it. "Yes, I know all about your love affair with Mykhalo. I find it surprising you gave in to him so easily being as you knew so little about his past. I see I may have to work a little harder to get you to expose your softer side to me."

"Is that what you want from me? I'm to be your lover?"

"Of course," he chuckled. "I have been accused of wanting whatever Mykhalo had. Well he had you. So now I want you."

My heart blazed with fury. "Never!"

"My dear, please don't dismiss me without giving me a chance," Farran teased. "Besides, I don't really give a damn whether I get your love or your blood. Fight me too much and I'll just take you any way I like. It makes no difference to me."

"I'll die before I give you either!" I said in fury. It was then I realized I had said the wrong thing.

Farran smiled, his eyes glittered dangerously. "As you wish."

He moved faster than I had ever seen. I felt a sharp, stabbing pain in my neck and pressure. Then something hot and wet began begin to trickle down my neck.

Oh my god! I thought in stunned silence. *He's actually bitten me.*

CHAPTER 12

Bree paced in the castle's great sitting room overlooking the hedge maze. She had spent a great deal of time there since the trip to town. She alternated between pacing and gazing down the lane which led from the castle to town. She'd barely eaten or drunk anything and only slept when she'd worn herself out from her incessant pacing. Every person who entered the room raised her hopes. Each time though, her hopes were dashed.

It was Bartal who entered this time. She had seen him briefly only once since her mother's capture, just long enough to tearfully relay her version of what happened. He'd been conspicuously absent since then.

Her heart leapt at the sight of him. But his expression was grim and he shook his head once. Bree visibly deflated.

"Bree, I need to talk to you. Please sit down," he said, gently gesturing to the plush leather chair behind her.

"Is it about my mother?"

"No," he replied.

"Then I don't need to hear it," she cut him off.

Bree turned her back, crossed her arms in front, and looked back to the scenery.

"Sabrina Tempest Miller, look at me!" Bartal said in a commanding tone of voice.

Slowly Bree obeyed, frowning in irritation.

"This is important," he said sternly. "It concerns you. Now sit down before I make you sit down."

Bree pouted but did as she was told.

"Fine!" she grumbled. "Happy now? What's up?"

Bartal frowned as he thought about the next words he would say to this petulant child. Finally he came up to Bree, took her hands, and knelt in front of her.

In as gentle a tone as he could muster, he said, "Bree, I have to send you home."

"*What?*" she exclaimed and bolted out of the chair, yanking her hands away. "You can't possibly be serious! My Mom has just been kidnapped and you want to send me away?"

Bartal scrambled to make amends. "I don't want you to leave. No one here wants you to leave. But it's what I must legally do."

She strode away and struggled not to cry. "You're not making any sense!"

Bartal sighed in frustration and scratched the side of his whiskered face.

"Look. You're a minor and you're in a foreign country. Your one parent is gone and you have no legally appointed guardian here with you."

"But the will..." Bree interjected and this time Bartal interrupted her.

"The will means nothing in this sense!" he spoke loudly. "You are a beneficiary of the will. It does not appoint anyone as your guardian. Only your mother can do that and she's gone."

Bree stomped her foot like an impatient horse. "I'm not leaving Germany!"

They were both silent for a long moment.

"What will happen if I refuse?" she asked in a softer, more rational tone of voice.

Bartal explained the process as he walked up behind her. He explained it quietly and gently.

"Then I will be forced to call the German politzei to escort you to the airport and put you on the plane. An American police unit will pick you up when you reach the States. If your mother did not arrange a legal guardian for you, then you will be put into the American foster system."

Bree covered her face in her hands and uttered one big sob.

Bartal continued. "Luckily for you though, your mother did arrange such a guardian and I took the liberty of calling her to come over the minute your mother was abducted. She's just arrived."

He left her side, went to the door, and opened it to allow another person in the room.

"Sage!" Bree cried in relief. "Oh Sage! Thank the Goddess!"

CHAPTER 13

Although it was spring, a fire roared in the fireplace. Staring into the leaping flames helped him to think through problems which annoyed him.

Bartal gave a tired sigh as Bethany Hess entered the room and closed the large door behind her.

"Is she asleep?"

"Yes, finally," she answered. "I think she'll be able to relax more easily now a familiar face from home is here."

Bartal nodded.

"And now we can talk," Bethany told him in a stern tone of voice.

Bartal heaved another great sigh. This was not going to be pleasant. He gathered himself, rose to his feet and turned to face her.

"Now," she turned on Bartal and her eyes blazed in a fury she had been holding in check.

"What the fuck happened back there?"

Bartal was ready for some sort of outburst but this caught him so much by surprise, he backed up a step. He could count on one hand how many times he'd ever heard Bethany swear. And those few times she had, it always shocked him to the core.

"I allowed Zan to come to Lion's Gate because I thought it would be safer here. We both knew she was being watched in the States. I thought being here would make it easier to protect her. And what's the first thing that happens?" Bethany stalked in a circle, throwing her hands into the air. "You lose her! And not just to anyone but to *them*!" Bethany bristled, cheeks red, her arms gestured wildly and her eyes shot sparks. He had never seen her this fired up before.

"I did my best…" he began to say.

"Well obviously your best isn't good enough!" Bethany continued in her tirade. "You sent her to town with two body guards. Only two? You're slipping, old man! You should have known better!"

Bartal softly cleared his throat. "Actually, I sent her to town with seven bodyguards. They only knew about the two. The others were in plainclothes scattered about wherever they went."

Bethany sniffed, unimpressed. "And what happened to them?"

Bartal hung his head like a properly chastised child. "First, someone picked their pockets and took their cell phones. When something went wrong, no one could call for help. Then they picked off my men one by one. Sigmund is the only one who survived."

Bethany nodded and crossed her arms in front of her chest. "Why didn't you go with them?"

Bartal hung his head and did not speak for a long moment. "I should have."

"Coulda, woulda, shoulda!" Bethany mocked him. "Where does it get us now? Nowhere!"

She shook her head and paced back and forth a few times. "Eighteen years ago I told you Zan would be important. Eighteen years! I was only twenty-one and I saw it in my scrying crystal clear as day. Do you remember that day, Bartal? I had just taken the oath."

"I remember," Bartal replied. "I also swore the same pact. Two hundred years earlier."

"Do you remember the words?" Bethany went on. "We swore to protect all of Hope's daughters, not from death but from ever becoming vampires. So when you heard my prediction, you gave me my first big job to prove myself. You charged me to watch and guard her. I did one better. I moved to Pennsylvania and befriended her, became her family, the only family the poor child had after her parents and her husband died. I kept her safe. And you informed."

"I didn't know who was after her!" Bartal struck back. "I knew she was being watched but I didn't know by whom or what their intent was. I didn't have enough information."

"Excuses!" Bethany exclaimed. "All petty excuses! I talked to Zan after the funeral. She said Ainsley was there. Now she doesn't know who he is but we do! Wasn't that enough of a sign? Couldn't you have figured it out by the presence of that greasy little weasel?"

She strode up to Bartal and began to hiss venomously in his ear.

"What was it all for? You lost her! What good did it do Zan? Now they've got her. And you know what they'll do to her. Bree might as well be an orphan! When she comes back...*IF* she comes back, she won't be Zan anymore. She'll be beyond all hope of saving. She'll be one of *them*!"

Bartal was breathing hard but said nothing. They just glared into one another's eyes. Then Bethany sniffed, spun on her heel and left the room.

Bartal stared after her. He clenched and unclenched his fists. He turned and went to the bar set along one wall of the room. He snatched up a liquor decanter to keep his hands from shaking. His knuckles were white from barely restrained emotions. He took a deep breath and poured a shot of vodka from one of the ornate crystal decanters. Slowly he walked back to the fire. Staring into the flames he downed the shot in one quick toss. He winced and wiped his mouth with an arm.

Then he shouted an expletive in another language and smashed the shot glass to pieces in the hearth. Flames roared in response to his anger. Bartal covered his face with his hands and his shoulders began to tremble. But no tears fell. It was not time for tears.

Not yet.

CHAPTER 14

Bree tried not to cry as she stapled the posters to the lamp post. The past few days she alternated between tears for her mother and grim determination to find her. Bartal had all his men scouring the countryside. She wanted to participate in the search. Somehow stapling posters and showing her mother's picture to people she could barely talk to, didn't quite seem like enough. She wanted a more active role in the search. Bree wanted to do something more. But she didn't know what.

She sighed and looked at her mother's face on the poster. Was she really gone? It didn't feel that way to her. Any moment she expected to turn around or open the door and there she'd be, smiling like none of this had ever happened. Bree prayed over and over. She hoped it was only a bad dream.

Bree stroked the side of her mother's face in the picture.

Where was she? What were they doing to her? Why did they take her?

The possible answers were just too frightening. She heard what they were saying in the castle when everyone thought she wasn't listening, especially Bartal and Sage. They whispered if they did find her, Bree wouldn't want her mother back. She'd be different, changed, a vampire. She wouldn't be Bree's mom anymore.

Bree didn't care. Live or dead, mortal or vampire, she wanted her mother back no matter what. She just wanted to know what happened. She wanted her safe.

Choked on tears that must not fall, Bree moved on to the next lamp post, stapler held like a weapon before her. She had barely gotten two staples affixed when she heard a laugh behind her.

A heavily accented German voice spoke to her back. "Poor little kitten lost its mother?"

The tone of voice was not kind. Bree set her jaw and turned around slowly.

A girl about her age and size stood with a lit cigarette dangling casually between two fingers. She wore heavy black mascara and was dressed in Gothic style clothing and had spike heels.

"I envy you!" she continued. Her accent was so thick Bree could barely make out the words. "I'd love to be rid of my parents!"

Bree shuffled the stack of flyers in her arms. She glared at the Goth chick and stalked away.

But her tormenter wouldn't be put off. Bree had only gone a few steps before she found the girl standing in front of her again.

"Walk away from me, will you?" she said as she cornered Bree. "No, no. I'm doing you a favor! You want to know what they're doing to your mother? Well, I'll tell you. They gonna fix her. They gonna make her perfect. She gonna be Nosferatu when she comes back."

Bree just stared angrily into the girl's eyes. "Ya, when she comes back, she be vampire. Then she gonna make me vampire and you vampire and then the whole world will be vampire. See?" The girl continued to taunt Bree by blowing smoke in her face. "We all be perfect then. No die, no get old or sick. We all stay young and beautiful forever. I jealous of you. You lucky chick. I wish my mother was vampire. Then I'd be princess. Doesn't that sound good? Sound nice? A princess in black!"

She laughed and blew more smoke into Bree's face.

"I hope you choke on your first sip of blood!" Bree said softly. She turned and walked away again.

"You American bitch! You come back here!" she snatched at Bree's arm.

Bree squealed as long black nails bit deep into her arm. Papers shot in an explosion of white leaves into the air. Bree was shoved forcefully to the ground, a stream of German expletives above her head.

There was a shout and another hand, a stronger male hand, ripped Bree free from her offender's grasp.

"Go home, Greta!" a man's voice ordered.

Bree rolled over and looked up through the shower of white flyers. A man stood between them. From the little she could see, he seemed not much older than her, lean and wiry. He wore torn and frayed jeans. But what she really noticed was his hair. It was shaved and styled in a spike Mohawk.

"I said, go home!" he repeated in a much more forceful tone before lapsing into a long string of German words. Whatever he said seemed to have an effect on her. The Goth girl he called Greta left in a hurry.

Bree picked herself up off the street and stared at the stranger.

"It's you! Mr. Mohawk!" she exclaimed. "The one at the concert!"

"Oh crap!" he swore. He slowly turned about to face her. He rubbed the back of his neck nervously as he awaited her next words.

"You're American," she said.

He nodded and shifted his weight uncomfortably from foot to foot. "Yeah, kinda sorta. You could say that."

Bree continued to stare at him while her thoughts spun.

"Where did you go?" she demanded. "If you'd stayed, you could've saved my mother, too."

He swallowed with difficulty. "There was a whole mess of suckers there. The minute you two got away, I got pounced on by a few more. They kept me from getting back to you."

Bree dropped her eyes to the pavement, crestfallen. "Oh,"

The awkward silence between them seemed a physical thing.

"This is the second time you've saved me," she said at last. "Thank you."

He nodded and mumbled something inaudible.

"Who are you?" she asked.

He took a deep breath. "Dante Fang."

She made a face at the name. "That's very Goth. I like it," she smiled.

Dante hesitated a moment only, then smiled in return.

"I'm…" she began to say.

"I know who you are," he interrupted.

A confused expression crossed her face.

At this he waved to the posters she had been stapling up. "The whole town knows who you are!"

He bent over and began to pick up the scattered posters. After a minute she joined him.

"You're the young American girl who's staying in Schloss Lowentore whose mother was kidnapped. Everyone is very concerned for you."

Bree sniffed. "I don't know why they bother. I'm not even German. I'm just a tourist."

Dante stood up and met her gaze. "That's silly! Germans have mothers, too."

He stopped abruptly. "Well that certainly sounded corny," he sighed. "What I meant to say was nobody likes hearing news of somebody's family member being kidnapped."

He turned his eyes back to the posters and scrutinized one for a moment. "Who did your English to German translation on these?"

"I did," she replied. "Mom's family was ex-Amish so I know a little German."

Dante shook his head. "You don't speak German. You speak Pennsylvania Dutch. They're not the same. Look here. You spelled 'mother' wrong."

"What?" she exclaimed and snatched the paper away from him.

"It's an easy mistake to make," he reassured her. "Every language changes with time. The English we speak now is nowhere near what English was a few hundred years ago or even a hundred years ago. Amish is actually a combination of German, Swiss and Finnish lingos and God Almighty I must sound like such a nerd to you!"

A small smile graced her face for a moment. "That's okay. I like nerds."

She turned her eyes back to the paper in front of her and growled. "I'm gonna have to change the whole thing. People here must think I'm an idiot!"

"Not an idiot. Just an American."

She glared daggers.

"You know, I can read and write German. I could help you if you like," he offered.

Bree frowned and thought for a minute. "Are you trying to make a pass at me?"

Dante became very serious. "No. Your mother was just taken from you. Now is not the time."

His voice lapsed into silence as her eyes went glassy with restrained emotion.

"First we get your mother back safe and sound," he reassured her. "I'll make a pass at you later...*Way* later!...If you like...If it's okay." And then he muttered under his breath, "Ooooh boy! I guess I should just shut up and forget I ever said any of that. Nice work, Dante!"

She narrowed her eyes at him and tried to frown. It didn't work.

CHAPTER 15

I came to wakefulness through waves of unsettling dreams which didn't want to leave me in peace, yet I could not remember the details. When I awoke, I was in a hospital bed. The room was better lit but there was no other furniture save the bed I occupied.

I took a deep breath and felt tired, oh so very tired. My limbs didn't want to move, my head felt as heavy as a bowling ball. I didn't even have the strength to roll over if I felt tired of the position I was in. My lids were heavy. I was cold. In spite of the blankets, I was chilled and shivered.

A memory of Mykhalo's voice tickled my thoughts.

"That, my dear, is but one small detail of what it is to be me, the aggravating, eternal cold. Pray you never experience it as I have," Mykhalo had told me.

Then it wasn't a dream, I really had been bitten by a vampire!

I felt my hopes plummet to the depths of my rolling stomach. I squeezed my eyes shut for one long moment. I opened them with a deep breath and tried to assess my current situation through tear-filled eyes.

The room had a huge, thick, iron door like the vault in a bank. My gaze drifted to the corner of the room near the ceiling. I noticed the security camera focused on me with the red light on.

He must have noticed I was awake because the heavy door opened and Farran came into the room. He came up to the bedside at once and sat down on the mattress next to me.

"What do you want?" I managed to gasp out in a venomous whisper.

I was amazed how much work it took for me to actually speak.

"To talk," he replied. "You seem to be better able to talk than fight right now."

I didn't want to talk. Oh, how I wanted to punch him in the mouth right then. But I could barely move. Is this how a person felt from just one bite?

"You are weak," Farran observed.

He reached out and stroked the side of my face tenderly. I felt my stomach heave in revulsion at his touch. "Do not worry. That will pass. It is only your mortality dying."

I squeezed my eyes shut in pain and told myself he must be lying. I told myself this to keep from giving up entirely. "What do you want from me?" I croaked.

His hand moved and he began to stroke my hair almost lovingly. I shivered at his touch. I felt the cold enter my heart. "To transform you into something better."

I tried my best to laugh. "You forgot to ask my permission."

Farran shook his head. "We both know you wouldn't have given it."

I couldn't fight him the way I was feeling. I couldn't even muster the strength to spit at him. I decided to try to appeal to his human side – if there was anything left of it. "Do me a favor and kill me, Farran," I said. "I don't want to be a vampire."

Farran smiled and narrowed his eyes. He didn't speak for one long moment. "You know, you weren't my first choice for vampire conversion," he told me slyly. "I really wanted your daughter. So young and naïve. So very young. I like the young ones. You're a bit too old for my taste."

Great! So my abductor was a pervert and a pedophile! Just perfect!

"But the Master didn't want your daughter. He wanted you. I didn't understand at the time but now I know why. Your daughter is a very clever girl. Smart of her to drink holy water every day. Now no vampire will want to drink her blood. She's poison to them. Which reminds me. Why didn't you drink the holy water?"

I had trouble swallowing. My throat was so dry. I decided I had nothing to lose by telling him. "She blessed the water herself. I wasn't sure it would work."

Farran smiled. "Impressive!" he declared. "Your daughter has many talents. Unfortunately it will only be her downfall. Now instead of biting your girl, most vampires intelligent enough to pick up on this will just kill her outright and be done with her. Not really worth it. I wonder how Kane knew this and I did not."

I tried to speak but coughed instead. The coughing turned into a fit, and I shivered uncontrollably. "I'm cold, Farran," I pleaded with him.

He only nodded. "Yes, the change has already started. Now it will take time. But soon you will become the most powerful vampire who has ever walked the night."

I shivered more. "The most powerful?" I repeated. "Is it really so important to you?"

He smiled widely, exposing fangs which had only retreated a little. "You were powerful as a witch." He said as he stroked the side of my face tenderly. His touch made my skin crawl. His words shocked me. Was I that obvious? He continued. "Yes, I knew what you were the first time I saw you. You will be even more powerful as a vampire. When I'm done with you, you will be a masterpiece!"

I tried to sit up. But I didn't have the energy. "But...you attacked the other dancer. So...I thought you hated vampires."

He shook his head. "That was what you and everyone else was *supposed* to think. I am a hunter, pure and simple. I cannot resist the lure of the chase. I hunted Mykhalo for many years."

My anger spiked at this.

"Then you must be pretty disappointed that you caught me so easily."

Again he shook his head. "No. I never hunted you. I have a whole different purpose for you. I just had to wait until you left your country and came to me. I knew you would eventually."

He sighed, thinking back. "I've hunted vampires because the world has too many of them. Hector didn't give much thought when he created more of our kind. He planned Mykhalo's transformation. But most of his children were made haphazardly."

He turned his eyes back to me and cocked his head like a curious dog. "I purify the ranks. There are many lesser vampires out there. I sift the bad from the good. The bad I feed on. The good I let go."

"And Mykhalo was a bad vampire?" I asked.

Farran nodded. "It started out that way. But then he became an extremely elusive and challenging prey. I pursued him for the sheer joy

119

of the hunt. I was very disappointed to find someone else bagged my quarry. Now I'm left with this feeling of not having completed my task. Which brings me to you."

He paused for a moment, leaned in close, and peered carefully into the details of my face. "I've never *made* a Nosferatu before. There had to be a good enough reason. A creature with all the powers of both witch and vampire? That's a good enough reason."

He withdrew his presence much to my relief. "The perfect gift for the Master's triumphant return."

I tried to take a deep breath but it was too much work.

Farran stood and turned to leave. "Kane will be pleased."

His hand touched the door and he paused. "It would be best for you to abandon all hope of rescue. Your friends will never find you here. This place does not exist. I'm telling you this to make everything easier for you. Your past is now far behind. You are my creation now."

The heavy door creaked open and shut quickly behind him with a ponderous clang. There was the sound of an enormous lock being turned. And then silence enveloped me like a heavy, wool blanket, crushing me in its weight. I was alone with my thoughts.

I felt a single tear slide down my cheek and start to dry on my skin. I was powerless to wipe it away.

* * *

I had no idea as to the passage of time. Was I dreaming or still awake? Or worse, was I going mad? No one came to rescue me. I couldn't tell the poisonous dreams from the venomous waking. I could not tell night from day. My only visitor was Farran.

Apparently he liked to hear himself talk. He especially liked talking to me because I was incapable of carrying on any lengthy conversation from the state I was in, the state he had put me in. I listened because I had to. I listened because I told myself he would slip up through talking and gift me with a gem I could use against him. If I ever got out of here.

So I listened as he rambled on. I listened and I thought. He could not keep me from thinking. My brain was my one weapon left to me and I was determined to use it.

If I could just live long enough.

And after each conversation, he would feed on me. And after each feeding, I would black out and awaken feeling more dead than alive.

One time he was talking and I pretended to ignore him. I found myself paying more attention to his words than usual. He was saying something which was actually interesting.

"Bartal was protecting you when I found you. Did he tell you about his 'friendship' with your vampire lover?"

Against my will, my eyes turned back to him.

"Ah! I see he did. Did he tell you he and Mykhalo were the best of friends? Loyal to the very end perhaps?"

I wondered what Farran was up to with this thread of conversation. Was he going to try to hurt me more with some shocking revelation such as maybe they were gay? As if it would have bothered me of all people! But knowing Mykhalo, I highly doubted it.

"You see I never quite bought the 'best friends to the end' thing from them. Especially knowing how they met."

I licked my parched lips and managed to croak out, "Bartal is a hunter."

Farran laughed and crossed his arms in front of his thin chest. "Oh is that what he told you eh? A hunter?" He shook his head. Then Farran leaned close as if he was divulging some great secret for my ears only. "Bartal was in love with Mykhalo's wife!"

In spite of myself, I gasped.

"Yes, all those years Mykhalo was married to Es, she was dabbling on the side with Bartal. The rumors among my kin even say Es was pregnant with Bartal's child when Mykhalo killed her. Of course we all know the story. Mykhalo was a newly turned vampire and Hector commanded him to do it. So he had no choice. But still…"

My fingers clenched the bedsheets spasmodically. My stomach felt empty and hollow.

Here Farran sighed and shook his head.

"If I was in Bartal's shoes, I wouldn't knowingly befriend someone who killed my lover, pregnant with my child. Or from Mykhalo's side, knowingly befriend someone who slept with his wife. Would you?"

I paused, preparing myself to say something long. "Well, I don't know. You see I'm *female*. Or did you miss that?"

"How I love your defiance!" Farran chuckled. "But you see my dear, I would only be a friend to such a person so as to get close enough to kill them."

I took a deep breath. "Bartal had too many opportunities. And time." I took another deep breath. "Maybe you just have trouble wrapping your brain about this thing called forgiveness."

Farran's smug look disappeared. "Oh. You're one of those people. Always one to believe that right conquers all, people are inherently good and all stories have a happy ending."

He sniffed in disdain and leaned in closer to my face. "Let me tell you something. I have lived nearly one thousand years and I can tell you from long experience, that is a fantasy. Especially with vampires!"

I met his gaze and lifted my chin as well as I was able. "Do you not agree then Mykhalo was not just any vampire? He broke the rules." I struggled to sit upright. "As do I."

Farran had nothing to say to this for a moment. Then he began to laugh a truly evil sounding laugh. The light switched off and I was plunged into darkness.

And then he attacked my throat again. But savagely this time as if he wanted to kill me.

CHAPTER 16

Bartal strode into the sitting room and up to the window overlooking the labyrinth. Bethany Hess was seated next to the window pretending to read a book. She found lately all she could do was skim the words. Her mind was on other more important things.

"Anything?" she asked him.

He shook his head in grim denial without even glancing in her direction and then heaved a great sigh of frustration. Outside the window, the pale green of spring was giving way to the darker green of summer. The roses on the trellis bloomed in full force and the daffodils had long since died for the year.

"What I can't understand is how she disappeared so completely without the slightest trace. We don't even have any idea of what direction to aim. It's as if she never existed in the first place."

"If she never existed then where did Bree come from?" Bethany sniffed in displeasure at his words.

Bartal grimaced and shook his head. He crossed his arms as he brooded on this problem.

"Holmes would be appalled at our lack of progress if he was real," he said. Then he turned to her. "What do your witch's senses tell you about this?"

Bethany closed her book. "They tell me she is in a deep dark place. I got no more details." She sighed and told Bartal softly, "Zan is in Hell."

He turned to face her. "I thought your kind don't believe in Hell."

Bethany only gave him a sharp look. "To be forcibly kept from her child is any mother's version of Hell."

"I stand corrected." He began to pace the room.

"So what you're saying is Zan is being kept underground, yes?"

"That's very likely," she nodded. "You have lots of tunnels and caves in this country, right? Places underground to store beer or salt mines and such. Have you looked there?"

He nodded, scuffing the expensive rug with a shoe as he thought. "We've searched every underground hiding place we know of locally. I'm ready to expand the search to places farther afield."

He turned once again to face her. "Bethany, we will get her back. Live or dead or otherwise, we will find her. I promise you."

She shook her head. "I know you'll find her. It's in what condition that I'm worried about."

* * *

I awoke to flickering candlelight. Farran had shut off the light above my bed and filled the room with white candles. Their soft light filled my lonely cell with shivering shadows.

The mood in the room was almost romantic.

I wished Mykhalo was there instead of Farran. I wished I was strong and human again.

Farran sat on the edge of the bed next to my side. He leaned close and peered intently into my face.

What was he looking for?

"We're almost there," he whispered. "I believe you're almost done cooking, my dear."

I grimaced in revulsion. I was certainly not his "dear"!

He cocked his head considering me for a long moment. He reached out and stroked the side of my face. His hand didn't feel quite so cold as it had in the past.

What was he up to? I wondered.

"Kiss me, Zan," he said softly.

My eyes flew open in shock. Kiss him? Never!

Farran's eyes narrowed and he smiled at my reaction. "I command it."

At this, I did something I thought I'd never do. My body betrayed me. I sat up and wrapped my arms about him lovingly and tilting back my head, I melted passionately into his arms while my mind screamed in denial. He took hold of my chin and looked into my eyes as if searching for any sign of refusal. Then he bent his head and his lips caressed mine.

I wanted to throw up. I felt sick to my stomach. Now I'd truly betrayed everything Mykhalo and I had done together.

Farran lowered me gently into the sheets as he continued to kiss me passionately. And my body, like a traitor, responded in kind. I tried not to think of what might come next. He traced the curve of my neck with his lips, tickling me. His hand stroked the other side of my neck and then went lower, diving slowly under my shirt. Against my will, I moaned.

He stopped suddenly and looked up into my face. His eyes had a mischievous gleam. Then he smiled and said, "Oh yes! You are almost there."

There was a gust of wind and all the candles were blown out at once. Then Farran left the room immediately.

* * *

"What are you doing just sitting there?" Sage berated Bree.

She hadn't left her room in two days, hadn't changed out of her pajamas, and her hair was disheveled as if she hadn't brushed it in a while.

Bree looked up from where she lounged on her bed with an expression of shock. "What do you mean?" she muttered. "My mother is gone. How am I supposed to act?"

Hands on hips, Sage ordered, "Get up, get showered, you're starting to smell funky, get dressed and for God's sake, stop stagnating!"

"Why are you yelling at me?" Bree fired back. "You're not my mo…" She suddenly clapped her hands over her mouth. "Ohmigarwd! Please tell me I didn't just almost say that!"

Sage just stood there with her arms crossed and toe tapping impatiently. "In the shower, young miss! Or do I have to do it for you?"

"All right! All right! Cool your jets! I'm going!" Bree grabbed a robe and disappeared into the adjoining bathroom. She returned a short while later to find Sage still sitting on her bed waiting impatiently.

"What's up with you?" Bree grumbled. She went the vanity and began to comb the tangles out of her wet hair.

"You've been moping!" Sage replied.

Bree rolled her eyes at her reflection in the mirror.

"Uh hello! My mother's been kidnapped and is in some bad place with God knows what bad person doing horrible things to her and I can't do anything about it! I think I have a reason to mope!"

"You have every reason to feel bad," Sage admitted. "You have a reason to feel angry at what was done, you have a reason to feel helpless and frustrated. But make no mistake. This is no excuse for you to disappear inside yourself and stop living."

Bree considered turning on the hair dryer to drown out Sage's words but thought better of it. "Well, what do you suggest?" she growled.

Sage smiled in an evil way. "You are to get dressed in something cheery with bright colors. Maybe something you bought in town with your mother. Perhaps we'll go there later today."

Bree frowned and crossed her arms in front of her chest. "I'm never going into that town again!" she said defiantly.

Sage growled and shook her head. "Yes, you are!" she insisted. "There are more pleasant things in town than vampire kidnappers! You've got to keep alive while waiting for them to find out something on your mother. But before we go into town, you are to go down into the armory and practice your dance."

Bree slapped the hairbrush suddenly down on the tabletop. "No!" she said firmly.

Neither spoke for a long moment. Bree refused to look at her reflection and kept her eyes on her hands.

Sage continued but in a softer tone of voice. "Honey, why don't you want to dance?"

Bree only frowned.

"Please tell me, child. You may have been new to dance but you were so talented. And you were learning so quickly. Why did you stop?"

She turned her big green eyes back to the mirror. "I dance when I'm happy."

"Ah!" Sage breathed as she nodded in understanding. "And since your mother's disappearance, you haven't been happy enough to dance, is that it?"

Bree's eyes were wide and shiny. Silently she nodded one time.

Sage quietly came up behind and hugged her. "Do you know how beautiful your mother thought you were when you danced? Beauty shouldn't be lost or kept from the world because someone we love is no longer there. Sometimes pain can make loveliness even stronger. Would your mother want you to stop everything you loved doing because she was no longer here? Would she want you to stop smiling or laughing or discovering new wonders and joys in life because she was no longer there?"

Bree dropped her eyes and did not answer verbally but she shook her head. "Mom's not dead," she said softly. "Why is everyone talking about her as if she's dead? She's not! I can feel it. And she's coming back. I can feel that, too."

Sage squeezed her shoulders reassuringly. "Of course she's not dead!" Sage agreed. She hoped her words sounded convincing. "Now we're going to go down into the armory and I'm going to show you a new spell. I'm going to teach you how to dance your mother back into your life. Only you'll have to do the dancing part because I can't. Then we're going into town and we're going to have fun and no one is going to get kidnapped because we'll be home long before nightfall. Agreed?"

Bree nodded and gave a brief smile. Sage squeezed her shoulders again and left her to finish getting dressed.

CHAPTER 17

"With tears of blood it begins,
With my tears, I shatter your soul,
With my tears, I break your will,
With my tears, I birth you into everlasting darkness,
With my tears, I chase away your light,
With my tears, shall you take the blood oath,
With my tears, you will become one with the dark,
With my tears of blood, your mortal life ends forever."

The chant commanded me to awaken. I obeyed. I was powerless to refuse.

Farran sat on my bedside with a smug look on his face. Tears of blood literally rained down his cheeks. He held a chalice under his chin to catch the flow.

"It is time," he smiled at me in triumph. "Sit up."

Although I was weak to the point of death, I obeyed his command.

He held out the chalice to me. "Drink."

I left my arms at my side and gave him the most poisonous look I could muster.

"Fine!" he sighed in exasperation. "You make me command you, then. *DRINK*! If you don't, I'll kill you and you will never see your precious daughter again!"

Against my will, I raised my hands. The heavy chalice was placed into my grasp. I tried not to think of anything as I raised it to my parched and cracked lips. His blood touched my mouth. I obeyed. I drank. I tried not to swallow the blood. But the vampire's magically charged life-force had already hit my stomach. In a moment the cup was drained. I dropped the chalice. It bounced off the mattress and hit the floor, clattering.

I began to convulse as if having an epileptic fit. Farran caught me and cradled me almost tenderly. I thrashed and kicked like a wild thing in his arms. He stroked my hair and face and whispered tender useless words to me as if this was an act of passion.

How I hated him! I promised myself if I made it through this, I would kill him.

My thrashing subsided and he lowered me gently back onto the sheets. Somehow the covers, which had been white, were now splashed in slippery, wet blood.

"When next you awaken, you will be with your daughter again," Farran said as he placed his blue, cold lips on my forehead. "Give her a kiss for me."

I moaned because I knew what he really meant. What a cruel joke!

"Welcome to the dark," he told me.

I felt like I was going to pass out. I gave in and let the blackness consume me.

CHAPTER 18

Her voice came back to me through the fog of my mind.

"Mom? *MOM*! Wake up! Oh please wake up! Don't be dead! Don't you dare be dead!"

It was Bree's voice.

I heard her. I was awake but I didn't dare open my eyes. I kept them squeezed shut. I felt the tears begin to come.

She shook me hard, making my head flop about. She even slapped me. I moaned.

"She's alive! Thank the Lady! She's alive!" I heard her sob. I felt her hug me tight.

I didn't want her to touch me, Bree, my own daughter. I was dangerous now. I might kill her. I was...damaged.

"Bartal! Over here! I found her!" Bree shouted still clinging to me.

Bartal was here? My mind scrambled furiously. Yes, of course! Bartal would know what I was. Bartal would save Bree from myself.

More tears. I had to look, I had to see my daughter's face one last time. I opened my eyes.

Bree still held on to me desperately. She peered into my face with a mixture of joy and worry.

How long had I been gone?

"Bree," I whispered. I touched her cheek to be sure she was real. She felt feverishly hot. Was she sick? Then another thought occurred to me. Maybe the problem wasn't with her. Maybe I was too cold. I looked at her again. Bree seemed to glow and shine with a luminescence from within. I looked about.

I was lying on the leafy floor of a forest. It was night-time. But every living thing was glowing from within, the trees the grass, everything. I squeezed my eyes shut and more tears came.

"No," I moaned in agony. I must be seeing things the way vampires saw things. Which could mean only one thing.

I was now a vampire.

"No," I groaned. Then I heard a rustle of dead leaves as Bartal came to my side. He paused and I heard him mutter some expletive in another language. I opened my eyes wondering what a dhampir would look like with my new gaze.

He looked normal, absolutely ordinary. Every living thing about us shimmered and glowed except for the dead leaves and Bartal.

"Come on, child. We need to get her inside quickly. It's not safe out here at night," he told Bree.

Bartal scooped me up as easily as if he was carrying a sack of dead leaves.

"No!" I mumbled as best I was able. "Don't try and save me. You need to kill me! Stake me before it's too late! Before I kill somebody."

Bartal laughed. "Hush Zan."

I realized he had never called me Zan before. It was always Mrs. Miller.

"I decide who gets staked and when." He risked giving me a tight squeeze as he carried me.

"Do you have any idea how worried we were about you?"

I whimpered helplessly and clung to him. I prayed this was all some very long, bad dream. I was still weak and dizzy. The rush of movement as he carried me was too much. I blacked out again.

* * *

Bartal had no memory of how they got to the castle so fast. Bree scuttled from side to side behind him trying not to lose sight of her mother's face. She was aiming a steady stream of questions at him which he fought not to hear and refused to respond. He had no answers himself.

They burst through the doors and were met by the very shocked Bethany Hess.

"Zan!" she squawked in surprise.

"Fetch Dr. Sullivan immediately!" he barked at her.

She hesitated only seconds then fled to do his bidding.

Bartal carried Zan into the main sitting room with Bree in close pursuit. A thought suddenly flashed into his mind.

He had to get rid of Bree. She still didn't know who Dr. Sullivan was.

"Bree child, your mother's cold. Go get a warm blanket from the laundry. Quickly now."

Bree blinked twice and said. "But that's at the far end of the castle."

"No argument girl! Just do it! Your mother is ice cold!"

Bree's face blanched white and she bolted from his presence. Bartal sighed in relief.

Moments later Dante stepped into the room. Bartal growled at his appearance. "Bree will be back any second! Put a mask on and cover your hair. Now is not the time to reveal yourself to her."

Dante sucked in his breath and quickly pulled a scrub hat out of his pocket and began to don his surgical mask. He stopped when he saw who lay on the couch. "You found Mrs. Miller?"

Bartal nodded and stepped back to let him do his job. "You need to take a blood sample from her and run your tests."

Dante held Bartal's eyes for one moment suggestively. He then knelt next to the couch and began to examine Zan's neck. "She's been bitten," he said softly.

"Yes," Bartal responded.

"Many times," the young doctor continued with gravity.

"I am aware of that," Bartal answered looking nervously at the door.

"Then why draw her blood?" he questioned. "She's been bitten many times and is not dead. We have our answer."

"Just do it!" Bartal insisted.

"I can't!" the youth said shaking his head. "There's no point! You know as well as I do what it means. The transformation has already happened. She's a vampire now."

"No!" he growled.

"Bartal, it's your rules. Even Mykhalo would agree. She must be staked. She's beyond my help now. Why are you hesitating?"

Bartal gave a nervous glance at the door and then stepped close to the young man to speak quietly. "Because it doesn't feel right. Something about this is wrong."

The young doctor uttered a growl of frustration muffled from behind his surgical mask. "What's wrong about this is she was never meant to be taken and turned. We've failed. There's only one thing we can do now. You know this."

Bartal's voice dropped to a whisper. "I can't stake her. Not now, not yet. So just humor me. Draw her blood and run your tests. Please! Do you want to tell Bree we have to kill her mother now that she just got her back?"

It was the doctor's turn to drop his eyes. He was silent for a long moment. "Fine!" he relented. "I'll do what you ask. But why I don't know. It's a waste of time. I already know the results."

"Just do it and be done with it! Quick, before she wakes up!"

The doctor sighed angrily but obeyed. He opened his bag and pulled out the necessary syringes, needles and tubes. He inserted the needle into the underside of Zan's arm just above the elbow. He collected three tubes of dark red blood. He put two in the case in his bag and began to steadily revolve the last tube up and down, keeping the blood flowing. "Now what do you want me to do?" he asked in a flat tone of voice.

"What blood type is Mykhalo's sample?" Bartal asked him.

The young doctor's brow wrinkled in confusion. He answered the question in spite of his bewilderment.

"Vampires do not have a blood type. Only mortals. Why do you ask?"

"I want you to give Zan a transfusion of Mykhalo's blood."

Sudden comprehension dawned on the doctor's face. "According to the tests I ran, a vampire's blood will accept any other blood type."

"You still have his donation, right?"

"I think it was just about to expire," he replied.

"Good! Then get it and do it! Hurry!" Bartal ordered.

The doctor thought briefly and then nodded. "That might just buy us some time. Good thinking," he said and went to get the bag of Mykhalo's blood.

"And make sure you're wearing your mask when you come back in, Bree doesn't need to know who you are just yet!"

CHAPTER 19

I awoke not much later in the castle, nestled on a couch in the sitting room while people buzzed about me. I felt remarkably better, stronger. I knew why in an instant. Someone had given me blood. I could smell it hanging in the air, a scent as strong as a fresh pot of coffee. It smelled metallic, like copper and iron all mixed together. I looked about and found my vision was clearer.

Bree was curled up on the floor next to me. A stranger in a white lab coat with his back turned was winding up intravenous medical tubing. The tubing was stained red.

Bree saw I was awake and smiled. "We gave you a blood transfusion. You looked like you could use it."

Oh my precious daughter! I loved her so much right then. She may have just bought them a little time and safety from myself.

Sage was there, too. I was so glad to see her. But she was avoiding my gaze for some reason. She fussed over tucking blankets in around me and muttered about how cold I was even though it was summer and said she was going to get me a hot cup of tea.

"Tea, woman? Are you mad?" burst out Bartal. "This lady needs something a whole lot stronger than tea. I'll see to that. You can bring the tea later. Way later!"

"Bartal, we need to talk." I began quietly.

"You need to rest, my dear," scolded Sage seriously.

I shook my head. All the bustle around me was making me dizzy. I closed my eyes and rubbed my forehead. "No, talk first, then rest. This is important!" I insisted with some force.

Bartal gave a quick nod and shooed everyone out of the room except for Bree, Sage and himself.

I sighed as the room stilled. Bree sat on the rug by my right side clinging to my hand with both of hers and looking at me as though I would vanish at any moment.

Bartal went to the liquor cabinet and poured something, I supposed it was vodka, into a crystal shot glass. I thought the drink was for himself. But he came around the corner of the couch and offered it to me. "Here," he said. "You really need to drink this."

I accepted without question and downed it in one gulp. Well, vodka it was but it was a whole lot stronger than I was prepared for! It numbed the roots of my teeth, the inside of my mouth and hit my stomach with the force of a mule kick. I coughed. Then it began to burn in my belly and I felt my whole body infused with an immediate and very pleasant warmth.

I shook my head. "What was that?" I said gasping and coughing. My very eyes were watering.

Bartal gave an amused half smile. "Never you mind. You looked like you needed it."

Bree chuckled. "You look horrible, Mom! Like a starved, runway model."

I bet I do, I thought to myself and I began to run my fingers through Bree's hair.

Bartal poured himself a shot of the same vodka and downed it in one huge gulp. "Now. Talk!" he commanded.

I nodded. "First, how long have I been gone?"

"A little over three weeks," Bree answered. "Everyone had nearly given up hope we'd ever find you again. Everyone but me!"

I stroked her hair and observed in wonder how it glittered between my fingers. "You were right to give up on me," I said in a distant voice. "And you never should have brought me back."

Bree looked stung. "Why on earth not?"

I smiled sadly. "Farran let me go. He let you find me. He's changed me. I'm a vampire now."

There was a stunned silence.

Bartal walked slowly up to me. The look from his eyes was stormy and dark. "Tell me what he did to you. Tell me everything."

So I did. I told him everything Farran had done to me and every word he had said. Although I omitted the part where Farran told me about Bartal and Esmerelda's relationship.

As I spoke a change came over Bartal. His face went blank. He approached the liquor bar as I drew near the end of my tale. He picked up the expensive Austrian crystal bottle which contained the vodka and walked back over to the fireplace in what looked like a numbed stupor. As my voice lapsed into silence, he closed his eyes and took several big gulps straight from the bottle. He swallowed with a hiss and a gasp.

Suddenly Bartal shouted an expletive in German and flung the bottle into the fireplace where it shattered with a splash. We all jumped in fright. Flames roared up greedily to consume the alcohol, then died back with a hiss and a pop.

"Once again I have failed to protect you. It was always personal between us, Farran and I. But this goes too far. I will kill him with my bare hands when I get the chance for what he did to you!" Bartal growled in a voice I had never heard. I hope to never hear it again.

"Get in line!" I replied. "As much as I'm flattered over your concern, I think we have a more pressing problem at hand right now." I sighed. "Farran sent me back here to trap you. I'm a vampire now and he probably expects me make a meal of either you or my own daughter. You need to take action and kill me, Bartal."

Bree became more agitated than I've ever seen her. "No!" she exclaimed "No, no, no, no! Don't even talk like this, Mom. Bartal, you and your troop of sucker hunters better stay away from my mother!"

"Honey..." I began but she shook me off.

"Mom, what are you saying? You can't be a vampire! I won't let you! There's gotta be some cure. You can't leave me now. I just got you back."

I shushed her and gathered her in my arms. She began to shake and sob.

"You can't be a vampire!" she whimpered. "You just can't!"

I rocked her and stroked her hair and kissed her on top of her head. My heart felt like it was going to break. I took a deep breath and sent the tears back to where they came from. Then I gave Bartal a very serious look. "I do not want to kill Bree. But when the hunger comes upon me, I may have no choice."

Bartal shook his head. "What you are is not yet certain. We have some time. I'm not willing to give up on you yet, Mrs. Miller." Bartal took a deep breath which seemed to suggest he felt every care in the world had been laid on his broad shoulders. "What I am more concerned about is why Farran felt he needed to turn you into a vampire. He planned all this out. That much is plain. But why?"

"He said something about presenting me to someone named Kane."

At the very sound of the name, Bartal and Sage exchanged worried looks.

"What's wrong? Who's Kane?" I asked.

"We need to call Gregori," Bartal said sternly.

"At once!" Sage replied softly and left the room hurriedly.

"Rest and regain your strength. You have been through quite an ordeal. We will talk more in the morning." Bartal told me.

* * *

I awoke with a start. I thought I'd heard Mykhalo calling my name. The clock said three-thirty. I was alone and the room was dark except for the flickering glow of flames dying in the fireplace. Bree slumbered away in the couch across from me. But something or someone had definitely been calling me. I felt wide awake and strong.

I sat up and swung my legs off the couch and onto the floor. I went to Bree and stroked her hair. She mumbled in her sleep.

My daughter was safe. I smiled in contentment. But something still called me. I straightened up and looked about. I felt compelled to follow the call. I left the sitting room. Some of Bartal's men wandered the halls on guard. I made sure to avoid them.

I traversed the spacious and vaulted hallways of the castle, alone and in secret. I wondered what it was I was following. I was afraid I might be pursuing Farran's command. But soon I realized where my feet were leading me. I was heading to the art room and the mirror.

The closer I came the more I dreaded it. Mykhalo was definitely calling me. What would I say? What *could* I say? I was different now; changed, damaged by Farran. And he had been unable to help.

All too soon the mirror stood in front of me. I stopped moving and stared at its back. I did not want Mykhalo to see me. I could feel him calling me in my head. All I had to do was walk around to the front of the mirror.

I stayed rooted to the spot, ashamed of what I was now.

I did not expect the mirror to move. But move it did. It had once been a long, double-sided mirror one could flip over to see a different reflection but one of the panes of glass was lost so now it only reflected on one side. The mirror creaked and flipped itself over on its hinges.

I jumped, startled and turned myself away. I did not want Mykhalo to see me or my face. He would know what had happened. I wouldn't have to say a word

"Zan!" I heard him say.

I whimpered and covered my face in my hands and my long hair.

"Zan, what's wrong? Zan, look at me!"

I began to sob.

"Zan. *LOOK AT ME!*"

I took a deep breath, wiped my eyes and turned around. But I couldn't meet his gaze. There was a stunned silence which seemed to last forever.

"He...didn't...." Mykhalo's voice was a dangerous whisper, heavily accented.

"He did," I whimpered, my voice catching in my throat. "What am I now?"

There was another, very long silence.

"Mykhalo," I managed to choke out. "Please say something."

I don't know what I expected to happen. But when it did, I wasn't prepared for the violence of its force. Mykhalo screamed. It was a sound full of frustration, despair and horrible anger. It was more frightening than any sound or any imagined sound I've ever heard before. Or ever hope to hear again.

The mirror shattered into a thousand glittering pieces.

I cried out in fright and collapsed in a terrified bundle to the floor. Shards of mirror fell about me like rain. The tall windows burst their panes and exploded into sharp powder. There was a loud crash and then another and another. I peeped through my fingers and saw the pictures being thrown off the walls and tearing free from their frames. The door to the room suddenly slammed so hard the frame cracked. I gasped in horror at the action.

My fear was replaced by anger. "Stop it, Mykhalo! You stop this instant!" There was a stunned pause in the chaos of the room. "How does this help?" I persisted.

One of the sheets which had covered the paintings rose up like a ghostly apparition and approached me. I scrambled backwards, scattering broken glass like snow from my body. But the sheet was not meant to scare or hurt me. It came close and was laid around my shoulders like a blanket in a comforting manner.

The air in front of me shimmered. Mykhalo stood before me then, misty and indistinct.

"I'm sorry. I didn't mean to frighten you."

I allowed myself to breathe again. The ghost of Mykhalo bowed his head for a moment.

"Farran took me and changed me. I'm sorry."

Mykhalo looked up and met my gaze. I had never seen such pain before in his eyes. They looked glassy and wet. Could a ghost cry tears? "Why are you sorry? I've failed you. I should have been able to protect you."

"How?" I asked.

The expression on his face told me more than his words. He had no idea how to help or protect me in this form. He crouched down next to me and reached out a hand. I felt his fingertips stroke the side of my cheek. I tried to touch his hand but my fingers went through the mist.

So he could touch me but I couldn't touch him.

I felt a huge sob welling up inside my throat. It broke free and I shuddered. I felt him wrap his arms about me. I wanted to hold him back, to cling tightly to him. But it wasn't permitted. I sobbed and cried big, hot tears of pain.

"What am I now?" I moaned to the empty room. "Vampire? Human? Undead zombie thing? Something else? What do I do with this?"

I gasped for breath. "Can you still love me like this?" I managed to get the words out in a whisper.

"Always," was the immediate response. "I don't care who or what you are. I will still love you."

The response made my heart ache and more tears come. I wiped my eyes. My mind scrambled for something to say. "I've got to find a way to use this to beat him."

I felt the ghostly Mykhalo nod as he stroked my hair. "I'm not leaving you again, Zan." There was a resolute sound to his voice.

I pulled back to look him in his transparent eyes. "Is it possible? Aren't spirits tied to a certain place?"

"Yes. And no," he replied.

"Well that makes perfect sense!"

He laughed briefly and then became silent. His ghostly hands stroked my own. "Keep that attitude Zan, and you can beat the devil himself!"

I smiled in return. "I don't believe in devils. Remember? Just people."

He smiled and gave me another tight squeeze. "Well, we have a devil to fight now and his name is Farran."

His mind scrambled for a plan. "I have to leave you, Zan but only briefly. I need to consult with someone else on this plane about how to handle this. But I will be back as soon as I can." I knew the look on his face.

"Wait a minute." I said and peered intently into his face. "You could have done this before but you didn't. You were afraid to. Why?"

He laughed. "My dear, you are a shrewd and perceptive woman."

My eyes prompted him to continue.

"There will be a sacrifice I will need to make. That's why I haven't done it until now. But now I'm forced to show my hand. I have no choice if I want to make sure you're safe. I've got to do this. I will be back and soon. I promise."

I rubbed my face and stood up. The door to the art room swung open softly.

I turned back to Mykhalo but he was gone.

CHAPTER 20

Exhausted by my emotional meeting with Mykhalo's shade, I returned to the sitting room couch, hoping to forget the events of the past in welcome, blissful slumber. But when sleep took me, it was far from restful.

I was troubled by strange dreams. My dreams took me to a familiar setting.

I stood in the Egyptian desert. Don't ask me how I knew it was Egypt, I just knew. The sun blazed down on me in all its oven-like glory. A hot wind blew, sucking the moisture right out of my skin.

Something was there with me. A lion snarled so close it sounded like it was right behind me. I spun around but there was nothing. The snarl came again. The phantom growl surrounded me on all sides.

I knew in an instant who the presence belonged to. "Sekhmet," I spoke aloud to the desert around me.

Again the growl came. "You gave up," The goddess's voice was deep and definitely did not sound pleased.

"What?" I said before thinking, for I knew exactly what she meant.

"When you were abducted, you gave up."

I had displeased a goddess! My heart started to pound with fear.

"I…I'm sorry," I stammered, knowing how meaningless my apology would be to her.

"You're a mother and you gave up." I hung my head in shame.

The leonine voice rose in volume and timber. "You're a mother. It is not your job to give up! It is your job to persevere no matter what the cost, no matter what the price. That's your job!"

I fell trembling to my hands and knees. "I'm so very, very sorry." I managed to stammer out in a terrified squeak.

"How *DARE* you give up?" Her voice roared in my head as if announcing her attack.

I sat straight up with a terrified gasp startling myself awake. I was bathed in sweat, the blankets were in a tangled mess about me and I had trouble breathing.

Sekhmet was angry with me. I felt like fainting at the thought. And she had absolutely every right to be!

CHAPTER 21

I awoke around eight the next morning.

Bartal, Sage and Bree were in the sitting room waiting for me to rouse. All the curtains were down, throwing the room into shadow.

"How do you feel this morning?" Sage asked.

I looked at each one of them in turn. "I...I'm not sure," I answered truthfully.

Bree stood up. "What if we pulled the curtains and let a little light in?"

There was a long silence. "Try it," I said.

She hesitated and then went the floor to ceiling window across from me. The room was silent. Everyone held their breath.

With a sudden motion of her arm, Bree yanked the cord. The heavy curtains flew back with a slight hissing sound. A beam of morning sunlight fell directly where I reclined on the couch. I blinked in the sudden brightness.

"How does that make you feel, dear?" Sage asked. There was a tiny tremble to her voice.

I tensed, half expecting to fizzle into ash in the next instant. But nothing happened. I sat up and leaned into the sunlight. Its warmth was delicious.

I sighed in relief. "It feels very good," I said and then pouted like an orphan in the musical *Oliver* and said, "Please sir, can I have more?" A half nervous, half relieved chuckle circulated around the room.

"Are you hungry?" Bartal asked me.

I thought a moment. "No."

"When was the last time you ate?" Bree asked.

I looked at my child and gave an apologetic smile. "When I had those amazing strudels with you, my dear."

"But that was…" Bree gasped in shock. She stopped herself and covered her mouth.

"Nearly a month ago the night I was abducted." I finished for her. "Yes, I know."

"Did Farran give you anything to eat while you were with him?" Bartal asked.

I shook my head in denial.

"You're sure you're not hungry?" Sage asked.

I nodded. "But I am thirsty."

Bartal growled unsettled.

Bree came and sat next to me on the couch. "What are you thirsty for, Mom?"

Suddenly Mykhalo's words from what seemed to be years ago, echoed in my thoughts.

"Of course I can drink things. It's the eating that gives me problems."

"You know, I think I could handle some coffee."

Everyone in the room heaved another sigh of relief.

Sage offered to get it herself.

Bree nestled a little closer and nudged me with her elbow. "With or without the 'Bavarian honey' part?" she whispered in a teasing tone. I made a scolding noise but laughed a bit just the same.

Sage returned with the coffee. I wound my cold fingers about the welcoming warmth of the cup. I breathed in the rich coffee smell and thought I'd never smelled anything so wonderful before in my life. I gulped a large mouthful and held it in my mouth, relishing in the flavor. Its heat traveled down my throat to my stomach. After no food or drink in so long, one sip of coffee felt like a religious experience. I didn't even realize the whole room watched with rapt attention, waiting for something sinister to happen.

I had almost drained the cup when Sage interrupted my ecstasy, "How is that sitting, my dear?"

"I'm fine." I replied, irritated with the intrusion. "I'm just fine."

Bartal nodded as if satisfied. "Your transformation is not yet stable."

"You mean…we can stop it?" Bree asked and I saw a wild hope leap in her eyes.

"No!" Bartal cut her off in a commanding tone of voice. He then sighed, crossed his arms and shook his head. "What has happened, happened. We cannot stop it or cure it. It is just taking a little longer for your full transformation to solidify. You will probably notice changes in your body. Your sleep schedule will alter gradually. Eventually you will be awake all night and rest during the day. Enjoy the sunshine, Mrs. Miller. Your time in the daylight now has an expiration date."

CHAPTER 22

I walked in the garden labyrinth. Bree and I had come to love losing and finding one another in its maze of greenery. We had spent so much time doing it, we had a pretty good mental map of its twists and turns.

But this time I strolled alone. It was an hour after sunset and night had completely fallen, but the moon was full and the sky cloudless.

I wasn't worried. Bartal's men were always close. Most of the labyrinth's pathways could be viewed from the castle windows so I felt safe.

I should have been more wary. I should have been more cautious especially with all I had been through lately. But it was a beautiful warm night and the full moon called to me. I walked around a turn, my fingers trailing affectionately on the shrubbery. I was immediately brought up short. My breath caught in my throat.

A dark robed figure stood about ten paces in front of me, its face shadowed and hidden completely by a heavy cowl.

It reminded me of something out of a long forgotten nightmare. The figure didn't move or make any threatening gesture. It simply stood there, quiet and still, allowing me to take a good long look.

"What are you doing here?" I asked trying not to sound as afraid as I was.

The cowl moved slightly and the figure spoke in a deliberate tone. "Susanne. Joel. Miller." It was a man's voice and it sounded like it hadn't spoken in quite some time.

I turned and ran. But I'd barely rounded two twists in the labyrinth when the figure appeared before me, closer this time. I turned and ran again this time taking two lefts instead of two rights. Once again the figure ended up in front of me. My heart pounded in my throat. I took a couple of deep breaths and ran again. My panicky mind lost all memory of how to escape the maze. And once again the figure ended up in front of me, this time close enough to touch me.

"Please stop," it told me. "I have no intention of harming you."

"How do you know my name?" I panted in fright. "What do you want?"

"I need to speak with you. *Alone!*" it said.

I took two sudden steps back as the figure moved. But it only raised its very mortal looking hands to its hood and eased the heavy fabric away to revealing its face.

He seemed human at first glance, not the terrifying creature from my dream. I relaxed somewhat. He was dressed like a monk but was unlike any monk I'd ever seen before. He stood no taller than myself. But he was extremely gaunt with hollow cheeks and deep set eyes. His hair was shaved but he was not bald. A mist of salt and pepper hair was growing back. His eyes looked Oriental but it was obvious he was no Asian. His face spoke of several generations of Asian and European people's blending. And his face was tattooed.

I had never seen such odd tattoos. They wound about the outline of his face, framing his features in bold lines and swirls. The art dove down from the center of his lower lip, went around his jaw on both sides, danced up across his forehead and then dove down the center bridge of his nose. The tattoos looked simultaneously similar and unlike anything I'd ever seen. Abstract lines loosely resembled tribal tats. The closest thing I could compare them to was the rendition of an elk tattoo I'd seen in an issue of *National Geographic*.

He stood there quietly, letting me fully take in his features by the light of the moon.

"Why do you need to speak to me alone?" I finally managed to stammer out.

An apologetic smile flickered briefly across his features. "Those of my order rarely speak aloud," he said. "We have learned to communicate through other means." I could not identify his accent.

He gestured for me to look at his face and stepped into the full light of the moon. It was obvious he wanted me to notice a certain facial feature.

152

As he turned, I saw his eyes flash in a strange way. They weren't dark but the palest shade of gray imaginable.

I gasped. I had seen eyes like that before. "You're Nosferatu!" I exclaimed and jumped back.

"No!" he corrected. "Not Nosferatu!" his accent thickened.

I had insulted him.

"But you're a vampire."

He nodded in reply. "I am a vampire, yes. Nosferatu never!" he clarified.

"I don't understand." I told him. "There's a difference?"

He nodded, then shook the heavy fabric away and extended a tattooed hand. "Words are clumsy," he explained. "Please, take my hand. I promise not to harm you."

I visibly shuddered. Mykhalo had spoken those exact words to me on one of our first meetings.

"Vampires do not honor their promises," I replied shivering all over with dread.

"*Nosferatu* do not honor their promises," he again clarified. "You are no longer mortal. You have been touched by the dead. You need to know our history. It is vital to your survival. But you must keep our secret. Take my hand, child."

How many times could I grasp the hand of a vampire before my luck ran out, I wondered. I took a deep breath to steady my resolve then extended my hand slowly. His cold hand clasped mind followed by his other laying gently but firmly on top. He stepped closer and whispered in my ear. "Now child, listen."

I gasped and started. It felt as if something jerked my soul roughly out of my body and took it someplace else, someplace frightening. I saw his thoughts.

Two can keep a secret if one is dead.

I began to tremble all over with fear as if I stood naked in the snow.

We are not an evil people. But only the evil survive. The righteous are hidden and forgotten.

My shivering eased. My mind spoke a question into the ether. *Who is Kane?*

He heard my thought and immediately responded.

Kane is not the biblical character. That's just the lie he wants everyone to believe.

I gasped at this revelation.

Kane existed long before the bible got its stories. He's not human. He never was. He is the last survivor of the first intelligent race which inhabited this planet. He was born in a time of darkness. Vampirism wasn't a disease to his kind.

Then the sun got stronger and his people began to die off. They found out if they bit the new evolving ape species, they became something like the first race. But vampirism to humans WAS a disease.

Many of Kane's people infected the ape population as a way of keeping their ways and their own culture alive. The first humans infected were the Kurgans, the people of the Black Sea. They found a way to control the blood lust and rage. They made an elixir from local plants and drank it or mixed it into the dyes for their body art, They found they could survive off animal blood in desperate times and only needed to feed four times a year. Most importantly, they didn't need to kill humans to do this.

The Kurgans were the very first human vampires. Mortal humans called them the Wise Who Walk At Night. They were not an evil race but looked up to as elders and sages.

This revelation shocked me. *But if they were honorable people then what happened?*

The monk smiled sadly. *What normally happens with many cultures; political discord. There was a faction of vampires, the Nosferatu, who refused to take the elixir. They liked the savage, lustful nature which would overtake them after a few centuries and willingly gave in to their carnal side. There was a war.*

He paused in his tale and was quiet for a long moment. I sensed a great and very old sadness from him. *Sometimes the bad guys win and the good guys lose. The Nosferatu, in this case, won.*

He sighed and continued. *Very few of the original Kurgan vampires survived this war. The Black Sea rose up and swallowed their city. All knowledge of the magic elixir was lost. After a few centuries most Kurgans had died out and were quickly forgotten. The only vampires to survive were the Nosferatu. Mykhalo never told you any of this because* he was unaware, like most modern vampires, this history ever happened. It had all been forgotten.

My mind spun with many possibilities. *But then how does Kane play into all this? Does he want to take over as leader and 'harvest' the humans?*

Yes. With him awake and aware again this is a very real possibility. The scattered clans will unite when they hear he is once more active. They believe in the power of the first of their kind.

I staggered, physically dumbfounded by this future outcome. *How do we stop him?*

The monk gripped my hands tightly in his own to reassure me. *It will not be easy. Because Kane is not human, things that normally give a vampire pause or kill them will not work on him. He does not like sunlight but it will not kill him. You must find something, a metal, a powder, which was abundant when the world was young and dark and use it for a weapon against him. I do not know what it is. But your modern friends might.*

One more thing. My people are a secretive race. We are very few in number. We have only survived this long because the rest of the world, even the Nosferatu, have no idea we exist. I'd like to keep it that way. Meeting and telling you these things will earn me a severe punishment from my order. But I felt it was unavoidable. Do not tell anyone anything about this meeting, not Bartal, not your daughter, NO ONE! This will be a test as to how well you can keep a secret. Do I make myself clear?

I swallowed with difficulty and nodded. *I will tell no one. I promise.*

He smiled quietly in the moonlight. *The Kurgan people...my people...are dead.* He paused lost in thought for a moment. *I have no name. I was never here. I do not exist.* He let go of my hands and melted into shadow.

Two can keep a secret if one is dead.

"But now two know the secret," I whispered aloud.

The invisible monk chuckled from the surrounding dark. *You still consider yourself mortal. How endearing! You are as dead now as the rest of us have been for centuries. This is your new reality, my dear.*

155

His words whispered in my mind as he retreated from my presence. *You will remember all this when the time is right. When it is needed.*

I looked up at the full moon overhead. "None but the dead walk here this night," I mused aloud almost to myself. It seemed so strange to include myself in the statement.

Yes... His words hissed into the silence of my mind.

I thought silently to myself, *Two can keep a secret if both of us are dead.*

CHAPTER 23

I didn't want to think about Mykhalo anymore. Thinking about him made my head and heart ache. I wanted to distance myself from him, even if he was still trying to protect us.

For the next few days I kept myself busy and around people. Bartal or one of his men guided me around the grounds and told me the castle's history. I experimented in learning German. I explored the gardens. More than a few times I got lost in its expertly manicured labyrinth.

Bartal showed me a rose garden Mykhalo planted by the light of the moon. Each rose bush was in memory of a dearly loved person he had lost. The rose garden was extensive.

Bartal eventually felt safe enough to allow us to venture off the castle grounds. I went into town a few times, always accompanied by Bartal and a mess of his men. But I decided I really preferred the castle. In town I always had to look over my shoulder. In the castle I felt safe. Bartal or one of his men were always within shouting distance, yet the grounds and castle were spacious enough to give me a feeling of being free and alone.

Eventually I realized I was waiting for something. What it was I didn't know, nor did I want to think about it. I spent my days avoiding the issue and distracting my attention by pretending to be on vacation in a strange and wonderful place.

Then one day I noticed I'd seen very little of Bree except at mealtimes where she ate while I drank coffee. She was always off exploring with some of the men in suits. Our conversations had become casual and of everyday things. I realized I needed to talk to my daughter, really talk, not just go through the motions of a normal life.

My life hadn't been normal for quite a long time!

I decided to corner her for a nice long chat the next day at breakfast.

It was foggy and threatened rain. Breakfast was moved from the outside veranda to an inside patio overlooking the garden maze. Bartal was just leaving when I walked in. He made a motion as if to stay but I gestured him to keep going. I told him I wanted to talk to my daughter. His eyebrows hopped at this but he shrugged.

"As you wish," was all he said.

I sat down to my liquid breakfast and was well engrossed in my third cup by the time Bree joined me.

I noticed a change in her attitude. She wasn't dressed in her sweats, yawning and trying to wake up. She seemed perky and cheerful as if she'd already had her morning caffeine. She had showered and dressed and even put on makeup and perfume.

Hmmmm. I thought to myself and narrowed my eyes at her.

She had earplugs in and was jamming to a beat only she could hear. That was normal enough for Bree. But this early in the morning? She shoveled food into her mouth with barely a glance at me.

I looked harder. There was definitely a new vibe about her, one which hadn't been there before. Sometime in the last few days when I hadn't been paying attention, my daughter had changed.

I finally slammed my hand down on the table so suddenly all the dishes clattered and in the same motion yanked her earplugs out with my other hand.

Bree nearly jumped out of her skin. "Ma! What the…?" she began in shock.

"What's his name?" I demanded in a firm tone of voice.

"Hunh?" Bree was still so shocked that her mind hadn't grabbed onto my words yet.

"Your boyfriend! What's his name?"

Bree just stared wide-eyed at me and blinked a few times. Her face immediately went red as a beet. "I…don't know what…" she stammered.

"Don't lie to me, Missy! You think I don't know the look of a girl in love?"

Her jaw flapped soundlessly a few times and I could see her brain scrambling to figure out a good excuse.

158

"Sabrina Tempest Miller! You tell me the truth! Out with it!"

She finally deflated with a huge sigh. "Okay Ma! I met someone. Are you happy now?" she spouted.

I sniffed. This was really quite interesting to me. My daughter was of age where adolescent girls get interested in boys whether their parents like it or not. The girls around her had all been dating several years. Bree had showed no sign of getting romantically involved with anyone. Whether I wanted her to date or not was beside the point. I found her lack of interest in dating highly unusual.

"Really? I couldn't tell." I raised an eyebrow at her. "Well? Spill the details. Is he German?"

"Uh no. He's from Boston actually," she finally confided.

"Uh hunh. We go all the way to Germany for you to meet another American. How ironic! So tell me more. I want details. What's his name?"

Bree gave another 'my mom is so lame' sigh, rolled her eyes and seemed to shrink inside of herself. "His name is Dante Fang."

My eyebrows went skyward. "Oh boy! A Goth. No mother in her right mind would name their kid that!"

Bree wrinkled her brows at me. "Like Tempest is a completely normal name?" she countered.

All right, she had me there. Touché.

"At least you didn't name me Moon-Feather or Snuggle-Bunny. That would have only been cool when I was five," she grumbled softly.

I ignored this quip and went on, thinking aloud to myself. "What's a young American doing in Germany all by himself?"

"He's taken a year off to see Europe before he goes into med school. He kinda liked it here so he stayed."

My eyebrows went skyward at the med school comment. So he was smart. This bit of news was even more interesting to me.

"Well med school sounds promising," I said thinking hard. "I guess he's cute, eh?"

Her answer surprised me.

"No," she said. "I mean, he's not ugly but he's no jock either. He's just really brainy."

"So he's a nerd and a geek," I supplied.

She made an apologetic face. "I like geeks as long as they're not creepy-weird or really odd. I mean it's like you always told me, there are many varieties of weird."

Okay, now she was using my own advice against me. "Yes," I sighed. "There's the harmless just very smart weird and then there's the weird where you grab you kids and cross to the other side of the street weird."

She nodded. "Yes, Mom. See? I do listen to you. He's harmless weird," Bree stuffed a fork of food into her mouth and thought a bit. "But you're still not gonna like him."

"And why?"

She whined a little, took a deep breath and then just blurted it out. "Because he has a mohawk, wears leather, and skateboards everywhere."

I was silent for a long moment digesting this. So my daughter had decided to date every parent's worst nightmare. Great! Just peachy! It was my turn to take a deep breath. "Now Hon. I didn't say I was gonna hate him. I do want to meet him though. And this is non-negotiable." I told her waggling a scolding finger.

Bree stomped her foot like an impatient horse. "I was afraid you would say that," she stuck her lower lip out. "When?"

I gave her the evil queen smile. "Today. And I don't want him to know I'm coming, understood?"

She started to sputter but I made a harsh noise in my throat and waggled my finger at her again. "Now finish your breakfast so we can go meet your sweetie."

Bree made a face at the term 'sweetie' but complied.

This new development in Bree's life produced a myriad of conflicting emotions inside me. On the one hand I was just so relieved Bree was acting like a normal teen. It was high time life got back to normal for her – meaning normal problems which had nothing to do with vampires or the paranormal underworld.

On the other hand I was highly apprehensive about meeting this kid from the description she'd given me. He sounded like a Goth and a rebel and a million things parents don't want their child to get involved in. And of course I was seeing all these traits in a negative light.

160

Then there was the fact this guy would soon be going to college. This meant he was older than Bree and illegally so. I would have to be extremely critical in my assessment of this guy. I *might* give my parental permission for them to date, despite the legal implications but it was a pretty weak 'might' on my part. He would have to be a knight in shining armor to pass my test!

Lastly, my little girl was dating! The thought made me whimper internally. The door was officially shut on her childhood. The adult years loomed closer than I wanted them to and with the realization that soon I would have to release Bree into the hands of the great, cruel world outside her childhood home. I emotionally wasn't ready for it yet.

I sighed heavily as we walked along thinking on these things. My stomach was all tied in knots. I looked behind me. At least Bartal's men were with me. They were dressed in plainclothes so as not to attract attention. But wherever Bree and I went in town, there were at least five of his men scattered about doing their best to blend into the crowd.

"Bree, you haven't been dating anyone before this have you?" I asked out of the blue.

She stopped and looked me full in the face with her brilliant green eyes. "Heck no, Ma! You would have known. I would have told you." she assured me.

"So what would Brittany have said about this Dante guy you're seeing?"

"She would have said he was a loser," Bree rolled her eyes.

I smiled in return. "A loser who's going to med school. Yeah, that makes sense!"

We were still laughing about it by the time we came to the city park where her beau would routinely meet her.

"So is this where you met him?" I asked as I looked about for odd-looking characters.

"Actually, you've already met him. He was the guy who helped us the night you were abducted."

This brought me up short.

"And he also chased a bully off me as I was putting up flyers when you went missing," she added.

"So he's a white knight who likes to save damsels in distress."

Bree shrugged and mumbled something in reply.

"Hey, Bree!" came a sudden shout.

We both turned about.

A young guy who looked about twenty ran up to us with a skateboard tucked safely under his arm. His dark brown hair was shaved into a tall Mohawk. He wore black leather trimmed in spikes and jeans with the knees ripped out. I didn't see any obvious piercings or tattoos and there was no makeup on his face.

He skidded to a halt the minute he saw me and his easy smile vanished from his face.

"Uh Dante, this is ..." Bree began.

"Your mother," he interrupted. "She looks just like you." He gave an uncomfortable laugh and shuffled awkwardly. I tried to smile politely at him.

"Mom, this is Dante Fang."

A hand wearing a leather glove with the fingers cut off and spikes across the knuckles, was extended my way and this Dante character gave me a stiff smile. "Pleased to meet you, Mrs. Miller."

I raised an eyebrow as he took my hand. Well, at least he had manners! The funny thing was I liked this guy immediately. He was dressed like a tough guy but smiles came easily to him. His voice was gawky and nasal. I sensed the clothes were just something to hide an introverted personality.

His handshake was strong but not too strong. But the same time I took his hand, I felt a strange sort of electrical charge from him. Something tickled my brain like a long forgotten memory. It flitted through like the quick beat of a moth's wings and then was gone before I knew exactly what it was. What in the world was it? I was left wondering.

"I didn't expect you to bring your mother along today," Dante said quietly, still giving me an awkward smile which tried to assure me everything was fine.

"Bree never told me she was seeing someone. I just had to figure it out on my own," I said.

"Mom, I just met him!" Bree whined and started to blush again.

An awkward silence fell on all three of us.

Dante finally said he planned on checking out the bands of a local street fair and would I be interested in coming with them? He was overly polite even though we all knew what the answer would be.

We turned and followed. Bree linked arms with him and Dante looked slightly uncomfortable. I was pretty sure his unease stemmed from the fact I was there. But he smiled and went along.

As the three of us walked and chatted I observed their body language carefully. Dante was obviously smitten with Bree, yet terribly shy about public displays of affection. He kept looking at her as if he couldn't believe she was with him of all people. Bree was cuddly with him and seemed to hang on his every word.

In spite of his looks Dante was an intelligent and sweet guy. He had wonderful manners. He was quick to open doors for both of us and pull out chairs for first myself and then my daughter. Again something I didn't expect from someone in Goth attire. I kept getting the feeling his appearance was just an act. I wondered why the clothes and hair screamed rebel but he didn't have a single tattoo or piercing to see. Something just didn't add up.

The band he wanted to check out was still setting up when we arrived. We stood there and watched them, suddenly seized by an uncomfortable silence.

I saw a nearby restaurant with tables and chairs set up outside. I suggested we sit and chat while we waited and maybe they could have a bite to eat. Bree and Dante agreed. After we were seated, I told Bree to go and order us something. My stern expression told her I wanted to speak with Dante alone. Quite out of the blue, Dante offered to pay for all three of us. I tried to refuse but he insisted and handed the necessary cash to Bree.

Bree gave me a disapproving look at my suggestion to leave us alone together. She leaned over and whispered in my ear, "Try not to have him for dinner, Ma!"

I just winked and made a shooing gesture. Bree frowned and slunk away. Dante faced me with an expression which told me he knew exactly what was up.

"So Dante," I started slowly. "How old are you?"

He smiled apologetically. "Uh, I'll be twenty-one in December," he said nodding, trying to keep his tone of voice light and casual.

I gave him a stern glare. I nodded and my fingers traced the pattern on the wrought iron table beneath me. "Old enough to drink, in America at least. Old enough for my daughter to be jailbait to you," I said in a low voice.

This pulled him up short. He swallowed with difficulty and I could see his brain scrambling to figure out the next most appropriate response but failing miserably.

"I realize that, Mrs. Miller," he said in a tone which was apologetic. "But like your daughter said, we just met. We might end up being friends and nothing more."

My eyes met his. I noticed he had brown eyes, big and soulful.

"She's not interested in you being her 'friend'. And I've seen the way you look at her. You are also not interested in being 'just friends' with her."

Dante hung his head in front of me. His words suddenly became awkward and fearful, almost like a dog who is called and expects to be beaten. "You've figured me out," he said. He gave a heavy sigh and squirmed uncomfortably in his chair. "Look, Mrs. Miller. I think your daughter is really cool. I never expected her to like me. And I know she's very young. All I can do is to assure you my intentions are completely honorable and that the future is yet unwritten. I have no idea where we're going in this relationship. I'm curious to see." He licked his lips and then looked me full in the face.

"I came to Germany to see the world, not to get girls. I'm no ladies' man nor do I want to be."

I arched my eyebrows. "And how many girlfriends have you had, Dante Fang?"

He leaned back in his chair as if he had said the wrong thing already.

"Is Bree your first relationship?"

He hung his head. "No," he admitted. "But look. It's about the depth of the relationship. I haven't dated many girls, I mean women. But those I did, I loved. And it hurts to talk about them."

I considered him through narrowed eyes. My accusatory gaze was obviously making him uncomfortable.

164

He relented with a sigh. "If what we have right now makes you that uncomfortable just say so and I will go away and never see Bree again. You have my word on this."

I tilted my head to the side and considered. It was a struggle to keep my face straight. I wanted to laugh out loud. But I didn't dare! I needed to put the fear of Bree's mother in him.

Damn it! I still really liked this awkward, gawky kid sitting across from me. He was just so adorable with his puppy dog eyes and his pretend Goth clothes.

I finally gave a heavy sigh. "Okay," I said.

Dante paused as if it hadn't been the answer he had been expecting. "Excuse me? Okay what? I don't understand," he turned his head to the side and squinted one eye.

"Okay," I repeated. "You may date my daughter. You may hold her hand. You may hug and cuddle her. You may even kiss her. More than this is not allowed at this time. Do I make myself absolutely clear on this?"

Dante fell back into his chair in shock and covered his mouth with his hands. Then a huge smile broke free. "Seriously? Really? It's okay?" he said. His relief and happiness could barely be contained.

"Are we clear on this?" I repeated.

Dante's mouth fluttered open and shut a few times before he could trust his voice. "Clear as crystal! Absolutely! Whatever you say goes! Thank you, thank you, thank you! Mrs. Miller, you're as fantastic as your daughter!" He was laughing and practically jumping about in the seat.

"Well I should hope so! Like mother like daughter or so the saying goes." I allowed my stern visage to crack and smiled in return.

Bree had returned by that time with our drinks and food. Dante bounded to his feet and in a second was at her side all smiles and compliments to assist her with our food.

I laughed at his relief and enthusiasm. Bree was looking from Dante to me and back in utter confusion. "What just happened here?" she said.

"Nothing!" Dante and I said at the same time.

"Let's just sit down and enjoy some good music," he said rushing to pull out her chair for her.

Bree seated herself between us. But she still kept looking back and forth in confusion. "Why do I get the feeling I just missed something major?"

CHAPTER 24

We returned to the castle around four in the afternoon. Bree was still glowing from her visit with Dante. She had become quiet and thoughtful but in a pleasant way. She said she was tired and wanted to go to her room to maybe take a nap before dinner.

"Thoughts of Dante interfering with your sleep?"

"Ma!" she whined. And then she rolled her eyes and shuffled her feet. "Okay, maybe a little."

"Go and chill." I smiled and squeezed her hand. "I'll come get you when dinner is served."

We parted ways. She went up the expansive stairway to the upper quarters. I watched until she disappeared from view and sighed quietly to myself. My little girl was becoming a woman.

In the sitting room, Bartal was talking on the phone with someone. The language sounded German. I went to a plush leather easy chair positioned next to a window overlooking the labyrinth. I gazed out the tall glass at the scenery and allowed myself to relax as I thought about the events of the day. I didn't notice Bartal had ended his conversation. I must have sighed again.

"Is something wrong, Mrs. Miller?"

"No, not really" I shook my head peacefully then smiled. "Bree's growing up. She's got a boyfriend."

But Bartal's reaction was not what I expected. "When did that happen?" his tone of voice seemed rather irritated.

My brow furrowed. "Apparently while I was gone. She met some boy in town."

Bartal nodded and the expression on his face grew darker. He turned his back on me to hide it but I had already seen.

"He's just a normal kid. It was bound to happen someday."

Bartal kept his back to me but the vibe I was getting from him told me he still wasn't happy.

"Good Lord, Bartal! Do you always have to get so upset about everything?" I spewed at his back. I was tired and not in the mood for dramatics. "I for one am relieved for the most part that Bree is finally behaving like a normal adolescent girl. What's wrong with that?"

Bartal made a sound like an angry bear growling. "Sabrina is not a normal kid!" he rumbled angrily. "And you are not a normal woman. You haven't been since before you were born."

I blinked in confusion at his inscrutable back. I suddenly wasn't all that sleepy anymore.

"Bartal, what are you saying?" I had a sneaky feeling I wasn't going to like the answer.

He sighed, shook his head and turned to face me. "You barely knew Mykhalo. But he knew you since before you were born. He had been keeping watch over you from a distance all your life, making sure you were safe. For most of your life he saw no need for you to know him. Until that day he came into your bookstore."

I shuddered. Why did his words bother me so much? "Why did he feel the need to watch over me? Why me? What made me different from the next person?" I asked in a voice barely above a whisper. I was afraid of the answer.

"Because he saw you as family. Part of the only family a creature like him could ever have." Bartal approached where I was seated and gripped the arm tightly. "Mrs. Miller, you are descended on your mother's side from Hope Bayer, the babe Mykhalo saved so many generations ago. He has tried his best to watch over her bloodline through the years."

More revelations! I was glad I was sitting down. My thoughts spun as I tried to take it in. Things still didn't make any sense. "And what does this have to do with anything?" I inquired. "What has this got to do with Bree dating and being a normal kid?"

"Quite a lot actually," Bartal told me.

"I didn't raise my daughter to be a nun!" As I said this I heard a panicky, desperate note come into my tone. What was I so afraid of?

"Of course you didn't!" Bartal agreed. He sighed, rubbed his forehead and knelt beside me. I had a sudden flashback to when I had tried to kill Mykhalo in my bookstore. He had knelt beside me as well.

"Mrs. Miller," he began in a low voice with forced patience. "You and Bree did a very nice job with Hector in the States. But do you really think you got all the vampires in one fell swoop?"

I paused to consider the truth of his words.

"There are other vampire families worldwide. Hector's clan was just one of many. And you did not kill all of his children. The ones who survived learned the lessons of their sire quite well. And one of the lessons he taught them concerns your family."

My throat felt like I had swallowed a chunk of ice. "Which is?"

Bartal bit his lip in concern and took my hand to reassure me. "The bloodline of Hope Bayer may live. They may grow and fall in love and bear children. But they are never allowed to hold a grandchild."

My thoughts flew to the sudden, unexpected deaths of my parents. I was pregnant at the time. My heart began to beat slower. "Hector put a hit out on my parents? The car crash wasn't an accident?" I heard myself say.

Bartal only nodded.

I was suddenly having trouble breathing. "Where was Mykhalo? Why didn't he save them?" I gasped. My jumbled thoughts came too fast to make sense of them. I wasn't thinking straight or I would have known the answer.

Bartal took my other hand and squeezed them tightly. "Because he was in the Middle East trying to save your husband. He tried and failed."

I felt like I was going to faint. I must have turned paler than normal because Bartal was telling me to breathe slowly. "There's more, Mrs. Miller." He went on. "I know it's going to be hard for you to hear it but you must find the courage somewhere. Deep breaths and hang in there."

I closed my eyes and breathed like I was giving birth. After a few moments I felt stronger. I sat back and opened my eyes. I didn't want to hear what he had to say next. But I had to. This was important.

"Now there are many of Hector's children who want revenge on you for killing their sire. But they will wait until the time is right because that's how he taught them. If Bree ever gets pregnant, either by accident or on purpose, they will come for you. They will try to kill you. If Bree gets with child, you die."

Bartal let go of my hands and stood up.

"I would advise your daughter to try very hard not to get pregnant."

CHAPTER 25

I knew I was dreaming. I was certain of it. But it was a very strange dream.

I was in the castle standing in front of the door to Bartal's personal quarters. I don't remember how I got there. But I do remember something, some other force, compelled me to get Bartal alone. I was powerless to resist. I had to obey.

But it was just a dream and dreams aren't real. So I allowed myself to be swept along.

The door opened abruptly enough to startle me. Bartal stood on the other side, looking equally surprised to see me.

He was dressed in a robe, pajama pants and slippers. His hairy chest peeked out a bit. It looked odd, even humorous to see him dressed so. I struggled not to chuckle.

"Mrs. Miller?" he said. "You took me by surprise. It's rather late. I was just going to bed."

"So I see," I replied blankly.

I nearly blushed. I hated disturbing people from their rest.

"Did you need to speak to me in private?"

Did I? I thought to myself. I wasn't sure. What was I doing here?

"Yes," the words were pulled out of me. I had no idea what I was doing here. But something kept me from apologizing and returning to my own bed.

"Well, come in, come in." He opened the door and welcomed me inside. "You know you can ask me anything, especially here. No one will eavesdrop in my own private chambers."

I stepped inside his castle apartment. "That's good," I replied. Again it seemed someone else was supplying the words for me because I had absolutely no idea what the next step was. Why was I here? What was I supposed to say? What was I supposed to do? All this was not my idea. Some other force subtly suggested to my mind not to worry. This was all a dream. Just go with the flow. I'll wake up soon.

I looked about Bartal's room, curious to see with what he chose to surround himself. The furniture was ornate, as befit a castle. He had many glass display cabinets. Each held an obviously old and very valuable chess set. All were beautifully cared for and lovingly displayed.

There was a table with two plush, green, leather chairs on either side. On the table sat a much newer chess set. The figurines were fashioned out of pewter on a lapis lazuli checkerboard. On closer inspection I found the figures to be from the *Lord of the Rings*. It made me smile.

This chess set was arranged as if a game had been interrupted. The pieces were scattered in strategic locations on the board.

"I see you like chess," I said softly, distantly.

"Do you play?" he asked.

"What me? No, I never mastered it. Bree is very good though."

"Ah! I shall have to challenge her to a game someday." Bartal said with some eagerness.

I stepped closer to the *Lord of the Rings* board.

"Please don't touch the pieces, Mrs. Miller," he warned.

I turned about. "Why not?"

Bartal shrugged and looked almost embarrassed. He came to stand beside me and traced the edge of the board in a loving, almost wistful fashion. "This was the last game Mykhalo and I played." Bartal heaved a great, sad sigh. "It's silly but I just don't want it touched. He was the last to touch the pieces."

I leaned over and looked at the figures closely. "Which side was he, Mordor or the Free Peoples of Middle Earth?"

Bartal smiled. "Mordor, of course," he replied. "I always beat him at chess. He always beat me at cards. He could have gotten himself into a lot of trouble with cards but it was all just a game to him. He never really needed the money anyway."

Bartal stood close to me as we looked at the pewter chess set, really close. The force pulling my strings wanted him closer and for him to turn his back to me. Why I had no idea. Then it got its chance.

"Ahhh! It's ridiculous I know…" and muttering this, Bartal turned away.

It was then the something else in me took over, dragging my body along like a helpless passenger. I felt a predatory presence rise to the surface. Knocking me aside, it took over my free will. A feral snarl rose up from the depths of my throat. I felt the teeth in my mouth change in an instant, becoming longer, sharper. I felt a sudden hunger of unknown origin.

I could smell Bartal's blood coursing and I wanted to bathe in it. I wanted to free his poor, trapped blood from its cage of skin and dance in its red rain. With a leonine roar I threw myself on the big man, aiming my fangs at the exposed side of his large neck. My reactions were quicker than his and my teeth found their mark. I sank them deep and began to drink hungrily.

Ahh! The taste of his blood in my mouth! It was the most heady elixir I had ever known.

Bartal gave a cry of surprise and tried to toss me off. He should've been able to. He was a big man and a dhampir. But I had latched on too tightly and he couldn't dislodge me. I felt him through my teeth, shout for his men. I clung tighter. I wound my arms and legs about him like a snake tightening its coils on a still struggling prey. He tried to pry me off but I clung too tight. I continued to suck down as much of his blood as I could. It poured in a red flood into my throat.

Bartal threw himself onto the floor and hit me in the head with something which felt like a metal club. It stunned me.

I was suddenly released from my superhuman strength and I let go. I rolled onto the floor and huddled into a ball as he scrambled away.

The pain brought me back. It felt like something had thrown me roughly back into my body. I woke with a jolt to the taste of Bartal's blood in my mouth and my blood running down the side of my face.

It wasn't a dream. No part of this was a dream. Every bit was real.

Two of Bartal's men had me pinned to the floor. One held a wooden stake to my chest.

I took in everything at a glance and wailed my pain to the world.

Bartal climbed slowly to his feet. He held a hand to his bloody neck. He said something indelicate in German. His men poured like an angry flood into the room.

"I told you to stake me when you found me," I moaned. "Kill me now before it's too late!" Tears and blood streamed down my face. Where were my gods now?

Then Bree shoved the men blocking the doorway aside and ran into the room.

I moaned in agony and squeezed my eyes shut, not wanting to see my daughter in this state. But what I expected to happen, didn't.

"Little mother, open your eyes and look at me," said a commanding female voice.

I knew the voice. *Sekhmet!* My eyes snapped open.

My daughter stood and gazed down upon me. But those were not Bree's eyes. Her form radiated the heat of the desert. The air was electric like the wind before a sudden summer storm.

Everyone in the room backed away from her. Everyone knew this was not my funny, adolescent daughter anymore but something else, something powerful and deadly. We all could feel it.

"Release her!" Sekhmet ordered.

The two men restraining me did so without question.

"Stand up, little mother. This is not the time to grovel before me."

I obeyed.

My daughter's body now housed the terrifying power of the goddess Sekhmet. She took two more steps towards me and stopped. "You were abducted by a vampire. He tortured and changed you. He sent you back to destroy your child and all those you love. That was his plan."

The air shimmered between us like a mirage.

Sekhmet smiled slowly. "Except it was not his plan. It was *MINE!* All those times you prayed and you thought no one heard you, *I* heard you. I did not abandon you to your fate. This was *MY* design, not his. He was supposed to think it was his plot to change you into a vampire. But it was *MY* plan to make you into a dhampir. This was the final step in your transformation. All the recipe needed was your first sip of dhampir blood to mold you. Your transformation is now complete."

Sekhmet turned her gaze to Bartal's men gathered in the room. "I created the dhampirs. They are my most glorious children. They are the positive to the vampire's negative."

Sekhmet turned her blazing eyes onto Bartal. She considered him proudly. "You are my soldier. Bartal is the best vampire slayer I have ever blessed although he knows me not. He will be your teacher, little mother. Together you three shall eradicate this ancient evil from the earth. If you do not, they will rise up and take over the world completely."

Sekhmet turned back to me. "This is why I have decided to change you. It was a painful gift I know, but a necessary one. Learn your new talents well and there will not be an undead who can stop you. This is a blessing and not a curse. Accept it."

She stepped closer to me and took my face in her hands. They felt as hot as the sunbaked desert sand. "I forgive you your despair. I am with you both and my blessings shall follow you wherever you go. You should thank me although I know you're not ready to do so yet. Give it time." She kissed me on my forehead. "Good hunting, little mother." Her lips burned my skin like the hot summer sun.

Then Bree's eyes rolled back into her head and she staggered as the spirit left her. I caught her just in time and lowered her gently to the floor. I sat there cradling Bree in my arms. Everything had become very quiet and still. I was almost afraid to breathe.

"That was Sekhmet," I finally said loud and clear. "She's an Egyptian goddess. She's helped us before. If it wasn't for Her intervention, Hector would still trouble the world."

I looked about the room. Everyone was frozen, just staring at me, like a movie set on pause.

"Please, somebody say something!"

My eyes searched the room wildly for a friend. They found Bartal. He had a look on his face I'd never seen before.

I shuddered and clasped my daughter closer.

Bartal approached and knelt before me. He reached out and touched the kiss on my forehead. I flinched in pain for it felt like a bad sunburn.

"Bartal, I'm sorry," I said squeezing my eyes shut. "I never meant to hurt you. Something else took over. I guess it was Her." I rocked Bree who had yet to come back to me. "Bree darling, wake up. Please wake up," I whispered, nearly sobbing into her hair. "What am I now?"

Bree's form stirred in my arms. "You are now the weapon, Mom. We won't need the dagger anymore." Bree turned around in my arms and hugged me back, hugged me tighter than ever before.

Then she turned her angelic face to Bartal. "Isn't that right, Bartholomew? Now look at my mother and tell me, is she a vampire? You would know right? You've seen hundreds of vampires."

He turned his dark eyes from me to my daughter. "No, not hundreds." He replied slowly, quietly. "I've slain roughly about a thousand."

Bree sat up. "Then you would know better than anyone. Shoot! You could probably smell them at a hundred paces!"

Bartal nodded. "Yes, I can," he replied very quietly.

"Then tell me. Tell this whole room. Is my mother a vampire?" Bree's voice was triumphant, confident. She already knew the answer.

Bartal turned his dark eyes back to me. He took my face in his hands. I shuddered at the touch of his big hands soaked in his own blood from the wound I had given him. He peered intently into my eyes for one long moment.

"You are not a vampire. A few moments ago you were. But that has changed already. Now you radiate dhampir energy. I've never seen such a thing happen before but there it is."

Bree smiled and gave me a reassuring shake. "See? My mother's a dhampir! We don't have to kill her!" Bree was almost in a celebratory mood.

But I could not take my eyes off Bartal. I had never seen the look upon his face before. Slowly he rose and turned his back on everyone.

Bree helped me get to my feet. I needed her assistance. I was stunned both physically and emotionally.

"It's late and I have a lot to think about," Bartal said in a muted tone of voice. "I need to be alone. Get out, all of you." He looked over his shoulder. His glittering black eyes punctuated his last words.

"Get out *NOW!*"

The room was jarred out of its paused state. Bartal's men scattered like roaches when the lights are turned on. People tripped over themselves leaving. Bree and I joined them.

I cast one backwards look over my shoulder before the great door shut, blocking my view.

He stood by the immense fireplace, one hand on the mantelpiece, a bottle of vodka in the other. His great shoulders were hunched. He looked tired and very old.

What have I done to him?

Chapter 26

It was two whole days and nights before either of us saw Bartal again. He showed up late one morning while Bree and I were pouring through the castle's extensive library. We had each found a particularly old book and were completely engrossed in its contents. Apparently he had cleared his throat twice, without either of us noticing. Finally he bellowed into the silence.

"Mrs. Miller, Sabrina!"

We jumped as if stung by a very large bee.

"Now that I have your attention, will you both please accompany me to the castle dungeon?"

We looked at Bartal, then at each other and back again. As one we left our respective books and slunk to him like dogs expecting a beating. While Bartal looked my daughter full in the face, he avoided my gaze.

He stalked away and we fell in mutely behind him like soldiers. Bree sent me a puzzled look, as if I knew what was going on. I told her wordlessly with my expression, I had no more idea than she what Bartal was up to.

Bree finally got her gumption up. "Are you going to lock my mother up in the dungeon?"

Bartal stopped abruptly. He paused a moment and then spun on her. Bree backed up a step in fright. "Now why on earth would you think that, child?" I saw genuine confusion cross his face.

Bree began to stutter incoherently so I stepped in.

"She means because I attacked you. She thinks you'll put me in chains."

Bartal finally met my eyes. The look of confusion remained. Finally it eased and a crooked smile softened his gruff countenance. "No, of course not." he explained gently. "I'm taking you to the dungeon because that's where our lab is. Dr. Sullivan wants to draw some blood from your mother for comparison to mine. That's all."

"Oh," we both said at once.

Why did this not reassure me at all? In fact all it did was make me more nervous. I was no lab rat! I wanted to protest but my words had suddenly left me dumb. All I could do was follow.

Bree must have noticed my concern. She took my hand and squeezed it reassuringly.

He led us down a flight of steps into a dungeon-like tunnel beneath the castle. The air became colder as we descended and it smelled funny. Our footsteps and voices echoed off the walls.

We came to a set of great oaken double doors with a smaller door cut into the right side. It looked to be an old brewery where wine and beer had been stored and aged.

Here Bartal paused. "Dr. Sullivan has worked with us for many years. He is an expert on all diseases of the blood. His specialty is identifying the vampire trait in blood samples no matter how early. No one knows more about vampire blood than he. We are very lucky to have him on our side." With this Bartal opened the little door and ducking his head, stepped through into the room beyond. Wordlessly, we followed.

"Mrs. Miller, I'd like you to meet Dr. Walter Conan Sullivan," he introduced in a loud voice.

We stood in a large room which had been fashioned into a scientific research lab. Medical paraphernalia flashed at us from every corner along with extensive glass and filing cabinets. Medical log books were open on just about every table.

A person in a white lab coat stooped over a microscope. He froze when he heard his name. Slowly he straightened up, turned, and came to greet us.

Bree gasped at the exact same moment I did. We recognized this 'Dr. Sullivan' in an instant.

"Dante?" Bree breathed in disbelief.

He looked much different. The mohawk was contained underneath a mesh cap. A set of spectacles perched on the end of his nose. But there was no mistaking the person who stood in front of us. He was the same 'boyfriend' Bree had been seeing.

His manner was completely different. No longer was he awkwardly hunched over. He stood straight, tall and eye to eye with me. His expression was much more serious. And it was obvious he couldn't possibly be on the verge of twenty-one!

I felt any small semblance of having a normal life disintegrate around me.

"Tell me something Doctor," I said in a stern tone when I regained my voice. "Just how old are you really?"

Dante's eyes flickered to Bartal who nodded. The young doctor before us sighed heavily, shuffled his feet a bit, then met my gaze with an equally steady one.

"I was born in December of 1884. I'm one hundred and thirty years old."

I felt like I had been punched in the gut.

Bree made a choked sound at my side. Dante turned to face her and his expression crumbled into one of intense pain. He took a step towards her and reached out. "Bree...I'm sorry," he began. His voice was soft and gentle.

Her face was ashen, eyes wet, and she trembled uncontrollably.

"You lied to me?" her voice quavered.

I reached out to her but she shook me off without looking.

"You lied to me!" she repeated with a venomous sound to her words. "How dare you lie to me?" Her whole body shook.

I had never heard such anger from my daughter except when she was overtaken by Sekhmet. It made me shudder. I tried to grab her arm but she wrenched herself away with a wail and a sob and bolted out of the lab. I directed Bartal to go after her and make sure she stayed safe.

Then I spun on the doctor in fury. I didn't care what big beautiful eyes he had, I was mad now! "Did you ever really care for my daughter or was it just a game to you?"

Dante still looked toward the fleeing Bree. When his eyes returned to me and saw the fury on my face, he took two steps back.

"No game. I really do care about Bree."

"Hunh! You have a funny way of showing it!"

He looked back the way she had gone and frowned. "Maybe it's just as well. My time is short."

This made me pause in anger. Mykhalo had said the same thing to me the last night we were together. "What do you mean?" I growled. "You look to be in your early twenties and yet you're way older than I am. Just what are you exactly?"

I circled him slowly looking him up and down. "You're not vampire. I'd know. Are you a predator?" I didn't know he was capable of such a serious glare.

"Yes," was the short answer.

"Are you a danger to my daughter, then?"

"No. I promised you I wouldn't physically harm her and I won't," he insisted.

"Then just what are you exactly?"

He didn't answer right away. He met my angry glare with one just as steady. "I'm a Mac Tyre," he said.

I furrowed my brows. "Excuse me? That term means nothing to me," I said.

"You're not Irish," he said. "The word means nothing to anyone except those who know the Irish legend and mythology quite well. The easiest way to explain is that I am an Irish lycanthrope from Boston."

Again I stopped moving. "You're a werewolf?"

He nodded. "In a manner of speaking, yes."

I mulled this over in my head. I wanted to dismiss such a notion as the ramblings of a crazy man.

But if vampires are real why not werewolves too?

"So every time the moon is full, you turn into this violent crazed, half man, half wolf monster?"

He gave a brief laugh which disappeared all too soon. "That's not exactly how the lycan trait works. I'm impervious to the cycles of the moon. I go on yearly cycles. Seven years I spend as a human. And then seven I spend as a simple wolf."

"So what did you mean by your time is short?" I began to get wrapped up in his explanation in spite of my rage.

He winced as if in pain and shook his head. "I 'go wolf' in December. When it happens, I will forget everything about my human

182

life. I'll be just as wary of approaching you and Bree as I would any other human creature. I won't be Dante Fang or Dr. Sullivan anymore."

"You'll forget all about Bree because you will be just an animal by then," I said.

He nodded. "Yes."

"Then why did you choose to get involved with my daughter in the first place?" I said. My rage at the deception returned.

"Because from the very first moment I saw her...I couldn't take my eyes away. She captivated me. No other woman has been real to me since. Except maybe you."

He took a big sigh and made his way back to his lab desk. "Don't you know it has always been this way with matters of the heart? It rarely chooses wisely."

He donned surgical gloves and held a tourniquet and needle with a yellow plastic cup in his hands. "With your permission Mrs. Miller..."

I sighed, nodded and held out my arm.

"So you're saying it was love at first sight?"

He shrugged. I could see a hint of the awkward Goth.

"Something like that." He tied the tourniquet securely around my arm just above my elbow, rotated my wrist, exposing the soft underside of my arm and tapped the skin where my vein stood out in blue contrast. He quickly stabbed the needle into the vein.

I winced and hissed in pain.

"Do you believe in love at first sight?" he asked. Dante's hands moved with swift confidence. He attached a medical tube into the port at one end and quickly loosened the tourniquet. We both watched the glass fill with my blood. He quickly switched to a second tube.

I had to stop and think. Did I? Was that what I felt the first time Mykhalo walked into my bookstore? Or was it just my sixth sense telling me to beware of a strange man?

And throughout my relationship I struggled to keep it casual and light, just friends with a fascinating, dangerous person. It hadn't exactly worked out that way. I realized every conversation held an underlying electricity which made my heart skip. Was that love at first sight? Some part of me believed in it. But had I experienced it?

"I...I'm not sure," I shivered. The big room was cold.

"I didn't plan to get involved with your daughter. It just…happened. I saw her and I couldn't look away. Do I need to apologize for what my heart did?"

I didn't answer.

"So you're not a medical student but a full-fledged doctor." I dodged the question.

"Yes," he replied. His concentration at the task before him never wavered.

I nodded. "And how long have you specialized in the blood of…creatures of the night?"

His smile deepened. "I was always a blood specialist." he replied. "When I found out I was…different…it just gave me more questions, more things to study. Blood is fascinating."

After drawing enough to fill several tubes, he seemed satisfied and he removed the needle.

I automatically drew my arm up to my body as if I had just donated at the blood bank.

"I would normally bandage it but I think you will find it is unnecessary in your case," he told me as he turned back to his desk.

I frowned and extended my arm to inspect the vein he had just stabbed. There was no wound or pain of any kind.

Dante still had his back to me. "Bartal's blood had some rather unusual anomalies. I'm curious to see if yours is just as unique. Before you, dhampirs were only born, not created."

His eyes turned to the lab's door and worry etched lines into his young face.

"Bree… I should go after her. I need to explain…" he made as if to leave. But I grabbed his arm and stopped him. "I understand how you feel and while it's commendable, it's exactly the wrong thing to do. You are the *last* person she wants to speak to right now. She wants to be alone with her thoughts. When she does speak, it will probably be to me, not you."

I considered my next words carefully. When I did speak, they were cold as ice. "You are her first romantic betrayal. I have no idea how she'll react."

His face looked ready to crack. He kept looking at the door.

I sighed and pulled up a chair. "Sit!" I commanded.

He crumpled, defeated into the offered chair.

"Tell me more about what you are." There was an uncomfortable silence. "Do you really expect my daughter to date you, dally with you and then, come December, put all her feelings on hold for seven years?"

Dante put his head in his hands. "No, of course not," he moaned.

"How have you handled this with past relationships?"

He looked up sharply. Yes, I knew there had been others. He couldn't hide the truth from me.

He crumpled a little more into his chair and spread his hands in helplessness. "Badly!" he said in frustration. "Look. What usually happens is a Mac Tyre is raised by his family to never get involved with anyone outside the so-called 'pack'. Romantic attachments are always complicated with my kind. Even if you do fall in love with another Mac Tyre, sometimes their cycles are outta whack. The one in human form usually guards the one in wolf form until their change comes about.

"I was orphaned as a baby. The people who adopted me had no idea about my parentage. I didn't even know I was Irish until I changed. My name was Smithson until then.

"Then, when I was twenty four and just graduated med school, I ran into another Mac Tyre. I didn't know who he was but he knew who I was. He bit me and the gene was activated. Now I change."

I nodded as I absorbed this information. "And how many women have you dated in all this time?"

He hesitated, not wanting to tell me at first. "Three before Bree." he relented.

"And where are they now?" I asked.

"Dead," he replied. "All dead."

I nodded again and pulled up a chair across from him. "Tell me about them." It was a demand not a request. I sat and waited.

He paused. "You want to know everything?" He retreated into the unsure young man I had first been introduced to.

"Oh yeah! Most definitely!" My expression left him no wiggle room.

Chapter 27

"How are you holding up, Zan?" Sage asked as she took hold of both my hands.

I gave a heavy sigh. "Somehow I never expected having children to be like this!"

We stood in front of the tall sitting room window in friendly silence.

"How come you never had any children?" I blurted out and immediately regretted it.

Sage and I had been close friends for many years. As far as I knew, she didn't have any children. I never dared to broach the subject with her. But she also never offered.

She looked like I'd slapped her for no reason. Sage dropped my hands and turned away. I suddenly had the feeling I'd asked the one question which must never be asked of Bethany Hess.

"I'm sorry," I hastened to apologize. "Forget I said anything."

But she held up a hand, halting my awkward words. "It's okay, Zan. I would never have told you if you hadn't come Germany, to this place. But now…with all that's happened…well, you deserve to know."

Sage took a deep breath. Her eyes blinked quickly, shiny with tears. "My parents died when I was six," she whispered. "They were killed by three vampires while I hid in the closet. I saw the whole thing through a crack in the door."

I gasped in shock and covered my mouth. Before I could stutter out an apology, she continued. "I must have made a sound, they must have heard me. One came and threw back the door. He saw me cowering there, scared out of my wits. He just stared at me. His hands were covered in my father's blood. I thought he was going to kill me, too. But he didn't. He just laughed at me. And then they all left."

Sage closed her eyes against the mental pain and swallowed with difficulty. She took a deep breath and plunged on. "Bartal found me the next morning."

"Wait a minute," I interrupted. "You already knew Bartal?"

Sage smiled and shrugged. "Of course, I'm one of Hope Bayer's daughters. He's been charged for centuries to protect her descendants."

My emotions were a whirlpool along with my thoughts. So Sage and I were related? Distant cousins, even sisters maybe?

"Bartal seems to do a bad job of protecting people!" was the first stunned comment I thought to make.

Sage shrugged. "Not always. Our enemies have just become... more determined lately."

She smiled in the face of my shock and continued. "Anyway, he brought me here and raised me like a father. I was understandably kinda messed up. For years I wouldn't speak. Not until puberty, but then I was a horrid child. Mad at everyone and everything. I'm sure Bartal wanted to lock me up in the dungeon for all the rotten hateful things I did and said. But around eighteen, things evened out. Bartal told me I needed direction and pushed me to go to college. I resisted, but later gave in to learn criminal investigation."

I nodded in immediate understanding. "You wanted to find who killed your parents."

She nodded.

"Wait a minute," I said. "Which college did you choose?"

Sage smiled. "Penn State."

"So," I mused. "You weren't born in Pennsylvania?"

Her smile increased. "No, I'm a Berliner born and raised. My father was an American G.I. who chose to stay because he fell in love with my mother. Does this surprise you?"

I'm sure my eyebrows hopped a bit at this. "Yes, because you have absolutely no hint of an accent. And I can usually pick out a non-native in a heartbeat."

Sage chuckled softly. "I was still mad at Bartal and I wanted to get away from him. Choosing an American college was a way to run from my problems. About the same time I discovered Wicca. Hanging around with all those New Ager's opened the floodgates for certain

188

talents I never knew I had. But I was careful to keep my Wiccan interests secret from my day job. Law enforcement barely accepts such notions now. If I could solve a crime psychically without telling anyone where my instincts came from, so much the better. Even today, only one cop knows I'm psychic. And he can barely believe it because I seem so grounded and normal to him. It's an act I work hard to present to the world. You see the other side of me because I allow you to. I trust you."

"And did you ever find the vampires who killed your parents?"

She nodded biting her lip. "Oh yes! And they've been dealt with! But what you need to hear from me is this: my parents died because I'm a direct descendant of Hope Bayer. As are you, my friend. We're distant cousins you and I. And both our families are targets of Hector's children."

My legs felt weak. I had to find a chair. "Is…this why you never had children?"

Sage took a deep breath and simply nodded. "Bartal helped me track down and kill the vamps who killed my parents. He's helped me all my life. When I was around twenty, I had a dream about you, another granddaughter of Hope and I was bound and determined to find you and protect you. I didn't expect to like you so much or to discover you were also becoming Wiccan. Somehow it just made things easier for me. Like it was meant to be I guess."

She turned her eyes away from the window and fixed me with a very narrow stare. "Zan, whatever happens to you I take very personally. You're more than my mission, more than my friend, you're kin. More than anything I wanted to prevent what Farran did to you. I was very angry at Bartal when you were first abducted. Part of me still is. Even though I know it's part of Sekhmet's sacred plan, I can't seem to get over the anger that every time I try to protect you, you're whisked away by something dangerous and deadly. I wish I could see the future in clear detail. All I want to know is that I will have a chance to blast something truly evil out of existence so I will finally have an end to all this anger and frustration I have built up inside."

My heart hurt for her. I took her hands in mine. "And what if it's still there afterwards? What will you do then?"

She sighed, withdrew and shook her head. "Probably find some vampire nest and go all Rambo on them."

"You may yet get your chance, Bethany Hess," Bartal said as he walked into the room.

CHAPTER 28

"Time for us to tell you our plans," said Bartal. A tall man with gray hair and a beard walked into the room. "This is Gregori." The new man stopped ten feet away and bowed respectfully.

I found myself rising to my feet, eyes riveted to this stranger's face. It felt like the day Mykhalo entered my bookstore.

"Tell me, Mrs. Miller, what are your first impressions of Gregori?" Bartal asked.

I still couldn't tear my eyes away. Although the hair on his head and chin were salt and pepper, his face looked young. Eyes as black as night glittered keenly at me as if a bird of prey was staring proudly down upon me from its lofty perch.

"Mrs. Miller?" Gregori addressed me. "I have heard so much about you. It is a great honor to meet you." His heavily accented voice was the deepest I have ever heard, like a Viking prince. He held out his hand to me as would a noble being introduced to an aristocratic lady. Without thought, I placed my hand in his grasp. He immediately bowed again and kissed the back of my hand, eyes never leaving my face.

An electric charge radiated through my body. I gasped in shock and tore my hand away. His hand and lips were cold as ice.

"You're vampire!" I jumped back.

Gregori straightened with a slow, smug smile. "Am I? It is daylight, you know." His dark eyes twinkled mischievously.

I took a deep breath and forced myself to think, not react like an animal. I felt his energy as best as I was able. "No," I finally said slowly. "No, that's not right. You're not vampire. But…what are you?"

"Your instincts serve you well," Gregori told me.

A shiver went through me when I realized Farran had said the same thing to me the first night he'd taken me hostage.

Sage caught me as I fell back into my chair.

"If you're not a vampire...then what are you?" I whimpered half afraid, half fascinated.

Bartal smiled, and came forward to take my hand. He rubbed it reassuringly.

"Well, done Mrs. Miller." "You sensed it without anyone having to tell you. Utterly remarkable. Don't you think so, Gregori?"

Gregori was nodded. "Very impressive. Not at all what I expected. This one has skills unheard of."

"Would you please stop talking about me as if I'm some germ on a microscope?" I demanded. "I apparently just passed some sort of pop quiz. Now what was it?"

Gregori's face broke into a wide smile. "And she has fire!" he commented. "Excellent! You're going to need every bit of it."

"Zan, Gregori is a dhampir like you." Sage told me.

"Like and yet unlike, my dears," Bartal corrected. "Dhampirs are born. Mrs. Miller was not born. A dhampir's greatest talent is to go completely undetected by the undead. If you had a room of vampires and one dhampir in their midst, none of those undead in the room could pick the imposter out. That is their strength."

Bartal settled himself in another chair and linked his fingers together. "Every vampire who walks the night knows about me. I'm the great traitor to their race, destined to be their greatest policeman. Instead I am now a pariah. Gregori here is our man on the inside."

I nodded in sudden comprehension. "You're a spy for the good guys?"

Gregori shrugged. "If you like."

"And how old are you?" I asked.

The corners of Gregori's lips twitched slightly. "Old," was his only reply. "Very old."

I nodded again. "And in all that time not one vampire has suspected you?"

"Those were dealt with quickly before rumors could spread," Bartal interjected.

Here Gregori shrugged yet again. "I have to eat sometime." He slid me a sharp look at this and a small smile.

I thought for a moment before speaking my thoughts. "Why do I need two instructors? Won't you do?" I said meaning Bartal.

He chuckled briefly. "Gregori is not here to instruct you. He is here to act as your body guard when you enter the nest."

My heart tripped and fell. "Nest?" I said. "What nest?" My eyes quickly flashed from one to another. I glanced at Sage. She took a deep breath and averted her eyes.

"What's going on here?" I asked.

"You still want to know about Kane?" Bartal replied.

I nodded without speaking.

"Well, Gregori here is our expert," Bartal waved his friend to a neighboring chair.

"You may need a drink for this, Zan dear." Sage told me. "Do you want me to get you one?"

I shook my head. I did not want my senses dulled so early on. "Not now. I'm good." I turned my attention back to the two dhampirs in front of me. "Tell me. Why do you expect me to go into their nest? That's the last thing I want to do right now!"

Here Gregori's face became dark and grim. "Because you will have to go into the nest to marry Kane."

I was glad I hadn't agreed to the drink.

"What are you talking about?" I exclaimed. "I have no intention of marrying anyone, least of all another vampire!"

Bartal growled and shot an evil look at his friend. "I would have eased her into it."

But the tall bearded man shook his head briefly. "We have no time to ease her into anything. This is going to happen and happen soon. She needs to be prepared or all our hopes are lost."

"Tact was never your strong point," Bartal growled in discontent.

"Will someone please explain this to me from the beginning?" I exclaimed.

Gregori swung his head to face me with his raptor gaze again. Once more I couldn't look away. "It's not a question of whether you *want* to get married, my dear," he told me. "Do not think this has anything to do with emotion. It doesn't. This is wholly a business arrangement. Farran turned you for this purpose only. A witch turned vampire is a powerful weapon for the Nosferatu. Your bonding to Kane will unify all the scattered clans of vampires under one single cause because you are their greatest human enemy now turned into an ally. They will join together when word gets out. This is Farran's great master plan, to turn you and then present you as a mate to the father of their race."

My heart forgot to beat. And my lungs to breathe. "Why do the vampires need to unify?" I whispered. "To what end?"

"World domination, of course," Bartal said. "When all the vampires have joined together, they will rise up and destroy the political system in every country."

"Some have done so already," Gregori interjected.

"With the political systems in ruin and vampires in control, they will be free to take over the human race," Bartal went on. "Mortals will become cattle to them, their numbers will be cataloged and controlled, their breeding will be arranged. They will be raised specifically for the purpose of feeding the vampire race."

I could not speak. My heart began to beat again but too fast. I was breathing like a horse who'd run a tough race. My mind felt numb.

"I'll get you that drink now," Sage said.

* * *

"Bree!" Dante called down a castle hallway.

Bree's eyes widened, nostrils flared, and her perfect little rosebud mouth became a stiff, hard slash on her face. She spun and hurried away.

"Wait!" Dante called again as he chased after her. "I need to talk to you!"

"I think we've done enough talking!" she said sternly, not even slowing.

Dante raced ahead of her and took her by the arm. Bree tore herself away and turned her blazing eyes on him. "Don't you ever touch me again!"

He raised both hands in mute apology. "Let me explain! Just give me a chance! Then you can leave and never speak to me again."

Bree growled, "Fine!" she heaved an angry sigh and relented. "You have just one chance! Better make it a good one!"

"Okay look, I wanted to tell you sooner but I just didn't know how." Dante closed his eyes and took a deep breath. "I mean there's no good way of saying, 'Hi! I really like you and want to go out with you but you probably won't like me anyway because I just happen to be a hundred and thirty years old and you probably think I'm outta my mind! Where are you going? I'm telling the truth!' See how it sounds?"

Bree's hands were on her hips, frown increasing. "I just wanted a normal guy and a normal relationship. Is that so much to ask?"

"C'mon Bree!" Dante smirked. A 'normal' guy couldn't handle you!"

"What?" she exclaimed in shock.

"Think about it. You're smart," he replied. "You're a teen-age American living rent free in the castle of a foreign country because a German aristocrat you're not even related to, a guy who also happens to have been a vampire, put you and your mother in his will. And your mother is a witch and so are you and from time to time an Egyptian deity possesses you. What 'normal' guy, even a nerdy one, could handle a relationship like that?"

"You lied to me!" Bree insisted. "You're over a century old. What am I to you? A baby? Practice? A sex toy to throw away when you get bored with me?"

Dante lowered his voice. "C'mon Bree. We haven't even gone there."

"Thank God not!" she spewed. "I'm so glad I found out your age before I made that mistake!"

Dante visibly winced. "So you think our relationship is a mistake? Age makes that much difference to you?"

Bree threw her hands in the air. "I'm seventeen! And you're a dirty old man!"

"Don't you believe in love at first sight?"

Bree turned her back on him. "Only girls believe in that."

Dante's face screwed up in confusion. "You had to have been told that."

"Yes. By Sage," Bree nodded. "Look. Whatever you are, I don't want to know. You could be my great grandfather. How could we possibly relate?"

Dante looked at Bree. "The first day I saw you, I fell in love with you. I didn't have a choice in the matter. I didn't know how old you were but I knew you were young. But then, compared to me, everyone is young!"

"I've never been interested in a quick roll in the sheets. That's not the way my heart works. Maybe other guys do but not me. If I'd wanted that from you I would have already taken it. Lord knows we've been alone together enough!

"But I want you to respect me. If you want me to go away and never speak to you again…well I won't like it but I'll do as you say. I'll honor your wishes no matter what you tell me to do. Just please give me a chance to prove to you my motives are honorable ones."

Bree looked deep into his eyes. He could see her doubt. She bit her lip as she mulled it over. "Tell me what you really are. No more secrets. And then I'll decide."

Dante nodded, took a deep breath and plunged forward. "My people are called the Mac Tyre. That means I'm an Irish werewolf. Except instead of turning into a wolf every full moon, I 'go wolf' for years. Seven years as a human, seven years as simple wolf."

Bree slowly digested this. "And when will you 'go wolf' next?"

Dante dropped his eyes in shame. "Sometime this December."

The expression on Bree's face became as cold as ice. "Then it's a good thing we've already broken up."

* * *

My thoughts were flowing as if in a fever dream. I'd always thought arranged marriages were a bad idea best left for the dark ages. I was grateful I lived in a culture who didn't believe in such things. But now I faced a prospect I despised intensely. And I was marrying the enemy. I had no idea how I could possibly get through this and survive.

Sage placed a shot glass in my trembling hand. I squeezed my eyes shut and gulped it fast, not caring what form of alcohol it was. I

196

slammed the glass on the table and demanded another. Sage refilled the glass twice more before I was able to talk.

I gasped, coughed and finally found my voice raspy though it was. "And what's my role in this?"

Bartal smiled. "Farran meant to make a powerful witch/vampire. But you are not that. You are something more. You are a dhampir touched by the hand of a Goddess. Deep within you lies a special fatal surprise for the Nosferatu. You will bond with their king. And then destroy them from the inside."

I understood. It didn't mean I liked what they were proposing. "I'm your Trojan horse."

"Exactly!" Gregori said with a wide smile.

"Did anyone think to ask the horse what it feels about all this?"

Bartal sighed. "Like Gregori said, we don't have much choice."

In a soft but menacing voice Gregori asked, "Would you rather it be your daughter?"

"No, of course not!" I raised my head in defiance. "Besides, she'll never be a vampire. She's drunk too much holy water. So said Farran."

Confusion crossed Bartal's face. "Where did she get holy water?"

"I taught her how to make it."

Sage spoke up. "Any witch worth her salt can make holy water. It's an easy enough process."

I began to whisper words to myself. "I should've been smart like Bree. I should've drunk it, too."

"Stop it, Zan!" Sage scolded me. "Stop second guessing yourself! If you *had* drunk the holy water, you would be no good to us now. It was meant to happen this way. Sekhmet knew what She was doing! Don't question the Divine."

I shook my head and turned to face the two dhampirs. "You have no idea what you're asking of me!" I was starting to panic now. "You need an actor for this. Not me! I have no idea what I should be doing."

"I'll show you," Gregori assured.

"C'mon, Zan!" Sage said. "You're a cat. You always land on your feet! You can do this."

My thoughts were coming too fast. "No!" I shook my head in denial. "There has to be someone else. I can't do this!"

Sage took me by both hands to steady me. "Zan dear, take it easy. Slow down and think rationally." She tried to reason with me. "There *is* nobody else, nobody with your history, nobody with your unique past. It has to be you. It's the purpose you were born to do, your sacred duty. We need you to stand with us."

I was still shaking my head. "I'll stand with you just fine as long as I don't have to marry a vampire. This is ludicrous!"

"Listen to me, Mrs. Miller," Bartal cajoled. "This is the purpose Farran created you for. We have to take advantage of his ambition and turn it to our benefit somehow. You will not be alone. Gregori will be with you as much as possible and warn you of what is to come."

My mind spun with dark possibilities. "Say I do this," I began. "Let's just say I go along with your madcap notion of saving the world from vampires…what happens next?"

Bartal and Gregori exchanged stern looks. Bartal dropped his head allowing the other to take the lead.

"Farran will summon you. When he calls, you must go. He is your sire and you must do everything he says. Or at least allow him to think you are obeying his every wish.

"Soon after he calls and is convinced the conversion has taken solid root, he will present you to his lord and master, Kane. You are to stay with Kane and find out as much as you can about his strengths and weaknesses."

Something didn't quite sound right about this and I said so. "If you're the expert on Kane, then why don't you already know all this?"

Gregori smiled. "Because you, as his dark bride, will have closer access to his mind than I ever will. It will be easier for you to investigate what exactly makes him tick."

I sighed and then voiced the one big unspoken fear which had been looming, huge and scary in my mind since this horrible proposal had first been ventured. "Am I gonna hafta sleep with the guy?"

Everyone exchanged uneasy looks. The men remained silent and averted their eyes.

Sage was finally the one brave enough to speak up. "I seriously hope it doesn't come to that!"

I sniffed, unconvinced. "I'll have to think about this," I said quietly.

"Of course you will," replied Bartal.

CHAPTER 29

I felt someone sit down on the edge of my bed. I opened my eyes to the darkness of night. The moon was either hidden behind clouds or in its dark phase. I had forgotten the passage of its cycles.

Dark as the room was, I could still see a blacker shape sitting on the edge of my bed.

I swallowed with difficultly and cracked my lips open to speak.

"Is this a dream?" I whispered to the darkness.

"Yes," the shape replied.

It swung its head about to face me. It was nothing but a silhouette and yet I could still see the gray eyes shining at me in the dark.

"Mykhalo?" I asked the shape.

He nodded.

"I am inside you now," he murmured softly to me.

I sat bolt upright.

"I'm pregnant?" I exclaimed in shock.

His lips parted and I saw his teeth flash briefly as he laughed.

"No," he replied. "I am incapable of impregnating any woman either as a human a vampire or even as a dream. I found that out many years ago."

His eyes turned back to me. "But I am still inside you."

I didn't know what he was trying to say.

"I…don't understand," I told him.

"No, you wouldn't. You were unconscious when it happened." He sighed softly and explained. "You remember when Farran released you and Bree found you?"

Wordlessly, I nodded and he went on.

"Well, you exchanged a few words and then passed out. That's when it happened."

I blinked still not comprehending. "When...what happened exactly?"

He sighed again. "When Dr. Sullivan gave you a transfusion of my blood."

I fell back into the pillows, stunned.

"He was only trying to help," Mykhalo continued and then faltered into silence.

"Did it work?" I replied.

Mykhalo's head nodded in the dark. "I'm not sure but yes, I think it did. I gave him the donation right after Sekhmet took my hunger away. I was different then, still a vampire but changed somehow."

My thoughts spun back over the past few days. "Do you know what I am now?"

He nodded.

"And do you know Farran wants to marry me to Kane? And Bartal and Gregori think I should go through with it?"

Here Mykhalo stood up and walked away from my bed, turning his back on me. He was silent for a long moment. "Yes, I know about that, too," he whispered.

My voice became hard. "I don't want to do it."

His back stayed turned to me. "You have to go through with it. There is no other way."

I shook my head forcefully. "The only person I want to marry is you."

He groaned as if I had punched him in the gut. And then he was back by my side and crushing me in the strength of his embrace. "I want that, too. More than anything."

"But you're dead."

He rocked me in his arms. "Quit reminding me!"

I heaved a heavy sigh of frustration. "Do you think I can do this?"

He released me from his embrace and touched his forehead to mine. "Of course you can! You're the strongest woman I know."

He kissed me then, deep and passionate and then he pulled away. "Do you know how much you've changed?" he told me. "I can see you differently as a spirit than I could as a vampire. When you were turned, a red light issued from you. But now that you're a dhampir, you shine like the sun. You burn my soul with the brightness of your light. I've never seen any dhampir radiate like you do now. You could bake the oceans into desert if you got really angry! You're so powerful now. You need to believe in your own strength and this will be a cakewalk to you!"

I laughed briefly. "But I don't know how to do a cakewalk."

It was a pathetic attempt at a joke for my part. Luckily he laughed. He rocked me in his arms and kissed me again. "Remember, whatever you go through, no matter how scared you get, you will never be alone." He placed a hand over my heart. "I am here inside of you. I swim in your veins. If you need my help, just wish me there and I will come to you in an instant."

He kissed me again and as he lowered me into the sheets, I felt my mind dissolve back into dreamtime. "I have to leave. *She* needs to speak to you."

I felt the pressure of his lips leave mine. "I love you Zan."

* * *

I flowed from this dream into a different one which took me away from my bed.

I stood with bare feet wriggled deep in cool sand. A million stars whirled overhead in the deep midnight blue sky. A chill wind blew and I shivered.

A deep rumble sounded behind me and a rich and throaty woman's voice spoke to my back.

"I never knew the transition for you would be so difficult. I only saw your strength. I'm sorry, my child."

I turned to look into the fathomless eyes of Sekhmet in all her red-maned glory.

I fell to my knees before her and began to sob.

"I don't want to be ungrateful," I began. But then the words spilled out of my lips before I could recall them.

"Take it back, Mother. Please take your gift back. I'm begging you."

Sekhmet purred and stroked my hair lovingly. "The gift has been bestowed," she told me. "I cannot take it back, Little Mother."

She touched my tears and they sizzled into steam. "I am truly sorry for all the grief this has caused you. But please listen to me, child. I chose you for this task years ago before you were born. This is the sacred quest you were set upon this earth to fulfill. I fashioned its beginning and I know its end. Please trust in me, little one."

I hiccupped a couple of times and tried my best to swallow my tears. My fingers dug deep into the sand in frustration as I sought to master my emotions. I took a deep breath in and out and forced the anger to go away with it. "But I don't even know how to do this," I gasped.

She gently took my chin in her warm hand and inclined my face upwards to look her in the eyes. "You're not supposed to know how!" she told me with a divinely wicked twinkle in Her eyes. "You're just supposed to do it."

She straightened and began to circle around me. "Kane can read minds. The secret to vanquishing him lies within you. But it is blocked from everyone, even you. If it is blocked, then no one can force it out of you. When the time comes, you will know exactly what to do. It will be instinctual. Trust me. This is how I designed everything which is to come."

"And what is my daughter's role in all of this?" I asked.

Sekhmet smiled. "Ahh! Your child," she breathed into the night. "She is the Pathfinder. She will find the way when all roads are lost. She will lead you when the time seems most grim."

"And a little child will lead them," I murmured softly to myself.

Sekhmet's smile increased. "Wisdom is still wisdom whatever the source. Truth does not change from one culture or religion to the next,"

She sighed. "I know you are plagued by self-doubt, about whether you can perform what is required of you in this situation. You must stop thinking this way. It is there deep inside you. I put every quality you need to carry out this mission into your very core. Even if you do not know what it is, trust me, whatever you have need of will be there. No more self-doubt. It kills success."

She faced me and looked keenly into my eyes. "You are my sacred warrior. I have blessed you with every skill needed to carry out this task. You must believe you will be successful. That is my requirement. Have faith you will accomplish this quest. If you doubt yourself, even for a second, you will fail. Do I make myself perfectly clear on this matter?"

I nodded and bowed my head. "Crystal clear, my Lady." I whimpered.

Sekhmet began to fade from view and so did the landscape around me. "Good. You are my message to Kane. This world belongs to Me, not him. You will conquer and destroy him, Zan. You are the most powerful woman who has ever been born and you have been blessed by the Goddess. None can touch you. No one can break you. Your destiny awaits. Embrace it."

I awoke from this dream with a start. I felt grit underneath my nails. My hands were clenched into fists around something. I raised my hands and focused my night vision on what it was I held. Slowly, I uncurled my fists.

Powdery desert sand sifted down onto the sheets from my fingers.

CHAPTER 30

Bree found me next morning sitting in my bedroom in a shaft of light and staring at a small glass cosmetic jar with the dream sand inside. I had no idea why but I felt the sand was important somehow. I had carefully swept up every grain and stashed it in the jar.

"What's that?" she asked innocently.

I smiled and turned the glass in my hands with a faraway look. "Sekhmet gave me a pep talk last night," I told her. "I woke up holding this."

Bree gasped and her eyes went wide. "You better not lose that! It's…" she began.

"Important?" I finished for her. "Yes, I know."

She was quiet for another moment. "Do you know what you're supposed to do with it?" she finally asked.

"No, and I don't care," I replied. "Sekhmet told me when the time came I would know what to do. So for now that's good enough for me."

A strange peace had entered my breast since I'd risen. I wasn't worried about anything anymore. Bree just looked at me for one long minute. Then she smiled and squeezed both my hands. There were no words needed. We both understood.

Bree finally sighed and changed the subject.

"I have a present for you, Mom." She handed me a small jewelry box. "It was supposed to be for Mother's Day but you were…away then."

She was referring to when Farran held me captive.

I smiled and quietly opened the small box. Inside was a gold chain with a rather singular pendant, a glass locket framed in gold filigree.

Inside it held a blonde lock of hair, braided and swirled into an intricate pattern.

I recognized the shade of hair in an instant. I gasped in surprise. "Is this...Mykhalo's?"

She grinned and bobbed her head excitedly.

"How did you get this?" I asked amazed.

"Well, I wanted to make you a necklace like we made during the ritual but from a lock of Mykhalo's hair. So the night before the funeral, I snuck down and opened his casket. But Bartal caught me. I can imagine what a sight I was hovering over a dead body with a pair of scissors in my hand! Anyway, you know what a bad liar I am. So I just gave up and told him the truth. I figured he would think I was some kind of crazy, grave robbing kid!"

My eyes prodded her to go on with her tale.

"But he was decent. Nice. He told me they used to have these things called memory lockets back in the old days. He thought it was a sweet idea. Except he said you needed something finer than a leather cord and a plastic vial! So he took the locket to a jeweler he knew and had him make this for you. I hope you like it."

"Like it? I love it!"

She beamed. "I kinda figured my vampire step-dad wouldn't mind. This way you can always keep a piece of him close to your heart."

I held back tears. Instead I busied myself with the clasp on the chain. But my vision was blurry so Bree jumped in to help me put it on.

I felt it rest cool and smooth against my skin. And then Bree was hugging me really tight. As I hugged her back, my gaze fell on the vanity mirror.

There in the mirror was the ghostly image of Mykhalo's face. Smiling.

* * *

Bree was alone in Mykhalo's rose garden Mykhalo. She wandered among the red blooms, marveling at their intense beauty and thinking on how he'd never seen his work in the light of day. The roses were so much more brilliant when touched by the light of the bright sun.

Bree leaned forward to sniff the scent of a single red blossom, larger than her fist. At the same time the sun hid its face behind a cloud. She shivered and became aware of an odd clicking emanating from the ivy climbing the wall behind the rose bush. She raised her eyes and stared into the glassy gaze of a high powered camera lens.

Her countenance grew cold. Bree straightened with a glare as the offending cameraman approached, no longer making any attempt to hide himself.

"What do you think you're doing?" she declared angrily. "Who gave you permission to take my picture?"

The photographer was slightly smaller than her and thick around the middle. He was balding and what was left of his lanky red hair was pulled back into a ponytail. Thick-paned glasses cloaked watery blue eyes. The more Bree backed away from him, the more he approached, clicking his infernal camera in her face.

"Stop that!" she demanded of him. "Go away! Who let you on the grounds?"

"No one lets me go anywhere," he giggled. He had a British accent. "I just help myself. Now I'm helping myself to you. You're such a scrumptious subject! C'mon! Pout a little more for me, love."

"Go away!" Bree said louder and then began to shout. "Bartal! Bartal!"

The little man put down his camera and laughed at her. "He can't help you, Sweetie. He's in town. So I've got you all to myself. Now show a bit more cleavage, my dear. I'm dying to get a shot of that!"

She began to circle away. But he only pursued her more, snapping away the entire time. "I'll break your damn camera, you little weasel!" she growled.

"So?" was his only reply. "I've got more cameras. Lots more. You know, I've got a whole wall of photos of you at home. It's just you now. I used to have lots of pics of your Mum, too. But she's changed recently. Doesn't record on film anymore. Did you know that?"

He lowered his camera and looked at her lecherously. "She's going to eat you someday," he told her in a softer, purposely more sinister sounding tone. "She'll drink you dry. Unless my Master gets you first."

Bree stopped. "Who is…your master?"

He smiled even wider, relishing the suspense. "Why Farran of course!"

Bree's face blanched white. She felt paralyzed with fear.

"Ah! That's the look I was waiting for!" he said in triumph. He brought the camera up and snapped away.

"Farran can't touch me!" Bree insisted with some heat. Her heart was pounding so loud she could hear it in her ears.

"Sure, sure! You just keep thinking that way," he said, clicking away on the shutter. "Besides, just because he can't drain you, doesn't mean he can't have some fun before you die. He likes to play with little girls. It's his specialty. He might even let me watch and take videos."

Bree was having trouble breathing. She was shaking all over.

"You are so pretty when you're scared!" he told her as he stuck the camera in her face. "I've got so many more scary things to tell you. Bad things are coming your way, little miss. Oh yes. Very bad things!"

A sudden roar sounded behind her. Before she had time to look, she was knocked aside. The man harassing her jerked backwards with a squawk. Bree rolled over to see what hit her.

Dante stood between them. The man's camera swung from Dante's fist by the strap. She had never seen him so angry. It chilled her bones.

"Get out of here, Ainsley!" he growled at the cameraman. "You've never been welcome here!"

"Give me back my camera!" Ainsley whined childishly.

Dante looked at the camera as if he just now remembered he had hold of it. He took it in both hands and squeezed. It began to snap, pop and crumple like a piece of paper. Dante wadded it up into a small ball and then tossed it to Ainsley.

"Here you go. Now, get out of Lion's Gate before I really get mad!"

Ainsley scrambled awkwardly to his feet. "Farran's coming!" he sputtered like a little boy having a temper tantrum. "He's coming for your mother. He'll take you too and do bad things to you! Your mangy cur can't be there all the time. Just you wait! He's not done with you yet! He's got something special in store for you!"

Dante just sniffed in scorn. "Yeah, so do we. Now get out!"

Ainsley fled.

208

Dante turned to Bree and offered his hand. She hesitated one moment only, then took it. He pulled her to her feet. They stood very close holding hands and looking into one another's eyes.

Then Dante let go and stepped back, dropping his eyes to the ground. "Did he hurt you?"

Bree shook her head and rubbed her arms. "No," she sighed in relief. "He just frightened me."

He nodded still not looking at her. "Ainsley is a weasel and a bully. If he bothers you ever again, I'll tear him limb from limb."

"But only if I give you permission, right?" Bree smiled.

Dante paused and met her gaze. He smiled in return. "Of course."

Silence fell between them.

"I didn't know you were that strong," Bree finally said to interrupt the quiet. "Have you been working out or something?"

Dante shrugged as if it was nothing. "Mac Tyres are stronger as humans than as wolves. But try to keep it to yourself."

There was another uncomfortable silence between them.

"C'mon," he finally said. "We have to tell your mother and Bartal what just happened."

Bree nodded and brushed the hair out of her face. She headed back the castle. Dante followed her close, his sharp eyes scouring every hiding place.

CHAPTER 31

Gregori promised to teach me how to be a proper dhampir. I didn't understand why but apparently this involved taking a walk through the castle woods in the hunting preserve surrounding the property.

It was about an hour away from dusk and the shadows were long. Gregori chatted about the history of the property. I was barely listening. Here we were in the woods to prepare me for challenges I would soon face and he was talking history? It didn't make any sense. But I was too polite to tell him so I just smiled and nodded at the appropriate places.

The woodland path wound us steadily downward until the sound of running water came to my ears. The well-tended trail curved off to the side at one point to end at the shore of a slow moving, wide stream.

"Ah! Here we are," Gregori said in triumph as if he had found what he needed.

I looked about. Other than being a very picturesque spot, I didn't see what he meant.

"Many times the local youths from town will break onto this property to come to this spot in the summer to swim. The water is deepest just fifty paces into the stream. Elsewhere it is too shallow to do anything but paddle."

"It's a very pretty place," I told him hesitantly. "But I don't understand why we're here."

He smiled. His smile did not reassure me. "It is here we are to begin your training." Gregori said. "Mrs. Miller, do you trust me?"

The question startled me. I looked into his face trying to determine what sort of answer was appropriate. His expression was stoic and didn't help me much.

"Well…since you're my teacher…I guess I'm going to have to," I said slowly.

He was silent for a long moment. I got the distinct impression I had said the wrong thing. "Very well then," he said. "Please take off your shoes and walk into the stream."

I imagine the look of utter bewilderment on my face was priceless but he didn't laugh at me. "Um. Why?"

"Just please do so. I will be right behind you."

"I'll get wet," was the only retort I could think of.

He nodded. "Yes, that's par for the course. Please, Mrs. Miller. I assure you there is a method to my madness."

I sighed, clenched my fists to stoke my confidence and did as he ordered. I slipped off my sneakers and socks and entered the stream.

The water was cold. It was not quite swimming season yet. I took three deliberate steps into the stream and found the ground dropped off steeply. The water was now at my calves and soaking the bottom half of my jeans.

I stopped and turned my head about to find Gregori had also slipped off his shoes and was following me into the water. He waved me to go deeper. I complied until I was standing in icy mountain melt water up to my knees. I stopped again and looked back to Gregori. He was two steps behind me. Again he waved me on.

I took a deep breath and advanced several more steps into the stream. The water was now up to my waist. My teeth should have been chattering. But I had to remind myself I was no longer human. I felt Gregori's hand on my back between my shoulder blades, urging me to advance further. I slowly obeyed. When next I stopped, the water was up to my chest. I should have been shivering uncontrollably but I wasn't.

Gregori's touch on my back suddenly changed from harmless to harmful. His hand was abruptly on top of my head and he pushed me forcefully into the water. At the same moment my feet slipped on a mossy rock and I went completely under. Icy water invaded my nose and mouth because I had forgotten to take a breath. I flailed with my arms and struggled. I gasped and coughed and bobbed to the surface.

"Do you think I'm trying to kill you?" as he said this, he pushed me under again.

Water entered my lungs and I tried to cough. I thrashed with my arms but he was still holding me down. Just when I thought my lungs would burst for want of air, he released me. I burst upward into the land of air, gasping and sputtering. Gregori stood there calmly. Before I could form words, he started speaking again.

"Think, Mrs. Miller! You are no longer alive *or* dead. You are somewhere between the two. You do not need to breathe, your blood does not need to flow, your heart does not need to pump. You can fake all these things easily enough but it is not necessary to your survival anymore. I cannot drown you if you don't let me."

As he said this, he took hold of my shoulders and forced my head underwater again. I resisted for a scant moment. Then the meaning of his words sunk into my brain. This time I went deeper, away from his hands and, hugging the uneven streambed, wriggled away from him like a salamander.

I did as he instructed. I emptied my mind of all thought and became one with the element of water. I stopped breathing. I willingly let the water take over my lungs. I opened my eyes and watched the last of my air bubbles float to the surface and burst.

I felt something, a perception of being, shift inside of me. I did not need to breathe. I took stock of what I had just learned. I was no longer mortal. I did not need my lungs to expand and contract.

"I cannot drown you if you don't let me." Gregori's words echoed in my mind.

I opened my eyes. My eyesight was different, too. The water was cold and dark. I should not have been able to see Gregori's legs because the water was so murky. And yet there they were before me, practically glowing with clarity.

Then I realized both vampires and dhampirs had night vision. My lungs ceased to hurt. In fact, nothing hurt now. I felt wholly different, strong, invincible even.

I hugged the streambed. The current was a little stronger here this close to the bottom. I allowed it to sweep me downstream and then, still hugging the bottom, I circled around behind Gregori's legs and crouched there waiting like a spider stalking a fly. I could hear Gregori from underneath the water calling for me. I could see him sway to and fro, eyes searching for me. I was sure if he turned around, he would see me. I crept silently up behind him and positioned myself perfectly.

Then I struck. I grabbed him by the ankles and jerked towards me.

I heard him shout and fall forward into the stream. Still holding one leg, I towed him underneath the water to where the current flowed the fastest. I let us both be towed downstream. I made sure he was submerged the entire time. I felt him kick and struggle against my grasp.

I smiled. It felt good to feel the struggle of one's prey in my arms. I realized what I was doing and, for the briefest of moments. I had allowed my dark side to control me.

I let go of Gregori's ankle. I watched as his flailing legs stabbed at the pebbled stream floor and righted his body. I heard him stand up, spluttering and coughing.

What had come over me?

I allowed the water to buoy me gently up and I felt my head break the surface with the quietest of tinkles as water rained off my head and back into the stream. I floated there, half my head exposed, the rest of me sitting on the pebbled floor for we were once again in the shallows. The water was still freezing but I didn't seem to care. I was part of the cold wet element and it was a part of me.

I gently expelled the water from my lungs and mouth. The current carried it away from us. I raised my head a little higher out of the water so I could speak.

"Don't you think the lesson was a bit…extreme?" I questioned him. "You could have just told me I didn't need to breathe and I would have believed you."

Gregori shook his head and water came flying in droplets off his hair. "No," he told me. "You've been human so long you have no idea how to act vampire. I had to shock your system into making your vampire traits rise up in self-preservation before you knew they were there." He stood up and began to walk towards me. "You also tried to hurt me."

"Yes," I admitted as I backed away from him.

"You have a dark side to you," he continued.

This topic bothered me. "We all have a dark side. What of it?" I growled back.

I held my ground as he stopped in front of me and bent down to jut his bearded chin in my face.

"You're dripping on me!" I glowered.

But he ignored my words. "It's very good you have a dark side," he told me. "When dhampirs have to pass themselves off as vampires, they must live in their dark side."

"But…" I began. "I don't want to."

"Get over it," Gregori frowned. "If you want to survive, that is."

CHAPTER 32

The light of the moon was blocked out by the dancing golden light of flames crackling up from the Berlin Group Home. Just an hour ago it housed some three hundred youngsters, many orphaned or from bad homes.

But the fire burned too quickly and none of the children or staff escaped.

A throng of people were gathered a safe distance away watching the conflagration. Most wept bitterly. Some had fallen on their knees and were praying for the souls of the victims. Several people tried to go inside to rescue anyone they could find. But the flames were too hot and the fire too strong. They couldn't get within a hundred paces of the building. The fire roared like a live thing and sent twisting tendrils and showers of orange sparks into the night sky to join the stars which twinkled peacefully overhead.

Sirens sounded in the distance from emergency vehicles rushing to the scene. All who watched knew they would not arrive in time to save anyone.

Far behind the throng of onlookers, well back in the shadows where no one could see their faces, stood Farran and Ainsley. The little British man was practically dancing in intense joy of the scene before him.

"What accelerant did you use to get it to burn that hot?" Farran asked.

He was amazed at the terrible beauty of the flames. He knew Ainsley, among other criminal talents, was an insane pyromaniac but he had no idea the little bastard was so skilled at setting such a huge, fast moving fire. Farran had observed since before the blaze took off. One moment it was just a very big old building which had stood for centuries. The next, it was a literal firestorm. Every floor seemed to have caught fire at once. It was as if the edifice itself exploded in flame.

"A magician does not divulge his secrets!" Ainsley declared proudly.

Wainwright was giddy and practically gleeful over what he had done, prancing about like a child who had aced some test and been congratulated by parents who rarely gave out compliments.

He abruptly stopped his capering as if something bad just occurred to him. "Will the Master be okay?" he asked.

Farran cast his gaze back to the burning building before him and smiled. "Ask him yourself. Here he is," he replied.

As he said this, a shadow separated itself from the smoke and flames. Unseen by any of the onlookers, it coalesced into a dark, solid human shape. They could see glittering eyes burning like the flames behind him as he surveyed the scene. Those eyes alighted on Ainsley and Farran and at once began to approach..

Farran could hear Ainsley gasp and shudder behind him. "Will I be able to walk through flames like that when I take the blood oath?" he asked in utter amazement.

Farran turned his face away so Ainsley wouldn't see his smirk of ridicule. "Of course you will!" he lied. "You'll be able to do anything you want then." Ainsley squealed in eagerness.

As the shape came closer it seemed to become more and more human in every aspect.

Farran fell to his knees and dropped his eyes to greet his lord and master. Ainsley followed suit.

"I hear the anthem of my people!" Kane declared as he came closer. "They sing the song of death and destruction." He meant the crowd gathered, watching the building burn.

"Kane," Farran breathed in awe. "You are flesh once again."

The shape towered over them both. "Yes, I have fed well this night."

Farran cast his eyes on the blazing edifice and shrugged. The lost innocent lives meant nothing to him. He told himself the children were probably all Turks anyway. This was the way he saw human death. It was a perception most vampires shared.

Kane turned his eyes from the burning building back to Farran. "I am now ready to take the throne. Has all been properly arranged?"

Farran never lifted his head. "Yes, my Lord. All the scattered vampire clans have united and eagerly await your rule."

"Including my bride?" he snarled. "Is she still mortal?"

Farran did not dare to look up. "No, my Lord. She has taken the blood oath. I am awaiting her baptism in blood before I collect her and bring her to you."

"What?" Kane exclaimed. "She has not yet massacred?"

"Not to my knowledge, Sire," he hastened to reassure his master his plan was still on track. "But do not be angry. I am sure she cannot hold out much longer. She will blood soon. I will know when it happens and present her to you then."

Kane nodded. "Do not delay when it does," he ordered. "I have changed my mind and now I am quite eager to meet this upstart young vampire everyone seems to love and despise so much. She sounds…intriguing."

Farran smiled to himself. "My Lord will not be disappointed, I assure you."

* * *

Gregori and I returned to the castle. He had already changed into new dry clothes, but I was still in a robe, busily drying my hair as I sat at the vanity in my bedroom. Bartal perched on the edge of my bed. Yes, I know how all this sounds but for some reason, I was no longer afraid of either of them.

We were discussing the recent events as I dried my hair with a towel.

"Am I going to be expected to kill?' I asked.

"Of course!" they both replied in unison.

I sighed in frustration and put down the towel. "Then we have a problem here." I turned and gave them both, in turn, a very serious glare.

I could tell by their expressions they weren't following me.

"Look, you two," I explained as patiently as I was able. "I'm Wiccan. I took a vow when I became a practicing witch as all witches must. 'Do as thou wilt and it harm none.'"

Bartal heaved a sigh of aggravation. Gregori made some sort of gesture which seemed to suggest he would handle this part.

"Mrs. Miller, I understand your hesitation..." he began.

"I'm not hesitating," I reiterated firmly. "You don't seem to get it! This isn't a hobby. This is my sacred pledge. It's how I live my life. And it's as important to me as anything the Catholic Church might have made you swear. You're asking me to break that promise? I will not kill."

Gregori stepped closer and pulled up a chair so he could sit across from me.

"Look, Mrs. Miller," he began in a soft, placating tone of voice. "No one is asking you to break your religious vows. I respect your devotion to your faith, really I do. The last thing I want is for you to feel you must do something which goes against your ethics.

"Vampires are not alive. They are not dead. They are caught somewhere between. Their souls have descended into the darkness that every person tries to rise above as mortals. They no longer think or behave as they would have if they were still alive. Killing a vampire is bringing a soul into the light, returning them to the good person they had forgotten they were. You will be saving them that way, not destroying them."

I attacked my hair with the brush and growled. I felt I was being pushed in a direction I did not want to go.

Bartal chimed in. "And you've forgotten that you still have to eat."

I stopped what I was doing and looked at him. "What do you mean?" I said. "I can eat just fine now that I'm a dhampir."

But Bartal shook his head. "You are still as much a predator now as when you were a vampire," he told me. "Look, Mrs. Miller. Do you think the lion feels sorry for the gazelle when he chases it down and kills it? If he did, he would never eat again. The gazelle is food, plain and simple. Well, you are a dhampir now. You may be able to eat food but you must supplement your diet with blood. And only vampire blood will do. If you don't do this, you will sicken and die. There's no other way around this."

"Vampires and dhampirs do not come in vegetarian, Mrs. Miller." Gregori added. "Somehow you must make this fit into your belief system. What do you think your Sekhmet would say?"

Oh, I knew exactly what Sekhmet would say! She would say this was all Her plan, it was fine and to get the Hell over it, more or less. I rolled my eyes and tossed my brush onto the vanity in submission.

The door to my bedroom popped open and Bree rushed in panting with Dante right behind her. "Mom! I have to talk to you! Good! Bartal's here too. I…"

Dante spoke up. "I caught Ainsley Wainwright in the rose garden taking pictures of Bree."

"What?" Bartal exclaimed in fury and stood up.

"What's the little weasel doing here?" I fumed. "And why is he taking pictures of my daughter?"

"Don't worry, Mrs. Miller," Dante hastened to reassure me. "I destroyed the camera and chased him off." He looked at me before he remembered not to and then cast his eyes down.

"Mom, he says he has pictures of you, too. Until you stopped showing up on film," Bree went on.

It was now time for me to stand up. "What? Why? Who is this little bastard?" I glowered before I remembered I usually didn't use language like that in front of my daughter.

"He is Farran's day walking spy," Gregori told us. "What did he do to Bree?"

My daughter had a stalker? *I* had a stalker? I was getting angrier by the moment.

"Nothing physical other than take her picture and try to frighten her," Dante said.

I turned my full attention on my daughter. I took hold of her arms. "What did he tell you?"

"He said he and Farran were going to do bad things to both of us…" She hesitated, shuffled awkwardly before blundering on. "…And that you were going to eat me," she said and her eyes got really big.

I hugged her close and tight.

"Of course I didn't believe him," she added, her words muffled by the terrycloth of my robe.

"So that's what he's waiting for," Bartal mused aloud softly.

"What are you talking about?" I growled.

Bartal began to pace the room as he thought things through. "He's waiting for you to blood," he mused as he paced. "He has no idea you are now a dhampir so he's waiting for you to make your first massive kill."

"Aha! That's our next step!" Gregori said in triumph.

Bree separated herself from me and put her hands on her hips. "Hello! It would be nice to hear this grand plan from the beginning!"

Gregori explained. "Every new vampire needs to massacre and to survive the consequences before being accepted into Nosferatu hierarchy. They get turned loose to deal with their new reality and the first time the blood lust comes on them away from their sire, they go crazy and kill everyone they come upon. If they do this and survive being caught and killed by an angry mob, their sire takes them into his clan and teaches them the ways of the Nosferatu."

Bartal stepped in. "Farran is waiting for you to kill Bree and everyone in this castle."

"But…" Dante spoke up, "that's not going to happen now she's a dhampir. Right?" he looked back and forth from Bartal to Gregori. "Right?"

CHAPTER 33

It was midnight. The moon had hidden its face behind the clouds. Zan slumbered in the great canopy bed.

Her bedroom door was gently and furtively eased open. Gregori approached the bedside silently. He peered intently into her face. He finally nodded, satisfied she truly was asleep. He returned to her door, opened it wide and gestured. Eight robed and hooded figures filed softly into the room. Gregori shut the door as seven took their places about her bed. The tallest monk removed his hood, revealing a man's face with a white beard and tattoos dancing around his hairline.

"I am sorry to make you speak but I do not share your gift," Gregori explained in a low voice.

Zan moaned and stirred restlessly. All froze in response, afraid she would awaken. Then the monk gestured to the others. Cowled heads nodded and they began to chant. Zan's breathing deepened.

"All who hear them will sleep," the head monk explained.

Gregori and the tall priest stepped to Zan's bedside.

"So you believe this one to be the chosen mother child the old prophecies foretold?" he asked in a stern voice. "We risk much exposing ourselves like this if you are wrong."

"I am not wrong." Gregori assured. "The prophecies foretold a time would come when a woman, a mother of a girl child, one who was new to the blood oath, one who remembered the old ways, would come. Her coming would coincide with Kane's awakening. She would be the only hope this world has for deliverance."

The priest gave him a doubtful look. "We have been trying to vanquish Kane for centuries. He always eludes us. And when he escapes, more of our order die. We are already so few in number. We cannot afford more loss. If you are wrong and she is not the one...." He paused and turned his gaze back to the woman who slumbered in the bed. His face was dark with deep shadows. "Then you have just signed our death warrant."

"Test her and you will see I am not wrong," Gregori insisted.

The monk sniffed skeptically but nodded. He gestured to one of the chanting monks. This one stepped to the head of Zan's bed across from Gregori and removed his cowl. If Zan had been awake, she would have recognized him as the monk who met with her secretly in the labyrinth.

"Since you too agree with this madness, you will test her," he instructed.

The monk nodded obediently and knelt by her bedside. He quietly took Zan's arm and drew it toward him. He turned her hand over so her palm faced up. He produced a bejeweled dagger from underneath his robes and slashed her wrist deftly. Blood immediately welled up and began to run from the wound. The monk raised her wrist to his lips and closing his eyes with a prayer, he drank.

Gregori and the head monk waited breathlessly. The others continued to chant.

Suddenly the kneeling monk rocked back on his heels with a gasp. His eyes flew wide open. "Father! She is the chosen one. But there's more besides," he said in utter amazement. "She's Kurgan!"

"What?" the priest exclaimed in disbelief. Some of the monks faltered in their chant. Zan moaned and stirred again. The head monk growled in irritation and motioned for them to continue with their task.

He turned back to the kneeling monk and glowered. "I don't believe you! Show me!" He produced a chalice which was tied to his belt. He passed it to the kneeling monk who nodded and obediently set about his task. He caught the blood running from Zan's wrist and passed it across the bed to the head of his order. The priest gave his disciple another glowering look of disapproval before turning his attention to the cup before him. He drank deeply of Zan's blood.

For a moment no one in the room moved. The other monks continued to chant. But they all waited for their elder's pronouncement.

Finally the head priest lowered the cup, staring into its depths as if he'd never seen it before. His incredulous gaze turned to the sleeping woman.

"The Kurgan people are extinct as a pure race," he murmured softly into the room. "They were exterminated or intermarried out of existence. But there's Kurgan blood in her. It's very faint, barely detectable. But it is there."

The kneeling monk raised her arm to show his master. "Look Father. She's already healed."

Gregori nodded and grunted in response. "Her blood is strong even if it is not pure. She will make a formidable weapon against Kane."

The kneeling monk stood. "Father! We must give her the marks."

Gregori refused. "Absolutely not. It's out of the question."

The monk insisted. "We must make the marks on her. It's her birthright!"

Gregori growled, "Her blood is dilute."

The kneeling monk rose halfway to his feet, "Please!"

Gregori became more combative. "The marks haven't been put on a new convert in centuries. Besides, if we mark her and someone sees, then you risk complete exposure."

The head priest raised his hands, gesturing for silence. "She will take the marks," he said with a tone of finality. "They will help and protect her in the time to come. And since she is the chosen one, it's a risk I am most willing to take. If she is to go up against Kane, she will need all the support we can give."

Gregori grumbled but relented.

"Do not worry," the other monk told him as he threw back his robes and produced a pouch which swung from his simple rope belt. "I have recently learned a new modern art form. These marks will only reveal themselves under the light of the full moon. And I will put them in places not normally revealed."

Gregori laughed. "Really? Have you seen the way women dress these days?"

The elder shook his head. "A series of marks will be placed on her for her safety during the following nights. We cannot hide all of them. Some will be in exposed areas. But as I have said before, it's a risk I am willing to take. Now proceed."

Gregori still seemed unconvinced. "Are you sure she will have no memory of this?"

"Quite sure," the head priest replied. "As long as the choir keeps chanting."

CHAPTER 34

I struggled to concentrate on Gregori's words. I told myself I had to pay attention. But I was tired and I yawned uncontrollably. I hid it as best I could.

In addition to my weariness, I was bothered by a strange rash that itched on the back of my neck and the inside of my arms. It was unnerving.

Again I yawned and this time Gregori caught me.

"Am I boring you?" he asked sharply. His tone was one of irritation.

I whimpered. I'd been found out. I chose to go with honesty instead of trying to brush it off. "I'm sorry, Greg..."

"My name is not Greg! It's Gregori!" His aggravation was now plainly obvious. "Why must you Americans always abbreviate things?"

I wanted to snap back, but with an effort I calmed myself. "I apologize, Gregori," I began again. "But I'm very tired and I don't know why. It's making it hard to concentrate on what you're trying to teach me."

His anger seemed to dissipate somewhat. "Your body is changing," he told me at last.

He had my immediate attention. "What do you mean?"

His tone became more patient. "Your system is trying to alter to that of a dhampir. You will need to be awake and alert during the night to pass yourself off as a vampire so it's trying to compensate by making you sleep during the day. It will take some adjustment to be awake both day and night. You will have to catch your sleep in small bits as time affords."

He paused another moment. "Go. Get some sleep. We'll continue your tutelage when you awaken," he told me.

I hesitated one moment only then eagerly bolted for my room. I felt his eyes following me as I left. My neck itched more.

* * *

"You look like you're doing research," Bree commented.

I was so involved pouring over books in the library that I had not heard her enter. "I am," I replied barely looking up from the book. "What do you know about the Kurgans?"

I felt rather than saw her face wrinkle. "You mean from the movie, 'Highlander'?" she said in a confused tone of voice.

"No!" I shot back impatiently. "*Real* Kurgans, the people. What do you know about them?"

She pulled out her new smart phone and began to peck away.

"Put away your infernal modern device!" Bartal declared as he walked into the room.

We both turned to face him.

"If you want to know about the Kurgan people, ask me," he said gruffly. "Not a book. Not a handheld machine."

I decided to take him up on his challenge. "Very well then," I replied. "Tell me about the Kurgans."

Bartal sighed crossed his arms across his broad chest and launched into his tale. "The Kurgans were a race of prehistoric people. At first they were migratory, herding their animals to pasturage around the region. Later they built small settlements and finally one large city on the shores of the Black Sea."

I absorbed all this information like a sponge. "Are there any still around?"

Bartal shook his head briefly. "No. An earthquake many centuries ago swallowed up their great city. It is at the bottom of the sea now. Those who survived intermarried and the Kurgans, as a pure people, became extinct, swallowed by the sands of time."

"Like Atlantis," murmured Bree.

Bartal turned his black eyes on her. "We know even less about the Kurgans than we do of Atlantis. Many theologians believe it never happened. It is just a story which cannot be proved or disproved."

Bartal turned his attention back to me. "Why this sudden curiosity about a dead race?"

I sighed and rubbed my face. "I had a dream about a people called the Kurgans and when I woke I couldn't remember much. I just had this insane desire to find out more. It's important somehow. But I have no idea why."

Bartal grunted. "I've told you all I know. They are a dead people. They took their secrets with them."

His words triggered a memory deep inside me.

Two can keep a secret if both of us are dead.

The random thought perplexed me even more. I wondered where it came from and what it referred to.

"If that is all, Mrs. Miller...?" Bartal didn't finish the sentence.

Preoccupied, I nodded and waved him away. I even forgot to say thank you.

* * *

Bartal left calmly. Once out of sight he rushed through the castle halls. He met Gregori going the other way and took the Russian by his arm with a sharp look. "Come with me."

Gregori looked confused but did not argue. Bartal led him Mykhalo's former personal chambers and unlocked the great doors. The two entered and Bartal relocked the doors behind them. He took Gregori to the old art room and shut the door.

"Mrs. Miller just asked me about Kurgans!" he told him in an apprehensive tone of voice. "She's beginning to remember. You told me it wouldn't happen!"

"Let her!" came a disembodied voice from behind him.

They both turned to see the image of Mykhalo staring back at them from the long mirror.

"Zan is like no other dhampir who has ever been," he told them calmly. "She was bound to remember eventually."

Bartal nearly fell to his knees in shock. He had heard stories of Zan running into Mykhalo's ghost. He'd tried not to feel jealous that she could see and speak to him but Bartal himself, who had known Mykhalo for most of his three hundred years, could not.

Mykhalo's shade looked him in the eye and smiled kindly. "Hello, blood brother. It's good to see to you. I have missed you."

Bartal stuttered a bit before he could manage words. His chest felt tight and his eyesight was blurry. With an effort, he mastered his emotions. "Why now? Why didn't you speak to me before?"

Mykhalo's expression in the mirror became apologetic. "Because before I could only speak to one person. I had to learn how to project myself in this form. I'm steadily improving. And this time I really need to speak to you both."

"Mrs. Miller needs to hold her tongue about the Kurgans," Gregori told him. "If too many people know we are not all dead…"

"She's Wiccan!" Mykhalo broke in. "She knows how to keep secrets!"

The tall Russian shut his mouth but frowned.

"Gregori, I need to ask your permission," Mykhalo said.

He turned his gaze back to the mirror.

"I need to be with Zan when she goes to meet Kane. She may need my help. May I borrow your form if things get...problematic?"

Bartal spoke up. "Gregori will be with her every second she is with Kane. He is among the trusted few in the highest inner circle closest to him. He knows better than anyone else what is needed."

"I realize that," Mykhalo reassured. "I'm not doubting his fitness. But I want to be there in case Zan needs my help. That's why I'm asking his permission."

"No," Gregori said suddenly.

Both Mykhalo and Bartal turned their eyes to the tall Russian.

"But I…" Mykhalo began again.

"I said *NO!*" Gregori reiterated in a furious tone. "My body is not some ghost's playground even if the ghost *was* my friend. No, you do not have my permission!"

He spun on his heel and stalked out of the room in anger. "No!" he repeated over his shoulder. "Never ask this of me again."

CHAPTER 35

"So how do I pass myself off as a vampire?" I asked of Gregori when next we were together.

He circled my chair in the library. He was quiet for a moment as he pondered his reply.

"Do you remember when I…'baptized' you?" he finally said.

"How could I forget?" I muttered.

He ignored my tone of voice. "We spoke of every person having a dark side," he continued.

"Yes," I replied. Somehow I had a feeling I was not going to like where this conversation would end up.

"You are going to have to embrace your dark side, Mrs. Miller."

I swallowed with difficulty. "Just what does that entail exactly?"

Now I knew I wasn't going to like the outcome!

"A vampire feels no fear," Gregori explained slowly. "They have no doubt, they do not worry what other people might think of their actions. Morals or religion do not govern their decisions. They are always confident and feel superior over every being they encounter whether it be vampire or mortal. Life is cheap to them. They do not feel remorse over the death of a human, any human. Pain is much like pleasure to a vampire."

He turned to face me and took hold of the arms of my chair. "When you are in the presence of Kane and the other vampires, remember to keep your head high. You are going to be welcomed as a queen of the undead. You must act the part!"

Apprehension welled up in my throat. "Uh…okay," I replied hesitantly. "Just how do I do that?"

Gregori resumed his pacing along with his explanation. "When the other vampires meet you, they will admire and despise you all at once. They will covet your position on the throne at Kane's side. They will be most eager to please you but they will be just as eager to take your place. Vampires know this is true of their own kind and therefore they trust no one. Killing another vampire is just another step up the stairway of their hierarchy.

"When they first bring you into their inner sanctum, they may try to test your resolve. They may murder someone in front of you to see if you will act shocked. You must appear anything but shocked. Kane may try to get you to feed in front of them to prove to all gathered that your conversion to the undead is real. I will try to discourage this if I am able."

I took a deep breath. This was going to be one hell of an act for me to pull off!

"So basically, I'm to act aloof and removed from everyone else. I'm better than anyone in the room and the only emotions I can show are sadism, seduction and annoyance."

Gregori smiled and spread his arms. "Exactly! Do this and you will fool everyone, even me."

I grumbled. "Sounds like playing with the mean girl bullies from high school!"

"That is a modern spin but a very apt description," he agreed. "Vampires are so self-assured that everything they do is right for them and it's all they really care about. They care nothing for right or wrong anymore. If it makes them happy, they'll do it. They feed on the fear and loathing from those around them."

"Need I remind you I haven't taken a single acting lesson in my life?"

Gregori did not seem bothered. "You are a dhampir now, Mrs. Miller," he said. "I think when you finally try to act the part, you will find it comes very easily to you. Dhampirs were designed this way. They wouldn't survive long if they weren't natural actors."

I tried to remember Sekhmet's words to me. *No more self-doubt. It kills success.*

I took a deep breath and tried my best to shove my apprehension away. I wondered what kind of an actress I was going to turn out to be. I needed to face my reality and prepare for my 'debut'.

"When will Farran come for me?" I asked.

Gregori stopped and raised his bearded chin a little. "When you have blooded."

I remembered when I had bitten Bartal and I winced at the memory. "But…I've already done that…" I told him but he interrupted.

"No! You did not," he clarified. "You only nipped him. Farran will come for you when have made your first kill. He will know when it happens. He is your sire. He will feel the rush of emotions inside of you and know you have killed. Then he will come for you."

I nodded. "Does it mean he can read my mind?"

Gregori gave me a very stern glare. "Yes. Be very careful of your thoughts when you are around him. Do not let him pick up on anything you don't want him to know. Don't let your thoughts stray."

I swallowed with difficulty. "Can Kane do that, too?"

He smiled. "Kane is even better at reading minds than Farran. The only thing standing in the way of him reading your mind is he is not your sire. It is easier for sires to read their spawns' minds than unrelated vampires because of the shared blood."

Gregori circled around me and stood behind me. Then he continued. "Please be careful of your thoughts when you are in their sanctum, Mrs. Miller. They can attack you from inside your mind. Remember this."

This was beginning to sound more and more complicated.

"How long is this charade going to take?"

He strode up to the great window and shook his head. "One night. Several. I'm not exactly sure. We will have to let the Nosferatu take the lead."

I grumbled. "So I'm going to need more than an overnight bag!"

Gregori turned to face me, gave an exasperated sigh and frowned. "Why do you cloak all your fear in humor?"

The question took me aback for a moment. I had to change gears to think about what he said. "Fear and humor have a lot in common," I told him. "We joke about things we are afraid of. Humor releases the tension."

I could see by his expression, he had not expected an answer and my words made him stop and think.

"You are quite correct now I think about it. Strange. You are so young and yet you say things which have not occurred to me in hundreds of years. You change my perspective. I see now why Mykhalo loved you so much."

I sniffed ruefully. "I hope Kane sees it that way, too!"

He waggled his head in a hopeful way and returned to the former topic. "You will need nothing," he explained. "Farran will come and collect you. We will follow. Here. Wear this ring."

He passed me a flashing bit of gold. It looked to be a signet ring. On its face was the etching of a roaring male African lion with tiny chips of blue diamonds for eyes and a slightly larger red ruby grasped in the canines of its mouth. A simple twisted design framed the ring.

"It is bugged. It will allow us to track you and listen in on your conversation when you are in their compound."

I admired the ring for a moment, then slipped it onto my middle finger. It felt warm and comforting like it belonged there.

"One more thing," Gregori added. "You may believe yourself to be safe from the vampires during daylight hours. But you will not be safe from Kane. He does not like bright sunlight, but it will not kill him. And he has slept for centuries. He no longer has any need for sleep. Do not let your guard down for one second, Mrs. Miller."

I stroked the beautiful lion ring where it sat couched on my finger. I knew it had been Mykhalo's. His presence still remained on the ring. "I think I'm going to need to pray," I murmured finally.

"We're all going to need to pray, Mrs. Miller."

CHAPTER 36

I knocked on the door. Silence greeted my ears. I rapped louder and again a third time.

Finally my ears were graced by the sound of movement inside. There was a mumble of acknowledgement, some scraping sounds and finally the door cracked open a tiny bit.

Dante's eyes peered out. He seemed surprised and slightly fearful to find me on the other side of the door to his personal quarters.

"What do you want?"

"Dante, I need to speak to you in private. May I come in?" I couldn't understand why he seemed so guarded all of a sudden.

There was a long pause.

"Wait a minute," he said at last.

The door shut and I heard more scraping sounds from beyond. I supposed he was tidying up a bit. Then the door popped open and he awkwardly gave me permission to enter his castle apartment.

"I'm sorry for the odd reception just now, Mrs. Miller," Dante apologized. "But when you've been hunted as long as I have, people knocking on the door tend to make one nervous."

I stepped inside and stopped. The décor of his place insisted one halt and just gaze about for a few moments. It was cluttered like I expected. But the mess was so…interesting. It looked like a college kid and a steamship pirate bunked together. There were rock bands and old horror movie posters on the wall. The bookshelves were crammed with more than just books. There was an odd assortment of hats scattered about. The first screamed steampunk. It was a top hat adorned with brass goggles. The overhead light fixture looked like it had been customized. It had started out as a hunter's chandelier fashioned from deer antlers. But somewhere along the way it looked like it had crashed through the parts supply of an antique clock repairman's collection. Gears, sockets and bolts shone from it and somehow the light fixture told time and had a working cuckoo bird hidden in an ingenious little alcove inside.

Dante noticed my close inspection and sniffed awkwardly. "My vain attempt at being artistic," he explained. "I get these ideas but when I sit down to do them, everything kinda goes crazy. People are either fascinated or disturbed by the results."

I just kept walking around, gazing up at the lamp from different angles. Every position of observation seemed to grace the watcher with a new little bit of discovery. "Definitely eye catching!" I commented. "It's very busy. There's a lot of things going on inside. But I think I like it. Um…what do you call…it?"

Dante just laughed. "Some things should not be named," he said in mock seriousness. "Bree likes it, too. She calls it my impossible, time-telling mess."

"My daughter has been in your bedroom?" My mind started to race.

He gave me a sharp look. "Yes, for about five seconds! She knocked on my door like you did just now and barged her way in. My 'mess,'" he pointed at the light fixture above us, "distracted her a bit. I told her she shouldn't be in here. Nice girls didn't do that sort of thing. Her mother wouldn't approve. I shoved her out the door and forbid her to ever enter my room again. If you don't believe me, please go ahead and ask her."

"Oh I plan on it!"

He nodded. "I'm not worried. You daughter is not the lying kind. You raised her better than that."

I knew he was just trying to stroke my ego. It worked. With an effort I pushed my maternal instincts aside. What he said still did not change what I was about to propose. He still loved my daughter. This made him the best person to ask. His words jerked me back to my real purpose.

"I need to talk to you about Bree."

The boyish countenance immediately disappeared from his face and he became an all too serious adult again. "You do know we broke up," he said quietly.

I saw no other place to sit which wasn't already occupied with something. So I sat on the edge of his bed. For some reason it was the most organized thing in the room, neatly made with the covers tucked in as if the maid had done the bed and nothing else. But it still seemed far too big and grandiose for this little wisp of a young man.

"Yes, she told me," I said gently. "But you still love her."

He turned his back to me and hung his head. "Yes."

"It's because of your love for her that I trust you most with what I'm about to say.

A look of confusion darkened his young features. "Go on."

I took a deep breath and began my proposal. "Look. Things are going to get very dicey in the next few days and nights. The time I was kidnapped by Hector...I thought I made it clear to Bree she was to stay with Bran. She didn't listen. She went on ahead and alone. She ended up getting captured by Hector's children. It was only by the grace of the Goddess she wasn't killed or turned into a vampire."

I paused and considered my words for a moment. "Bree is young and impulsive. She charges in where angels fear to tread. A lot!"

I met Dante's gaze with a very stern maternal glare. "Stay with her. Whether she is willing or not, you stay with her, whether you have to be open about it or stalk her movements like a thief in the night, you stay with her. Guard my little girl."

Dante's face looked like it was going to crack. And then he was suddenly on his knees before me, holding both my hands in his firm grasp. "Mrs. Miller, I promise you, if I have to die to save her, I will!" he swore.

I laughed briefly. "I hope it doesn't come to that!" I said. "But listen carefully, Dante. Farran has no use for Bree save as a knife to stick into me and twist. He cannot convert her. She's drunk too much holy water. So he will mean to kill her. If he can do it in front of me or Kane, so much the better."

I pulled my face in close to his and stared him straight in the eye. "Don't you dare let him do that," I warned. "If she dies because you fell down on the job...then I really *will* give in to my dark side! And you'll be the first person I come after. Understood?"

He swallowed once. "That's not going to happen, Mrs. Miller," he assured me. "I'll keep her safe. I promise you. I'll always keep your little girl safe even if she hates me forever for it."

"Well, make sure that you do. I for one do not want to know what I'm like when the dark side of Zan comes out. I'm not sure the world can take it."

CHAPTER 37

Kane stalked through the halls of his compound. He was not happy. Something was not right.

He cast his eyes about at the throng of vampires gathered to socialize near his presence. They all looked up at him hopefully.

He ignored their eager faces and searched the room.

Somebody was missing. Kane smelled the air.

"Where's Ainsley?' he growled at no one in particular.

A red-haired lady seated close by sniffed in disdain and rolled her eyes. "That little poser?" she scoffed as she tossed her red mane over milky shoulders. "He said something about setting up more surveillance cameras around the Lion's Gate. Night vision lenses or something or other."

Kane spun on her. "And you let him go?" he exclaimed.

The woman drew back slightly, not sure of what she had done to anger him so. "Well yes," she retorted. "He's not my pet!"

Kane marched to her in a threatening manner. She drew back at his advance. She had been reclining on a long couch, her hands behind her. She wore a strapless red and black lace gown which left her shoulders and much of her chest bare, almost indecent, and the milk white mounds of her breasts bloomed above her bodice. The expression on her heart-shaped face with full red lips suggested she didn't know whether to prepare to surrender or defend herself from Kane.

He stopped two steps away from her. "What is your name?" he demanded.

"Katya," she replied at once.

"Well, Katya." Kane told her with a smug sneer. "Go get that idiot Ainsley Wainwright and bring him back here. Any way possible."

Katya blinked at him in confusion. "But…he's Farran's cur!" she complained. "Let him do it!"

Kane's eyes narrowed and with a snarl he picked her up by the arms and shook her until her head snapped back and forth. Perfectly coiffed red curls flounced about her face.

"Do you see Farran here right now?" he shouted. He flung her back onto the couch then hovered until she cowered with her arms up defensively and turned her face away.

"Farran has been told to keep his dog on a short leash!" Kane scolded her. "He was strictly instructed to keep him away from the castle. I will deal with Farran. You deal with the mortal. Bring Ainsley Wainwright back here as soon as you can. Or you will be the entertainment for the evening! Is it clearly understood?"

Katya peered up at Kane between red polished fingernails.

Kane had embarrassed her in front of all gathered. Her eyes glittered dangerously as she set her perfectly painted lips in a hard line. Katya rose to obey.

CHAPTER 38

Things were happening too fast. The weight of what was expected was a heavy burden. I couldn't rest and I couldn't stop thinking. How did I get to be the expected savior? I didn't want the job! I wanted someone else to do it.

I tried to think of what Sekhmet had told me, that self-doubt would kill any chance of success I had in this 'mission'. But at the moment, I lacked any confidence at all. Inescapable. Insurmountable. It was too big. I didn't want to deal with it. I wanted to run away from it all.

I wanted my mother to hold me.

I found my feet leading me to the art room and the mirror. I needed to talk to Mykhalo. I needed him to embrace me with his words if nothing else. Before long I stood in the dark before the mirror. The shadowed room was briefly lit by flashes of an approaching storm.

"Mykhalo?" I called out into the darkness. Only rumbles of thunder answered me. "Mykhalo, I need to talk to you," I said a bit louder.

A flash of lightning lit up the silent faces in the paintings around me. "Please talk to me. I feel so overwhelmed by everything. I really need to hear your voice."

Silence was my only answer. A great pang of emptiness welled up deep inside my chest. Why was he not speaking to me? I thought of the conversation we had previously where I berated him for hanging around as a ghost and interfering with my grieving process. Maybe he'd heeded my angry words and truly left me for good. I did not feel his presence anywhere.

A thunderous crack of lightning crashed right outside the window. I jumped, startled at the violence of it.

No one answered my pleas either living or ghost. I was completely alone in a room surrounded by paintings of people long dead. Now Mykhalo was one of them.

Rain began to fall outside in angry sheets.

There was no one to console me. I sank to my knees and began to cry. The lightning flashed again and I noticed something in the wild light.

I was weeping tears of blood.

* * *

It was nearly midnight. Dante hovered over his microscope. From time to time he looked away to log his observations. It was late and he was very tired. But still he pushed himself to finish this last task before retiring. Outside the rain poured and lightning flashed. It would have been eerily quiet but for the din of the weather. He could feel the thunder through the soles of his feet. Even this far underground the air had changed. It smelled electric, almost like burned wire and old wet stones.

Dante looked up from his work. Something wasn't right. There was a strange scent in the air undetectable to most. But not to Dante. He closed his eyes and breathed in, trying his best to ascertain the source of the smell.

Then his eyes flew wide and he stood up so quickly his chair toppled over with a clatter. At the same moment, Bartal burst into his lab, drenched with rain and holding a backpack slung over one shoulder.

"It's time!" he said breathlessly. "There's a vampire on the property!"

"I know. I sensed it, too," Dante said.

"You know what to do?" Bartal asked quickly.

Dante gave one short quick nod. The young man tossed Bartal a set of keys. "The cabinet to your right," he directed by pointing. Dante headed to his desk across the room.

Bartal opened the medical cabinet to find it full of plastic bags with sloshing blood agitating so it wouldn't clot. He snatched out bags by the handful and stuffed them into the backpack.

"Pig's blood?"

"No, it has to be human otherwise Farran will know," Dante informed him. "Don't worry. It's clean."

Dante opened a desk drawer. Slowly, almost reverently he removed a leather bag tied securely with a cord. The bag was about the size of a large baseball. Dante chanted a brief prayer in French as he picked it up.

"Ready?" Bartal asked.

Dante nodded. "Has she killed yet?"

Bartal held up a hand signaling for silence. He listened for a moment. "Not yet," he whispered.

"We will have very little time from she kills to when Farran collects her," Dante replied quietly. "We need to start *now!*"

"Luckily most of the staff have already left for their homes," Bartal said. "There are only twelve people to take care of before he gets here."

Dante was listening but he'd already taken the lead, headed straight for the servants' quarters.

* * *

The rain subsided as the storm passed. Bree had been awakened by the fury of the storm but couldn't get back to sleep. She tossed and turned until finally she got up and decided to take a walk.

Her insomniac steps led her outside. She stood for a moment looking up into the night sky devoid of stars. Thunder sounded distantly and there were flashes of light from over the trees far away. From time to time clouds dripped fitfully, unwilling to stop. Everything was shiny and wet save for her.

Bree shivered and pulled the small throw blanket close around her shoulders like a shawl.

Her wandering bare feet led her to the embankment of a small pond on the property. During the day ducks and swans floated gracefully and colorful koi flashed just underneath the water's surface. But it was night now and the waterfowl were asleep with heads tucked under wings, and the fish had buried themselves deep in the mud.

Bree looked at her dark reflection in the pool's glassy surface. All was quiet and still. She sensed rather than heard a presence stalk up behind her. She turned quickly. She started and then laughed. It was only Dante.

"You frightened me!" she giggled nervously.

But Dante had the most serious look on his face she had ever seen.

"I'm sorry, Bree," he said. "I'm so very, very sorry for what I must do."

The smile vanished from her lips as he spoke.

"I love you, Bree," he said softly. "Remember that. I have always loved you from the very first moment I saw you."

He took a step closer, eyes glittering dangerously in the dim light of the faraway lightning. Dante took hold of her arms and kissed her tenderly once on her forehead.

"It's time for you to go, Bree." He extended his palm face up toward her and in one short quick burst, blew a powder into her face.

Bree went suddenly stiff all over and couldn't move. She heard Dante chanting something which sounded vaguely French. There was an ominous sound to the words. They wound themselves about her like serpents, cold and deadly. She couldn't even close her startled wide eyes.

And then he shoved her forcefully backwards.

She felt herself falling. She was unable to stop it from happening. She felt her back slap the smooth surface of the pond. The water closed over her head and she was sinking, sinking down into the dark, murky depths of the pond where the turtles and the fish slept peacefully in the mud.

And she couldn't do a thing about it.

CHAPTER 39

Katya had trailed Ainsley's scent since she first arrived on the castle grounds. Her vampire senses could still pick up his pungent aroma despite the rain. Wet droplets hung like dew on her hair and clothes adding a slightly crystalline feature to her appearance.

She was close to Ainsley now, so very close. He was just around the next turn in the hallway, around the next corner of the architecture. She was sure of it.

Then another scent distracted her attention. Someone was standing behind her. Katya could feel eyes on her back. She stood up straight and tall and turned to face this new threat.

A woman stood dressed in a filmy purple robe which fluttered as delicately as a moth's wings. Her long straight hair was black and her eyes were an unusual shade of pale gray. She gazed at her with the innocence of a young child.

Katya recognized her in an instant even though they had never met.

"It's you, isn't it?" Katya said quietly. "The betrothed of our Lord and Master."

The woman said nothing but continued to stare at her.

Katya began to circle as she looked the woman up and down.

"You certainly don't look like much," Katya told her. "I expected someone taller, more imposing, more…queenly." Katya turned to face her again. "You're so…raw. As if you're still cooking."

She laughed briefly and tossed her hair about her shoulders. Crystal rain flew off her form and sparkled in the dimly lit hallway. "You're going to need to get some initiative if you intend to survive long as Kane's bride." Katya told her. "I could teach you, my dear. You could be my pet. Or maybe I'll just take your place myself."

Katya stepped closer to Zan and gently brushed her hair back from her face. At the slight contact of red nails brushing the skin of her neck, Zan's eyes rolled back in her head. She breathed in the scent of the vampire woman in front of her.

And then her hunger could no longer be contained. With a catlike snarl and blinding speed, Zan took hold of her by the arm and spun Katya about until the red-haired woman was facing away from her. With her other hand she clutched Katya's chin, yanked her face sideways and hugged her body close. And then her fangs were buried to the hilt in the vamp's milk white neck. Blood gushed in a wild river into her throat almost too fast for her to drink.

These motions took the briefest of seconds for Zan to perform. Her reactions were so fast and so unexpected, Katya never had a chance. She struggled but could not break away. Zan held her too tight. She kicked and thrashed but it did her no good. She fought to say one word. But the syllables choked and drowned in her throat.

The blood continued to flow and Zan continued to drink the rich red tide which rushed to greet her. Katya's movements grew less desperate and more sporadic. She twitched now rather than kicked. Zan could feel her growing weak and more feeble. She sagged in her arms and began to slide to the ground. Zan followed her, supporting the dead weight as she slowly knelt on the highly polished marble floor. The rush of blood began to slow. Gently Zan eased her to the floor. She released the vampire's neck from her cruel teeth. Cradling her head softly, she spread her form on the cold floor.

Katya gasped one word in desperation before the ghost of her dark spirit fled from its cold home. "Dhampir!" she hissed helplessly.

Zan smiled and began to lick Katya's blood from off her fingers.

* * *

Mom! Help me!

The thought intruded into my mind and with a jerk, brought me back to the present.

My hands and arms were covered in blood. I licked it off of my skin like a cat grooming itself. Before me was the body of a strange woman

I'd never seen before. She was beautiful, red hair, milk white skin, perfect body. She looked like a Parisian model. But she was splayed across the floor in a stilted position, her fastidiously coiffed locks flung dramatically about her face, her mouth frozen open revealing vampire fangs and eyes wide with fear.

And there was an enormous jagged tear across her neck made by the canines of some cruel beast.

I squawked in horror and scrambled backwards away from the body until a wall stopped my progress. I was unable to look away.

I had done this! I was the cruel beast who had killed her.

Do as thou wilt and it harm none.

This was the first thought which sprang into my head. I was certain, vampire or not, this classified as harming.

The strange blood in my mouth turned to bile. I bent double in revulsion at what I had done. I wanted to throw up, to expel the vampire's blood from my body and burn the incident from my memory. But my body was now dhampir. I could feel the new part of me refuse to reject the vampire's essence. Blood made it strong. Blood nourished me. Blood was now my life. I was not allowed to let it go away. I sobbed in shock of what I had just done. Emotions assailed me from all directions. I hardly knew what to think or feel.

I was different now. I was a killer. I had drawn first blood. And I must accept it.

I gasped for air, trying desperately to get ahold of myself. The strange new part of me told me air was needless. I no longer needed to breathe. But breathing was what I was used to so I gasped and sobbed.

Mom! Help me! I need you!

Oh. My. God. Bree! She was in danger.

I shook the confused chaos out of my head and forced myself to focus. My daughter needed me. Where was she?

The blood stranger inside me offered to help.

Every mother knows the scent of their offspring. It told me. *Follow her smell.*

I closed my eyes and took a deep breath.

Outside. She was outside the castle. I sensed something wet. She was near water.

Help me!

I opened my eyes and bolted to my feet. I forced myself to think of nothing else. I had to find my daughter. My feet carried me at a sprint through the different corridors of the castle by memory. I took no notice of anything but finding Bree. I ran through the main entrance of the castle. This put me on the stone causeway which led up to it front the road. I sniffed again.

Down the steps to the side, some inner instinct told me.

I did not question but followed immediately. The steps were wet from a summer storm and I was barefoot. They should have been slippery. I did not falter once. I flew down the stairs like a deer. My feet hit the wet grass at the base.

The pond. Go to the pond. She's near the pond.

I obeyed without question. I saw the pond. There was no one standing near.

Where is Bree? I thought to myself.

There was something floating in the water.

Help... The voice in my mind was very faint.

I suddenly realized, in a panic, what it was.

Mom, help me! Get me out of the water!

Bree wasn't *near* the water. She was *in* the water!

"BREE!" I heard myself scream. The water splashed about my blood soaked body and dragged at my legs, keeping me from reaching my daughter as quickly as I wanted. I flailed against the liquid and reached out for her. The waves I was making seemed to push her further away.

And then I felt my fingers thread through the belt loop on her jeans. I yanked her close to me. Her form floated face up, open eyes blank and staring blindly at the stars. I heaved her into my arms and staggered out of the pond with her. I felt my feet and legs sink deep into the mud from our combined weight.

No! The water was not going to claim my daughter! I furiously tore my feet free from its sucking grasp and staggered the both of us up onto the embankment.

I cradled her in my arms and called her name in desperation. There was no response. I listened to her chest and heard nothing. I touched her lips, waiting for the tiny gust of air, something which would tell me she was still breathing.

Nothing. Her skin was very cold. Her eyes saw nothing. I shook her and moaned her name.

She couldn't be dead. Sekhmet wouldn't let it happen. Not to Bree! I looked into her face. I tried to feel her spirit. It seemed detached from her form.

If Bree was dead, wouldn't I know it? Wouldn't I feel it in my mother's heart? If she was dead, then why did I still hear her voice in my head?

CHAPTER 40

Farran found Zan outside the castle kneeling on wet grass at the edge of a duck pond. She was covered in blood spatter, rocking and moaning in pain as she clutched something tightly to her breast.

He crept quietly to her side and gazed down at what she cradled.

It was Bree's lifeless body.

Farran smiled. He was surprised and yet pleased. He didn't think she had it in her.

"Zan, leave her. She's an empty husk now. Your place is with me, your sire."

Zan moaned and shook her head in agony.

Farran knelt beside her and placed a cold white hand on her shoulder. "Zan listen to me carefully," he whispered quietly in her ear. "Come with me and I will show you a whole new world of dark pleasures where you need not ever die. Leave this world and all its troubles behind. I will raise you up as a queen. Forget this place and its little people."

Zan continued to rock her daughter and sob great tears of blood.

"Come with me." He spoke as if it was a request she could refuse. But it was no request.

Zan placed the body of Bree gently on the ground. Slowly she rose to her feet. Her expression was blank. Farran took her by the hand. She allowed herself to be led away. She followed him silently down the lawn which wound away from Lion's Gate.

They finally met up with the main road leading into town. At the bottom of the hill, at the entrance of the castle road, a black limo sat with its motor idling and all its lights off.

Farran opened the door for her and quietly guided her into the back seat. He followed her in and sat on the plush black leather across from her. Reaching behind, he tapped on the window which separated him from the driver. The limo pulled away from the side of the road and headed off into the dark.

"Well Zan," Farran said to her when they were finally well on their way. "That was quite a display back there. There were bodies all over the castle and blood everywhere."

Farran took note of her blood-splashed form. "You are quite a messy diner!" he commented. "We will have to get you some new clothes. I can't present you to Kane looking like this!"

Zan blinked several times and as she did so, her white eyes returned to their more natural shade. She reacted as if shaking off a spell.

"My daughter," she whispered and then spoke louder. "My daughter is dead!"

Farran frowned. He had hoped to avoid this topic. "Yes, bad sport that," he muttered. "What a waste! She would have made such an excellent vampire!"

Zan glared at Farran.

"Well," he continued on. "Your daughter would have been right here at your side if she hadn't gotten the ridiculous notion to drink holy water! Wonder where she got that idea from?"

Zan's eyes blazed at Farran. "I taught her how to make holy water!" she told him forcefully.

But Farran only laughed. "Really?" he chuckled. "Well that was certainly a stupid thing to do! I hope you turn out to be a better vampire than you are a mother."

Zan growled and hurled herself toward him. But Farran only smiled raised his hand. She was suddenly thrown back as if by some unseen force.

"You cannot hurt me, Zan," he told her with a smug look on his face. "I made you. That means I can now command you."

Zan growled, angled her body away from him and cast her eyes out of the window into the rainy black night. Farran only laughed at her.

She refused to speak or even meet his gaze the rest of the ride. They drove on for some time into the night before they reached their final destination.

The limo crept to a nearly silent stop in front of what looked like an abandoned railway tunnel entrance. Farran got out and then offered his hand for assistance. Zan refused to take it and stepped out unassisted. She looked at their surroundings.

"This is it?" she questioned him. "The great Lord and Master lives in a railroad tunnel?"

Farran sneered at her. "It's an underground cellar which used to store beer," he explained. "It's much bigger inside than it looks to be up here."

Zan raised her head and scoffed at him. "Mykhalo lived in a castle and you expect me to be satisfied with catacombs? Oh how the mighty have fallen!" She gave him a challenging glare. "I much prefer my little castle to this hole in the ground!"

Farran was shocked she spoke so boldly. "You will be returned to your beloved castle and this time you will have a throne to seat your delicate little rump on...right next to Kane's. Until then, my lady will have to do as I say. Now march!" He gestured sternly to the tunnel entrance.

Zan aimed one more venomous look in his direction before she obeyed.

* * *

"Bree! Wake up!"

It was an hour before dawn. The sun was just beginning to tinge the edge of the night sky with light.

Dante held Bree's limp body in his arms and shook her gently.

"Come on, Bree! Get up!" he pleaded.

"What's the matter?" Bartal said as he came up behind the young doctor.

Dante was breathing hard and his face was creased with worry. "I think I overdosed her!" he told him quickly before he turned back to Bree. "I gave her less than everyone else so we could get her away before the police showed up. But she's not rousing. Not at all!"

Bartal grunted and motioned to Dante that he should let him examine her. Dante stood up and backed away. He paced in a panicky

253

circle and ran his hands through his mohawk in desperation. "She has no eye reflexes. I can't find a pulse or a heartbeat," he told him.

Bartal raised a hand to steady him. "Calm down, Doctor," he soothed quietly. "You're letting your emotions run away with you. You know your job and you do it well."

Bartal touched Bree under the curve of her jaw on either side. "The powder you used is supposed to slow the pulse and the heart to a rate where a doctor cannot detect it. It's *supposed* to give the appearance of death."

Bartal held up Bree's arm by the wrist and flopped it about. "See there?" he reassured. "It's been hours since you drugged everyone. If Bree truly was dead, rigor mortis would have already set in. But she's still limp. The drug did exactly what it was supposed to. You did exactly what you were supposed to. Quit worrying."

Bartal gently scooped Bree's body into his arms and stood up. "Come now," he ordered. "We need to get in the old bomb shelter. The police have been called. They will be here any minute and we have to be out of sight."

Just as he said this, they heard the wail of sirens on the road coming from town.

Bartal with Dante close behind, speed-walked to a certain dark corner of the castle wall and kicked a particular stone. There was a creak and a groan and the stone wall opened inward, revealing a flight of stairs which led down into darkness.

"Besides," Bartal mused as they headed down the stairs. "Even if she *is* dead, you can do some of the hoodoo voodoo stuff you know to bring her back, right?"

Dante coughed. "I'm not interested in a zombie girlfriend!"

Bartal only laughed. "Well now, aren't you two a pair! She doesn't want you because you're too old for her and you're not interested in her if she's a zombie. You're made for each other!"

Dante frowned and growled, "Shut up, Bartal!"

The sirens screamed louder as they pulled up the lane in front of the castle. The flashing lights reflected on the outer wall's stones. The hidden doorway creaked close with a shudder and a snap.

Slowly Bree awakened. She found herself on what looked to be a crude wooden bed hung from the wall with chains, the kind of bed which would have been found in a medieval dungeon's jail cell. A light mattress, pillows and blankets made it seem less Spartan. She tried to sit up and found her limbs too leaden to move.

"You'll gain control over your body soon. The drug is starting to wear off. For now, you should be able to talk and move your head a bit," a familiar voice from her right said to her.

She was able to tilt her head just a little and saw Dante sitting on the stone floor next to her propped up against the wall.

She made several attempts before she was able to speak. Her voice croaked like a frog. She felt like she was recovering from a sore throat. "You…you tried to kill me," she managed to croak out.

"No!" Dante said and then he sighed and cast his eyes downward as if ashamed. "It's very important that everyone believes you to be dead, though."

Bree was silent a moment considering everything which had happened. "You know voodoo," she said. It was a statement not a question.

Dante looked at her in mild surprise. "You figured that out by yourself?"

Bree tried to laugh but found herself unable to muster any more than a small smile. "I *am* the daughter of a witch," she told him. "Where did you learn that?"

Dante looked away and said nothing for a long moment. "In Haiti. I met Mykhalo there. I was the doctor for the workers of his coffee plantation. I was told by the supervisor I could experiment on the black workers as much as I liked, they were replaceable."

His paused and his eyes grew distant and faraway. "I never liked him much anyway. I found him a cold-hearted, cruel person. Anyway, I treated the African workers like people not slaves. I did all I could to help them. They returned the favor and taught me their magic. That's where I learned hoodoo."

Bree tried to move her arms. She found she could twitch her fingertips just a little. "I guess you could do anything you wanted to me right now," she said quietly.

Dante turned his head and gave her a concerned look. Then he got up from the floor and sat beside her on the bed. Bree expected him to take her hand but he didn't. In fact he didn't touch her in any way whatsoever.

"Bree, listen to me," Dante told her in a serious tone. "What I did to you just now I had to do. Right this very second, the German police are swarming all over the castle above us investigating the scene of the crime. We are in a section of the dungeon which can be accessed by a secret tunnel only a few people know about. They threw people in here centuries ago to forget about them."

"You mean we're in an oubliette," Bree interrupted.

Dante nodded. "Now you can scream if you want to and let them know all about you being trapped down here. But I'd rather you didn't. It certainly wouldn't help your mother any and it would spoil all the plans Bartal made."

Dante sighed. His eyes caught hers and refused to let her look away. "I promised your mother I would keep you safe. And I will. But I also promise you I won't ever hurt you. I love you, Bree. And whether you choose to return that love or to go your own way and find love somewhere else, I will always honor your decision. I will not touch you unless you give me permission."

Bree thought hard about what he'd just said. "You're one hundred and thirty years old."

Dante dropped his eyes briefly. "Actually, if you minus all the chunks of seven years I was a wolf, it's more like eighty."

Bree frowned. "Whatever! Why do you look only twenty?"

He sighed in frustration. "A Mac Tyre stops aging the first time they are bitten and go wolf."

"So you've looked twenty all these years?" she asked.

He nodded. "I certainly don't *feel* twenty! I'm not twenty here or here." He gestured to his head and his heart.

"Then," Bree began again, "how am I supposed to feel when I age and you do not?"

Dante heaved a very great sigh. "Bree, I live in the moment because that's all I've been given. The rest of time is just smoke and mirrors to me."

Bree cast her eyes as far sideways as she was able to. She noticed the door to the ancient cell seemed to be rusted wide open. "The second I'm able to move, I'm going after my mother and save her," she said still looking at the open cell door.

"No, you are not!" said a gruff voice forcefully.

Bartal stepped out of the shadows. He strode through the doorway of the cell and up to her bedside. Crossing his big arms in front of his chest he looked down on her frowning.

"I don't remember asking your permission," she fiercely shot back at him. "Besides, I've done it before."

"You didn't save her then," Bartal fumed. "Hector nearly killed the both of you. I heard the story. If you go after your mother now, you will ruin everything." Bartal scolded her.

"Let her," Dante interrupted.

They both looked at him in surprise. Bartal started to protest but Dante raised a hand, stopping him. "No wait. Hear me out," he interjected. "Zan expected this. She knew Bree would be impulsive enough to disobey everyone's orders to stay behind. That's why she asked me to guard her."

Bree struggled to move. All she could manage was to clench her fists. "Look, you two. I nearly lost my mother once. I had to sit here and wait while all the adults were doing important things and still not finding her. I'm not going through that again. If you're mounting a rescue attempt, then I want to be included this time."

Bartal turned to Dante and muttered, "Do you have more of that voodoo dust?"

Dante threw up his hands in frustration. "I'm not double dosing her."

Bartal snarled in exasperation and gave Bree his stormiest glare.

She faced him as boldly as she was able to. "I'm going." she insisted. "And there's not a damn thing you can do about it."

CHAPTER 41

It was several hours after Farran had taken me from Lion's Gate castle. The blood of my nightmarish slaughter had been scrubbed off of me. I had been directed to don a black dress which somehow reminded me of the curve-hugging attire of Morticia Addams. My hair was simply brushed and left straight and still slightly damp to hang down my back. I wore no makeup.

I stood before two great oaken doors far underground in a beer cellar. Farran flanked me on one side, Gregori on the other. Beyond those great doors was the vampire king himself, the first of his kind, Kane.

There was no turning back.

I fought the urge to look at Gregori. I wanted him to smile at me in encouragement, take my hand and squeeze it to bolster my courage, pat me on the back with a little, "I know you can do this," gesture. But he couldn't do any of these things and I couldn't treat him in any way which suggested we knew each other. As far as Farran or anyone else knew, Gregori was as much a stranger to me as Kane and I must behave accordingly. So I did not look at him.

I fought to keep my heart from pounding. I struggled to not breathe. I must act like I was a vampire. The farce must be convincing. If anyone suspected for a moment I was a…

I didn't finish the thought. I scolded myself to keep from thinking the word, 'dhampir'.

"When I introduce you to Kane you will kneel before him," Farran said.

I glared at Farran.

"But only if you wish to keep your pretty head attached to your neck," he continued. "And you will do or say nothing which makes me seem a fool in front of him. Understood?"

I turned back to the doors. "If you wanted me to kneel, you should have given me a dress with more gussets. I'm going to bust a seam if I try to kneel in this sausage skin!" I growled.

"Then I'm sure we all will enjoy the view, my dear," Farran replied. His words reminded me I was going to be the only female in a room of three, sadistically minded males. Well, except for Gregori. I tried not to feel endangered by the mere thought.

There was a creak and a groan and the doors suddenly opened inward. The room beyond was poorly lit by torchlight flickering from sconces along the wall. The walls were decorated with curtains and drapery positioned a safe distance from the sconces. In the exact center of the room was a raised dais with a large, throne like chair. Seated in the chair was a man.

His features were shadowed by the dim light of the room. Gregori left us at once and striding in long steps, took up his position behind the throne, standing like a silent sentinel. He leant over and whispered briefly to the man in the chair.

The seated man beckoned for us to approach.

Farran jutted out his elbow for me to take. I slapped it away and marched myself up to the throne leaving him behind. I heard him trotting behind me to catch up. Five steps before I reached the dais, the seated man waved his hand briefly.

I paused.

The pillar torches at the base of the platform blazed into life chasing away the shadows from the person seated. I did not look at his face. I immediately dropped my eyes to the floor and knelt on both knees before him.

"My Lord and Master Kane," Farran stated now he had caught up to me. He spoke with a flourish and a deep bow. "May I present Zan..."

"No!" I said furiously and rose quickly to my feet, my eyes blazing at him. "You do not get to call me that. You have not earned the right to call me Zan."

"Your name is Mrs. Susanne Joelle Miller. Is that not right?" Kane spoke at last.

We both fell silent and turned to look at him. Behind the throne, I saw the corners of Gregori's mouth turn upward for just the briefest of moments and then the smile vanished.

I chose this pause in the action to look Kane full in the eyes and observe the features of the creature I faced. He seemed to be lean or it could have been the illusion of his long legs stretched out before him. His skin was dark but his eyes were the most unusual shade of pale olive green. His nose was hawk like and his lips thin.

The light which burned within his eyes was decidedly not human.

"Yes, that is my name," I admitted.

Kane nodded and looked over my form with renewed interest. "Has anyone ever called you Joelle?" he asked.

I blinked and thought briefly. I had always been told by my parents, my grandfather would have called me Joelle…if he had lived.

"No," I replied.

Kane nodded again. "Then, with your permission, I will address you thusly," he told me.

Without thinking, I bowed my head in submission.

Kane's eyes shifted to Farran. "Thank you. That will be all," he ordered and waved him away. He then inclined his head back into the carved pattern of the wood in his chair and aimed his next words to Gregori.

"You as well. I wish to speak with her in private."

Gregori stepped in front of the throne bowed low and deep one time, spun on his heel and left to follow the very confused looking Farran. As he passed me, he smiled and winked one time.

The doors closed behind me with a dismally final sounding *boom*!

Kane heaved what sounded to me like a very relieved sigh and rose to his feet. "Ah! That's better, isn't it?" he told me.

I did not answer him.

He approached and began to circle me, looking my form up and down critically, "So you are the witch turned vampire who I have heard so much about," he mused as he walked. "You're not at all what I was expecting in appearance and more than what I was expecting in personality."

I wasn't sure whether I should be flattered or insulted. So I continued to say nothing.

"So you're to be my 'Eve'!" he said with an amused chuckle.

"Actually I think I'm supposed to be your Lilith," I told him.

He smiled at me. His smile gave me chills. "Ah, you humans and your little stories! You are so fond of them aren't you?" he said.

"I suppose." I tried to think fast. "Why do you speak as if you are not human? Have you been a vampire so long you've forgotten what it's like to be human?"

He really did laugh at this. I felt the room get colder.

"You're so young and innocent!" he told me. "It's quite refreshing." He strode away from me and up to one of the torches. He made sure I was watching and then he stuck his hand straight into the flames and left it there. He watched my expression. And I watched his. I noticed his hand did not seem to burn nor did he seem to be in any pain whatsoever.

I felt like a little girl being teased by an older boy to get her to scream. I gave him no such satisfaction.

"My dear, I was never human to begin with. To you, vampirism is a disease. You catch it from being repeatedly bitten. I was born this way. It's what I am," he said quietly.

He removed his hand from the flames. It was untouched.

"Are you an alien?" I asked.

Again he laughed at me. "Why is it when you creatures stumble on a life form you've never encountered before, you always assume it's from some other planet?"

I narrowed my eyes at him. "Then educate me."

He turned to face me as if my response had surprised him. "This world is far older and stranger than you humans ever conceived of in your puny little minds. Has it never occurred to you there might be another race who inhabited this planet long before your ancestors hauled themselves out of the primordial ooze? I am as much a native of this world as you are. I am just the last of my kind. The rest of my people could not survive the increasing light from the sun in the time after what you creatures so quaintly call the K-2 event."

I found myself getting fascinated with his story. "Then why do you look human?" I asked.

He sniffed and I could see his thoughts reaching back over a millennia. "My original form was worn out. It was never meant to live this long. The body crumbled but the spirit was very much alive. I had to sleep for quite some time. When I awoke, I needed fuel, lots of it and the potent kind. The blood of children always rejuvenates me. When I ingest enough, I take on the form of the species I devour. I am not human. I just have a human skin."

I stepped back. The bully had done his job. He had shocked me. I was to be bound to a killer of children.

"My true name I have long ago forgotten," he continued. "But your forefathers have ingratiated me with the name of Kane, a name from one of their oldest creation stories. And I must admit, it flattered me. So I accepted it."

"Why would you not want to be called Abel?" I asked. "Abel was the hero of the story. Kane ended up coming to a bad end."

Here he laughed. "Do I look angelic or saintly to you?" he said spreading his hands wide. "Besides, the villain makes the story, not the hero."

"But the villain always dies!" I put to him.

He smiled and shook his head. "By your people's interpretation, I am already dead." He kept walking around me as he spoke. But he had seemed to discover what he wanted from my appearance so now he stared intently at the floor, pondering something with his arms crossed in front of his chest while he paced.

"Do you want to marry me?" he asked quite suddenly.

The question startled me for a moment. I tried to ascertain what was the intended answer.

"Do *you* want this marriage?" I countered to stall him.

He turned to face me and waggled a finger in an admonishing way. "I asked first!"

I stared at him while my brain scrambled for a reply which wouldn't get me killed. Finally I sighed and gave in to the truth. "I have no intention of marrying you!" I declared.

Kane smiled widely as if I had said something which pleased him. "Excellent!"

Somewhat encouraged I blundered onward. "And I certainly have no intention of bedding you!"

His smile grew even more. "Perfect!"

I opened my mouth to continue and then tripped into silence, surprised by his reaction. "Wait a minute! What did you say?"

Kane just laughed. "You don't want to marry me and I don't want to marry you. And I wouldn't bed you if you were the last of your kind on this planet…"

"Just wait a second," I interrupted him. "I know I'm no supermodel but I'm also not particularly hideous to look at…"

It was his turn to interrupt me. "Looks have nothing to do with it. You're not even my own *species*. The idea of joining with you is abhorrent to me. That's why."

My face was still screwed up with confusion. I wasn't sure what I was supposed to think. Part of me was relieved and the other part insulted beyond belief and still another part was telling me to quit thinking so hard, just to go with it. I was a little bewildered by it all.

"Tomorrow night is the first night of Midsummer, you and I will marry," he told me. "It will be a business arrangement *only*! There will be a masquerade ball immediately after. It is the important part of the evening. You will bond yourself to me in front of all the scattered vampire clans and be seated at my side as queen. This will unify all the clans under my rule. This is the true purpose of this marriage."

He seated himself once again in the throne and linked his fingers together. "I think you will find I can be an extremely permissive mate. You will be permitted to do anything you wish as long as it does not interfere with the agreement between us. And please continue to be interesting. If you damage the business arrangement or proceed to become boring…"

Here he turned his eyes to me and fixed me with a rather stern look. "I will rip your throat out in front of everybody!"

CHAPTER 42

I was delivered to Gregori after this first meeting. He was to see to my creature comforts.

"Is it safe to talk?" I asked in a hushed tone as he ushered me from Kane's 'throne room'.

He paused. "Keep it brief," he instructed in an equally hushed tone of voice.

I counted to ten to settle my nerves. "Where are you taking me?" I asked.

"To your day quarters where you will be expected to sleep until nightfall," he informed.

"When will I see Farran again?" I asked.

"Tomorrow night just before the evening's festivities," Gregori told me.

He stopped in front of what looked like a cell door. Turning to face me he gave a stern look. "He is not pleased with you right now," he said.

"I'm aware of that," I replied.

Gregori nodded. He opened the door and gestured me inside.

The room was no cell but a spacious lady's bedroom. A fully curtained canopy bed stood against the wall along with a large wardrobe and a vanity with a mirror set on the other side. The walls were draped with colorful velvet curtains to give the illusion of windows where there were none.

"Be careful, Mrs. Miller," he counseled me. "Farran is not nice to deal with when he becomes temperamental."

I smiled at Gregori. "Don't worry," I reassured. "I am no longer afraid of him." And I meant it. There was a much bigger predator who concerned me now.

It was midsummer night, the night of my wedding to Kane. I sat at the vanity and brushed my hair. I had risen early because I could sleep no longer. I could sense the other vampires in the compound all beginning to stir. It was creating a peculiar sensation inside of me. I was ravenous.

With a bang, my bedroom door was thrown open with such force I jumped nearly out of my skin. Farran stood before me and his eyes were blazing in fury.

"I told you!" he growled at me. "I told you not to disrespect me in front of Kane. And you did it anyway!"

The hunger within me surged. I shook my head to try to get control of myself. I could not give in to my hunger yet, not here, not now, not with Farran. If I did, then all would then know what I really was. I channeled my hunger pangs into anger.

I rose quickly to my feet almost toppling the chair over. I clutched it desperately to keep my hands from shaking. "What are you going to do about it?" I challenged him. "Kill me? Tear my throat out?"

I laughed at him. "You can do nothing! I don't belong to you anymore. I belong to him! And I think he likes it when I sass you in front of him!"

Farran's eyes widened in shock that I chose to face him. "Why you impudent little spawn! I'll teach you to talk back to your sire!" he sputtered and he threw the back of his hand at my cheek to slap me.

But the intended blow never struck home.

I didn't flinch. I didn't blink. I didn't even step back. I caught his hand in midswing and stopped him.

I smiled slowly and angrily. "You can do nothing to me anymore, Farran," I told him softly. "Your job is done. By making me, you've outlived your usefulness. You have no purpose anymore. Your time is just about up. And I couldn't be more thrilled about it!"

I threw his wrist back at him. "Leave me!" I ordered. "I need to get dressed for my wedding."

Farran just stood there sputtering for a moment. Then he spun on his heel and left the room slamming the door behind him.

I crumpled, deflated onto the chair. I had done it! I had stood up to my jailer. I wanted to sigh in relief.

The door opened again but much less forcefully this time. I looked up to see Gregori standing before me with another woman. She was a vampire. I could smell her blood. It smelled like ambrosia.

"This is Sonora," he told me. "She will help you get dressed." And with this he left me with her.

We looked at each other. She had short brown hair cut in a pixie bob. Her dark eyes were painted heavily with kohl and she wore black lipstick. She was small and thin. I could sense she was a very young vampire maybe one newly turned, fresh and naïve.

She looked delicious. She made my mouth water.

She smiled briefly at me, suspecting nothing. She turned her back to me and went to the wardrobe. She opened the great doors and began to rummage about inside.

I don't remember rising to my feet. I don't remember crossing the room in mere seconds. I don't remember thinking anything.

I just remember ripping her head to the side and snapping her neck in one smooth motion. Before she even had time to slump, I caught her in my arms and buried my fangs deep in her throat.

Then there was her blood on my tongue in blessed great gouts of it. I nuzzled my face closer, heedless of the red spray as my teeth readjusted their position to gulp more of the delicious red tide. I drank and swallowed hungrily as if I could never get enough. I felt her life pass before me in colorful snatches of memories. I reveled in the strength of her youth, a strength I now stole from her as I drank her dry.

It may have been seconds, it may have been minutes but I eventually came back to the present. I found myself cradling the body of a skeletal creature with skin stretched taunt over its bones. With a screech of horror, I dropped the body I held and crab-walked as far away from it as I could get.

Gregori must have heard my cry. He burst into the room. His appearance had changed. He now wore a very baroque outfit shot through with gold and red ribbon and there was a matching mask hiding all but his eyes from the world. It was by his eyes I recognized him.

He looked at me and then at what used to be Sonora and assessed the situation in moments.

"I'm sorry…" I half stammered, half sobbed.

"Don't you dare!" he admonished me. "Don't you dare be sorry for this. This is what you were meant to do. You've given her spirit peace now."

He stooped low over the body to inspect my work. "However, your timing isn't the best," he muttered.

"I…got hungry," I explained. "Suddenly."

He sighed in exasperation. "Yes, I know. It happens to new dham…To new ones."

He waved me to the mirror. "Clean yourself up!" he instructed me. "I'll find you a new outfit. And dispose of the body and the mess."

I silently obeyed. There was a basin and a pitcher on the vanity. I hurriedly began to wash the blood off my face.

He rummaged about in the wardrobe and finally with a satisfied grunt, tossed a red and black laced number with an enormously full skirt like a bell out onto the bed. "Here. Put it on quickly. They'll be suspicious if you're too late," he instructed.

He scooped up the body and deposited it in the wardrobe and shut the doors.

"I can't wear this!" I wined in a panic. "It's got lacing in the back!"

The dress Gregori had chosen was a very gothic style garment with a corset-like torso which had to be fitted by intricate lacing.

"Look. We don't exactly have the luxury of time. Put it on and I'll lace it up for you. I promise to keep my eyes away from your prize. Hurry now!"

I stammered but obeyed. Gregori turned his back while I shucked off the blood spattered Morticia dress and wriggled into the alternate dress. I held the corset tight over my bosom and told him to turn around. I felt his cold fingers deftly go to work on my laces. He pulled and tugged and threaded until I was grateful I no longer needed to breathe.

"Done!" he finally said in triumph. "Let me see you."

I turned around, shyly covering the white mounds of my breasts which were blooming out of the top of the red and black bodice.

Gregori frowned and slapped my hands away. "Stop hiding!" he scolded. "You've got nothing to be ashamed of! And vampires aren't exactly shy." He took hold of my bare shoulders and looked me straight in the eye. "Mrs. Miller, look at me," he said gently.

I obeyed.

"You just stood up to Farran. You just killed another vampire. You are a queen. Hold your head high. Act the part! You can do this!" His eyes held no judgment, only admiration. He offered me his elbow.

"Come. Let us go and meet your subjects," he said.

I forced myself to smile and lifted my chin. I took his arm.

"Vampire or mortal, dark or light, you look very beautiful, Mrs. Miller."

CHAPTER 43

Gregori led me through the maze of barely lit tunnels until we at last reached two large wooden doors which looked like they belonged on the main gates of a castle.

"You must do your best to control your hunger," Gregori whispered to me. "The room beyond is full of vampires. I hope you are sated for the time being."

I fervently agreed with him! I closed my eyes for a moment and prayed to Sekhmet for strength. I instantly felt Her presence at my side. The Divine was with me. I had no need for fear.

"No prayers either," Gregori counseled. "They can hear your thoughts."

As if in answer to this, Farran appeared out of the shadows. His anger was thinly veiled. "You're late," he growled.

I sniffed and raised my chin defiantly at him. "You ever tried getting into a corset?"

He frowned and offered me his arm. Gregori dropped his and stood back.

I stood there for a moment, my hands balled into fists at my side, wordlessly refusing.

"He is your sire. Take his arm," Gregori ordered in a cold tone of voice.

I gave Gregori an irritated glare and turned my eyes back to Farran.

He growled in haste. He angrily snatched my hand and slapped my palm on his arm, holding it there with an unkind grasp. "You will obey me tonight!" he demanded.

I softened my expression but not my words. "Of course," I said to him. "I can give you one last gift before you die." And I turned my eyes away from him.

As I glanced away from his face, my gaze flickered briefly across my hand.

The golden lion's head ring flashed from my finger, exposed through Farran's hard grasp. The blue eyes glittered up at me. I tried not to think about the hope it represented.

The doors opened inward.

There's no turning back now, I thought to myself.

"Indeed," Farran said in reply to my thoughts. "Here is where you leave your old life behind."

I raised my chin and tried to look regal.

The room beyond was lit with chandeliers hung from the ceiling. There was a clear path leading from the great doors to a distant throne upon which Kane was seated. The aisle way was flanked on either side with people dressed to the nines in flamboyant ball gowns and gothic attire. Everyone was masked except for Farran, Kane and myself.

And they were all vampires.

I felt faint as the emanations from them swirled around me. My stomach jumped and twisted, my fangs grew and my knees were shaky. I shuddered and staggered at the enormity of these feelings.

Gregori noticed and stepped to my side immediately. I saw him clench his fists to keep from offering assistance in front of all these new eyes upon me.

'*I must not appear weak!*' I thought to myself. '*Not in front of everyone!*'

How do you take a deep breath to steady yourself when you're not supposed to be able to breathe?

A bolstering thought appeared in my brain. '*I am a queen among insects,*' I thought to myself. I stood tall and proud and lifted my chin.

From far across the room, Kane smiled. We stepped into the great underground hall.

I held onto Farran's arm and cast my eyes before me. I did not look to the left or the right. I felt if I looked into the myriad of vampire gazes which were upon me, I might lose my nerve. I tried my best to stand tall and straight and step with confidence. I felt like I was walking a gauntlet but instead of being beaten by clubs, I had to withstand the scrutiny of all those undead eyes.

The promenade up to the throne seemed to take forever. But at last I stood before Kane.

Farran took my hand and extended it to Kane. He spoke aloud to Kane and all those gathered. "I deliver to you my daughter of blood, Joelle, for you to take as your consort for as long as you desire."

I wanted to look at Gregori who stood behind the throne. But I dare not look anywhere but into Kane's eyes.

"I accept your gift," Kane replied. He took my hand and Farran stepped back.

"And do you willingly agree to be my consort of the night, Joelle, blood daughter of Farran?" Kane asked of me.

I paused. I tried to think without thinking.

'Don't tremble! Don't breathe! Don't fight it! Don't think about what you want. This is supposed to happen. Play the game.'

"I bond myself to you willingly for as long as our night together lasts." I hesitantly blurted out in a voice which sounded too loud to me.

"You mean 'nights'," Kane corrected.

"Excuse me?" I said breathlessly, too fearful to know where I had erred.

"You meant to say 'nights' plural," he explained. "For our nights together will be endless as long as you don't displease me." He smiled as he said this.

I tried to brush it off with a shaky smile. "Of course that's what I meant!" I said hurriedly and then dropped my voice. "There's just a lot of people here and public speaking was never my strong suit."

I sensed horrified shock from Farran standing behind me. But I dare look nowhere else than at Kane's face.

His smile increased.

"Have I amused you, Sire?"

"Always!" he replied. "I am most pleased at this joining."

Kane then turned his attention to Farran.

"Farran, it is time for your reward in finding me a suitable mate. Please approach the throne," Kane ordered.

Farran obeyed without question. Kane then turned his attention to the throng gathered about. "Let us seal this union in blood," he announced to all.

I was instantly suspicious.

Before Farran or I or anyone could react, Kane snatched him by the shoulders and drove his fangs deep into Farran's throat. Farran shrieked in shock and began to struggle.

Kane turned into smoke. Farran's arms seemed to be pinned behind him by some unseen force. He was lifted high into the air as a dark storm coalesced about him. He screamed and contorted, he danced in pain in the air while a tumultuous wind howled about him. His body began to shrink, his muscles wasted away before our very eyes and the skin turned black and seemed to melt onto his bones.

Farran was abruptly tossed out of the whirling tornado before us. What was left of him was dumped rudely on the floor, a steaming charred wreck of what used to be a vampire for all to see.

The black storm clouds condensed before our eyes into a solid form. Kane stood before me once again. He was gazing at me in amusement.

"Consider this my wedding gift to you, my dear."

'Don't you dare look shocked!' I scolded myself.

I frowned at Kane and sniffed in disdain at what was left of the corpse. "I wish you had saved me a drop or two."

Kane laughed at this response. "You are indeed my ideal mate!" he told me still chuckling. "What a fine queen you will make. For a short time at least!"

I shot him a suspicious glance but made no other reply.

Kane gestured to an orchestra sitting off to the side. They struck up a classical number. "We shall start off the evening's festivities by leading everyone in the first dance. Joelle, if you please," he offered me his hand.

I noticed his lace-cuffed sleeves still had blood spatter from Farran on them. I took his cold hand in my own.

I barely knew how to dance let alone do ballroom dancing. But I knew it would be pointless to refuse. So I passively let him lead me out onto the dance floor.

I did my best not to wince in distaste as he swung me close into his arms in some semblance of a romantic embrace. I tried to look at the floor as it spun by. But his words pulled my eyes back to his face.

"I know you did not want this," he told me. "Neither did I. It's a game we must play to stroke the ego of those here assembled. They so enjoy their pomp and circumstance. So play the role well and you may yet survive this."

I glanced about as other couples joined us on the dance floor. They looked so much at ease. My position was correct but stiff. I did not care for this style of dancing.

"And how long do you expect me…to survive this?" I repeated.

He swung me about in a stylish twirl and then pulled me in close again. His face was near my own.

"That all depends on you, my dear," he said. "I can be a very lenient mate. You may dance with any of the other vampires. You may even have clandestine meetings with them if you so desire. I certainly don't have any use for you in that fashion."

My eyes met his. He had my attention and I knew it was how he wished it to be.

"But be warned," he scolded me in a voice as soft as a lover's. "If you betray me in any way whatsoever, I will have no problem terminating your life in the most painful way I can think of." He stroked my face gently with the back of his hand in feigned tenderness. It was all for show, a spectacle for those gathered to notice. "I do not love you nor do I plan on ever beginning to love you. You are a trifle to me and no more. Do not forget this." As he said this, he spun me out of his arms and I was suddenly flung into the arms of another waiting vampire.

I danced as best as I was able to with this vampire and carried on polite small talk. All the while I was inwardly reeling from the emotional threat Kane had just issued.

Then I was spun into the arms of another vampire and another and another. I saw Kane watching from halfway across the room as he conversed with a small group of what appeared to be Nosferatu dignitaries. He seemed amused at my predicament.

My eyes searched for a savior. All I wanted was to get away and alone. I wanted to breathe. I saw Gregori speak to one of the musicians furtively. Then I was spun about and lost sight of him. My eyes searched for Kane. I saw him turn his back to me and move off into the throng surrounded by the other dignitaries, obviously to conduct some business.

I was spun about yet again and the vampire turned me loose to be flung into the waiting grasp of yet another flashily dressed masquerader.

But this time I found it was Gregori who held me.

At the same time the orchestra struck up a new tune. I recognized a piece by Johann Sebastian Bach.

I nearly breathed a sigh of relief before I remembered not to.

I recognized the music and it jarred me. I remembered Mykhalo had known the classical composer personally.

"Forgive me, Zan," Gregori said. His words brought me up cold.

But…Gregori never called me Zan. It was always Mrs. Miller. And…his voice sounded so strange.

My eyes met his. Gregori had never looked at me the way he was looking now. His eyes were the most unusual shade of pale gray I had ever seen.

I gasped in surprise as realization dawned on me.

"Mych…" I began.

He stopped me with a finger held to my lips. "Shhhh! Don't speak my name! Not here, not now," he said in a hushed tone.

We danced closer to the center of the throng of dancers. I looked at him in amazement. It was Gregori's form but I could almost see the mirror image of Mykhalo's face transposed over his own. My heart leapt in joy.

"Gregori told me not to do this," Mykhalo's voice said. "He expressly forbade it, in fact. But he gave in. I told him all I wanted was one dance with you. He had to give me that."

I felt tears brim at my eyes.

He took hold of me tighter and I willingly gave in. "I'm here with you, Zan," he told me. "You are in a nest of vipers. But your friends are coming. Do not be afraid. Soon you will have an entire army of supporters scattered everywhere in this room. Don't lose hope."

He swung me about in a flurry of black and red lace skirts and gold ribbon.

"I...miss you," I nearly sobbed. I nestled my head next to his neck. "Where were you? I went to the mirror to talk to you and you were gone."

"The mirror no longer holds me, Zan," he whispered. He readjusted his hand on my back so he could hold me closer to him. "I had some loose ends to tie up. I heard you. But I was busy. I'm sorry." Mykhalo pressed his cheek into mine. I did not feel Gregori's beard but only Mykhalo's smooth cheek touching my own. I bit my lip as the emotions surged inside of me.

"You're in a very dangerous place, Zan," he whispered to me. "I had to be here in whatever form I could manage."

I felt a lump coming into my throat. I nodded without saying anything.

And then I sensed a sudden shift in Mykhalo's attention. He pulled away from me just a bit.

"Kane is returning. He's suspicious. I have to leave," he said quickly.

He pulled away from me and stared longingly into my eyes. I didn't want to look away. I wanted to kiss him one last time. I saw the same yearning mirrored in his eyes.

And then I felt his spirit vanish into the space between us. It was only Gregori holding me. Mykhalo's essence was gone.

He dropped my hands as if he was holding acid, separating any contact between us and looked at the floor in shame. I felt much the same way. There was an awkward feeling as strong as if it was a tangible thing. In the briefest of moments the emotional bond had been cut.

I looked back in the direction of the throne to find Kane standing before it staring narrowly at me. I didn't like the look he had fixed on me.

Gregori noticed Kane's attention the same moment. He stepped back and lightly touched the small of my back with his palm, gesturing me to the throne beside Kane. I gathered up my skirts and obediently made my way up to the dais to join him.

"Did you enjoy yourself?" Kane hissed at me.

I met his eyes for one second only. He was no longer pleased with me. "No," I replied simply. "Your man can't dance." I seated myself at once without waiting for him.

I felt his suspicious glare upon me as he followed my action. I refused to look at him and gazed out into the crowd of paired up dancers.

Kane almost growled at me. Instead he raised a hand and the music stopped. "I think it is time for our queen to prove her loyalty to us," he announced.

He gestured to the guards at the door.

"Please usher in our honored guest," he commanded.

The great doors were opened. A small round figure stood beyond them blinking in the bright lights of the ballroom.

I recognized Ainsley Wainwright in a second.

He hurried through the throng of gathered vampires. They whispered and chuckled at his presence. Puffing and blowing at the exertion of the walk, he stopped at the foot of the platform and bowed low before Kane. The light shone on the balding patch on his forehead.

"Ainsley Wainwright has dreamed of being a vampire all his short life," Kane told me. "Please, my dear, reward him."

I steadied myself for the challenge before me. I rose to my feet.

Ainsley bowed lower.

I took three steps until I stood before him. I looked down on him and sneered in disgust. "I don't eat junk food!" I said quietly. I returned to my seat.

Kane's smile returned. "So she has standards!"

"Please, my Lord!" Ainsley pleaded, groveling. "You promised to make me one of you."

I leant forward. "You've been duped, Ainsley! Vampires never keep their promises."

He half rose from where he crouched. "But..." he stammered looking from me to Kane and back. "But...you promised...." His voice took on a panicked note.

Kane gestured once.

The sharp report of a gun rang out. The bullet ripped through Ainsley Wainwright's knee. He spun about with a howl of incredible agony. "No!" he sputtered in confusion. "This is not supposed to happen! Not to me! You promised…"

Kane rose to his feet to tower over the wounded man. "Did you really think any vampire here would sully their fangs with you?" he told him. "You're cannon fodder! You always have been! I will paint my steps with your blood. But no one will feed on you. And certainly no one wants to convert you."

More gunshots rang out. Ainsley wailed as the shots tore through his torso. He jerked like a fish on a line. A vampire strode up to him bearing a long hook meant for hauling hay bales. He stabbed it through Ainsley's shoulder and drug him, shrieking and crying out of the throne room leaving a long blood smear behind him.

The doors shut with a final sounding boom cutting off the stricken wails.

I tried not to act shaken as Kane turned his attention back to me. "Nicely done," he complimented me. "None here would have touched that greasy man. I'm glad to see there is a point you will not cross." He waved to the orchestra to continue and then gestured me back to the dance floor.

"Please," he urged. "Continue to amuse yourself. I have business to discuss." Two of the Nosferatu he had previously been conversing with had approached him again.

He waved me away as if I was a mere plaything to him. Then I realized I was.

I strode to the center of the dance floor which was clustered with other couples. The music began again. They all resumed their dancing. But they were casting judgmental looks my way. I felt like a high school outcast tossed into the mix of popular people.

"Madame?" spoke a voice behind me. I turned to find a masked vampire attired in gold, bowing low before me. "May I have the pleasure of this dance?"

I extended my hand to him and he swung me into his arms. I noticed he wore white gloves on his hands and his mask was particularly ornate, hiding any view of the skin of his face except for his glittering eyes. They looked familiar somehow.

"My lady, do you not know me?" he spoke softly.

I stared into his face for a long moment as we swirled and danced. Then I remembered and I gasped.

"That night in the labyrinth!" I said in a hushed tone of voice.

He was the Kurgan monk who had spoken to me then in the moonlight.

He nodded. "You were a vampire when last I saw you. Now you are more. So much more," he said in pride. His dance steps directed me to the back of the room where there were less people. "I had to speak with you," he told me in a furtive whisper. "Your…mate…is distracted with business affairs. But still I have very little time."

He glanced about to make sure none of the other couples were too close to pay attention. He pulled me nearer so he could speak into my ear.

"Your family is here," he told me.

I did not know what he meant. "I don't understand," I hissed. "My whole family is dead."

"No, your family is all undead," he corrected.

We spun about together again as the music swelled. He pulled his face in close until he was cheek to cheek with me. "You are Kurgan," he told me in the softest of whispers.

I pulled away from him in shock of the revelation. His eyes flickered once to the crowd about us, signaling for secrecy.

I nestled closer to him and bent my head into the crook of his chin so I could better converse with him.

"How do you know this?" I whispered in return.

He smiled. "My Lady, I have tasted your blood while you slept. It is faint but definite. You are one of us. You are Kurgan."

"Stop saying that! Someone will hear!" I hissed.

"Indeed," he agreed. "I am only here to tell you this. Your family is with you. They are scattered throughout this room ready to die in your honor. I am also here to warn you. Stay out of the moonlight. You now bear the marks of your race. If any assembled here see them, they will know who and what you are. Stay out of the moonlight, my Lady."

He spun me about and stepped back away from me. He bowed low, kissed me once on the back of the hand and melted into the colorful ranks of the revelers around me.

I turned and made my way back to the throne. Couples stopped dancing and bowed to me as I passed. I took no note of them.

Kane looked up as I climbed the stairs and seated myself beside him. "Is there a problem, my dear?" he asked, raising a questing eyebrow at me.

"I tire of dancing and music," I told him. "I am bored. Entertain me."

Before he had time to react, Gregori stepped to his side and whispered something in his ear. He then straightened and purposefully walked past my chair to circle around to take up his position just behind the thrones. As he passed me, he aimed a secretive wink in my direction. Something was about to happen.

Kane looked at me and smiled. He waved away the Nosferatu he had been talking to. "How convenient," he mused. "It seems my guards have just picked up someone snooping about the front door. Shall I have you play with them?"

Without waiting for an answer from me, he waved at the guards. The doors opened and two vampire sentries dragged a very unwilling person with them. He kicked and struggled in their grasp. They hauled him bodily up to the steps of the dais and dumped him unceremoniously on the floor before us.

Kane leaned forward peering at the crumpled personage who remained prostrate and panting on the floor before us. Kane muttered. "Joelle, do you know this person?"

I arose from the throne and stepped cautiously down the stairs. The man huddled before me in torn and ragged jeans. His head was partially shaved and his long lank dark hair covered any of his facial features. I wasn't sure if his clothes were in bad shape because of fashion or because the guards had roughed him up a bit before they hauled him into the throne room. I could smell his sweat and his blood intermingled. The scent hung heavy on the air, like salt and copper.

I bent low over him and grasped his chin with my fingers. I forced his head up to stare me in the face. I could only see one brown eye but it was all I needed to recognize him. I shuddered before I remembered not to.

It was Dante.

He peered up at me from his one visible brown eye, the other was swollen shut.

I was staggered. The last of the color drained from my already pale face. In an instant I reminded myself to erase the emotion. All were watching. Someone would notice.

And then he tore his face from my grasp and huddled with his arms over his head.

I straightened slowly and quietly looked about the room at all the assembled vampires.

"I sense a dog in our midst," I said clearly.

I heard a rustle of fabric behind me as Kane arose from his chair.

"Indeed? A werewolf has come sniffing at our front door? Rather unlucky for him I should say."

He paused and looked at me. "Kill him," he ordered briefly.

"*NO!*" I squeaked before I could stop myself. I gulped and my mind scrambled to correct its words. Gregori flashed me a glare of warning before he shielded his expression the next instant.

"I mean...why?" I added. "Didn't I just tell you I was bored? And here comes the perfect court jester to amuse ourselves with. Can't we all have some fun with him before he dies?"

I strode up to Kane's side and pressed myself lovingly into his form. "Please, darling?" I cooed. "I've never seen a werewolf before. Please let me play with him. You can kill him later, I promise."

I batted my long eyelashes at him seductively. Kane sneered in distaste. "Very well," he muttered. "If it will keep you from fawning over me."

He ordered Dante bound and chained. A very small cage was then brought into the room and placed at the foot of the stairs where all could see and Dante was stuffed forcefully into it.

Kane laughed as he twisted about inside his cage struggling to find some position which wasn't cramped.

"That's right," he mocked. "Sit there and enjoy the view while my children poke and tease you. This is what happens to nosy curs who come sniffing about our front door!"

Under the circumstances it was the best I could do for him. Dante sat curled in the corner of his cramped prison and refused to look at anyone, especially me. Other vampires gathered laughing about the cage. They stuck the sticks of their masks through the cage and tormented him. He snarled and growled at them like some wild thing, not the doctor I knew he was.

I felt ashamed. It was my fault he was in the cage. I wanted to go up to him and apologize. I wanted to tell him it was better than being killed and I would free him as soon as I was able.

But I couldn't say anything. His cage was too much in the open. If I spoke to him, it would raise suspicion. At the moment I counted myself lucky Kane was not pressuring me to go and join the new game of 'piss off the werewolf'.

And then Gregori bent low and whispered in Kane's ear again. I realized another unexpected prize was in store and my heart began to pound with dread.

"It seems we have another bit of entertainment planned for this evening, my dear," he told me.

I tried not to look as apprehensive as I felt.

"A young girl appeared on our doorstep this evening," he proceeded to inform me. "She wants to be converted." Kane sighed bemused. "I expected this," he said. "Once word gets out I have taken the throne, there will be many such new, would-be converts turning up at our doors. This one is just the first. I leave it to my children to decide whether to indulge them or use them as an evening meal."

He turned his eyes back to the great doors across the room from us. "But before she takes the change, this one said she would like to entertain us on this our most auspicious of nights. She wants to perform a dance for our amusement."

He waved to the door wardens. "Let her enter," he directed.

The great doors opened slowly. Beyond them stood a thin figure shrouded in red lace which glittered and flashed over a garment of shadowy black.

I felt my heart stop. I knew the very essence of the figure. I could feel her magic as it entered the room before she even began to move. It was familiar and welcoming. It was borne from my own magic.

My daughter, Bree, strode gracefully into the very center of the room.

I gasped and struggled to maintain my composure. I could not react. I must not react. I could see Kane out of the corner of my eye gauging my emotions. *I must be the ice queen,* I reminded myself.

Her face was hidden from all due to the floor-length shroud which covered her head to toe. But I knew it was my daughter.

My daughter was alive! Thank the Goddess! Bree was alive!

Don't react. Don't breathe a sigh of relief, don't cry in joy, don't do anything! I scolded myself.

Bree was alive and well and mercifully still human. I could smell the mortality on her

Bree was alive!

Part of me was shocked, the other part didn't care how or why.

She came to the center of the room and stopped. She motioned briefly to the orchestra and the violins began to play a soft tune which almost sounded like bees buzzing. She knelt and then prostrated herself on the floor facing both thrones. The red shroud fell into a glittering pool of red color about her like a puddle of shiny blood.

The music swelled and she raised her arms to the heavens. Slowly, in time with the music, she rose to her feet and began to spin. Her winding circles increased in speed and rotation and the shroud flew out about her like wings.

I dared a quick glance about the room. All were transfixed by the gracefulness of her motions. Kane was leaning forward, mesmerized by her skillful moves.

She began to undulate and shimmy. The fabric about her glittered and flashed and threw off sparkles of color to dazzle the eyes.

I risked another quick glance at Dante. He had twisted himself about to get a better view of her. He too seemed caught up in the spell her expert movements commanded of her audience. And then he shot a wary glance at me.

For just a split second, we held each other's gaze. He gave the briefest of nods to me. I could only blink in reply.

Whatever big thing was going to happen, it would happen soon. Be ready. This was the message his eyes sent me.

I turned my eyes back to my daughter's dance. I began to notice a slight hum growing in the room. I looked about in haste. It was not coming from the orchestra. They continued to play on heedless of any strange noise. They did not hear the hum.

I glanced again at Dante. He twitched and swatted at an ear as if a bug was irritating him.

So he could hear it too, but not the assembled vampires.

Bree continued her ebb and flow motions, each once matching the music perfectly. I caught brief glimpses of her facial features as she spun closer to me, through the veil before her face. She was dancing with her eyes closed, moving as one with the music as if in a trance. Her lips moved silently as if muttering words none but she could hear.

The air in the room literally began to vibrate.

Again I looked about only to find no one else reacting to the emanations I felt. I suddenly realized what was going on. Bree was casting a spell with her dance.

I gazed with new appreciation at my talented daughter and wondered where she had learned the skill. I could feel the spell clearly now as if I was sitting right next to the huge speakers at a rock concert. My skin tingled with its power and I felt more alive than ever before.

Bree's form suddenly began to glow with a red light from within. I felt the spirit of the Divine enter the room.

I gasped in awe of the feeling. Sekhmet was coming!

There was a sudden boom and a flash of light which knocked everyone to the ground in surprise.

When they all looked again, a figure knelt on the floor before us, a figure who was definitely not Bree.

Slowly Sekhmet rose to a standing position, unfolding Her tall frame. She raised Her head and opened Her eyes. She passed Her fiery gaze about the room at all gathered. It finally came to settle on Kane. She raised an accusing finger in his direction.

"This world is mine!" She told him. "It will never be yours!"

Kane came to his feet and faced Her. "I know who you are," he replied to Her challenge. "You are the spent deity of an infant race. I am far older than you will ever be. I claim this world as my own. You are nothing but a fantasy to me."

Sekhmet clenched Her fists at Her sides and roared in fury at him. She threw one of Her fists across Herself and a fireball seemed to explode next to Dante's cage. It shattered into pieces.

Kane only laughed at Her temper tantrum. "This world is mine! Its people are cattle to me!" Kane declared to her. "My children will swarm over you and crumble you into the dust of the past!"

Kane waved to the assemblage. The vampires picked themselves up and, fueled by his words, charged the goddess.

She spun on them and muttered one word. A word I had never heard before. The room was suddenly thrown into darkness. A chandelier lit itself from the center of the room, casting a weird blue light into the throne room.

I realized at that panicked second, Kane was staring at me in horror. An unearthly light seemed to be issuing from below me. I looked down.

There were marks all up and down my arms and hands, glowing in the black light cast by the chandelier.

I looked about. My fear could no longer be contained. It was then I noticed vampires clearing away from certain members of those gathered. Scattered among the revelers were other vampires whose arms and faces glowed with flowing marks.

The Kurgan people had been revealed!

Sekhmet spoke in a loud voice. "You are betrayed, Kane! These people were never your own! Your kind is long dead and crumbled to dust. You will be that way soon enough. You are no deity! It takes more than incredible age to earn the right to be a god. And that you will never be!"

The room was thrown into darkness. I fell to my knees on the floor to escape whatever punishment Kane would throw my way. My sight went blurry for the merest of seconds while it switched to night vision.

I saw shapes thrown into turmoil. The revelers had transformed the throne room into a battlefield. There were sounds of fighting from every direction around me. I heard shrieks of pain and anger and smelled blood as it was spilt. I had no idea what direction to turn.

Then I heard Gregori shout a warning to me. I was shoved roughly out of the way and ended up toppling down the stairs. A shadow behind me roared in fury. I had no idea whether it was Kane or Sekhmet. I came to a stop in a puddle of lace and silk. Something came tumbling down the steps after and bumped into me. I spun about with a cry…

And looked into the dead eyes of Gregori. His throat had been torn to shreds.

I cried aloud in horror and scrambled away from his body. Someone grabbed me from behind and clapped a hand over my mouth to stop me from screaming any more. I smelled the pungent odor of sweat and blood.

"Hush! No more screaming!" I recognized Dante's voice.

I clutched him in desperate relief.

"Where's Bree?" I hissed.

"I don't know," he replied. "But I think Sekhmet will take care of her. We need to get you out of here."

"No!" I said and shook off his grasp. "We need to stop Kane. That's what we came for!"

I felt rather than saw Dante shake his head. "They are the same thing. Kane is no longer in the room and this place is a war zone! We have to find out where he went."

Something chose the moment to bump my feet. I looked down.

It was a glass tube filled with what looked to be desert sand. I snatched it up at once.

"Bree said you forgot that," Dante told me.

I clutched the glass close to my heart. "I know what I have to do," I said to him. "Can you figure out which way Kane went?"

In the dark I saw Dante smile. "No vampire can track someone better than a Mac Tyre!" he declared proudly. "Follow me." He took my hand and we crawled to the perimeter wall.

The great doors were slightly ajar. We burst through into a hallway lit with incandescent lights.

Dante sniffed briefly. "He went this way."

I followed him down the tunnel. Over the next few breathless moments, he proceeded to lead me through a maze of doorways, branching corridors and assorted dark and lit tunnels until my sense of direction was completely bewildered.

We came at last to a heavy metal door. Dante wrestled it open. He took one sniff and paused briefly.

"Mrs. Miller, it's a good thing you're already dead," he murmured. "There's poison gas down this tunnel."

I stepped into the tunnel and paused. Dante followed me.

"What about you?" I asked in a furtive tone of voice.

"What? Me? Poison gas won't bother me...much. It will take a lot to affect me. Don't worry." He sniffed one more time. "Kane is very close now. I can smell him. Like dust and smoke."

I didn't like the look of the tunnel. The first half was lit. The far end was cloaked in shadow. We strode forward cautiously, Dante leading. He was right. I knew Kane was in this tunnel. I could feel him watching us.

The sharp report of gunfire rang out from the silence ahead.

"Get down!" Dante said and threw himself over me.

Bullets ricocheted along the walls around us and I felt Dante shudder.

The gunfire stopped as abruptly as it began.

"I know that sound," he said as we stood up. "He's all empty now."

I detected the scent of fresh blood. I looked at Dante. The shirt on his side was torn and the frayed edges were stained with blood.

"You idiot!" I scolded. "Why did you do that? The bullets won't hurt me!"

"It's okay really, Mrs. Miller," he told me with a grunt. "I just got grazed."

He paused. "I think you'd better go on alone. It's you he wants anyway. I'll guard the entrance."

I shook my head at him. "You idiot!" I repeated.

"It's only a flesh wound!" he insisted, "Go!"

I turned away and headed down the hallway on my own, clutching the glass of dream sand under my voluminous skirts.

My way grew progressively darker as I went. I finally came to the spot where if I took one step more, I would be plunged into complete blackness. I took a deep breath because breathing was what I was used to and stepped into the dark.

My sight immediately altered to night vision. I heard a scuffle before me and peered in that direction. I thought I saw a figure standing before me in the dark just out of range of my dhampir eyes.

"Kane?" I spoke aloud.

The misty shape turned to face me. "I told you what I would do if you betrayed me," he growled from the shadows before me.

I took another deep breath and advanced another step into the darkness. "What did you really mean to do, Kane? Take over the world and harvest all the humans? Set up blood farms for your children to survive off of?"

A mocking laugh rolled off of the walls around me. "I want my people back," he roared and he was abruptly standing right in front of me.

His eyes blazed in absolute rage. "But that will never happen now, will it?" he said to me. "I am the last of my kind. And when I am gone, we shall never come again."

"What do you want, Kane?" I persisted.

He sighed and relented. "I want all your silly useless political systems to be torn down and replaced by the Nosferatu royalty. Mortals will be thrown into concentration camps to be harvested. But it will ultimately fail. Vampires were never meant to be farmers. They will fall to bickering among themselves like they always have. There will be a revolution. Too many mortals will be consumed at one time, depleting their food source. In several generations they will have eaten and fought themselves out of existence."

"Leaving you the only intelligent life on this planet," I finished for him.

"Yes," he agreed. "If I cannot bring my people back then I want you all to die and leave me alone. That is what I want. Complete extinction of your whole stinking race."

"Sounds lonely," I mused.

He growled. "What do you know of loneliness? You who haven't even been alive one century! How could you possibly relate to the loneliness of countless centuries?"

"Let me try," I told him.

"How?" he snarled.

I smiled. "We still have to consummate our marriage."

There was another growl of disgust. "I told you I would never bed you," he said.

"I'm not talking about that," I said. "In my species, no marriage is complete without a kiss. That is all. Just a simple kiss. What has one like you to fear from a kiss?"

I stepped closer to him. He held his ground. I took another step nearer still. He was watching me closely. "It is a pointless gesture," he said. His tone of voice had become softer, less angry.

"Yes, it is," I admitted. "Pointless and harmless." I touched his arm. He didn't move. He stood there like a wild stallion about to jump away at any second. I slid my arm around to his back. I leaned my face up to his. He was staring intently into my eyes.

He took hold of my chin in a hard grasp. "What are you up to, little queen?" he murmured to me his eyes glittering dangerously in the dark.

I did not know what else to say. I sensed my moment was about to escape me. So I closed my eyes and just went for it.

My lips touched his with the gentleness of a fluttering moth's wing. At the same time I brought my other hand about with the dream sand and smashed the glass on his chest as if it was a dagger.

I felt his scream inside of me. Kane started to pull away. I clung closer, tighter. I felt his essence condense into smoke and flow into my mouth. I breathed him into me. My skin became fire. His form began to shrink within my grasp. When I tried to tighten my grip, his solid form vanished in my hands. I felt his spirit rush into my body.

I didn't know this was going to happen. I didn't want him inside me. But then I heard Sekhmet laughing in triumph in my mind. I gasped and felt myself falling.

CHAPTER 44

I opened my eyes somewhere between consciousness and dream time.

I could still hear Sekhmet laughing.

"Why did you do this?" I shouted to the ether. "I don't want him inside me!"

Her laughter stopped. I heard her voice purr behind me. "You consumed him, little mother. That's what you were *supposed* to do. Look within yourself. Does his spirit exist there?"

I stopped and obeyed her words. I dropped my consciousness deep within myself and searched. "He's not there. Why is he not there?" I asked.

Her purr rumbled about me. "Hate cannot survive where love exists," Sekhmet's voice told me. "Especially a very old hate. When it is exposed to love, it is either utterly consumed or healed. Kane could not be healed. He didn't want to be healed. So you consumed him. This was your task, your purpose, to expose him to a goodness which had long ago been erased from his soul. His essence could not survive in the face of your strength. The light within you is nourished by his evil and transforms it into your inner strength. He is truly gone from your body and this world. Kane is dead."

I listened to her words and felt my apprehension leave me like the passing of a gentle breeze.

"You need to return," Sekhmet told me. "I have left your daughter's form and she is looking for you. She will need her mother very soon. Her man is hurt."

I obeyed the words of the goddess. I closed my eyes. I felt my spirit being hurtled back into my body.

* * *

"Mom? Mom! Where are you?"

I heard Bree calling my name.

I sucked in a great gulp of poisoned air and roused myself. I felt so very strange. My skin tingled with energy and power. I forced myself to my feet and staggered as the world swam about me. I put out a hand in the dark to steady myself against the wall. Some dim part of my mind told me there was light at the head of the tunnel. I searched for the light and saw it. I headed in the direction. The closer I came to the exit, the more my vision cleared and the better I felt.

I saw Dante standing just inside the metal door. He looked strange, too. He was slumped against the wall, head bowed, holding his stomach. He looked up at me and I noticed his skin had gone gray in color. Beads of sweat stood out on his forehead.

"Mrs. Miller?" he panted when he saw me. "I think I lied to you back there. It's not just a flesh wound."

And then his eyes rolled into the back of his head and he crumpled like a wet rag onto the floor. His hand fell away and I saw a huge pool of blood staining through his clothes.

"Dante!" I shouted and bolted to his side. "Bree! I'm here!"

I heard footsteps pounding down the hallway towards us. I couldn't let Bree come in this tunnel. The gas might not bother me but it would certainly hurt her.

I looped my hands under his armpits and tried to drag him out of the tunnel expecting it to be difficult. Instead he seemed very light in my arms. Then I remembered I had dhampir strength. I immediately swung him into my arms and carried him out of the tunnel. I laid him on the floor just outside and turned to shove the door closed on the evil gas.

Just at that moment, Bree came bursting around the corner with Bartal close behind.

"Mom!" she shouted in relief and then stopped as her eyes took in my appearance.

"You look…different!" she commented.

"Never mind that!" I scolded her. I realized the great expanse of my skirts hid the doctor from view. I moved to the side and knelt beside the stricken man.

"Omigod!" Bree screeched. "Dante! What happened?"

"He took a bullet for me. He told me it was only a scratch. He lied."

I could see the emotions as they played across Bree's face. She wanted to hold him and she was afraid to move him. "There's so much blood!" she gasped. "Tell me he's not dying!"

Bartal bent low over Dante and inspected the wound.

"He's not supposed to get hurt," Bree was crying and shuddering all at once. "He's a doctor. He's supposed to fix people. The doctor isn't supposed to get hurt."

"He will die if we don't get him some help and quickly," Bartal muttered.

Bree wailed when she heard his words.

Bartal grumbled and went to pick him up.

"Stop! Don't touch him!" a voice behind us said.

We all looked up.

A small knot of vampires stood in the tunnel beyond us, just underneath the light so their faces were thrown into shadow. "We can help," said one of them. He stepped forward revealing his face to us and I breathed a sigh of relief.

They were Kurgans.

He knelt by Dante's side and took in his injuries at a glance. He then turned a severe stare to me. "We will do what we can. Leave him alone with us," he instructed.

I drew Bree closer to me and hugging her to my side, guided her away from Dante.

"But Mom!" she protested. "They're vampires!"

"No," I told her. "They're Kurgans. And they're family. They will tend to him. Let's go." All I wanted was to get my daughter out of these tunnels. Bartal fell in beside us. "How many vampires are left?" I asked him.

I had a tight hold on Bree. She wanted to turn around and go back to Dante.

"Those few who escaped Sekhmet will soon be found and taken care of by my men," he informed me. "Where's Gregori?"

I paused in my steps. "He's dead."

Bree sobbed once, staggered by the news. Bartal froze in place, shocked into silence.

"I liked Gregori," Bree moaned dismally.

I glanced at Bartal's face. It had become shadowed and dark. He did not need to tell me they were close friends.

"And Kane is…." Bartal asked in a low voice.

"Dead. Really and truly dead. I saw to that," I said.

"Are you sure?" Bartal said as if he didn't know whether or not to believe me.

I closed my eyes in stress. I was so tired. "Yes, I'm quite sure," I told him with a touch of irritation creeping into my voice. "I ate him."

I could sense Bartal and Bree just staring at me for one long, incredulous moment.

Bartal sighed in immense relief. "Well, that's a blessing."

I nodded. I still felt tired. Oh so very tired. "I think I'm getting too old for this adventure thing," I mused.

Bartal's eyebrows raised and with a wry smile, he snorted. "How do you think *I* feel?"

CHAPTER 45

"He's resting now," the Kurgan monk told me as he shut the door quietly behind him.

We were in the oubliette of Lion's Gate castle because dawn was approaching fast and the Kurgans needed a place to do their work underground. Here at least they did not need to worry if their work went overtime into daylight.

Bree made as if to rush into the room but the monk stopped her with a stern hand on her arm. "He sleeps now. Let him!" he scolded. "You may sit with him but please do not wake him. The only way he will survive this is if he is allowed to recuperate."

She bowed her head, nodded and then rushed into the jail cell just on the other side of the door. I sighed at her departure and then turned my attention to the monk.

"How is Dante really?" I asked him.

The monk shook his head once. "He's lost a great deal of blood," he told me. "Enough to have killed a normal person by now. But you and I both know Dante is not normal."

He sighed and then continued. "The young doctor is a werewolf which means…in his human form…he is stronger than any mortal I know. He should recover well in a few days. He is nothing if not a survivor."

I smiled, knowing he was just trying to reassure me. "Did you give him any of your blood?" I asked.

He laughed at me. "You do not give a werewolf vampire blood!" he laughed scornfully at me. "Our systems are incompatible."

He considered me quietly for a moment. "We Kurgans know much of the healing arts. We have known many things that mortals are just now beginning to realize. People have always sought us out because of it. And vampire blood does not cure everything!"

He paused and gave me a meaningful glance before he continued. "It does nothing for a broken heart."

I wondered if he meant myself or my daughter.

Then he smiled and the gravity of the situation lifted. "It has been a long night filled with great deeds and emotional highs. We are all tired. I suggest you and your daughter get some well needed rest. We will do the same." He turned to leave. The shadows swallowed him up.

"Remember, Mrs. Miller," he called out to me. "My people are here if you should ever need us again for anything, great or small. You have only to ask. You and your daughter are no longer orphans. We Kurgans take care of our own." The silence followed his passing.

I uttered a very heavy sigh and rubbed my face. I had just one more thing to do before I could seek rest for myself. I opened the door and entered the room.

Bree was sitting by Dante's bedside holding his hand. She jumped when she saw me and immediately let go and sat back in her chair.

"I…wasn't trying to wake him," she told me. "Really. I was just talking to him."

I smiled, too worn out to scold her. I turned my attention to Dante. He appeared to be sleeping. His face was peaceful and relaxed. He looked so young and innocent.

I reached forward and brushed the hair out of his face before I remembered not to.

I sat down on the other side of the bed across from my daughter. We held each other's eyes for one long moment. "You seem very concerned for someone who just broke up with him," I said softly so as not to wake him. "Are you having second thoughts?"

Bree smiled apologetically and dropped her eyes to her lap. "He took a bullet for you."

I nodded. "If the situation had been different, he would have taken one for you, too."

She nodded still without looking at me. "I know."

I considered my daughter quietly for a moment. "Whatever he may be…Mac Tyre or not…he's a good man," I said. "I know he's got skeletons in his closet. Shoot. He's probably got an entire graveyard in there. But he's still a good man. He loves you enough to let you go away. He won't control you. He's not the jealous type. He's certainly proved to me he's heroic and will protect you with his last dying breath. He honors and respects you. And he adores you. What parent wouldn't want their daughter to fall in love with a person like that?"

A shy smile curved her cheeks. "And the fact he's way older than me...doesn't bother you in the least?" she murmured softly.

"O my darling little bookworm!" I gently said. "Every relationship has its drawbacks. It's not always skipping through a field of spring wildflowers. And I'm hardly one to be advising you to stay away. Look at me. I dated a three-hundred year old vampire. You told me to stay away from him."

Bree sniffed. "Yeah, but that was before I knew said vampire would agree with me."

She shook her head and turned her concerned eyes back to Dante who slumbered on, oblivious to our conversation. "I told him all I wanted was a normal boyfriend. He told me I couldn't handle a normal guy!"

I laughed softly. "He's probably right! Not with the experiences we both have had lately."

She nodded. "Do you ever think things will go back to normal for us?"

I sighed and thought for a long moment about her question. "Probably not. We've been touched by the extraordinary. It's changed us. You and I aren't the same people we were before Mykhalo walked into our lives. We'll probably always attract weird things now.

"At least we now have family and new friends like us to rely on and surround ourselves with. We're better equipped now to deal with such things than we were before. The Goddess will take care of us. She always has."

Bree nodded. She looked at Dante and frowned. "I still love him," she admitted. "Is that wrong? To love a man I know won't be here in a little while?"

I shook my head sympathetically. "No kitten. How you feel about him isn't wrong. But what you do with what you feel could be. I know you're trying to protect yourself from any heartache. And if we all could see the pain coming, wouldn't we choose to avoid it?"

Bree bit her lip in worry. "But seven years, Mom! Seven years is such a long time! Anything could happen to me during those years! My feelings toward him might…change. I might meet someone else. I might become someone else…"

"Oh no. Not might. You *will* change into someone else. Years do that to you," I told her.

"Then why get involved to begin with? If I know I'm only going to get hurt, why not just stop it right now before I get my heart any more involved?"

I got up and came around the bed, seated myself on the mattress next to her and hugged her tight. "Because humans are meant to feel," I told her. "We're meant to love with our whole body and soul, with every fiber of our being. It's how we experience all the beauty there is in life, not by living safely…but completely, with all the joys and sorrows that entails. To do less would reduce the utter richness of the experience. And besides, there is no guarantee tomorrow will be there for you or me or Dante or anyone. We all could live until one hundred. Or we could die tomorrow. Give your heart a chance to breathe, my child. You deserve to be loved deeply, fiercely, completely by someone other than your mother."

I felt her nod in my arms. "But Mom…I'm afraid," she whispered.

I squeezed my eyes shut and kissed her on the top of her head. I hugged her tighter.

"I am too, kitten," I said. "I am too."

* * *

And so I rested. I relaxed. I thought about all that had happened since I first set foot on the German soil at Lion's Gate castle. I avoided people because I wanted to be alone to process all which had happened to me. Bartal seemed to suspect what I needed and kept people away. Bree didn't come near me because she was so concerned about Dante, she rarely left his bedside.

I let her be. She had a lot of thinking to do as well.

After three days, I found my feet taking me to the art room. I closed the door behind me and crossed the room. I pulled back the curtains from the large windows. Then, surrounded by all the pictures of Mykhalo through the years but without even glancing at one of them, I came to the center of the room and sat down on one of the small backless benches museums usually had scattered about the room. I rested my elbows on my knees and stared vacantly at my hands.

"I told you, the mirror no longer holds me," I heard Mykhalo's voice say behind me.

I did not turn around to face him. "Maybe I just came here because I like the room," I replied.

He was silent for many minutes. "Zan, what troubles you?" he asked.

I shrugged and did not speak for a long moment. "Am I still a dhampir?" I said at last.

I felt rather than saw, his ghost circle around to stand in front of me. I cast my eyes to the floor so I could not see his misty, indistinct feet.

"Yes," he answered.

I frowned. "I do not like killing people," I said in a flat tone of voice. "Even if they are vampires. Even if they are evil and had it coming to them. I don't like being a dhampir."

He was silent for a moment. "I didn't like being a vampire," he told me. "I never did like it."

I growled in irritation. "Well there's the difference between you and me. It's done and in the past for you. I'm still dealing with it."

I thought a bit before I continued. "When I first found out what you were…I pitied you. Poor vampire always at war with his conscience over the countless wrongs he's done, the innocent lives he's taken."

His shade knelt in front of me. "But you changed all that," he consoled. "You rescued me from a predatory existence."

I still refused to look at him. I just nodded. "Un hunh," I mumbled. "So who gets to rescue me? Where's my hero?"

He didn't have an answer.

I blundered on before my nerve left me. "I didn't want to be a vampire. I don't want to be a dhampir. I've done my job. Now someone set me free," I said.

He stood up. "What are you saying, Zan?" he asked in a whisper.

I heaved a very long, heavy sigh. "I'm saying I'm no longer interested in being the hero. I want to retire. Someone else can have the job. I'm done, in here," I poked a finger at my chest. I stood up and began to cross the room to the door. "Who do I speak to about resigning?" I said.

Mykhalo didn't stop me. Nor did he answer. He simply said nothing at all.

I left the room without once looking at him.

* * *

Bree sat in one of the comfy chairs in the library in front of a large window. A book was open in her lap but she wasn't reading it. Instead she was looking out of the window. Her thoughts were a million miles away.

"Bree?" a voice called from the doorway.

She turned her head about and with a gasp, jumped to her feet. The book toppled out of her lap and onto the floor.

Dante stood in the doorway. He looked very shaky, bracing himself against the door frame with his hands. He smiled and began to make his way slowly over to her. He looked very pale.

Bree started to run to him but he held up a hand stopping her. "No, let me do this myself," he cautioned.

He wove drunkenly closer, taking a very wobbly route so he could steady himself on every piece of furniture between them. He staggered weakly when he was only a few steps away. She squeaked and caught him in her arms. Carefully she guided him into the chair she had just occupied and then knelt on the floor before him.

"Did you come downstairs all by yourself?" she asked.

"No, they wouldn't let me do that," he said with a bashful laugh. "I've been working on getting here…with lots of help…for the past half hour. I think I'll stay put for a while. That is if it's all the same with you."

Bree smiled and laid a head on his knee. "You can stay here forever as far as I care. And I'll stay right here with you," she cooed in adoration at him.

Dante laughed again and blushed. "Well I might have to visit the facilities a few times during forever."

They both laughed in unison and then fell into an awkward silence. Both avoided the other's eyes.

"Did you really mean it, Bree?" Dante finally said. "That you want to stay forever?"

Bree took a deep breath and bit her lip. "I…think…er hope…so," she said slowly. "Although what exactly it entails in this instance has me kinda scared."

Dante nodded. "It should. It's a pretty big thing."

Bree nodded in return and repeated in a very small voice. "Yes, a really big thing."

Dante reached out and took hold of her chin in one hand. He stroked her cheek with his thumb. She met his eyes for a long moment. They could not take their eyes off each other. "I'm so glad you didn't get hurt," he told her. "I don't ever want to see you get hurt."

Bree's eyes grew shiny. "I could say the same to you. But then you *did* get hurt! Don't ever do that again!" she scolded.

"At least I know how you really feel about me now," he told her.

The smile vanished from Bree's face and her eyes seemed to well up a bit. "If I fall apart for this, how am I gonna handle you going wolf in a few months?" she asked.

Dante sighed wearily and let his hand drop. "You'll handle it like I do, like the wolf does. One day at a time."

Bree laid her cheek against his knee and hugged his leg a bit tighter. "But what if you come out of it seven years later and I'm not there anymore?"

Dante closed his eyes and inclined his head back into the plush leather of the chair. "I'll cope. Somehow. We both will have to cope. Somehow."

He was quiet for a minute as he thought about it. "Listen to me, Bree," he finally said. "You like to show the world the bubbly bouncy side of you. And many people think that's all there is. But I've scratched the surface and I know better. Inside of that funny exterior there's a strong woman. A woman who can overcome anything she sets her mind to. I told you before, you don't need a normal boyfriend. You need someone who tests and challenges you. I think you can handle the challenge of loving me. In fact I don't think, I know you can."

Bree felt her eyes beginning to leak. She stood up and squeezed herself into the chair beside him even though it was a snug fit for the two of them. She wrapped her arms around his neck and hugged him so tight he could barely breathe. "And if, in seven years, I'm not there anymore?" she mumbled into the side of his neck.

Dante hugged her back. "Then I will do my utmost best not to judge you. It's a long time. Life goes on. So must you." He tightened his arms around her as the emotion of the moment began to get to him. "All we've got is now. Tomorrow is just empty promises. Let's enjoy the now together."

He prayed time would stop and not let this moment leave. His lips found hers. He felt her melt into his arms. He was so happy right now. And at the same time he felt his heart breaking. He buried his face in her neck before the tears began.

* * *

My suitcases were open and all laid out on the great canopy bed. I folded and stuffed my clothes into every available corner. I shook my head, not satisfied. I still needed more room. Bree and I had come to Germany with two small cases of clothes, enough for maybe a week. It hadn't exactly turned out that way. How had I accumulated so much more stuff?

The door opened and Bartal walked in carrying a spare suitcase which appeared by his heft to be empty. He flung it onto the bed and opened it.

I hurriedly covered up my underwear which I had been packing with a pair of jeans and glanced at him.

"You really are leaving this time aren't you?" he muttered. He sounded like a boy who had just lost his puppy.

I sniffed and turned back to the dresser. "You act like I'm never coming back again!" I laughed.

He seemed uncomfortable. "I'm just worried for your safety, that's all."

"I'm dhampir now," I said softly. "I daresay I can look after myself better than before. I no longer need a bodyguard."

"Maybe I liked being your bodyguard," he muttered in return. "And planes can be dangerous." There was an uncomfortable silence between us.

"People fly on planes all the time and survive," I reassured him. "Besides, Dante is coming with us."

"He is?" This apparently was news to Bartal.

I smiled. "Yes. I think Bree wants to show him off to all of her friends back home. Does it make you feel better about us leaving?"

He thought about this briefly. "Yes," he finally said. "You will have a doctor with special talents guarding you."

I laughed. "You know the real reason, Bartal! They want to spend as much time together as possible before he goes wolf."

Bartal sniffed gruffly. "Dante just doesn't want to let your pretty daughter out of his sight!"

I smiled and shook my head. "Bree could do worse, a lot worse. I'm okay with Dante. Even with all his skeletons."

Bartal's tone became extremely serious. "Are you coming back?"

So that was the real issue!

I sighed and turned to face him with hands on my hips. "Bartholomew Sebastian Bathory," I said using his full name. "Pennsylvania is my home. I have a house and a business to run there. I have to manage my own life." I turned about and zipped a suitcase. I started to fill the spare he brought me. "But, I have grown to love Lion's Gate castle. I'll be back. Soon. And frequently."

I paused in what I was doing and turned to look Bartal in the eye. "It seems I now have family here. And I must work to keep those new ties secure."

I smiled at him. Slowly he returned my smile.

"Besides," I added. "I'm thinking of opening a second Batty Belfry Books here in Germany."

Bartal snorted in scorn. "What? A chain of batty bookstores?"

I tsked at him in an admonishing way. "Perish the thought! Do you really think I'd do that?" I scolded.

Bartal was silent for a moment. "Speaking of books..." he finally said. "Mykhalo wanted you to have this."

I sniffed as I turned away from him to add more clothes to the suitcase. "He's already given me everything. What more could he possibly have to give...?"

My words trailed off into space as I turned about and saw what Bartal was extending towards me. He held a large thick book with an old-style cover and stitched spine so one could add more pages to it.

"Is that what I think it is?" I said slowly in a low tone of voice.

Bartal smiled and stroked the cover lovingly. "It is. This is Mykhalo's journal he kept of his entire life both living and undead. It is so thick because I just finished translating it. I hope you can read my writing."

The articles of clothing I held spilled to the floor, completely forgotten. My hands shook uncontrollably as I took it from his grasp. I too stroked the cover fondly. I closed my eyes and smelled the scent of old pages and inkwell strokes. I opened my eyes and opened the old tome. The first page was written in bold strokes. I couldn't decipher it. It was written in German. But the accompanying page next to it was written in someone else's handwriting, in ballpoint pen and it was in English.

I closed the book quickly, without reading a single word. I squeezed my eyes shut and hugged it close to my chest. My eyes began to water.

"What a treasure," I whisper.

Bartal nodded. "Mykhalo told me he wanted you to know all his secrets. And then he died before he was able to divulge them to you. This way he can still keep his promise."

I shook my head and forced myself to laugh. It only made the restrained tears fall hot and fast. "That beautiful, impossible man." I moaned.

Bartal nodded and I could tell by the shine in his eyes he felt much the same way. "I thought you would be pleased." And then he took hold of my arm. "I will miss you," And I found myself being drawn into his big bear hug.

I laughed and hugged him back tightly. "I'll be back!" I assured. "I promise. Besides, didn't you tell me Lion's Gate has a tendency to call its people back?"

"You are Hope's daughter," Bartal told me. "You now have two homes. Go home to Pennsylvania and read Mykhalo's journal. Then return and if you still have questions, I will do my best to answer them."

I smiled and nodded as I wiped the tears away from my face. Here I was about to go home and instead I was thinking of another trip. I suspected my next journey would be into the past in between the pages of this book I now held grasped within my embrace.

I found myself hungry for visions of Mykhalo's faraway past. What would I find in the leaves of his journal, Mykhalo the vampire demon or the knight in dented armor? Or would I find both within the same skin?

I did not know.

OTHER BOOKS BY THE AUTHOR

DEADLY CONVERSATIONS
Book 1: Zan Miller meets Mykhalo, a 300-year old Bavarian vampire. She tries to keep the relationship casual but suddenly finds herself beset by problems only he can solve. Complicating matters further is her teen-aged daughter Bree who questions her faith and battles the gift of magic inherited from a very old power. Bree holds the secret to ending Mykhalo's torment… but at what cost to her mother?

WANDERLING'S CHOICE
Once upon a time there lived a farm girl named Rhiannon who dreamed of having adventures and didn't want to get married---EVER! So she acquired a fine horse from a mysterious trader and ran away to find that exciting life. All would have gone very well if she hadn't been abducted by a cruel young king and kept hostage in his large castle filled with soulless servants. She has only two options for escape, marry the tyrant…or become a zombie slave.

Available in eBook and Print

www.ingramcontent.com/pod-product-compliance
Lightning Source LLC
Chambersburg PA
CBHW021309250626

47155CB00002B/458